DAMAGED
GOODS

DAMAGED GOODS

JODI BLASE

iUniverse, Inc.
Bloomington

DAMAGED GOODS

iUniverse books may be ordered through booksellers or by contacting:

iUniverse
1663 Liberty Drive
Bloomington, IN 47403
www.iuniverse.com
1-800-Authors (1-800-288-4677)

ISBN: 978-1-4759-5207-0 (sc)
ISBN: 978-1-4759-5209-4 (hc)
ISBN: 978-1-4759-5208-7 (ebk)

Printed in the United States of America

iUniverse rev. date: 10/05/2012

Dedicated to the world's best grandparents:
Anthony & Marie Bruno, Billy & Edna Cogan

PROLOGUE

THE DECISION

Karen Sherburne sat on her worn out leather couch, mindlessly swirling a glass of scotch. She had been waiting for this moment since September 12th, 1980. For the past sixteen years, she had lived in a depersonalized state, divorced from reality. On particularly challenging days, the world around her sounded as if it was under water. Voices echoed Charlie Brown's gurgly teacher, *Wah wah wah wah wah,* and she struggled to translate the garbled language. Had it not been for the sound of her heartbeat, she could easily have thought herself dead.

When Karen first lost Meg, she had hoped that she would be fortunate enough to die from heartache. And when it didn't happen, the rage came, and Karen willingly let it course through her. Over the years it died down, residing just below the surface of her skin. Anna the psychic had been right about Karen having been around the killer for a long time, but she was wrong about Karen's rage.

Rage was good. It was a two-handed death grip necessity.

If it weren't for her pent up rage, she'd have lived in a constant state of grief, which was too much to bear. Now, with the discovery of Meg's killer, the dormant rage bubbled to the surface and Karen welcomed it like an old friend. It encouraged her to act quickly, before she could change her mind, before a coherent thought could interrupt and make her question her motives. Karen was right to stay toxic because if she hadn't, she wouldn't be able to do what she was about to do.

She was about to plot a murder.

She took a sip of scotch and giggled.

This must be what it feels like to go insane.

Her life had turned into a tsunami of events that included ghosts and abuse and gingerbread houses.

SIXTEEN ODD YEARS AGO

It was during the height of her career that Karen began to feel like a walking contradiction. A highly regarded social worker known for her determination and resourcefulness, her number one priority was ensuring kids be placed out of harm's way and into safe environments. Her dedication to her work came at the expense of her own daughter, Meg, who had spent a good chunk of her childhood as a latchkey kid.

As a single mother of an only child, Karen justified Meg's long stretches of unstructured time by telling herself that she was a professional in her field who was fully aware of her family's needs. And she had no trouble expressing this confidence, however misguided, to anyone who challenged it.

"You're a workaholic."

"I'm a single mother, Dad."

"What's that got to do with working fifty hours a week? Have Meg take the bus to my house where she'll at least have company. The kid sits alone all afternoon," her father, Carl, would complain.

Meg's welfare had become a frequent topic between the two, with Carl adopting an edgy, judgmental tone parents use when they disagree with their children. Karen took her father's attitude in stride; after all, this was a man who once believed a woman's place was in the kitchen. Carl was ten years behind the times. How could she blame him for not understanding today's world? There was nothing wrong with what she was doing. And she wasn't about to hurt her father's feelings by disclosing that Meg had declared she would rather stick needles in her eyes than spend afternoons at her grandfather's house.

"Are you kidding me? No way am I going to Grandpa's every afternoon. Capital B for boring!" she'd told her.

"She's perfectly fine, Dad. I know exactly what I'm doing."

When Meg entered the tumultuous teen years, Karen admitted defeat and resigned to clean up the dysfunction that had become her life. She promised herself that her latest client, a very troubled Frankie Ortiz, was going to be the last case she'd accept on her already burdensome workload. The upcoming months would be devoted to quality time with Meg and finding a work/life balance.

This was a decision that Karen made a bit too late.

Because not long after, while Karen was at work, Meg was murdered.

Talk about corset-constricting mother's guilt.

To be exact, she experienced furious surges of rage and despair that caged her lungs like a metal vest, gripped her soul, and slowly squeezed her essence so that the breath felt like it was gone from her.

The hunt for Meg's killer was short lived, and Karen blamed sloppy data gathering for the lack of evidence in her daughter's investigation. She hired a private detective who promised her results, but who came up empty. In desperation, she visited a section of town where should-be condemned houses were inhabited by sketchy characters. She found herself standing on the walkway of a tiny white ranch. Carefully negotiating her way through the creaky planks of the rotted out landing beneath her, she made a fist and knocked on the front door.

A small, squat woman in her mid thirties greeted her with a suspicious, "What do you want?"

Her eyes searched behind Karen for signs of . . . *what* . . . the police, drug dealers, bill collectors . . . Karen couldn't say.

"Someone told me you were the best psychic in town," Karen replied, opening her still clenched fist to reveal a fifty dollar bill.

The woman stepped aside and allowed Karen entry into a tiny room, lit only by a table lamp covered with a tan colored silk scarf. She led Karen to a small circular table, its centerpiece a crystal ball. Motioning toward a beat up wooden chair with missing back spindles, she said, "Have a seat."

Karen sat in the rickety chair. Hoping it would hold her weight, she cursed herself for listening to Sarah's suggestion that she come here.

"What's your question?" she asked, staring directly into Karen's eyes. The woman had a square jaw, raven hair fashioned after Stevie Nicks, and sleepy gray eyes.

An avid non believer, Karen decided to test this lady's skills. "I want to know about my job."

It was a blanket statement that didn't leak any information about her. She leaned back, crossed her arms, and waited for the so-called psychic to make a fool of herself.

"Well, you've had a rough few months, that's for sure," she said, in a strong Boston accent. "Your job is draining and quite frankly, you think it sucks. If you don't find a hobby to keep you busy, you're gonna disintegrate," she cautioned, nodding toward an ashtray beside her, "like the ashes of a cigarette."

Was she really paying for this crap?

Ashes of a cigarette? *Who* speaks like that?

Karen rolled her eyes and slowly shook her head from side to side, indicating to this woman that every word that came out of her mouth was a total crock of B.S.

This seemed to amuse her and she smiled, showing off small yellow teeth accented by full lips and deep dimples.

"What's so funny?" Karen asked defensively.

"What'd you expect? You lied to me."

Her cheeks flushed with a heat of embarrassment, and Karen lied about her lie.

"I did no such thing."

"Oh, pah-lease. Lady, you didn't come here to talk shop."

"Then what did I come here for?" Karen challenged.

"To find your daughter's killer."

Holy sweaty palms, queasy stomach, lightheadedness, floating out of her body, muscle twitching people who see things.

"What's your name?" Karen asked, swallowing over a hard lump that had formed in her throat.

"Anna, but," she winked, "I don't need to know yours. I know it begins with a K, so I'll just call you Kay."

"Please, Anna, do you know who murdered my Meg?"

"And how did I know that was coming next?" sighed Anna. "Truth is, I can't see who murdered your kid. What I can tell you is that the killer is male, he lives nearby, and that you'll be seeing him again." Anna paused, and with a baffled expression said, "Huh, that's odd."

"What's odd?" Karen asked hopefully.

"You'll see him more than once over the course of quite a few years. You won't know it's him right away, but when you do find out, oh boy," Anna whistled, "Oh honey, it's gonna be a hot mess."

"So, you can't even give me a name, a first initial like you just gave me? Can you at least describe him? Where will I see him? How will I know?"

Anna looked at Karen with pity and shrugged.

"I only know what I know. The best way I can describe it is that I see this puzzle with pieces everywhere. Some of them ain't even turned over. A lot of it doesn't make sense. Must mean you're not meant to know right now, maybe you're not *ready* to know."

Right here is when Karen felt the inclination to grab Anna's five dollar crystal ball and beat her over the head with it until the puzzle pieces did fall into place.

"Stop thinkin' of hatin' on me," said Anna. "It's so awkward and uncomfortable."

Karen's mouth dropped open.

"I do have one more thing," she offered.

"If you can't tell me who the killer is, we're done here," said Karen, sliding her chair back.

Anna leaned in and gently grabbed Karen's wrist. "I gotta warn you of something first. You're full of disease."

"Disease?"

"Yeah, the disease of revenge. If you don't watch it, it's gonna destroy you."

Karen tried to control her voice, which was steadily rising.

"You're kidding me, right? Let me make sure I've got this straight; you're concerned about my rage *destroying* me?"

"That's right," nodded Anna.

"Well, let me tell *you* something. If the image of my daughter's body lying slack on a cold metal slab at the morgue didn't *destroy* me, nothing will. So if the best you've got is a warning for me not to be pissed off," Karen giggled cynically, "I'll be on my way."

"When the time comes, and I promise you the time will come, don't do it."

"Do what?" Karen huffed.

"I'm a psychic, Kay. You're lying again," Anna scolded. "In the end, it won't just be his blood; it will be your blood as well."

"Then my blood it is," spat Karen.

She stood, tossed the money on the table, and headed toward the door.

"Kay, wait! Listen to me, you've gotta let it go. It will eat you alive," said Anna, following Karen.

"Save it, Anna. Let's both agree that I don't need a psychic to know this is one story that's going to end badly," Karen said, waving her off with her hand and storming out of the small, dark room.

In her abrupt exit, Karen missed Anna's reply. Anna pocketed the money and grabbed a cigarette from the box in front of her. She walked over to the window and watched Karen peel out of the parking space, leaving skid marks in her wake. "Lady Kay," Anna said somberly, "bad doesn't begin to describe how your story's gonna end."

PART I

The Collective Past

MEG

Two Months before the murder

"I said no, Meg."

"Why not?" Meg shouted.

"Because I'm not going to allow you to turn into one of those kids who gets whatever they want. You'll grow up aspiring to be nothing. You'll end up lazy, turn to drugs for relief, have no ambition, and eventually kill yourself because you won't be able to cope with failure. Then I'll blame myself for giving you too much."

Karen stood firm, arms crossed.

"That's such a load of crap, Mom! Tell me you're shitting me," Meg said, in a *duh* tone.

"I shit you not, potty mouth. I'm imposing limits on you for your own good, and that's that," Karen nodded triumphantly.

"You're off your rocker," spat Meg, "I don't see why I can't have an Atari."

"Because you don't need an Atari. It will rot your brain."

"Rot my brain?"

"Yeah, Pac Man will rot your brain."

"Oh, please, you loved playing Pong at the arcade."

"That's because it's like an exciting tennis match."

"Exciting? It's snoresville!"

"Anyway, that was at an arcade for fun. Not in your own home."

"Well, what do you suggest I do while you're at work?"

"Clean your room."

"For like, ten hours?"

"By the time you wake up it's noon. Clean your room, read a book, take a walk, call a friend, watch TV for a small amount of time, do a

3

jigsaw puzzle. And hey, feel free to cook dinner. That should bring you pretty close to six o'clock."

"Yeah, except for when you're home by seven or eight or nine."

"How about spending one day a week at Charlene's house?"

"And do what?"

"Whatever it is you kids do these days, Meg."

"We shoot up."

"Well, make sure you don't share needles."

Meg looked at Karen and squinted her eyes just enough to make it a judgment.

"Oh, I see. I'm a bad mother for working. Well, guess what? This is the deck we've been dealt. I have to work. You know that."

"Not obsessively."

"I do the best I can, Meg."

"An Atari would ease the blow of being here all alone."

"You're making the choice to be alone. Grandpa would love to have you every day. He even offered to pick you up."

"Oh, there's a fun filled afternoon."

Karen huffed and threw her arms in the air.

"What do you want from me?"

"An Atari."

"Forget about it."

Meg walked casually over to the coffee table and started to shuffle through the stack of magazines until she found the one that said, *How to Say No to your Child.*

"Aha! I knew it!" she shouted, shaking the magazine in the air. "This is bullshit! I'm not one of your nut cases."

"It's okay to be angry with me, but it won't change my mind. You'll thank me later when you're compassionate, kind, and non-materialistic. So it's no, for sure."

"Fine. I'll just ask Grandpa to buy it for me."

Karen put her hands on her hips. She wished someone would inform her who replaced the old easy going Meg with this fresh-mouthed teen she barely recognized.

"Oh, really, Little Miss Smart Ass? We'll see about that. Now, come on," she said, waving Meg into the kitchen. "I wash, you dry."

"You ever hear of a dishwasher?"

"I have one named Meg."

"What if I washed and dried for a month? Would that earn me an Atari?"

"You're wearing me down, Meg. I'm going grayer by the minute."

After the kitchen was cleaned, Karen had one appointment, but promised to be back within the hour. Meg watched the station wagon drive down the street before opening the window and lighting a Parliament. She leaned onto her elbows and blew smoke rings into the cool, crisp evening air. She took a few puffs then put the cigarette between her thumb and pointer finger and flicked it out onto the street. She closed the window and marched toward the phone. It was time for a business call.

"Hi, Grandpa."

"Hey, Meg, how's my girl!"

"I'm good," she replied, in her best sullen voice.

"Is something wrong?"

"Nothing. Just bored," she sighed.

"Is your mom home?"

"No, she's out as usual."

"She is, is she?"

"Yep. Apparently, some head case is more important than me," huffed Meg.

"We both know that's not true, Megan."

Uh-oh. Grandpa used her real name. Better change tactics.

"It's just that summer days can be long and I'm finding myself bored. I think too much TV is tacky, don't you? Sometimes I wish I had a game to play. Something like, uh, I don't know, an *Atari?*"

"I see," said Carl.

"Yeah. And in case you don't know, it's a video game system for the television. Atari. Mom likes to play, too. She loves Pong on Atari," added Meg enthusiastically.

"Let's see now. I do have some housework that's been neglected and there is always yard work to be done."

"Look no further. I'm your girl!"

"I never had to bribe your mother to do chores."

5

"Times change."

"How about I pick you up tomorrow and we go and get this Atari. What's your mother's late night?"

"It varies, but usually Tuesdays."

"Okay then, as payment, you can come over every Tuesday for a month to do whatever chores I need. Then we'll eat dinner together. Deal?"

"Deal!"

Meg hung up the phone and jumped around. She knew her grandfather all too well; he'd make her do one day of solid labor and then call them even. She grabbed another cigarette and did a victory dance toward the window.

"Atari, Atari, I'm going to get an A-t-a-r-i!"

KAREN'S PAST, IN BRIEF

Whether it was genetics or shit poor luck, Karen was an unfortunate combination of her good looking parents. Although she would never have admitted it, it disturbed Vicki that her daughter didn't inherit her good looks. Karen surmised her mother felt this way from statements such as: "Are you going out in public with your hair like that, honey? I can fix it up if you'd like," or, "Tuck in your shirt to show off that tiny waist of yours," and, "You'll grow breasts someday, dear!" as well as, "Let me show you how to pluck that one eyebrow into two separate ones."

Karen sometimes felt she was God's joke on Vicki, because although she didn't care if she had the figure of a boy, one eyebrow, and untamed frizzy hair, these physical traits seemed to cause her mother mental anguish. None of what Vicki said was meant to be cruel, nor was it an indication of how much she loved her daughter. In fact, Karen didn't think it possible that any mother could love her daughter more than Vicki loved her. Her mother's egotistical remarks, Karen knew, were fear based and carried over from her own childhood. Every night until she was twelve, when Karen felt too old and gently began refusing her mother, Vicki read Karen a bedtime story. After she closed the book, she'd wrap her arms around Karen and cuddle her close.

"Look at those deep brown eyes, so brown I almost can't see your pupils. Who has better eyes than you?" Vicki would say proudly

"Your eyes are pretty too, Mamma," Karen would tell her.

"But your eyes carry this awareness of something that I can't quite put my finger on, Karen. You see, I'm not so very bright," Vicki meekly admitted.

"But you're pretty," Karen said, feeling pity for her mother, a woman for whom the Pope would resign his post to marry.

"It's okay, honey. You don't need to feel bad for me. I'm happy in my own skin. I just want you to be happy in yours. Are you?"

"I guess so," Karen said, wondering if this were a test and she should have said *I need thinner eyebrows.*

"Of course you are," Vicki smiled warmly. "And you know what? I have a feeling that someday you'll be someone very special," she said, lightly tapping the tip of Karen's nose.

The most influential adult during Karen's teen years was her tenth grade social studies teacher, Mrs. O'Hara. *Listen up kids,* she told them, *there are only two types of people in the world . . . movers and shakers, and do-nothings. Do-nothings are like malignant tumors. They sit around and complain about the state of the world and do nothing to change it. Movers and shakers are influential individuals who take action to change social and/or economic situations for the betterment of society.* Karen swore Mrs. O'Hara looked directly into her eyes when she said, *Which will you choose to be?*

"I'm going to be a social worker," Karen announced at dinnertime.

"Why not a schoolteacher?" asked Carl.

"I don't want to be a schoolteacher. What's wrong with being a social worker?"

"Nothing's wrong with it," said Carl, taking a bite out of a pork chop. "But it's not the cleanest occupation."

"Clean?" Karen questioned.

"It can get a bit dirty. Now a teacher, there's a proper, fitting job for a woman."

"You mean more traditional?" asked Karen, a bit sarcastically.

"Exactly," said Carl, pointing his fork at her.

"Don't you care about social consciousness, Daddy?"

"Social *what?*"

Karen looked at her mother for support, who raised both hands in surrender and said, "You're talking over my head, honey."

"But isn't helping others the main reason we're here?" asked a confused Karen.

"The reason we're where?" asked Carl.

"Here, on earth. The reason we're born."

"Where did that harebrained idea come from?"

"Carl," interrupted Vicki. "She is not a harebrain. Our Karen is a smart girl."

"I didn't say she wasn't smart, Victoria, I said the idea was harebrained. Now don't you two go ganging up on me," he said, defensively.

An infantry man for three years, Carl was wounded at the Battle of the Bulge. The shrapnel that hit his right leg left him with a slight, but permanent limp. His main focus was, and always would be, on his family. Everyone else, as far as he was concerned, was on their own.

"Daddy, we have to think about others."

"Karen, I do think about others. I think about you and your mother and how I'm going to stay middle class American. I can't be worrying about everyone else's problems."

"Well, can I be a social worker, or what?"

"You can be whatever you want, honey. Isn't that right, Carl?"

Carl looked at his wife. She had been the number one support in his life; agreeable, submissive Vicki had never challenged her husband. Carl knew this was a lioness protecting her cub situation and that he, although king of his den, better think twice about his answer. He met his beautiful wife's stare. Her sharp, blue eyes beseeched him to listen to his daughter.

Carl stuck a piece of meat in his mouth and, without taking his eyes off of Vicki said, "Karen, you can pick whatever profession your little heart desires."

"You mean whatever profession her big heart desires," grinned Vicki, who bowed her head slightly at her husband before picking up her fork.

"Thanks, Daddy!" Karen smiled. "Now, can we talk colleges?"

"Gee whiz," Carl sighed. "I can't do it all in one night, Karen."

Karen shrugged and said, "It's okay. We'll talk later."

By nine o'clock, Carl had fallen asleep on the couch. Vicki was perched on the loveseat with a TV tray in front of her that held rollers, bobby pins, and a comb. She wedged a bobby pin between her front teeth and picked up the comb.

"Hand me a medium roller, will you honey?" she asked, the bobby pin stable between her teeth.

9

"So," said Karen, sitting on the edge of the loveseat, "You think I'll be a good social worker?"

"Are you kidding? How could you not be? What better profession is there for a socially conscious girl such as yourself?"

"I can't think of anything else," grinned Karen.

"So, we're agreed?"

"Agreed," Karen nodded, squeezing herself in the small space between the arm rest and Vicki so that she could rest her head on her mother's shoulder.

On May 2, 1964, while at Simmons College, Karen hopped into the back of a friend's hunter green VW and drove to Times Square to participate in the first major student demonstration against the Vietnam War. On the ride to New York, she envisioned marching through the Square to the United Nations. She smiled widely to herself and thought, *I am going to help change the world!* What Karen forgot was that she was direction challenged. Upon arrival, the group merged into the crowd and Karen somehow managed to lose sight of every one of her friends. She ended up near tears in front of an ancient coffee shop called Big Ed's Black Brew.

"You waiting for anyone in particular?" a warm voice asked her.

"I'm all set, thank you very much," she said shyly, trying to recall if she had recently taken the time to pluck her one eyebrow into two.

"If you're all set, why do you look lost?"

Wanting to appear confident in her light brown peasant shirt, bell-bottoms, and a tie-dye headscarf, Karen looked him square in the eye, intending to say something clever or pompous, or both.

"Look," she began, rather firmly.

"At what?" he questioned, looking around.

"What?"

"What?"

"No, what to you," she repeated.

"What, *what* to me?" he smiled.

"Go away. You're bothersome," she told him, but she couldn't take her eyes off him.

"Yeah, well, you're annoying."

"Then why are you still here?"

He leaned in and whispered, "You look lost. I feel bad."

Karen's defenses fell slightly. He smelled delicious, a combination of cinnamon and the first day of spring.

"So?" he questioned.

"So, what?"

"So, are you lost?"

"Only kind of lost," Karen answered.

"Define kind of."

"Okay, yeah, I'm pretty lost," she admitted, tossing her hands in the air.

He held his hand out and said, "I'm Michael Humble."

For the first time in her life, Karen wished she had her mother's beauty. Michael had steel gray eyes, a perfect nose, square chin, slightly crooked smile, and reddish blonde hair that seemed to alternate in color by every other strand.

"Karen Sherburne," she said, extending her hand to meet his.

"Care for a cup of joe?" he smiled.

"Just a quick cup," she smiled back. "I've got to find my friends."

A quick cup lasted three hours, and Karen learned that Michael was just finishing his teaching degree at Boston College. He told Karen he was an only child and that both his parents had died in a plane crash two years earlier. He had received money from the accident and a small inheritance that would provide for his college tuition and, if all went well, a starter home. They reminisced about their childhoods, exchanged embarrassing stories, and talked about what a blessing and a curse it was to be an only child. Michael asked for her number and told her he'd call her soon, soon being exactly two days, twelve hours, and thirty seven minutes later.

Karen and Michael began seeing each other every weekend. Being the era of free love, they freely slept together and, after two months, Karen realized she was right after all; she could change the world.

By becoming pregnant.

"Well, I guess that's it for you. You went and ruined your life. I told you to be a teacher, not screw one."

"Carl!" exclaimed Vicki, who was slowly learning that being vocal or disagreeable wasn't such a bad thing. "That will do. What's done is done."

"It's done all right," he groaned.

Michael was ecstatic.

"Let's get hitched!" he cried, swinging Karen around in his arms.

If asked, Karen would describe the next few years as the best and worst of times. On August 5th, 1964, Michael and Karen were married at Somerville City Hall. The only people in attendance were her parents and Michael's best friend, Samuel. They moved into a two-family house in Somerville; it was the perfect location and size for a family of three. Michael began teaching third grade at the Bingham School. For the next eight months, happiness followed more happiness, and just when it didn't seem possible that there was any more happiness to be had, Megan Jane Humble was born on April 22nd, 1965.

"I hope you're planning on staying home to raise your girl," said Carl.

"But if you'd like to attend a few classes, your dad and I will baby sit for you," added Vicki enthusiastically. A baby wasn't about to prevent her from giving up on the dream of her daughter making something of herself.

Carl was sitting with his elbow propped on the table, his cheek resting in his fist. "Oh geez, Vicki, isn't it bad enough she kept her maiden name? Meg's going to be confused enough as it is, what with her mother being Karen Sherburne and her being Meg Humble. Will someone please tell me what the point of being married is if you're going to have two different last names?" he muttered, unballing his fist and dropping his forehead into his open hand.

"Of course she won't be confused. She's too smart to be confused," said Vicki.

"She's only a baby. How in the world do you know what she is?" Carl sighed.

"I can tell by looking at her that she's brilliant, just like her mother," beamed Vicki.

"But people won't even know they're related."

"But we'll know, Carl," she said lovingly, "And that's all that matters."

November 30th, 1965, was no different from any other morning. After toast with jelly for Michael, toast with peanut butter for Karen, and plum baby food for Meg, Michael kissed his wife goodbye.

"I'll call you at lunchtime."

"Sounds good, honey," smiled Karen, who was wrestling with Meg over the jar of baby food.

Michael was an inefficient multitasker. With a piece of toast between his teeth, he was shrugging on his jacket and grabbing his bagged lunch of ham and Miracle Whip. He turned toward the door and hit the side of his hip on the edge of the counter.

"Yowch!"

Karen laughed. "You'd better pay attention to one thing at a time or you're going to get yourself killed!"

"I like to live on the edge," he said, rubbing his hip.

Karen filled the bathtub so just enough water covered the bottom and placed Meg in the tepid water. She sang Sesame Street's *Rubber Ducky* while Meg giggled and cooed, her tiny hands flapping up and down beside her waist.

Michael stepped outside and looked up at the sky. It was dark and cloudy and he had forgotten his umbrella. At the bus stop, he felt two droplets of rain hit his nose, and by the time he reached the school, a steady rain had begun to fall. He stepped off the bus and decided to make a run for it, his briefcase and lunch haphazardly swinging back and forth. Just before he reached the school steps, he jogged past a set of construction workers who were debating whether to continue working in the rain. Sidestepping nail guns and ladders, Michael jogged passed Ed, the second grade teacher and Sue, the fifth grade teacher.

"Slow down, Mike!" joked Ed, "You almost took me out!"

Michael laughed and waved him off. "I'll save a spot on the radiator for your soaking wet clothes!"

There were two sets of cement stairs going into the school, with a landing dividing the sections. Michael took the first set two steps at a time, hopped onto the landing, and started for the second set. His foot hit the first step of the second landing, and as he propelled himself over the second step to reach the third, he missed by a smidge, his balance resting on the strength of his big toe's grip on the wet cement stair. He hovered in mid air for a split second, his arms out to the sides and his knee bent precariously in front of him. As he leaned forward, his shoe slipped on the wet stair and Michael went tumbling backward, his body flipping like a pancake, alternately hitting the left side of his body, and then his right. In an attempt to stop the painful momentum, he put out his arm, and his body rotated half a turn lengthwise. By this time, he had reached the bottom of the landing and his final blow was to the back of his head.

The fall broke his neck, but it wasn't enough to kill him.

What did kill Michael was a nail from the construction site that had found its way to the exact spot where Michael fell. Angled perfectly for mishap, it punctured his airway and penetrated the back of his broken neck.

Karen was told it was an unfortunate series of events that led to her husband's death. She never fell apart, but did have flu like symptoms that only a heavy workload seemed to cure. Outwardly functioning, she lived with an ominous belief that prevented her from ever trusting that her life wasn't meant to go from bad to worse. What others perceived as workaholic behavior, Karen perceived as a sanity saver. To save herself, she made sure that her platter was beyond full so that she didn't have time to think about Michael.

Or the promise of a wonderful life that was stolen from her and her daughter.

KENDRA AND AUGUST, 1980

"Tell me about your father," Kendra asked August.

"What is there to tell?" August said, dismissing his granddaughter with the wave of his hand.

"I want to know how he died. Is it true what they say, that his own wife, a.k.a. your mother, shot him? Is it really true, Gramps?"

"Who would this *they* be, Patatona? Who the hell's been telling you this?"

"I overheard Ms. Rizollo gossiping to Mrs. Stills. They were talking about the old days, and then Ms. Rizollo told Mrs. Stills about the day your father died, how your mother shot him in cold blood and all."

August and Sheri Rizollo had lived in the same neighborhood for forty years. Sheri had the figure of Wonder Woman and the face of a peacock. Mrs. Stills was no better, at six feet tall and shaped like a bowling pin.

"Those two ninnies," mumbled August.

Kendra scooted her chair closer to August and whispered, "If you told me, I wouldn't be wondering about sordid family secrets."

August sighed. "I'll tell you if you don't pester me no more about it."

Kendra darted to the television and turned down the volume, then raced back to her chair.

"Well, come out with it," she pressed. "Did he beat you? Was he a bastard? How did he treat your mother?"

"He was a bitch and a bastard. He thought all women were slaves and should walk behind him."

"Why would he ever think that?"

"How should I know? That's what all the Italians in my family used to think. He wanted everything his way," August said.

"Did he have a job?" she asked, almost too excitedly, as if this were the Montel Williams Show and not her actual lineage.

"He was a carpenter. He was good at it; a real craftsman, my father was."

"So, how did the murder happen?"

"She killed him."

"Der, I know that. Did she suddenly decide to go out and buy a gun one day and—bang?"

"She didn't hafta buy nuthin'. She shot him with his own gun."

Kendra grabbed an Oreo off the plate in the center of the table. Twisting the cookie open, she asked, "Why did she kill him?"

August felt like someone had lit a match in his gut. For a moment, he turned bright red and looked as if he were choking. Kendra braced herself for what she referred to as an "August fit". Instead, he let out a giant sigh.

"She shot him because he was trying to kill her."

"Oh, my!" Kendra said, clasping her hand over her mouth in surprise.

"And don't go thinking my mother was a bad woman. She was practically a saint. She worked all her life at the laundry factory. She would come home with sores on her body from the hot irons. A saint," he said, defending her crime.

"Were you there? Ms. Rizollo said you were there, and that's why you're such a miserable old bastard."

"Sheri Rizollo's an ugly old goat," he barked.

"But is she a correct old goat?" pressed Kendra, twisting another Oreo open.

"The old goat is correct," nodded August. "I was on the third floor asleep in my room when it happened."

"And?"

"I dunno. All I can remember is noise, confusion, and then the police banging on our door."

Kendra leaned forward. She wanted another Oreo, but settled for chomping on her cuticles.

"Were you afraid, Gramps? Did you hide?"

"What was there to be afraid of?"

"Of all the commotion."

"What did I know? There was always fighting. I was confused, just like I told you," he said, sounding exhausted.

"Did you like your father?" Kendra asked.

"I didn't hate him. He wasn't horrible to me, but he wasn't the nicest àncora on the street, if you know what I mean."

"Did he beat you?"

"Oh, Sweet Jesus, you kids don't know the meaning of words. Back then no one cried abuse. What happened to you, you dealt with."

August thought a moment before adding, "He may have mistreated me, or he may not have. I had chores to do and I made sure I did them so I wouldn't have to worry about getting in trouble."

He leaned toward Kendra and swatted her raw cuticles away from her mouth.

"What kind of chores?" She asked, backing away and switching fingers to chew on.

"Like carrying wood and picking dandelions to eat for dinner . . . get your goddamn fingers out your mouth. What are you, a cannibal?"

August batted at Kendra's hand. She ducked back and continued to chew on her skin.

"I'm a nail biter, Gramps. Get used to it."

"Sweet Jesus," he said, squeezing his eyes shut and pinching the bridge of his nose.

"So, you ate dandelions?" She asked, wiping her fingers on her shirt. "Cause you were poor?"

"Not because we were poor, because they were the thing to eat back then. A bunch of us used to go to an area in the city that was full of them. Me and Tony Hopper . . . we called him Hopper cause when he was a baby, he fell down a flight of stairs and he walked with a hop . . . we'd bring a little knife and some tin pails and we'd scoop the whole root," he explained with a nostalgic grin.

"Seriously? You ate dandelions?"

"Sure we did. Now, you don't want flowered dandelions. One time I brought back a flowered dandelion and my father . . . oh, the hell with it," he sighed, noting Kendra had grown bored with talk of dandelions.

"Speaking of which, back to your father," Kendra pressed.

"Once I got to be a big boy, my father didn't bother me no more. He was afraid of me because I got vicious. I was a real teppista," he said.

"What's a teppista?"

"A thug," said August, placing extra emphasis on the 'g'.

"But you're not a thug. You say the rosary," Kendra pointed out.

"Mobsters say the rosary, Patatona."

August signaled for Kendra to hand over the remote control. "Now get the hell out of here, Mass is on soon."

Kendra examined her fingers, chose the outside edge of her ring finger to sink her teeth into, and peeled off another piece of cuticle.

August winced. "Who's gonna wanna put a ring on that finger?"

Kendra smiled and bounced to her feet. She pinched her belly and said, "My cuticles are the least of my issues, Gramps."

She leaned over and kissed the top of her grandfather's bald head. "I'm going to do my homework. What's for dinner?"

August picked up his rosary and smirked at his granddaughter.

"Dandelions, Patatona. We're having dandelions."

JULY, 1980

Seven weeks before the murder

"It's all yours," said Sarah, plunking down a folder on top of the mountain of paperwork already on Karen's desk.

"Retread?" Karen asked, noting the folder's thickness.

"Marty said you'd love this one. He's high priority. Take a peek when you can."

"Gee, I can hardly wait."

Because she preferred not to be confined by the boundary of time, Karen didn't wear a watch. When she finished with one case, she would get up and stretch, have something to drink, sit back down at her desk, and take the next in line. Her department's rule of no overtime pay didn't deter Karen from putting in fifty-hour work weeks when her contract was for thirty to thirty-five hours. She flipped to the first page and began to read:

Frankie Ortiz, aged 15. Truant for two weeks. Suspected that mother is aware of truancy. Assault resulting in hospitalization of a 16-year-old boy. Victim was knocked unconscious and suffered a broken nose, cracked ribs, and two black eyes. Arrested for petty theft and loitering, and two B&E's. In 1978, Mom was charged with heroin use. Father is absent, with history of past abuse.

Frankie was supposed to be doing supervised community service helping to pick up trash at Prospect Hill Park, but was a no-show.

"Sarah?"

"Yeah?"

"What happened to the other social worker?"

"She was the sensitive type."

"Meaning?"

"He called her a butt ugly bitch and told her to eat shit and die."

"Huh, is that all?" asked Karen. "What a wuss!"

"That's why you get all the good ones!" laughed Sarah.

Karen dialed the Ortiz home. She didn't expect, so was surprised, when someone answered it.

"Hello?"

"Is this Mrs. Edna Ortiz?"

"I don't have the money," she spat.

"I'm not looking for money. My name is Karen Sherburne, and I'm the new social worker assigned to your son, Frankie. I was wondering if I could stop by later today to meet with you both?"

"Today's no good," slurred Mrs. Ortiz.

"There's no time like the present, Mrs. Ortiz, don't you agree?"

"Oh, I don't know about this. I no feel so well."

Karen ignored this comment and said, "How about 6:30?"

"Does my son have to be here?"

"Yes. That would be the point of me coming," said Karen, with a hint of impatience.

"Okay then, I will tell him to be here, but sometimes I no can control him too well."

Karen left the office at five and ran home to cook dinner for Meg.

"Wow, you're actually home before six?" said Meg, who was on her belly in front of the TV, her hand manipulating a remote control box that looked like a game console.

"Not really home for the night. I have an appointment. I just came by to say a quick hi to . . . Megan, what is that?"

"Atari."

Karen licked her lips and closed her eyes. She took three deep breaths before impatiently asking, "Where did you get it?"

Meg rolled on her side and looked at her mother innocently.

"Grandpa. I'm cleaning his house every Tuesday for a month. Didn't I mention it to you? I thought I did," she said sweetly.

"Grandpa?"

"Yes."

"I see. Did you happen to mention to him that I already said *no*," Karen barked, her voice picking up steam.

"I cannot tell a lie. I did not mention it," Meg smiled weakly. "But look, you're going out and I'm alone again, and . . ."

Karen threw her arms in the air and looked up at the ceiling in frustration.

"Argggggggghhhhh!" she grunted. "Do you see how sneaky this is?"

"But Mom—"

"Oh, don't give me that crap, Megan. Don't start the 'I'm all alone and locked up kid' crap with me."

Meg shrugged and turned back to the TV. "Take a nutty, why don't cha?"

When Meg turned her back, Karen raised both hands and aimed them at Meg's neck, mock strangling her daughter. She glanced at the clock on the wall and thought, *shit.*

"I've got to go. This discussion isn't over."

"You mean this dictatorship?" Meg said, looking over her shoulder at Karen.

"Argggggggghhhhh! You are so frustrating! I want to kill you sometimes, you know that?"

Karen spun around and slammed the door behind her. If she believed in corporal punishment, Meg would be a goner by now. By the time she rounded the corner, she remembered the reason she had gone home . . . to cook supper for Meg. She pulled over to the nearest phone booth.

"Hallo," said Meg.

"I'm still mad at you, but I forgot to feed you. There's money in my underwear drawer. Order a pizza or something. I'll be back from this appointment in an hour."

"Don't you mean you'll be back from the sicko in an hour?"

"Give me a break, Meg. In fact, give yourself a break. You're already in it neck deep."

"But how could you blame me for asking Grandpa for an Atari?"

"Oh, I don't know; maybe because I said no to begin with."

"I'm not a bad kid, Mom. I could be drinking my brains out or taking drugs. I could be snorting lines on the kitchen table as we speak while you're out saving the world. Did ya ever think of that?"

"What I'm thinking is that you're self-inducing brain damage in front of the television."

"If you must know, I felt guilty when you left and turned it off."

"And I suppose you're sitting on a chair with your hands folded in your lap?" Karen teased.

"No, I'm not," Meg paused before adding, "I'm snorting cocaine."

Struggling to maintain composure, Karen spoke deliberately, taking a breath between words.

"Just—order—the—pizza."

"I'm ordering drugs, too. I'm calling the dealer first."

Then it happened.

Meg released an infectious giggle and before she knew it, Karen was snickering into the phone.

"That's super, honey. Save some for me, because I have a daughter who is driving me crazy."

"Mom?"

"Yeah, Meg?"

"I'm sorry I went behind your back."

"You should be."

"You want me to order pepperoni or plain?"

"Pepper and onion."

"Good choice."

"Meg?"

"Yeah?"

"Make sure you drink some milk with dinner."

"Mom?"

"Yeah, Meg."

"We're so dysfunctional."

"I know. Isn't it wonderful?"

"I love you, Mom."

"I love you more, Meg."

Karen hung up with a heavy conscience. She promised herself that this was the last case she was going to accept until at least two or three others had cleared. She pulled onto a narrow side street and parked in front of a house whose front yard resembled a junkyard. She had to sidestep broken glass and serrated tops of tin cans to get to the door. On the third knock, she was greeted by the blank stare of a very handsome boy.

"Frankie?" she smiled.

He stared blankly at Karen for a moment before turning his head and shouting, "Ma. The lady is here."

"You can go in that room," he said dully, pointing to a kitchen that looked Board of Health condemnable.

"Thank you," she smiled again.

When he didn't reply, she said, "You are Frankie, right?"

"None other," he muttered, folding his arms and leaning against the wall.

Karen was used to bullet answers, she was used to defiance, and she was used to being told to fuck off by seven year olds. What she wasn't used to was paying a visit to a boy who was clearly a mess on paper, but who looked like a teenage heartthrob. Frankie's olive complexion framed his thick, almost white hair that was cut in a headbanger hairstyle that hung loose at his shoulders. His eyes, an unusual mix of amber and copper, looked at you with disinterest, while at the same time demanding your attention. In his loose fitting jeans and ripped Judas Priest tee shirt, Frankie carried a look of mistrust. His stance was defensive, his arms crossed in front of his chest, and his eyes were fixed on anything but Karen. Although the chart said he was fifteen, he could easily have passed for twenty-one.

When Edna walked in, Karen knew immediately that this was a woman who had been abused long and hard. Her front bottom tooth was missing, she smelled of alcohol and urine, and was wearing stained, worn out clothing.

"Mrs. Ortiz," Karen began, "We've received reports of truancy and failure on Frankie's part to show for appointments with his DSS caseworker."

"What dickhead turned me in this time?"

Karen took a deep breath and replied, "You know the routine, Frankie. You've failed to comply on your community service. There was also that incident . . ."

"Blah, blah, blah. You people can eat shit and die," he said calmly. "I'm fifteen now."

"Yes, Frankie, and I'd very much like to see you spend sixteen, seventeen, and the rest of your life outside of jail."

That shut him up. Frankie's expression shifted from one of anger to one of acknowledgment.

"What do you want from us?" Edna moaned. The woman was clearly on multiple substances.

"Let's start with getting you clean, Edna," said Karen.

Edna snorted.

Karen ignored her.

"I also want to meet with Frankie weekly, and with the two of you monthly."

Edna glared at Karen like she was demon spawn. She had the same amber eyes as her son, only they weren't as sharp. Years of living with abuse had dulled them to a bloodshot, dried out appearance that was more pitiful than angry.

Karen reached across and lightly touched Edna's arm, "You don't want to lose your boy, do you?"

Edna's eyes filled with tears.

"Life isn't so good. He is not so good all the time."

"Shut the hell up, Ma!" yelled Frankie. "You'd just love to blame me for your entire disgusting life, wouldn't you?"

"Don't you talk to me like that, you son of a—"

Karen put her hand in the air.

"People, please. Let's not do this in front of the social worker. It's been a trying day and I don't have time to referee your battles."

She stood up and handed them each a copy of the service plan. She turned to Frankie and said as calmly as she could, "I want you to read your service plan, Frankie. I've already looked at your school records. With the amount of time you've spent outside of the classroom, I was surprised to see that you've managed a B average on every test score. Not one C or D, Frankie. You know what that tells me?"

When Frankie didn't answer, Karen continued. "It tells me you're smart, maybe exceptionally smart, but of course with continued absences, you're bound to flunk out of school."

"And I care because?"

Karen ignored him. "I've spoken with the principal and have arranged for you to make up the work you've missed. You won't have to repeat this year if you complete it. You want out of school the right way, don't you?"

"Does it require effort?"

"I hate to say this, but with your intelligence probably not."

"So what do I need to do?"

"I suggest you do the work, get out the right way. No use backtracking and worrying about a GED years from now when you're stuck working at some fast food place mopping the floors, right?"

Karen expected a giant fuck you from Frankie, but he surprised her.

"If it gets me out, I'll do it."

"Smart move," she nodded. "See you next week."

Once inside her car, Karen pulled out a moist towelette and vigorously scrubbed her hands. This wasn't because she was a germaphobe. She was washing away the filth of the meeting. She gave her head a slight shake to clear out any residue from the meeting, then turned on her cassette player. If Meg were in the car, she'd call her mother a queer for humming to Louis Armstrong's *What a Wonderful World*.

"You're so queeaarrr," she would tease.

Karen would answer her by breaking out into the full song.

FRANKIE

Frankie sat on the edge of his bed and read through his service plan:

1. Edna must have weekly random alcohol and drug tests.
2. Weekly visits will be established by Karen Sherburne, LISCW.
3. Edna must provide nutritious meals for Frankie three times per day.
4. Edna must attend individual substance abuse counseling.
5. Edna must attend weekly AA meetings.
6. Unless ill, Frankie must attend school five days a week.
7. Frankie must be enrolled in an after school activity, such as the Boys and Girls Club.

Go to school daily? Is she kidding?

The only reason he went to school was to fulfill his basic needs for warmth and hunger. His attendance was always higher during the winter because he needed to stay warm throughout the day to survive the frigid nights at home. And when Edna forfeited her entire paycheck for alcohol or drugs, Frankie waited for the cafeteria to clear out before rummaging through the trash for half-eaten sandwiches that he could stick in his backpack for later in the day.

The incident that the social worker lady was referring to, the one that landed her at his front door, was a violent assault on Tim Ashley, a sophomore and bully, just like Frankie. What wasn't written down on paper, and what Frankie was too ashamed to admit, was the reason for the attack. Tim forgot his math book in the cafeteria and had caught Frankie red-handed eating out of the trash.

"What the fuck, you spazz! You want a takeout dish for supper?"

The shame that engulfed Frankie was one of the most horrifying that he had ever felt. Watching Tim laughing loudly while aiming his finger at Frankie's face caused something inside Frankie to snap. He reacted without thinking. Frankie dropped a half-eaten sandwich back into the trash and pounced on Tim. His fist met Tim's face, stomach, and kidneys. While Tim lay in a heap on the floor, Frankie threatened to kill his mother if he ever told a soul what he witnessed. The only reason Tim wasn't worse off was because old lady Gleason, the cafeteria lady, called school security. When asked why the incident occurred, a bruised Tim, minus one tooth, thought protectively of his mother and pleaded the Fifth.

Frankie crumpled up the service plan and tossed it into the corner of his bedroom where it disturbed a clump of dust bunnies. This lady was high if she really expected a wastoid like Edna to sober up. His mother had as much chance of getting clean as did a shit stain on white underwear. And by being her son, most people considered Frankie guilty by association. He'd never get anywhere as long as he was stuck in this hellhole. The apple, Frankie told himself as he lit a joint, wasn't allowed to fall far from the tree.

KENDRA AND MEG'S BRIEF, LIFE CHANGING ENCOUNTER

The day of Meg's demise

Kendra announced resolutions year round.

"Gramps, I've got a new resolution."

"It can't wait until New Year's?"

"Nope."

"Let's hear it then."

"A no judgment rule."

"Why?"

"Because once you begin to compare and judge others, you become imprisoned by their opinions and belief systems, which are detrimental traps to the human psyche."

"I don't even know what you just said. Do you know what you said?"

"Sorta."

"Oprah?"

"Yeah."

"Patatona, would you do your old grandfather a favor?"

"Sure thing."

"Make like an egg and beat it."

"Are you judging me?"

"Yes, now scram!"

At four-thirty, Kendra plopped herself on top of her checkered bedspread to read a trashy novel brimming with promiscuity. Ridiculously handsome men rescued blindingly gorgeous damsels in distress and the word nipple was used ad nauseam. Just when she was getting to the juicy sex part, August poked his head inside the doorway.

"I need you to walk down to the corner store for milk and breadcrumbs. Fried chicken for dinner."

"Anything for a gazillion calorie greasy meal," Kendra replied, closing her book and hopping off the bed.

Because fried chicken was one of Kendra's favorite meals and she planned on consuming the same amount of calories as a famished construction worker after a hard day's work, she decided to ride her bike to the larger grocery store across town. The bike ride, she told herself, would cancel out the large amounts of grease she was about to consume. Arriving at her destination at five o'clock, she locked her bike on a small rusty rack, and because this wasn't her side of town, she tested her bike lock twice. Entering the store, she had a near collision with a girl who was exiting. Luckily, Kendra was paying attention, and the two ended up brushing shoulders. This inconsequential event would spark a connection, something neither would be aware of for years to come.

"Whoops!" said the girl, turning sideways.

"Oh, sorry," replied Kendra, but the girl hadn't heard her. She was busy humming to her Sony Walkman and digging around in her purse.

Kendra momentarily watched the skinny blonde with strawberry highlights walk confidently away, her head bouncing to whatever song was playing in her ears. She couldn't see her face, but her confident strut probably meant she was pretty. Kendra sucked in her stomach and mumbled, "Well, excuuuse me." She would have mumbled more, but remembered her no judgment rule.

While searching for breadcrumbs in aisle five, Kendra bumped into more good news: Mrs. Stills and Ms. Rizollo. She had forgotten they preferred to shop at this store, claiming the sales prices couldn't be beat by anyone else in town.

"Hi, Mrs. Stills, Ms. Rizollo," she said politely, because if anything else, Kendra Bruno was polite.

"Hello, Dear," they replied in unison, clutching their carriages like nursing home walkers.

"Why, you are looking more and more like your mother every day, Kendra," smiled Ms. Rizollo. Then, as if Kendra couldn't hear the blatant Irish whisper, Ms. Rizollo leaned toward Mrs. Stills and said, "You remember her mother don't you, Gloria? Sullen type, dressed in all black, heavy makeup?"

Mrs. Stills turned her bulging, fish-like eyes on Kendra.

No judgment she told herself, grateful that although raised by August, she didn't share his explosive nature. She looked at the two women with compassion and wondered at what age one slowly begins to go retarded; the age when verbal filters malfunction and whispering equals talking normally. Maybe someday she'd uncontrollably blurt out her inside thoughts to the general public or even worse, she might become like these two . . . a fashion 'don't' with bright red lipstick bleeding around her mouth like a smear of red frosting.

"Okay then," she said to the two women. "Have a nice day."

"You too, dear," said Ms. Rizollo, who clucked her tongue and loudly whispered, "That poor child."

"That old bat," said August, when Kendra told him what happened.

"That didn't bother me because they have no idea what my parents were really like."

"That's right, Patatona."

"But you know."

"Know what?"

"C'mon, Gramps. Was my mom some kind of witch or something?"

August couldn't bear to tell his granddaughter anything close to the truth.

"No, of course not. Rizollo ain't nothing but an out of her mind idiota. I'll grab that goddamn cane of hers out from under her next time I see her," shouted a red-faced August.

Dodging his angry spurts of saliva, Kendra calmly replied, "No, you won't, Gramps. Forget it. She's old and lonely."

"Yes, Patatona, you're so right. And if anyone is a witch, she is. Who does she think she is picking on my granddaughter? *Pfft*, like she is so perfect. That's why she's an old maid. She never understood how to be considerate. She's one sour woman, that one."

Throughout dinner, August continued to rant about the two old goats. Kendra, who had grown bored with listening, decided to ride her bike to the library.

"I'll be back before nine."

"You going to meet some friends?"

"That's right," she lied.

Poor August actually thought his granddaughter had friends. Over the years, she'd fabricated stories about friends from school and fake invitations that she turned down just so he wouldn't pity her. It wasn't that Kendra was disliked; on the contrary, kids found her quite amusing. She made a decision to mentally separate from her peers so that she didn't feel the sting of pain over their normal upbringings. Normal, meaning they had a mother and/or father who didn't abandon them.

The library was a small stone structure that smelled of must and burnt leaves. It was outdated and run by retired college professors who recommended books by Voltaire and Dickens as light reads. Kendra browsed the occult section, looking for anything having to do with witchcraft, palmistry, or experiencing visions. When she was convinced that she had read enough to conjure up a summoning spell that would bring her parents home, she checked out a couple of books and rode to the smaller market for spell supplies. The summoning spell called for funkier herbs than the supermarket offered, but she didn't see the harm in substitutions. After all, isn't that what people did for cooking recipes? How different could casting a spell be?

She waited until August was asleep, because if he found her casting a spell he would A) douse her with holy water B) probably die on the spot. When the coast was clear, she positioned herself on the edge of her bed. From her pocketbook, Kendra produced a small bottle each of dried basil, thyme, and oregano. On her bedside table was a paper cup of August's wine, which she had stolen from the pantry while he was watching an *Archie Bunker* rerun. According to the book, the wine was supposed to be in a chalice, but what supermarket had a chalice?

She figured the spell wouldn't care if the wine were in paper, pewter, or glass. She raised the paper cup to the heavens and with head up and eyes glancing at the open pages on her nightstand, recited the *The Wiccan Rede,* a poem she found by some woman named Lady Gwen Thompson. She recited the last few lines with as much passion as she could muster, "True in love ever be Unless thy lover's false to thee. Eight words ye Wiccan Rede fulfill—An' it harm none, Do what ye will," and then gulped the bitter wine a bit too quickly. Kendra felt slightly woozy as she placed the empty cup on her bedside table. She walked over to her mirror and stared intently at her eyes. She took a deep breath, exhaling slowly, trying to hypnotize herself with her own reflection.

Nothing.

She went back to the bedside table, lit a candle, and turned off the lights. Then she walked back to the mirror and tried to bewilder the magic to happen.

"Beauty unfolds the blue sky above, bring me the people that my heart so loves. I love movies, food and trees, will my loved ones please return to me?"

Zippo.

"Just as I suspected," she said, giggling from both the wine buzz and her own stupidity.

MEG'S LAST DAY

"Hi, Sarah. Is my mother in?"

"You just missed her, kiddo."

"She asked me to call her if I go out because she doesn't trust me."

"Have you ever thought she's just worried about you when she's not around?"

"That would be 90% of the time," Meg said sarcastically.

"Give her a break, Meg."

"She thinks I'm defiant."

"Are you?"

"Of course I am. I'm a teenager."

Sarah suppressed a giggle. "I'll tape a note to her computer that her defiant, but adorable daughter called."

"Love it. See ya, Sarah."

The grocery store was approximately a nine-minute walk. Meg walked slowly, puffing on a Parliament. She arrived at four forty-five, snuffed out the cigarette, and flipped her headphones around her neck. At five o'clock, she paid the cashier, secured her headphones to her ears, and accepted the gallon of milk from the bagger. Humming Blondie's *Heart of Glass* and rummaging through her purse, she brushed shoulders with a girl who was entering the store as she was exiting.

"Whoops!" she said, shifting sideways.

Meg dug out another Parliament and stuck it between her lips. With the unlit cigarette sticking out of her mouth, she searched her Walkman for a good song. She stopped when she heard *Another One Bites the Dust* by Queen, and then her eyes were back in her purse searching for a book of matches. She lit the cigarette and exhaled. *This is the life,* thought Meg, enjoying the beat of the music and the sensation of smoke-filled lungs. On the corner of Main and Alpine,

Meg had two choices: go straight down Main Street, or cut through an alleyway.

Looking down the narrow alleyway, Meg had one of those spine-chilling, foreboding moments that warned *this may not be a good idea.*

But she chose the cut through anyway.

A quarter of the way down the alley, two boys startled her by jumping out from behind a dumpster. One was tall and exceptionally good looking; the other was short and twitchy, and reminded Meg of a nervous rat.

Cute Boy was saying something, but she couldn't hear him through the Walkman. Maybe he was asking for her phone number, which she would actually consider giving to him.

She pulled her headphones away from one ear and said, "What?"

"The purse. Give it over."

"No way!" she barked, turning away her shoulder with the purse on it.

"Look," he said, his voice thick with impatience, "You've got two seconds."

"Eat my shorts!" Meg spat, her chin protruding upward in defiance.

"You gonna take that from her?" asked Rat Boy.

Before she realized what was happening, Cute Boy leaned in and grabbed her purse. After a small struggle, Meg felt something pierce her side. She let go of her purse, and as Cute Boy pulled away with it, she felt an odd, warm sensation in her side. It was sort of like a booster shot. Confused, she looked from one to the other.

"What was that?" she wondered aloud, her hand automatically drawing to her side.

Rat Boy looked at his friend and said, "What the fuck?"

"Shut up and let me think," replied Cute Boy, pushing his friend in the chest.

As they argued, Meg, who was now woozy, was still occupied with finding out exactly what had poked her. She felt around until her finger found a tiny hole no larger than the tip of a pencil.

"Oh, Christ, there's blood on her fingers!" panicked Rat Boy.

Meg glanced down and sure enough, tiny specks of blood were on her shirt and fingertips.

"Will you shut up and just help me!" growled Cute Boy.

While the boys continued to argue, Meg grew more disoriented by the second. Her body slid helplessly down the wall she had been pushed up against during the struggle for her purse.

There, she thought, *much better.*

From that moment on, things became blurry for Meg. She felt the boys grab her under her arms and lift her to her feet. They laughed loudly as she was led staggering to a car. She attempted to shout, "Please, somebody help me, I'm hurt!" but was surprised when her plea came out no louder than a whisper.

While being placed into the backseat, Meg recalled the warning police officers emphasized to grade schoolers . . . *Never get in the car . . . Never let them take you away . . . You don't come back.*

"Take me home, please," she mumbled, not sure if she could be heard over the blaring music.

When there was no acknowledgment, Meg tried again.

"I have money at home. I'll give you all my cash. I promise."

At this point, Meg wasn't even sure she was speaking out loud. Her head was bobbing up and down of its own accord, and with each bounce she thought for sure she would vomit.

"Pull over here," she heard one of them say.

The humming of the engine ceased and Meg felt herself being carried away. After what seemed an eternity, she was placed face up on a hard, moist surface that smelled of dirt and fresh air.

Cute Boy was giving instructions. "Easy, don't just drop her."

"You assholes can't leave me here," she whimpered, struggling to grab one of the boys by the pant leg.

"She's coming after me!" cried Rat Boy. "Get her off, get her off!"

"Just move, you dip shit," said Cute Boy.

Rat Boy stepped sideways, out of Meg's reach.

"Assholes, she mumbled, closing her eyes. "I'm going to get you both."

The boys walked quietly away so not to disturb nature. Because she could clearly hear the car being started, Meg surmised the road couldn't be far away. This was confirmed when she smelled exhaust and heard tires grinding over salt and sand. Fear of the boys harming her further was overridden by a sinister doom that whispered to Meg that she was probably going to end up as road kill. For the next few hours, she passed in and out of consciousness. She woke in the darkness to an awful pain in her side, listening to the *wrrrrr, wrrrrr, brrrmmm, beep* sound of traffic.

Shit, she thought, *they dumped me on the highway. I hate highways!* From her vantage point, signs weren't visible. *Is this 93 north or south? 128? 495? Route 1? I-95?*

Meg decided that it didn't really matter where she was because judging by the way she felt, she would probably be dead by the time anyone discovered her.

MEG

Roadside Trash, Day 1

Highways are nothing but yellow lines of hypnotizing pavement decorated with roadside trash, and for the past few hours, I've been the trash. When I was a kid, I hated being in the car, especially for long rides. The mere sight of a highway sign sent me into a tizzy. The click of the directional was all it took for me to scream: "Is this the highway?"

Mom tried everything to quiet me. She bribed me with food, she sang stupid songs, she told jokes. Nothing worked. Finally, she thought of something that held my interest.

"See those trees over there, Meg? See the bright colors at the very top? God painted those this morning just for you."

"He did? What are their names?"

"Over there is Mr. Pine. This one coming up on my side is Mrs. Maple, and over there, I think that could be a Sir Evergreen."

From that point on, highway trips were turned into tree trivia games; tree names, tree colors, tree leaves . . . and the highway, though it was still nerve wracking, became doable. Did you know that trees keep their knowledge inside their trunks in a bunch of rings? You can't see these rings unless you slice them open, but they're way cool because they can tell you things about the past, like if there was a volcano that erupted or a fire that happened or a glacier or a flood or an earthquake. It can even tell you about insects in that area.

Pretty awesome, huh?

Ever since, I've been a tree hugger. I can't imagine anything more beautiful than rows and rows of multi-sized afros in brilliant orange and burning red and all sorts of green.

Can you?

When I was around twelve, I got it in my head that somewhere along the barren trash littered sides of the road, the trees wanted me to find this dead baby. I'd make myself carsick, my forehead pressed against the cold window, searching the sides of the road and thicket of forest patches for a lump shaped like a newborn. I was certain someday I would find that almost dead baby, abandoned by a fifteen-year-old girl who was too afraid to tell anyone she was pregnant. She would later turn up at a hospital having been brought there by a friend, who happened to be a special kind of stupid, and who suddenly figured out her friend was bleeding to death. Charges would be filed, but she wouldn't have to go to jail or anything. It would be more than a slap on the wrist, but less than what I would have given her if I were the judge. If I were the judge, I would sentence her to death by lethal injection. Then I would dope slap her alleged friend for being such a dumb ass.

Ooo, I just created a pretty good movie of the week. Mom used to say overexposure to Creature Double Feature and Twilight Zone over stimulated my imagination about my baby on the highway obsession.

Considering my current circumstances, I guess we can both agree that I wasn't overreacting.

P.S. About the lethal injection thing, I know you're not supposed to want to kill another person, but if someone kills a defenseless baby for any reason, including not wanting to admit they did the dirty with their boyfriend . . . well, they deserve to die . . . an eye for an eye.

At least that's my take on it.

FRANKIE

The Night of the Stabbing

No one had ever promised Frankie that life would be easy, but no one told him it would be one shit storm after another either. He tried to make good decisions, but for some reason always ended up making disastrous ones, landing in the wrong place at the wrong time. As he paced the confines of his room, uneasiness swelled into panic and remorse. He didn't intentionally mean to hurt her.

Questions haunted him: *How bad was it? Could she identify me? Were they going to find his fingerprints anywhere?*

He had been very careful not to touch her, and though he did lean into her when the mini screwdriver punctured her side, no skin-to-skin contact was made. He only hoped that moron Adam didn't fuck up and smear his fingerprints everywhere. Eighteen and still in tenth grade, Adam had the mentality of an earthworm. Frankie only hung around with him because he had wheels.

"What the fuck, Frankie! You were only supposed to threaten her, not stab her," said a panic-stricken Adam.

"Did you want the purse or not?" he defended.

When the girl sunk against the wall, she looked as if she were in a drug-induced trance, which gave Frankie an idea. If he and Adam could somehow get her to Adam's car, they could transfer her to another site, and if ever questioned, Frankie would deny he'd been with Adam. It would be Adam's word against his, and Edna would provide him with a sound alibi. She was usually filled with so much booze she didn't know when Frankie was home; all he had to do was say, "Tell them I was here, Ma," and Edna, who despised authority, would oblige. It seemed like a win/win situation. Frankie bent down to where the girl was slumped and disoriented. There was the smallest of stains on her shirt and a bit of blood on her fingers. He gave Adam explicit instructions and then gave him a moment to let it all sink in.

"Whatever you do, Adam, try not to touch her. We're going to scoop her up under the arms with our elbows and direct her to the car."

There was a slight pause before Adam's face turned pale with understanding.

"Are you crazy? I'm not touching her and she's *not* getting in my car!"

Frankie ignored him and said, "And I need your baseball hat to cover her hair."

"No fucking way," snarled Adam.

"Pick her up," Frankie said, his voice edged with a danger that caused Adam to wince.

"All we have to do is get from point A to point B. Point B is your car, and it's right behind us down the side street. No one will even notice."

Adam dug his heels in a minute longer before nodding his head in agreement. If anyone noticed anything, it was two teenage boys helping a drugged or drunk someone in a baseball hat and farmer's jeans down a side alley. When they reached the car, Frankie opened Adam's glove compartment. Because of his prolific love for pot, Adam carried a stash of medium-sized plastic baggies.

"Here," Frankie said, handing Adam two baggies. "Put your hands inside so you don't leave any prints. And grab that blanket you have in your trunk and put it on your seat."

They drove down I-95 and at the first sign of minimal traffic, pulled over.

"What if we already left prints on her when we took her to the car?"

"Did you touch her or scoop her?"

"Scooped her."

"Then we'll have to hope for the best," said Frankie, fitting a baggie onto his hand.

Frankie and Adam used the corner of the blanket to pull the barely conscious girl out of the car. Once she was on the ground, Frankie directed, "Hurry. Take her legs and we'll bring her down the slope."

They scooped Meg under her armpits and carried her down a steep path.

"Why is she so out of it?"

"Beats me, but I'm not complaining," said Frankie.

The girl's eyes were glazed and her breath reeked of sour milk, which Frankie tried to avoid by turning his head sideways. He was keenly aware that he was abandoning an injured human being, but he told himself this was a necessary evil. By the time she made her way up the hill, they'd be long gone.

Placing her on moist dirt among rocks and leaves, he gently took off her denim jacket.

"What are you doing?"

"Taking any evidence."

"She'll freeze."

"Nayh," said Frankie. "She'll be climbing up this hill within the hour. Now, let's go. With any luck, she'll forget what we look like."

As they pulled away, Frankie was eighty percent confident that she'd never be able to fully identify them.

Then something he hadn't thought of crossed his mind.

What if she died?

Killing a person was much different than killing a cat. Killing a cat could land you in juvie, but killing a person could land you dead. Frankie glanced back. The girl was well hidden. He didn't have the luxury of dwelling on what ifs. He told himself the girl would live to tell the story of how she got mugged. Period.

When they parted ways, Frankie threatened Adam that he'd kill him if he ever breathed a word to anyone. He could only hope the threat was enough to keep him quiet, because none of what just happened was inside of Frankie's comfort zone.

This didn't mean he wouldn't take the appropriate steps necessary to protect himself if Adam fucked up. Frankie was all about self-preservation.

"You need to wipe down the car with bleach," warned Frankie. He confiscated the baggies, Adam's baseball hat, his blanket, and just to be sure, his coat. Because he lit a bonfire at least twice a week to stay warm, none of his neighbors would think anything of seeing a fire in Frankie's backyard.

He burned everything, including his underwear, to a pile of ash, and then sat on the edge of his bed to surf the evening news. At eleven thirty on Channel 5, he found what he was looking for. A perky brunette with hungry eyes reported: "A truck driver discovered an injured girl on route I-95 north tonight. Just before ten o'clock, the driver said he was distracted by a moving object and quickly realized it was a girl crawling on her hands and knees. He pulled over and assisted the girl to his truck, where they both waited for help to arrive. The girl appears to have suffered head trauma and has no recollection of the day's events. The parents of the fifteen-year-old, whose name is being withheld, stated that the girl is expected to make a full recovery.

It had to be the same girl. But how did she suffer head trauma?

Maybe she stood up and fell backward, hitting her head on the ground?

Maybe she slammed into the guardrail and smacked her temple?

He wished they had given a description or showed a picture or something. Frankie let out a giant sigh of relief. He couldn't have wished for a better outcome. Alive with amnesia! And with any luck, she wouldn't remember a thing. He settled into bed and vowed he would never stab another person for as long as he lived because the next time, he may not get so lucky. If he were caught, this is exactly what people would have expected from a boy like Frankie. And Frankie didn't intend to be trailer trash forever. If it was the last thing he did, he was getting out of this hellhole.

WAITING FOR MEG

Karen and her father sat vigilant by the phone, occasionally checking to make sure the ringer wasn't turned off. They kept conversation light and avoided any speculation or fears they had of Meg not being found alive. She tried to banish the negative thoughts that swirled around in her head by replacing them with positive affirmations. This only worked for a short time. Since Meg's disappearance, Karen lived with a dull pain in her chest and a constant pool of vomit at the base of her throat. She saw Meg's face everywhere: her shiny silver braces, her wide-set eyes that were the same slate gray as Michael's, her perfect nose inherited from Vicky, and an award winning smile, compliments of Carl.

The day after Meg's disappearance, Karen left Carl in charge of answering the phone. She rode to Meg's school and parked at the front of the building. While waiting for the dismissal bell, Karen thought that this could all be one giant mistake. Meg could have forgotten to tell her she had slept over at a friend's house. She waited long after the last students had left the building before driving home empty-handed. Bypassing her father in the living room, she headed for Meg's room and locked the door. She sat on the edge of her daughter's bed, inhaling the air. It was a unique smell she knew she would never be able to replicate, and one she feared would fade over time, especially if Meg was . . . she picked up a teddy bear that Meg aptly named "Teddy," and inspected the stuffing leaking from its foot. Meg had begged her many times to sew him, and Karen promised she'd get to it eventually, but she never did. Now, Karen's world stood still, and she had all the time in the world to mend Teddy's torn foot. The minor surgery came in the form of a bad stitch job, but at least the foot would survive. Karen held the bear in front of her and smiled to herself, knowing that Meg would be very happy when she saw it. She leaned Teddy against Meg's pillow, picked up the purple fuzzy blanket at the end of her bed, and left the room. She went into the kitchen and poured herself a cup of coffee, then grabbed a chair, which she positioned two feet from the front door. In an effort to contain the sorrow that engulfed her, Karen hugged the blanket fiercely against her chest. She sipped her coffee and willed herself to stay awake, fearing that if she closed her eyes, she'd slip to some faraway place, to a reality that didn't include Meg coming home.

MEG

Roadside Trash, Day 2

I feel way restless, like when you can't sleep at night. Like when you're lying in bed and your eyes pop open, and you feel like you're on speed. You know those nights where you toss and turn and punch your pillow a couple of times so that it fits your head better? You try every position imaginable; your back, your belly, your side. One leg out straight, one leg bent, one leg dangling off the bed, an arm slung over your eyes like a mask to force them shut. You punch the pillow again, swearing at it for doing you wrong. That's how I feel right now, and on top of all that, I'm achy and sore and hot and cold, all at the same time. I'm scared, especially when I hear animal noises. I imagine a bear or coyote tearing me to bits, or Jason and his freaky mask creeping up on me and gutting me alive.

Although I'm not near Crystal Lake, so that only leaves bears and coyotes.

And bears are kind of far-fetched for this neck of the woods.

If forced, I think I could take a coyote, but how much would it suck if I was like two seconds from getting rescued and some mangy coyote started gnawing on my leg?

It would, in every sense of the word, bite.

I keep dreaming Mom is sitting next to me, rubbing my hair and spooning me chicken soup. Her nails are lightly scratching my head and it causes me to doze off. It all feels so real until my eyes open and I'm back here in pain, the trees dropping their leaves in an attempt to blanket and protect me.

But wait.

What if I'm dead?

What if this is what dead is?

This so sucks if this is what dead is.

Either way, I want to be found. If I'm not dead, then they can fix me. But if I am dead, they can bury me. And then maybe I can find Grandma Vicki, because she's dead, too.

Grandma Vicki used to say, "We all meet in heaven, Megan," and this sure as shit ain't heaven.

Unless I'm not going to heaven.

But why wouldn't I get into heaven?

I wasn't that much of an A-hole.

Was I?

I was an altar girl, and I did strive for verbal resolution over violence (except for that one time I let Sheila have it, but let's be honest, she deserved a fist in the mouth).

Before she could worry further over her circumstances, Meg lapsed into unconsciousness.

WHERE ARE YOU, MEG?

Karen sat on her couch picking at her cuticles. They weren't exactly the type you'd show on a Palmolive commercial; her nails were bitten down to the stub and her thumbs were broad, like a man's. Tiny slits formed between her fingers and along her knuckles from too much hand washing and not enough cream.

"Where are you, Meg?" she said aloud, ripping the cuticle off her left thumb, drawing blood from the small tear in her finger.

Karen's boss, Marty, told her to take all the time she needed, but being still was never her strong point. She went to the liquor cabinet and fixed herself scotch with a splash of water. Taking the bottle with her, she went back to the couch and sat down, bringing her attention to a stack of work folders she had brought home in the hopes of keeping her mind occupied. She grabbed the first folder:

Martha, 40, divorced, mother of two children. Girl is 8, boy is 10. Dad convicted of and served time for molesting a young boy. Dad is out of jail. A 51A filed by family friend because Martha is allowing dad unsupervised visits with kids. Martha is easily manipulated by ex-husband, who pays extra child support in exchange for sexual favors.

She threw it down and grabbed the next folder: *Susan, 28-year-old single mother of four. Alcoholic. Boys in home are 18 months and 5 years. Two older boys, ages 10 and 6, have been permanently removed. Father in jail. 51A filed by Susan's mother for neglect, possible drunk driving with kids in car. After interviews with pediatrician, grandmother, and daycare provider, 51A was substantiated. Neither child has had regular medical checkups, and 18-month-old has never been vaccinated. Home filthy, house empty of food. Children's stomachs bloated due to malnutrition.*

She reached for a pad and pencil and began to write a service plan, but couldn't think of one thing that would save this family. In an

47

attempt to quell the inward seething that was rising from the pit of her stomach, Karen gulped down the scotch. Her father had been right; social work could be dirty business.

"And these are the people who get to keep their kids when mine is missing," she mumbled bitterly.

Karen tossed the notepad on the sofa, poured herself another scotch, and closed her eyes.

Where are you, Meg? Where could you possibly have gone?

MEG

Roadside Trash, Day 4

By the early morning of day four, Meg had an unquenchable thirst. She was trembling from the cold and hallucinating that her mother was coming out of the trees, a heated blanket in one hand and a cup of hot chocolate in the other. She had tried to stop the pain in her side by pushing against it, but barely had any strength left for ample pressure. The tiny, angry wound seeped milky pink pus onto her hand. Yesterday, in an attempt to crawl, she managed to roll from her back to her side. Unfortunately, she was on a slight hill and when she tried to bring her top knee beneath her, she rolled onto her stomach, burying her face in a pile of leaves.

"Owwwww," she moaned, tilting her head at an awkward angle in an attempt to see up the hill to the highway.

"Help," she pleaded for the millionth time to no avail, her hoarse voice barely audible.

She turned her head back to the most comfortable position she could manage, and there, in direct alignment with her eye, was a small rock. It looked exactly like the pet rock Roberto had given her, the one she named Rocky.

"Rocky," she forced out the words. "Can you help me get up, or go for help or something?"

The rock remained silent.

"Have it your way," said Meg, struggling to turn onto her side. She managed a slight turn, but was now facing downward. Her feet were toward the traffic, hidden by the slope of the hill.

"Rocky, this sucks. Can you help me turn on my back?"

When Rocky didn't answer, Meg said, "I understand. But I have to tell you, my ass looks big from this angle. When they find me, they'll be referring to me as Jane Doe, the one with the big fat ass. I need to be face up with my head to the left. According to *Tiger Beat's* profile test, that's my best side."

She chuckled lightly, inhaled dirt and spat it out, her wound feeling like it was going to blow wide open.

"I just thought of something. I'm filthy. Now I'm going to be a dirty, big-assed Jane Doe with huge, frizzy hair. They'll probably think I'm a dead prostitute."

She managed another chuckle, and just before losing consciousness said, "Rocky, my skin feels like the inside of a giant freezer. I'm scared and I wanna go home."

Hours later, Meg woke to a strong, cramping pain in her stomach and a tremendous weight pressing down on her, as if a Sumo wrestler were sitting on her chest. A wetness between her legs told her that her baby had died. She looked at Rocky, and wished he had legs so that he could help her.

"I was right all along," she told Rocky. "I always told Mom that I would find a dead baby on the side of the highway. I just never thought it would be inside me; a pregnant, soon to be rotting teenager. Where are all the rubberneckers anyway? Am I the only person who searches for dead bodies along the highway?"

She didn't expect Rocky to answer.

"Rocky, can you imagine the look on my mother's face when she finds out I was pregnant? On the bright side, I don't have to worry about her killing me or taking away my Atari."

Though Rocky was only a rock, Meg derived comfort from it. She dozed in and out of consciousness until a loud shuffling noise startled her awake.

"Rocky, did you hear that?" she asked.

Beyond Rocky, where she could see more than just dirt and leaves, stood the outline of a girl. Meg blinked a few times to adjust her vision. The girl was transparent, like a ghost.

"It's an angel," she whispered.

The angel had long black hair and green eyes that sparkled with brown flecks in a starburst pattern, *like a kaleidoscope*, Meg thought.

"I'm Meg," she gasped.

"Meg?" the angel stammered.

Meg wasn't sure what to expect, but it certainly wasn't the reaction she got.

The horrified angel jumped a mile, hollered like a screech owl, and stumbled backward.

"I'm Meg. Please," she begged, forcing out the words, "Send someone for me. Don't forget me."

The angel closed her eyes and frantically shook her head.

Meg persisted, wondering why God would send her a retarded angel.

"I'm Meg. Have you come for me?"

The angel clasped her hands over her ears and disappeared.

"Rocky," chuckled Meg, because really, even she could see the humor in her tragic situation.

"Did you see that? The only one who knows where I am is a poor, retarded angel."

The next time Meg shut her eyes, it was with a slight smile.

And this time, her eyes remained closed.

FRANKIE'S COUNTDOWN

Frankie told himself that after seven days if no one came looking for him, chances were they weren't going to. He had been keeping a low profile, going to school and coming right home. It had not been easy being here with his mother, but it was a necessary evil. He figured if she saw him around all week, she wouldn't be able to discern a timeframe for when he was or wasn't home. Today was day six of watching his mother drink and smoke herself to death. Frankie couldn't wait for day eight.

Later that evening, with his mother intoxicated and passed out in a heap on the bathroom floor, Frankie heard the most unsettling news of his life. He was watching *Buck Rogers* on TV, only half listening because when she was really stoned, he used the other ear to make sure his mother was still breathing, when breaking news interrupted the program. The same hungry-eyed brunette appeared on the screen:

"Earlier this evening, a pregnant woman discovered the body of a teenage girl on I-95 north when she pulled over to the side of the road to walk her dog. *I was waiting for Patches to do his business and looking at how the leaves had turned such lovely colors when Patches started to bark like crazy. I looked around and saw a sneaker and then I saw the sock in the sneaker and then I saw the ankle, and that's when it hit me; there was a body attached to it,*" sobbed the hysterical woman, unconsciously rubbing her giant belly.

"The girl, identified as fifteen-year-old Megan Humble, had been missing for six days. According to the coroner's report, Ms. Humble is presumed to have been dead between twenty-four and forty-eight hours. Authorities are unsure as to whether last week's incident is related to this one. The other girl, whose name has not been released, remains hospitalized and in stable condition, but as of yet, she has no recollection of what happened. So far, there are no suspects in either case."

"Fuck me," Frankie mumbled, when the news ended and no photo was shown.

THE SPELL THAT
WENT WRONG

Upon further research, Kendra found that some spells are more effective if you do them consistently. Intent on bringing her parents home, she performed the spell nightly, ending in front of the mirror with, "Beauty unfolds the blue sky above, bring me the people that my heart so loves. I love movies, food and trees, return my loved ones now to me."

On this particular night, September 16th, 1980, all sorts of weirdness broke out. Kendra's unsophisticated spell techniques had worked magic, but not the kind she had hoped for. Whether it was the phase of the moon, the tides of the ocean, or simply the fact that she was the last person beside the killers to come in contact with Meg when she was alive, Kendra became the first to come into contact with Meg while she was transitioning from this world into another. When she finished reciting her mantra, the back of her neck got the prickles. Looking at herself in the mirror, she swore her hair turned red/blonde and her eyes changed color to a steel gray. She ran and grabbed her rosary beads, which she had placed on the bedside table, just in case something like this happened. She blew out the candles and flicked on the overhead light. With the beads clutched against her chest, she walked slowly back to the mirror to make sure she hadn't been possessed by a demon.

"Oh. My. God," she exclaimed, leaning closer to the mirror, "I'm getting a frigging zit!"

She turned and began walking toward her bed, but was stopped in her tracks by a strange noise. Slowly, Kendra turned her head, then her body. There, as if the mirror was a two-way window, lay a girl in fuzzy surroundings.

"Aeeeeeeeiiii, holy shit!" Kendra screamed, stepping backward and tripping over her schoolbooks.

"I'm Meg. Please send someone for me. Don't forget me," she said softly.

"Meg?"

"I'm Meg," the girl repeated in short quick gasps. "Have you come for me?"

Kendra stared wide-eyed and slack jawed into her mirror.

Please let this be a wine hallucination.

"Please," said the girl named Meg, "don't forget me."

Kendra closed her eyes and covered her ears to shake off whatever brain aneurysm was happening, and when she opened them again, she was thankfully staring at her own reflection.

August knocked before opening the door. Eyeing the room suspiciously, he asked, "Patatona, what's all the ruckus about?"

"I have a zit," she said, pointing at her chin.

"Mary, Mother of God," he said, closing the door. "Come and eat. Dinner's ready and I wanna watch a movie."

"Be there in a minute," she replied, her hands behind her back so that August couldn't see her death grip on her rosary beads.

As he shuffled away, Kendra heard him mumble, "Kids. A damn pimple should be the least of my problems!"

Kendra sat on the edge of her bed and tried to compose herself. The best way to handle a situation like this was to forget it ever happened.

She was going to put it right out of her mind and pretend she didn't summon ghost girl from Spooksville, nor would she worry about the fact that there may not be a ghost and that she was completely insane.

She wasn't sure which dilemma would be worse.

During dinner, Kendra distracted herself by asking August more personal questions.

"So, what happened next with your mother?" she said, biting into a ravioli.

"What happened next when?" asked August.

Watching August eat was like watching a reenactment of a barbaric caveman on PBS. The man put whole meatballs into his mouth, chewed twice with his mouth wide open, and then swallowed.

"After she shot your father did the police take her away?"

Kendra watched August inhale another meatball. When he spoke, food particles attacked Kendra from every angle. "Why the hell you bringing this up again? Didn't I tell you enough already?"

"Just tell me," she begged, aching for a distraction.

"She got arrested, but she didn't exactly go to jail. She lived with the sheriff and cooked for his family."

"How long did she have to do that for?"

"Sixteen months."

"Did they let you see her?"

"Maybe once a month."

Kendra poured herself some soda and August some wine.

"Where did you and your sisters go while she was in jail?"

"My two sisters went to live with my uncle and became housemaids. I was sent to live with my aunt's father and mother."

"Were they bastards to you?" Kendra queried, prepping for all sorts of drama.

"Nayh. They were good people, but they were old. They sent me to school and fed me and I had a bed to sleep in. I was better off than my sisters were."

"But they must have loved you a teensy bit?"

August swigged a full glass of wine.

"Love? Listen, as far as my relatives were concerned, we were cheap pieces of furniture. They only took us in because they found a case of money that my father stashed down the cellar. It wasn't for love, Patatona. It was for money."

Kendra's eyes welled with tears.

"Didn't anyone love you?"

At his granddaughter's obvious distress, August softened.

"My Aunt Angelica loved me."

"She did?"

"Sure she did, but her husband was a bastard," he said swallowing a meatball.

"Were all men bastards back then?"

"Every man I knew was. They were thugs with guns, and when I grew up, I became a thug, too."

"You're not a thug now. And I love you, Gramps."

"Aww, go on now. Get the movie ready while I clean up."

August watched Kendra walk toward the living room. Without her, his life would be meaningless.

Even though his granddaughter had come to him in the worst possible way, he was grateful she was here.

FRANKIE'S PAST, IN BRIEF

Frankie slipped through the social system cracks as easily as a breadcrumb. The first 51A was filed by a next door neighbor with an allegation of abuse and neglect when the neighbor witnessed Frankie's father smacking his then one-year-old son for uprooting a marijuana plant. The police arrested his father, who didn't serve much time, but at least he never moved back home.

Throughout his elementary years, Frankie's teachers, neighbors, and relatives filed reports to local authorities that Frankie was being abused. Somehow these reports always managed to be screened out. Frankie went to school for relief, but didn't find much. Knowledge of his home environment predisposed his being thought of as a behavioral issue, so teachers were reluctant and cautious around him, and he was the first to be blamed for a disrupted classroom. He smelled from lack of care, and even though he was the tallest kid in his class, he was often bullied.

Until he earned the position of King Bully.

Frankie's mother, Edna, was born in the Dominican Republic and held a sixth grade education. Edna had the remnants of a true beauty, meaning that if you looked closely, you could see the fine curves of a young girl, curves that were now replaced with a tight side bulge. Her dark hair was a salt and pepper gray, her face was saggy, and the flesh around her eyes displayed battered, blackened circles. She had the slumped walk of a woman with low self-esteem and was as bitter as the darkest piece of chocolate. Frankie's biological father, whom his friends called Whitey, was close to 6'4" with almost albino features and skin that turned as red as his temper. He paid a visit only when he needed money, which Edna promptly gave him so that he would leave as quickly as he came.

Then Ray moved in when Frankie was three years old.

Ray was like a seven-year shit show. He had probably damaged Frankie more than any of the other men who had been in their lives. Here was a typical Ray statement: "You stupid, useless bitch! You and your son will never amount to anything. You're both big fat zeros! You're mistakes, is what you are."

Then Ray left.

Then Ray came back.

It wasn't that Ray didn't want Frankie around. He was more than happy to use the boy for drug drops. The rest of the time, he wanted Frankie invisible, silent, and perhaps, Frankie thought, dead.

"Quiet, Frankie," his mother would whisper when Ray was in an especially bad mood. "If we're quiet, it will be okay."

"Momma, do something," Frankie begged her on a night when Edna decided that sitting on their front steps in the shivering cold was better than facing Ray's foul mood.

"If I stand up to him, it will no turn out good."

Frankie knew his mother endured as many hits from Ray as he did. After a while, he stopped questioning the beatings and started to believe what Ray said; Edna really was a dumb bitch. After all, she allowed Ray to hurt her son.

Only a dumb bitch would do that.

Frankie's neighbors tried to intervene, but gave up when they discovered that their offers of help fell on deaf ears. One neighbor, Mr. Watts, called the authorities at least six times, but Ray was smart. He never kept anything in the house. Each time the police came there was no evidence that any man was living with them. After a while, even the people who had tried to help Frankie looked at him like he was white trash.

Then Ray left again.

"It's just you and me, Frankie. From now on we're a team," Edna told him, holding him close.

Unfortunately for Edna, the mother-son bond had been annihilated. Frankie shunned his mother's touch and walked away.

Ray didn't leave without giving Frankie something; an education in the art of cruelty. When Ray was mean to Frankie, Frankie was mean to nature. At four years old, he began torturing and killing insects. By seven, he had graduated to field mice, and when he was ten years old, he killed a stray cat with a slingshot. Right about the time he turned fourteen, Frankie became that which he hated most. He became a man like Ray.

When Edna tried to reprimand him about his truancy, Frankie raised his hand and caught his mother on the side of the cheek.

"I said shut up, you stupid bitch!"

After slapping his mother, Frankie stormed out of the house toward the woods where he would take out the remainder of his blind rage on a small animal. The way he looked at it, it was either Edna or the animal.

It wasn't that Frankie didn't understand the concept of right and wrong; he just never had the opportunity to observe any right in his life. And no one, not even his mother, had taught him how to express himself otherwise.

AN ALTERNATE REALITY

Karen had managed to lie to herself whenever a panic attack emerged: *Meg was a fifteen-year-old with a healthy social life who was playing runaway with a friend, or Meg was just sleeping over Charlene's house and I forgot.* But by the third day of Meg's disappearance, her occupation barred her from continuing with this train of thought. Karen had handled too many cases over the years not to wonder:

> *Was Meg being kept by some psycho as a sex toy?*
> *Is she being tortured in someone's dark, dingy basement?*
> *Worst of all, is she dead?*

And although Karen may have been able to temporarily alter her mind by telling herself Meg would be home any minute, her body betrayed her. If she settled down and allowed herself one moment's rest, a wave of butterflies infested her stomach and a looming migraine attacked her forehead. She chewed gum to alleviate jaw clenching and scrubbed every piece of woodwork in her house. She hummed to try and drown out the voice in her head, the one that told her she may never see Meg again. This horrible, obstinate thought fell to the small of her back causing a dull ache in need of a heating pad.

Six eternal days after Meg went missing, Karen was woken by the continuous *ding dong* of her doorbell.

"Meg!" she shouted, hopping out of bed. She charged toward the front door, halting to a lifeless stop when she saw the familiar silhouette of a police officer through the window. She stood and listened to the doorbell's ring, thinking how strangely reminiscent this was of the day she found out about Michael.

Feeling like she was floating out of her body, Karen opened the door.

"Please," she begged, "Tell me you've found her alive."

The officers glanced at each other, and then looked at Karen with a cavernous pity. After a dramatic plunge to her knees and a near fainting spell, the officers helped her to her feet. She raced to the bathroom to vomit in the sink while simultaneously discharging a nasty bout of diarrhea. When the physical reaction was over, Karen called her father and asked him to meet her at the medical examiner's office. They were taken into a room and brought to a table where a body lay wrapped in a white plastic bag. The coroner unzipped the bag, first width-wise, then length-wise. When he opened the flap, a rancid smell permeated the air, exposing Meg. Karen whimpered and Carl made a noise that sounded like a wounded animal, both of them bringing their hands up to cover their mouths.

"Is this your daughter?" asked the examiner.

"Dear God, yes, it is," Karen said weakly, staring at the faint scar shaped crescent moon that went from Meg's left eye to her cheek.

Karen leaned back onto Carl, who was standing behind her. He held on to both her arms and she allowed him to bear the full brunt of her weight. Her daughter's eyes were closed, her face filthy and bruised. Her frizzy hair was matted to her head and knotted with leaves and bits of twig. Her lips, full with a wide flare on each end, were partially open so that her silver braces peeked through. Her fingers were blackened from fingerprinting and a tag with the number 35564 was tied to her big toe.

Karen stepped up to the table and leaned in as if she were going to touch Meg, but then pulled herself back.

"How did it happen?"

"We're not sure yet," said the coroner, "but we did find an entry wound."

"I'd like to see it," Karen said flatly.

The coroner walked over to Meg's right side and lifted a corner of the sheet exposing a dark bruise with a tiny hole. It reminded Karen of a bull's eye.

"That's it?" Karen sounded stunned. "That tiny hole is what killed my daughter?"

"We'll need your permission for an autopsy."

"You have it," she said absently.

"We're sorry for your loss, ma'am," said one police officer.

Karen placed her hand on the top of Meg's head. She stroked her hair a few times, kissed her daughter on each cheek, and then rested her own cheek on Meg's forehead. When she stood up, she said, "Her name is Meg Humble."

The coroner nodded in sympathy.

"Megan Jane Humble," she repeated, looking around to ensure that everyone acknowledged her announcement.

The policemen shifted uncomfortably.

"Megan Jane Humble is my daughter."

"Karen," began Carl, giving her arms the slightest shake.

"Megan Jane Humble is my daughter. She's fifteen years old. I'm a social worker. I should have been home instead of out saving the frigging world."

"Let's just go," said Carl, gently pushing her off of him and walking to her side to take her elbow.

Karen ignored her father and continued.

"Megan Jane Humble should not be lying here right now. She's done nothing wrong. I've spent my life working for a system that fails over and over again. A system I never gave up on, where I've worked tirelessly with slime who have committed such awful crimes that if they were shot, no one would have missed them. But thanks to our super wonderful system, they get to walk the streets," she said, tossing her arms in the air and then letting them slap at her sides.

"And," she grinned bitterly, her pointer finger waving erratically around, "this is my payment, is it?"

Karen turned to Carl and asked, "Daddy, can you solve the million dollar question?"

"Karen, don't do this."

"No? Okay."

With wild eyes, she directed her attention to the policemen.

"Any of you care to venture a guess on why this happened?"

She didn't give anyone a chance to respond before splaying her hands in front of her and saying, "No takers? Well, then, allow me," she said, her tone maniacal. "My payment from the system I work so hard for is having my only child murdered. I get a daughter with a toe tag! Can any of you gentlemen please tell me what's wrong with this picture?"

"Thank you, officers," Carl cut in. "Karen, let's go."

As Carl guided her by the shoulders, Karen saw the coroner move toward Meg, and something between incomprehension and horror passed across her face.

"Don't you dare zip that up!" Karen screamed, her finger aimed at the coroner's face like a loaded gun.

"*Shhh*, Karen . . ."

"No, Daddy!" she wailed. "What if she begins to breathe again? How is she going to breathe all zipped up? She's not a sandwich. Give her a sheet, for Chrissake!"

Carl swiveled Karen around so that she was facing him.

"Listen, you wait right here."

Karen watched as Carl calmly walked toward the coroner. He kept his tone low so that she couldn't hear what he was saying, but the coroner nodded and left the bag open. He went to a closet and took out a white sheet, which he fluffed over Meg. He folded the sheet under her chin, so she looked like she was sleeping.

"Thank you, Daddy. They'll check back on her, won't they?" she sniveled.

"Of course they will," Carl lied, putting his arm around his daughter's shoulder and escorting her toward the door.

Just before she crossed the threshold, Karen wriggled out of her father's grasp and warned in a voice loud enough to shake the building, "You check back on her!"

As soon as they left the room, the policemen asked the coroner what Carl had said.

"He told me he was afraid if I covered her in front of her mother that he'd be back here identifying his own daughter, and he couldn't bear to go through another tragedy."

For the rest of her life, Karen would have nightmares about the day she had to identify her daughter. She would dream of Meg lying there with twigs in her hair, dirt on her face, and stuffed in an awful white bag, a single toe hanging out of the zipper with a giant tag attached to it. And she dreamed of the noticeable smell upon entering the room, indescribable to anyone who has never experienced it, and unmistakable to anyone who has. And it was this dream that propelled her toward what was fast becoming her life's goal:

1. Find the killer.
2. Kill the killer.

And though she never spoke a word about what it felt like to see her daughter lying dead on a cold metal table, she did find herself, on occasion, compelled to discuss the distinct and unique smell of death.

PART 2

The Shift

MEG, SOMEWHERE
IN LIMBO

Wow, what a difference, Meg thought. *I feel great!*

Pain free and filled with a gladness that paralleled Christmas morning, Meg sprang to her feet.

"Grandma Vicki?" she called. "Yoo-hoo, Grandma Vicki! Am I dead?"

"Mom?"

Maybe I'm in a coma in the hospital.

"God?"

"Helllooooo?"

She shrugged into the silence, unable to feel frightened in the midst of the beauty that surrounded her. She stood in the middle of a hunter green field with rolling hay bales and bright, colorful flowers. Just behind her was a giant oak tree and under the tree, Rocky was waiting for her.

"Hello, Rocky," she smiled, squatting next to the rock that seemed to be leaning against the giant tree stump. "Have you come to keep me company?"

Meg stroked the smooth surface of the rock and sat back against the tree.

"By the way, thanks for being there for me in my time of need. I really appreciated not having to die alone."

Inhaling and exhaling deeply, Meg lifted her face to the sky, feeling such indescribable peace that she began to laugh out loud. As she closed her eyes and tilted her face toward the bright sun, she heard a woman's voice, "See you soon, Megan."

Meg's eyes popped open. She sat up and cried out, "Grandma Vicki, is that you?" but no one responded. She looked at Rocky and said, "Want to know why I want to see Grandma Vicki so badly? No, not just because I loved her, silly!"

Meg leaned closer and whispered, "I killed her, Rocky. I killed my own Grandma."

THUGS

"So tell me about the thugs, Gramps."

"You're either going to be a serial killer or a screenwriter," laughed August.

"Neither. I'm going to be an artist."

"Drawing ain't going to pay your bills. You draw for fun, not for a career," frowned August disapprovingly. "This is what you do; you get yourself one of them business degrees and then you get married, have kids, and fatten up. Use the degree when the kids go to school. You want to be able to take care of yourself in case things go wrong with the husband. Then when you're an old lady with nothing better to do, you draw."

"Okay, first, no. Second, fatten up? I'm already fat, Gramps. And third, don't curse my future husband or marriage. Now, tell me about the thugs."

"Fat? You? You must be blind, Patatona."

"And you must be in need of glasses. Now, thugs?"

"Thugs this, thugs that! You have an obsession with thugs. Don't go marrying a thug."

"But I could by accident if you don't tell me what to look out for."

August sighed in defeat. "What do you want to know?"

"Did they have guns?"

"In my day, every man had a gun."

"Did you?"

"I had three."

"Three?"

"Yeah, I had two until my mother-in-law asked me to bury my father-in-law's gun in the backyard. I told her I did, but I kept it for myself."

"Who was the biggest thug you knew?"

"Cosmo DeLuca, otherwise known as Dukes DeLuca, on account he was always putting up his dukes."

"Was he dangerous?"

"Sure, Dukes shot quite a few people in his time."

"What happened to him?"

"Live by the sword, Patatona. He was shot by the cousin of a guy that he shot. The cousin seduced him and took him to a hotel where the wife of the guy he shot was waiting, and then they both let him have it. It was a brutal killing. I heard they each shot him four times; once each in the face, the groin, the heart, and the top of his head, just to be sure."

"Egads!" exclaimed Kendra. "Were you still a thug when you met Nonie?"

"I was still a thug after I married your Nonie," August corrected.

"You didn't," Kendra paused theatrically.

"Didn't what?"

"Gramps, you never killed anyone, did you?" she asked, in a squeaky, dramatic voice.

"Of course not! Whadda you think? I may be simple, but non sono stupido! I was no killer, Patatona, I was a gambler!"

"But you don't gamble."

"Not today, I don't."

"What did you gamble on?"

"Everything."

"Like?"

"Oh, you're killing me!"

"Stop being vague then."

"Jesus, Mary, and Joseph, she's the death of me," August mumbled, pressing his fingertips to his eyelids.

"So you gambled on horses? Cards? Dogs? What?"

"Everything, Patatona."

"Define everything."

"I would go to the ballgame and bet on the pitch and the hit; I would bet on whether the next guy up to the plate was going to spit or not. I bet on card games. I bet on who was gonna fart when. You get my drift?"

"How much did you win?"

"Win?" August laughed. "I never won!"

"Never?"

"Anything I'd win, I'd spend."

"Okay then, how much did you lose?"

"A lot."

"Why didn't you just quit?"

"I couldn't."

"What, like you were addicted to it?"

"Sure. I could stop drinking or smoking, but as far as gambling went, it was in me. I used to leave my wife and boy for an entire weekend to go gambling. I had it bad."

"When did you quit?"

"I quit when Willie got killed."

"Who was Willie?"

"He was a bookie. One morning he held back on the book and when he opened the door—POW—two guys put five bullets in his head. They never caught the guys. I didn't want to be next. From there on in, I kept my nose clean. I stayed home and gambled with my in-laws for nickels, and I still got the hit I needed."

"Sweet heavens!" exclaimed Kendra, reaching for a bag of chips. "This is just like the movies!"

"The movies it ain't," said August, wagging his finger at Kendra. "In the movies they make it all glamorous. Trust me, dead ain't glamorous, Patatona."

Kendra was quiet for as long as it took her to finish the bag of chips. Wiping her mouth with the back of her hand, she said, "Gramps?"

"What now?"

"What was my mother like?"

August would have preferred 'name the women you've had sex with' to this question.

"Another day, Patatona. Mass is on TV. Now do me a favor and hand me my rosary."

Kendra did as she was told.

"Now," said August, lightly pushing her aside, "make like an egg and beat it."

MEG'S SECRET

When they found Meg, Karen thought, *Oh no,* and *Thank God,* all at
once. She had feared becoming one of those missing children parents,
the ones forced to live in perpetual limbo. When you can't find your
child, it niggles at the mind in psychotic ways while leaving open an
eternal hope that maybe the child is alive and well. On the nights you
manage to fall asleep, there are dreams of the ruinous decay that was
your child, a languid remorse unfolding the path destined to be your
entire life, because no matter where you go, you're haunted by places
where your child could be . . . alleyways, train tracks, city dumps,
locked in a psycho's basement.

When Karen was told Meg was most likely alive for up to four
days lying in a pile of leaves, she decided to cremate her daughter. The
thought of putting her in the ground would only remind her of Meg
being left for dead *on* the ground. Karen decided to have a wake for the
sake of the people who wished to pay their respects. She had a closed
casket that she filled with Meg's favorite things; roller lip gloss, purple
socks and lollipops, an empty pizza box from their favorite pizza parlor,
and her new Atari game. Last year's school photo sat on top of the
casket. Her possessions would be buried next to her father, a gravestone
marking her having lived in this world. During the service, Karen
and Carl stood side by side, Karen clutching a heart-shaped necklace
containing Meg's ashes. It seemed as if the entire student body had
come to mourn the loss of her daughter. Her basketball team and track
buddies, kids she had never met before who cried on her shoulder,
teachers, even the janitors and cafeteria ladies. Meg's very best friend,
Charlene, was inconsolable and almost fainted when she walked into
the room.

"There is no question our Meg was well-liked," said Carl, placing his arm around Karen's shoulder.

Karen nodded and scanned the crowd of teenagers, huddled close together and whispering how awful it was that Meg was dead.

"How are you doing?" asked Charlene's mother, Jen, who had come to relieve Carl alongside Karen.

"I'm okay," Karen replied. "Do you think you and Charlene could stop by afterwards?"

"Of course we can," said Jen, giving Karen's upper back a circular rub.

Within five minutes, Jen, who would rather be shot than seen without makeup, had turned into a bit of a mess in the receiving line. She had faded purple eye shadow clumped in the creases of her eyes accented by drippy black mascara that was smudged top to bottom. She was obsessively dabbing her bright red nose with a tissue and clearing her throat rather loudly. Karen thought she looked like a rabid raccoon.

"I think I'll take a break," Karen said to her. "Just need some air."

Outside of the funeral parlor the line traveled for what seemed miles. Karen slipped in between a couple of parked cars and sat on the curbstone. She couldn't wait to speak with Charlene afterward. If Meg had confided in anyone, it was her best friend.

When the county coroner asked, *Did you know your daughter was pregnant, Ms. Sherburne?* Karen's expression didn't waver. Through a heavily beating heart, she forced a swallow over what felt like a hairball in her throat, and without so much as a wince replied, "Yes, I did."

And forward she went, silently questioning how and when her fifteen-year-old tomboy of a daughter could have possibly gotten herself pregnant.

And because Karen lied to the coroner about her knowledge of the pregnancy, she found herself lying to the police as well. It was as if all rationality escaped her.

"Yes, I knew she was pregnant. He's a long-time family friend. He'd be here now, but they've moved to Europe. And please, don't mention this to anyone, especially my father. He's going through enough as it is."

Karen realized that the killer may very well have been the boy that got Meg pregnant, but it didn't matter. If this boy was a suspect, if justice needed to be served, Karen didn't plan on involving the police. She made peace with her lie and told herself that if caught, she would deal with the embarrassment later. For reasons she couldn't explain, her ego was bruised and swollen, and it refused to deflate at any cost.

After the wake, Jen, Charlene and Karen sipped Earl Grey tea and reminisced about Meg. When Karen felt the timing was right, she looked at Charlene and said, "Can I ask you something, Charlene?"

"Sure," said Charlene, her sapphire mascara smudged as much as her mother's from a day's worth of crying.

"Did you know that Meg was pregnant?"

Charlene's crimson face answered her question.

"What do you know about him?"

"I can't tell you," Charlene whispered, before breaking into a heavy sob.

"That's ridiculous, Charlene. You tell her right now!" scolded Jen.

"It's okay, Jen," said Karen carefully, not taking her eyes off of Charlene. "It's not like Meg's going to get mad at you. Right, honey? I just want to know, for me, for closure. Can you understand that?"

Charlene wiped her nose on her sleeve and nodded.

Karen leaned in and, in an attempt to center the girl and keep her focused, lightly touched Charlene's forearm.

"This boy, do you think he could have been the one who harmed Meg?"

"Oh, no!" blurted Charlene. "He would never have done this to Meg!"

"Who would never do this to Meg?"

In a traitor's voice, Charlene responded, "Roberto."

"Roberto who?"

"Roberto Conti."

"Was he at the wake?"

"No."

"Why not?"

"He moved."

"When?"

Charlene blew her nose into an already used tissue that was crumpled in her hand. "He moved to New Mexico, just afterwards."

"Just after what?" wondered Karen.

Charlene looked at Karen as if to say, duh.

"Oh! Afterwards, *afterwards*."

"It was his going away gift," she sniffed.

"Going away what? Are you kidding me?" scoffed Jen, shaking her head disapprovingly at her daughter.

Karen ignored Jen. "Did Meg really like this Roberto?"

"Yeah."

"Did he know she was pregnant?"

"No. He moved away before she found out. She was going to talk to you about it the other day but you were—" Charlene paused and looked down, her right thumb chipping off the bright pink nail polish on her left thumb.

"It's all right, Charlene. You can finish the sentence."

"You were working late again."

"I know she wished I were home more," Karen said, "but I thought we had all the time in the world. I thought I needed to protect the kids who were really in trouble. And look what happened," she said, releasing a spastic laugh, "My own daughter needed me, and I wasn't there!"

"Don't do this to yourself. Meg knew you loved her," said Jen.

Karen wiped her nose on her sleeve.

"Was he cute?"

"You wouldn't have thought so, I didn't think so, but I didn't tell Meg that. He was too grungy for me," sniffed Charlene.

Karen smirked. "Grungy, huh? What's grungy look like?"

Charlene proceeded to tell Karen everything she knew about Roberto Conti. When she was feeling less fragile, Karen would attempt to contact this boy's parents to inform them about Meg's death, but there would be no need to mention the pregnancy. After all, what was the use in having a conversation about something that would never come to fruition?

GRANDMA VICKI,
AS TOLD BY MEG

"On my twelfth birthday, I ruined my family's life. Me and Grandma Vicki were going to Sears to pick out a birthday gift. I knew when we got there that people would not pay one bit of attention to me, because Grandma Vicki was very pretty. She was so pretty that anyone in her vicinity was rendered invisible. Wherever we went, men would stop and look at her. Even young guys whistled at my grandma! Mom used to tell me I was so lucky that I was the spitting image of my father, but I would have preferred to look like Grandma Vicki. We were on the highway and I was doing my usual scanning for signs of dead babies when I thought I saw something near the medium strip wrapped in a ratty old blanket.

"*Pull over! Stop the car!* I screamed.

"I was so convinced that I saw something that I unbuckled my seatbelt, lunged forward and grabbed Grandma Vicki's arm.

"Alarmed and taken by surprise, she yelled, Meg, stop it!

"I pleaded for her to pull over and tried to turn the wheel. I yelled, *We're passing it. We're going to miss our chance!*

"Either I was stronger, or Grandma Vicki was weaker than I thought. Even when we swerved from our lane and onto the dirt headed straight for the tree ready to bear its brunt, my only thought was to rescue the dead baby.

"*Meg, you have to let go of the wheel this instant!* Grandma Vicki squealed.

"I let go too late.

"It wasn't the crash that killed her. It was her heart, they told me at the hospital. I, on the other hand, just about went through the windshield. What saved me was the death lock Grandma Vicki had on my upper arm. My only injury was a scar that went from under my left eye to the top of my cheekbone. Mom said it looked like a crescent moon and it symbolized a kiss from Grandma Vicki.

"*Did they find the baby?* I asked my mother.

"*What baby, Meg?*

"*The one on the highway. We drove right past it,*" I explained.

"*Hush now, get some rest,*" she said soothingly.

"No one had the faintest idea that I killed Grandma Vicki. They all thought she had the heart attack before we drove off the road. They thought I was unbuckled because I was trying to control the swerving car. They applauded my bravery and I, being the coward afraid to go to jail, went along with it.

"I killed her, Rocky, and I can't wait to see her so I can apologize."

Meg shrugged when Rocky didn't answer. She brought her hand up to shield her forehead and squinted at her beautiful surroundings. The vast field was overflowing with brightly colored flowers, tall blades of thick grass and rolling hay bales. The sky was bluer than any she had seen before and the climate was perfect, almost as if it were custom made to match her body temperature. She wasn't hungry, thirsty or tired. Everything, Meg thought, was perfect. She settled back against the tree and closed her eyes, and as she did so, the magic of the field blanketed her. It washed away her fears and doubts and filled Meg with a sense of peace so profound that her mind went blank. She forgot about anything that might cause her pain, including poor Grandma Vicki's untimely demise.

KAREN, 1980

The three months following Meg's death

Karen knew that even on the best of days, with flowers and wreaths and a beautiful landscape, cemeteries were merely deserts of solitude. The caretakers could dress them up all they wanted, but at the end of the day, they housed corpses. Even though Meg was not in the casket, the tombstone counted as tangible evidence, proof of her existence, and Karen was drawn to visit like a moth to a flame. No giant statue or special scribes along the edges, no corny sayings about angels in heaven, Meg's epitaph read:

> *MEGAN JANE HUMBLE*
> *April 1965-September 1980*
> *Beloved Daughter, Granddaughter*

On her first visit, Karen stayed for fifteen minutes. The next day, she stayed a bit longer. With each passing day, Karen increased her stay by a few minutes. On the fifth day, as she was turning to leave, guilt stabbed her in the chest, sucking the air from her lungs. For her next visit, Karen packed a beach chair, lunch, Meg's boom box, a book, and a blanket. She arrived at ten in the morning and didn't return home until five-thirty in the evening. For the next two months in rain, sleet, and frosty chill, Karen set up camp at the cemetery, staying anywhere between two to seven hours. Every day she followed the same routine: unpack, settle in, play Meg's favorite music . . . Madonna, Blondie, AC/DC . . . have an in-depth conversation with her daughter as if she were standing next to her, read, grab her blanket and take a nap, eat lunch, drink her thermos of hot cocoa, chat with Meg some more, drive home and retreat to Meg's bedroom where she would take a nap.

It wasn't until her father caught her in the act that she began to wonder if what she was doing was, indeed, sane. It began with a phone call.

"Hey, kiddo," said Carl. "Where have you been? I've been trying to reach you for days."

"Spring cleaning."

"It's not spring."

"It's just a figure of speech, Daddy."

"Where you been cleaning?"

"The uh, basement."

"Really? Because I stopped by twice and you weren't there."

"Really? I must have been out at the store buying groceries," she lied.

"Really? Because you don't cook," said Carl suspiciously.

"Really?" began Karen, before Carl interrupted, "Enough with the *Reallys*. I'm stopping by Friday afternoon. That's two days from now. If you plan on being in the basement or at the grocery store," he said sarcastically, "try to do it in the morning."

The following afternoon, Carl happened to stop by the cemetery.

"Karen?" he questioned, looking at her settled into the chair with a blanket and reading *Love Story* for the fifth time.

"Oh, hey, Dad," she said, casually. "Fancy meeting you here."

"Yeah," he answered wanly, smoothing out the grass with his shoe. "Say, how long you been here, honey?"

"Oh, not long," she said, looking up at Carl. "Maybe since ten o'clock."

Carl looked at his watch.

"It's four."

"Mmm, hmm," she said, turning the page of the book, like six hours was a reasonable amount of time to be sitting in a freezing cemetery.

"You been coming here a lot?"

"Sometimes," she lied.

"Is this where you are when you're cleaning the basement?"

No reply.

Carl put his hands in his coat pockets, gave a little shiver, and blew out a puff of cold air.

"Thinking about leaving soon?"

Karen laughed lightly. "What are you, the cemetery Nazi?"

"Well, this ain't no personal campground, kid. You're not going loony on me, are you? What about your job?"

"I'm taking time off to concentrate on other things."

"Other things? Like what, squatting by a tombstone?"

"No. Like taking time for the little things," Karen said, shaking the book at him, "like finally reading and relaxing."

"By a tombstone," Carl said darkly.

Karen stood up and flung off the blanket. She had been looking for a good argument to release the pent up emotions that were clouding her sanity.

"Don't push me," she screamed. "Don't you dare try to push me!"

"What do you want me to do?" Carl asked gravely. "Should I ignore the fact that my daughter is spending her days holed up at a cemetery so that she can hide from her responsibilities? C'mon, Karen, this is crazy time."

"Well, excuse me if reality has battered my belief system. Maybe I don't want to recover. Did you ever think of that? Maybe I'm done being Miss-Service-to-All! Let someone else shovel the shit for once. I certainly don't see any service being given back to me," she said, kicking over her chair.

"I felt this way when your mom died."

"No offense, Dad," Karen snarled, "but losing your spouse is far different from losing your child. I should know. I've lost both."

"And I'm deeply sorry, Karen. But you persevered without Michael because you had Meg, and I hope you'll persevere without Meg for yourself, and selfishly, for me. You see, you're my baby. You're all I got, and I don't want to lose you. It's you and me kiddo, a team."

Karen reached out and firmly grabbed her father's forearm. "I'm broken Daddy!" she screamed.

Carl drew Karen to his chest and she buried her face against him. "And you don't know how to come back, do you?" he asked.

Karen surveyed the area. There were food crumbs scattered everywhere, books, blankets, a boom box, the tipped over chair. Carl was right; she was treating the cemetery like a campground.

In barely a whisper, she replied, "No, I don't know how to come back. Why can't I hide here for a while where it's safe? I deserve that much."

"Let me ask you something. How long is enough? When will it be safe enough?"

"When was it safe enough for you? How long did you have to wait for this horrible pain to go?"

"I'm still waiting. Consider it a side effect. The blessing of such a profound love brings a sense of profound loss, but at least you felt the profound love. Some people never get that."

"You did not just make that up." Karen sniffed.

"Course I didn't. Jack said it to me when your mom died when I asked him the same thing you just asked me."

Karen grinned. "I thought it kinda sounded out of your element."

Tears glistened at the corners of Carl's eyes. "Well, I guess if I had to say something original it would be what can ya do?"

"That's definitely more you," Karen nodded. She wiped her nose on her sleeve, then bent down and folded up the beach chair, which she handed to Carl.

"I could go for Chinese."

"Onward and upward," he said hooking his elbow into hers.

"Through the fog," Karen finished, walking away from Meg's grave, which, from that day forward, she would only visit periodically.

MEG AND ROBERTO

"January 5, 1979," Meg explained to Rocky. "That was the very first day I laid eyes on Roberto Conti.

"He transferred from California and ended up in my math class. Do you know how lucky that was, Rocky? I might never have met him otherwise," she said dreamily.

"Roberto was the most beautiful person I've ever seen in my entire life. It took over a full year before he noticed I even existed. To catch him, I did the one thing I swore I'd never do. I sold my soul and resorted to wearing skin-tight Bonjour corduroys!" she giggled.

"March 21st, 1980, that's when he asked me out."

Meg stared at Rocky, and then admitted, "Okay, maybe I asked him out."

As if the rock had posed the question, Meg said, "How did I finally snag him? Funny you should ask. I stalked him. Me, my Bonjour cords and my basketball bounced past his house for one whole week. On day four, just as I was about to give up, I saw him sitting on his front steps. I had on dark blue Bonjours and a ridiculously tight red tee shirt. Roberto was reading a car magazine. I stood at the foot of his walkway with my basketball tucked under my arm and my boobs sticking out as far as I could push them, which, I confess, wasn't very far. I waited a good thirty seconds.

"I know it was thirty seconds because I silently counted *1, 2, 3 . . .* and he would not look up from that stupid magazine.

"After fifty seconds, I struck the best supermodel pose I could manage and said, *Uhm, hi.*

"He looked up, gave me a head nod, and went back to reading. *Whatcha reading?* I asked."

Meg shifted positions and looked at the rock. "See, this was a clever tactic on my part, Rocky; to appear curious in order to inch my way onto his property, because really, I didn't give a shit what he was reading.

"He told me it was a car magazine and I told him it sounded interesting then flashed an award-winning grin. Honest to God, Rocky, it really was award winning. In preparation for this very moment, practicing my smile had become a nightly ritual. Anyway, he never looked up to see it," Meg sighed.

"I said goodbye and when he didn't answer me, I stormed down the street, slamming my ball so hard it's no wonder I didn't crack the pavement."

Meg shifted positions. Facing the rock, she lay down on her side and leaned on her elbow. "But I couldn't let it go. Three houses away, I stopped bouncing and crouched down to tie my sneaker.

"It was already tied, but I wanted to give Roberto time to notice me and my good looking butt. But he never looked up from that dumb mag."

Meg sighed and flopped onto her back, one hand cradling the back of her head like a pillow, the other on her stomach. Roberto, with the black wavy hair, light skin, and emerald eyes; Roberto, who was probably an inch shorter than she, but it didn't matter. Roberto, who, when he smiled, could light up a starless summer night, and who made her tingly in all the right places.

"I'm not usually one to give up, but Rocky, I was humiliated. Then I remembered what Coach Hayes said right before our playoff game: *Keep your eye on the prize, girls, eye on the prize.* So I jogged back up the sidewalk, ball bouncing in perfect unison with my stride."

"*So, Roberto,* I began to say, but he looked up and gave me an, *Oh God, she's back* look which threw me off only slightly. I said to him, *So since you're not asking, I am. Let's go out sometime. Unless you're gay or something. Are you gay? Cause if you are, I'm cool with that.*

"That made him smirk, which made me sweaty and warm, and I prayed that my armpits didn't have visible sweat rings on my bright red shirt.

"He told me he wasn't gay which made me flush head to toe. I mean, shit, I could've done that weeks ago and saved myself the hassle of tight jeans! I think wearing those stupid pants cut off at least ninety percent of my circulation.

"A couple of days a week, I went to Roberto's after school and did homework on his front stoop while he worked on his car. Every few minutes, I'd look up to admire his beauty. And oh, what beauty it was! His entire torso leaning into his 1967 Mustang, a cigarette hanging from the side of his mouth, his muscles flexing with each movement. He turned me into a hot and bothered horny teenager who was ready, willing, and able to screw his brains out. He even got me to change my taste in music. Before Roberto, I was like, *The Ramones* who? But soon enough, he turned me into a groupie."

Meg looked at Rocky and blew out a lust-filled puff of air.

"I never told Mom about Roberto. He dressed like a punk in ripped jeans and leather, smoked, and barely got C's in school. He even had an earring. My mother would have taken a nutty if she knew I was seeing a boy like him. But I couldn't help myself. On the days I went to his house, I told Mom I was at the library. I mean, it's not like she was ever home to check, right?"

Meg let out another sigh.

"I didn't exactly love lying to Mom, but I got used to it. I did everything I promised her I wouldn't do: I smoked ciggies, drank, enjoyed the occasional joint. I was an unsupervised kid for Chrissake, what did she expect from me?"

Meg sat up and pulled her knees into her chest.

"August 5, 1980. That's when we had sex. That's also when he told me he was moving to New Mexico.

"But you just got here! I wailed.

"It was his father's stupid job. He had no choice. I smacked him on the arm and asked him why he didn't tell me sooner, and you know what he did, Rocky? He grinned, and that's all it took. I melted like a chunk of cheese in a fondue pot.

"He asked me if I wanted to fool around. His parents weren't going to be home for at least two hours. Now, don't judge me, Rocky. I was hot for him. I didn't give a fart about all that your body is a temple crap.

"I said, *Hell yeah, I wanna fool around!*

"Roberto put on the Sex Pistols' *God Save the Queen* and poured us a glass of vodka mixed with orange juice. He told me he wasn't trying to get me shitfaced; he just wanted me to relax.

"Before he could warn me not to guzzle, I downed a full glass in like two seconds. Man, oh man, stomach burn followed by insta-buzz. My head was woozy and my body light and airy. We fooled around a while and then we did IT. A week later, we broke up, because long distance relationships don't last. Roberto handed me a pet rock, which I named Rocky," Meg said, tapping the rock lightly.

"The day we said goodbye, we huddled together on his stoop and talked about how he would call me every day. We promised that when we were older, like 19, we'd get married. Then we shared the longest French kiss in the history of French kisses."

Meg leaned back on her hands and arched her back. She sat forward, absently rubbing her belly.

"I found out I was pregnant on the day I was killed. This may sound twisted, but once I realized I was dying, I was relieved that I wouldn't have to tell Mom about the baby. That would have been one monumental fight for the records."

She flipped over onto her stomach, bending her knees and cupping her chin in her hands while alternating toe dips on the soft, green grass.

"I'm glad I didn't die a virgin, Rocky. As it is, I'm going to miss proms, graduation day, college, first job, marriage, and kids. At least I can check first love and sex off the list," Meg sighed, dropping her head down to rest on her arms.

She recapped the morning that she took the pregnancy test, which was upsetting enough. Then, without warning, memories of the rest of that fateful day drizzled in, inciting anxiety. With a shaky voice, Meg began to recount her murder.

"I was so scared," she began to sob, "I was just lying there and . . . hey, ho!" she cried, distracted by a dragonfly that landed on the point of her elbow. "You know," she said, staring at the vibrant fuchsia insect, "these are supposed to be good luck." Overwhelmed by the beauty of her surroundings, Meg's tears disappeared and she completely forgot about her past.

"Rocky," she asked, "Do you smell that? Brownies! What say you, me and Mr. Dragonfly go exploring?"

DECEMBER, 1980

Sarah greeted Karen with a tearful hug

"If we can do anything, anything at all, let us know."

"I think just getting back to work will help. Taking all that time off did me more harm than good."

"Well, don't faint when you see your desk," grinned Sarah. "You know we always save the best for the best."

Karen's workstation was piled high with a mountain of untouched paperwork. As she sorted through folder after folder, neglect to abuse to abandonment cases, one solitary thought crossed her mind:

How on earth am I going to do this? How am I possibly going to give a crap?

Since Meg's death, Karen had settled into the role of victim. In her car, she searched the radio for songs like *It's a Heartache*, and *All Out of Love*. She rented tearjerker movies just so she had an excuse to cry. It wasn't going to take another social worker to alert her to the fact that she needed to get out of her own head. And since she had no hobbies to speak of, work would have to be the intermediary between her bitterness and whatever else lay ahead, be it more turbulence or a reprieve from this feeling of indefinite sorrow.

At noontime, Sarah poked her head into Karen's cubicle. "Care to grab a bite?"

"There is nothing I'd love more, but I'm so far behind that I don't dare stop now."

"Then how about I bring you back a sandwich and you break for ten minutes? I'm not fussy, I'll take whatever time I can get," Sarah winked.

"A Ruben on rye with herbal tea sounds good."

"Lemon zinger?"

"That's the one."

"You got it."

Over the next couple of months, Karen worked tirelessly, scheduling appointments day and night. Even Marty, known for working people into an early grave, seemed concerned about her late hours.

"Look at you. You're exhausted. You do realize we don't give out A's for effort?"

"You don't give out anything, Marty," she snorted, not bothering to look up from her desk.

"How's that case coming with the older kid? Is he complying?"

"Frankie? I'm just catching up on my visits, but according to these reports, he's not complying. It's a sin," Karen shook her head. "This is a smart kid, but his mother's a real piece of work. Leaving him at home isn't doing either of them any favors."

"You can't save everyone, Karen."

"Find the hole, save the kid," she yawned.

Marty leaned in and knocked his knuckles on her desk.

"I know times are tough, but don't burn out, kiddo. Take care."

Karen stopped writing and looked at Marty. "This *is* how I take care."

Before he turned to leave, Marty reached inside his coat pocket and pulled out a purple lollipop, which he threw on Karen's desk.

"Now you can't say I never gave you anything," he winked.

Meg loved purple lollipops. Karen pulled the pop out of its wrapper, took a few careful licks, and then bit with purpose, crunching and chewing a rush of purple, a rush of Meg.

* * *

"Oh, it's you," Frankie said flatly, opening his door to Karen.

"Well, it's good to see you, too," Karen said, hearing the sarcasm in her own voice.

Frankie stepped aside and shouted down the narrow hallway.

"That lady's back."

A moment later, Edna staggered out of the bathroom.

"Mrs. Ortiz," Karen said, inspecting her closely.

"Hello," she said, fumbling with the button on her pants.

Frankie looked at his mother in disgust.

"Jesus Edna, could you have fixed yourself before you came out?"

"Excuse my manners," she slurred, wobbling into the wall.

"What are you on, Edna?" asked Karen bluntly.

"Me?" she said. "De nada."

"She's totally shitfaced," said Frankie.

"Oh, go and play with yourself," spat Edna.

"Shut up, you whore!"

"People, please," said Karen calmly, holding her hands in the air. Karen turned to Edna, "Sometime over the course of this week, you'll be receiving a phone call for a drug test. I'd get clean if I were you." Then she turned to Frankie. "Once again, you're delinquent in your community service."

Frankie towered Godzilla-like over the two women, his arms crossed in front of his chest, intent on being a threatening presence. Without indicating that she felt an ounce of fear, Karen said, "This wasn't the deal, Frankie."

"Who are you, anyway? You come here and then you disappear. They send in some schmuck to replace you, but they don't come cause they're scared of us. And now you're back? Why don't you people do me a favor and screw."

"I apologize for my lack of visits. It won't happen again. And please, watch your mouth."

"Sure, I'll watch my fucking mouth."

"You do that," Karen said calmly.

"Looking forward to spending scads of time together," he lisped in a mock tone.

Karen ignored the sarcasm and smiled widely.

"Excuse my son," said Edna, who appeared to be sobering up with each belch.

Karen ignored her.

"Frankie," she said, in an amused voice, "did you say scads?"

"What?"

"Now that's a word you don't hear often. You read?"

"He does," Edna cut in, "He reads all the time. He got books all over . . ."

"Shut the hell up! Who the fuck asked you anything?" he barked, balling his hands into fists.

"There are better words to use in the English language than curse words," Karen offered. "Please, watch your mouth."

"You mind your business and I'll watch my mouth," he snarled.

Karen pulled herself up to her full height, "According to the state, you are my business, and I am at my boiling point. Are we clear?"

This was not how Karen worked, but this boy needed discipline and he wasn't going to get it from his stoned mother.

"Crystal," he snarled.

"Good. I'll see the two of you next week."

Her usual courtesies replaced by a brusque nod, Karen turned on her heel and walked out the door.

*   *   *

The following week, Karen drove to the Ortiz home. She knocked five or six times, waited a bit, and then knocked some more. When there was still no reply, she rechecked her date book. In the notes section on today's date she had written, *Follow up at Ortiz home, 7pm.* She closed the book, placed it in her suitcase and stared dumbly at the door. Maybe it was because every light in the house was on, or because Karen thought she heard a tiny whining sound similar to that of a cat, or perhaps it was mother's instinct that alerted her that something was wrong. She put down her briefcase and leaned over the porch to gape in the window. There was nothing in the kitchen but a stack of filthy dishes. Nothing in the living room but scattered magazines on the floor, and nothing as far as she could see down the hall . . . *wait.* Living room, far corner, just behind the recliner; someone was there, and that someone wasn't moving.

"Fran-kie!" yelled Karen, tapping on the window. "Open up! Can you hear me? I said, open up!"

Frankie remained still.

"Ed-na? Ed-naa," she cried, turning her head left to right, "Are you in there? It's Karen Sherburne. Open the door, please."

Instead of following the rules of logic and phoning the police, Karen did exactly what she was wasn't supposed to do; she went back to the front door and slowly turned the knob.

It opened.

The dim house reeked of ammonia and rancid food. As she walked deeper into the room, Karen could hear mice scattering back to their cubbyholes. Dressed in a long black trench coat and ripped Levi's, Frankie was slumped against the wall. His head was turned to the side, almost touching his shoulder, shadowing his face.

Karen squatted next to him and caught a strong whiff of alcohol and vomit.

"Frankie?" she said, gently shaking his shoulder.

When he didn't answer, she shook a bit harder.

"Frankie!" she said, raising her voice.

"What?" he startled, lashing out with his long arm that Karen dodged just in time.

"It's Karen, your caseworker. Where's your mother?"

"Who?" he asked, barely coherent.

"C'mon. You need to stay alert, Frankie. I need you to wake up. Where-is-Edna?"

"How the fuck should I know?" he slurred.

Karen stood, put her hands on her hips, and looked around the room. On the floor by the coffee table was an empty vodka bottle.

"I'll be right back," she told Frankie. "Try to stay awake," but he was already dozing off.

The kitchen was alive with fungus and grease. Dirty dishes were piled in the sink, the floor looked like it hadn't been washed in years, and the table was smeared with food. Karen shuddered at the filth and continued down a dark, narrow hallway that led to a closed bedroom door.

Call the police. Don't go snooping on your own warned the little voice in the back of her head.

She turned around to dial the authorities, then curiosity got the best of her and she knocked on the door.

You are such a dumbass, Karen. Turn around.

"Ed-na?" she called, waiting a minute before easing the door open.

With the push of her fingertips, the door creaked open and Karen peered around the empty room. Once inside, she had to maneuver her way around lumps of strewn clothing. She walked over to a bare mattress covered with brown stains. There were no sheets or pillows. A thin, worn out blanket lay crumpled on the floor next to the bed. A bureau with drawers hanging off the hinges stood in the corner of the room. Across from the bedroom, the bathroom's thick, pungent smell rivaled a subway restroom.

Unacceptable was the only word Karen could think of. She went back to Frankie and shook him awake.

"I'm going to call for help," she told him. "I need to know when you last saw your mother."

"I don't need help," he mumbled, swatting at her like a bothersome insect.

"I need a number, a location, where I can reach Edna."

Frankie turned his head toward Karen. He was barely recognizable with two black eyes swollen near to close, a nose that looked broken, and dry, crusty blood covering both cheeks.

"What happened?"

"There was a bit of a mêlée," he sniggered, in a faux French accent.

"I can see that," she mumbled, scanning the room for a phone.

"Yeah, hi, this is Karen Sherburne. I need to report a child at risk. We're at 1422 Glenrock. He's going to need medical care and immediate placement."

Karen followed the ambulance to the hospital, relaying what little information she knew about Frankie's medical, emotional and psychological history.

Was he allergic to any medications?

She wasn't sure.

Any surgeries in the past year?

She couldn't say.

How much alcohol had he consumed?

The bottle was empty, was all she could offer.

Was he on drugs?

No clue.

After flushing Frankie with an IV, he was treated for two broken ribs, a broken nose, and a small gash on his left cheek shaped like a crescent moon. It wasn't nearly as big as Meg's, but it was, Karen noticed with a pang in her chest, most definitely a crescent moon.

*   *   *

Karen had to pull a few strings along with some serious begging for Frankie's placement, but her wish was granted. He was taken to the home of Aileen and Hal O'Malley, an older Irish couple who had been fostering children for eighteen years and who had experience with older teens with histories of drug and alcohol abuse.

While Frankie was recovering in the hospital, Karen purchased half a dozen white and black tee shirts, four pairs of jeans, six pairs of socks, seven pairs of underwear, deodorant, razors, toothbrush, toothpaste, mouthwash and aftershave. On the way to the register, she passed the bedding department and, remembering what Frankie was accustomed to sleeping on, couldn't resist purchasing the largest, fluffiest pillow she could find. She dropped the items off at the O'Malleys before Frankie arrived to avoid triggering an, 'I'm not a charity case' response from him. For all he knew, this stuff could be part of the fostering package. After being discharged, Karen gave Frankie a couple of days to adjust before paying him a visit at the O'Malleys. Hal greeted her with his usual gruffness.

"One wrong move and he's out."

"Why, it's good to see you too, Hal," Karen grinned, giving him a friendly squeeze.

Hal blushed and cleared his throat. "He's out on the sun porch," he said, in his thick Irish accent.

Frankie was sitting cross-legged on a wicker loveseat and doodling in a notebook.

"Hey," she said, taking a seat across from him.

"Hi," he grunted.

"Nice place, huh?"

"Whatever."

"You know, one wrong move and you're out."

"So they say," he said, exhaling a loud, bored sigh.

He had heard this same warning from both the hospital personnel and the liaison that had dropped him off at the O'Malleys, as well as from Hal O'Malley himself.

Frankie looked physically and emotionally beaten. Karen knew there was a good chance she might never find out exactly what occurred in those few days before she found him passed out and beaten to a pulp, but she was glad that he was finally away from his mother.

"The rules here are no cursing, attending school, obeying curfew . . ."

"I get it," he frowned, shifting in his seat.

"Good, Frankie, I hope you do get it, because you're too old to be shuffled through the system, and too young to be on your own."

Frankie didn't reply, nor did he look up from doodling.

"So, what happened?"

"My fucked up mother happened."

"Hey, hey, language," Karen warned, glancing behind her and hoping the O'Malleys were out of earshot. She would be at a total loss if Frankie lost this placement.

"I'm not kidding. The O'Malleys are sticklers with their rules."

"What the fuck," he mumbled.

"Look, I know it's difficult, but please, just pretend you can never say that word again. Pretend it's extinct."

Frankie sucked in his cheeks and blew out a puff of air, his breath directing a straggly piece of hair away from his bruised face. Beneath the discolored black and blue surface, Karen noted his perfect bone structure. He cleared his throat and spoke slowly, as if Karen was an idiot.

"My alcoholic, drug addicted mother allowed Ray into our home."

Ray? Karen spun her mental wheels . . . Ray, Ray, Ray . . . oh, man, the bastard who burned him with cigarettes. There was also a question of sexual assault when Frankie was six years old.

"Did you and Ray fight?"

"I tried to kick the fucker out . . . I mean it was an *uncomfortable* situation, so I asked him to leave."

"And what did he say?"

"Not much. I asked him with my fist, and he responded in kind with his fist. He didn't look much better than me," said Frankie, his eyes gleaming with pride.

"You sound happy you hurt him."

"Oh, you bet I'm happy."

Karen didn't say it or show it, but she was happy too.

"Where was your mother?"

"Shitfaced on the couch . . . I mean," he cleared his throat, "She was incoherent and drunk, unable to assist me."

"We haven't been able to reach her. Do you know where she is?"

"I couldn't say," he said, blinking innocently at Karen, "but if I had to venture a guess, she's giving multiple blowjobs in the bathroom of some pub for a quick buck."

Knowing this was probably true, Karen didn't respond.

"Did you try to call your dad?"

Frankie let out a contemptuous laugh.

"You're joking, right? That dirtbag only comes around when he needs money. I'd be surprised if he knew my name."

"Do you know where we could find him?"

"Dear ol' dad can always be found tying one on at the Powder Keg."

Karen looked at Frankie and frowned. He was responding exactly as she had asked, but with a smug edge to his answers, as if he were saying *fuck you* without really saying it, which was even more aggravating.

"Okay, I get it. Can we cut the crap now?"

Frankie folded his shoulders toward his chest in a slouch. His voice changed tones.

"I don't know where Edna is. She left with Ray."

"When?"

"Sometime before you found me. Could've been that day or the night before, I don't know."

"Did your mother know what kind of shape you were in when she left?"

"Since she was present and accounted for when we were pounding the crap out of each other, I'd have to say, why yes, she did know," he smiled.

Karen peeked at the notebook, expecting to see juvenile doodles of pot leaves, skulls, favorite band names.

"Hey, that's not bad," she said, admiring his artwork. "Not bad at all! Does that car exist, or did you make it up?"

"It's a De Lorean DMC-12."

"What kind of doors are those?"

"Gull-wing."

"Never seen anything like it. Sweet drawing!" she smiled, examining the detail of his work. "You ever think about taking art classes?"

Insulted by her compliment, Frankie snapped the notebook shut.

"I'm no art fag."

"For your information, artists aren't fags. They're talented people who express themselves through their craft, and let me tell you, you can draw. This picture looks 3-D," she said, tapping on the closed notebook.

"I just doodle."

"Yeah," she nodded. "And you *just* read too, right? What kind of books do you like?"

"I don't like books."

"I don't get it. Why hide the fact that you like to read?"

"I told you. I don't like to read."

"Then why does Edna think otherwise?"

"Oh, right. Edna," he said, looking up and bringing his pointer finger to his lips as if he were in deep thought. "Let me tell you about Edna and why I read, why I never fail in school."

"I'm all ears."

"I first began reading to avoid hearing my whore of a mother jacking off some drunk in the middle of the night. Turning up the radio wasn't enough, but I found that along with the music, if I read the same boring schoolbooks over and over, I would eventually fall asleep."

Regardless of how many years she'd been in the system, this was the stuff that turned Karen's stomach sour.

She tried to lighten the thickness in the air with a halfhearted joke, "Imagine if the radio wasn't on, you would have gotten straight A's!"

Frankie stared at her dumbly.

"Yeah, but then I would've heard her moaning when the guy was boning her."

Karen was shocked into silence. Her eyes moved across his face to his cheek. The crescent moon cut would turn into a slight scar, just like Meg's did. Without thinking, she touched her own face.

"It doesn't hurt, if that's what you're thinking," he said flatly.

"What, your face?" she said, trying to hide her embarrassment by scratching her cheek. "I'm glad to hear it."

Karen leaned toward Frankie and placed her elbows on her thighs.

"I want to ask you something, Frankie, and you need to think carefully about your answer. If we can locate your mother, I'm going to request her rights be terminated. Once that's done, your father will be asked to surrender his rights as well. Doing so would allow you to be placed in permanent foster care with the possibility of adoption. The thing is, because you're fifteen, you do have a say in the matter."

"What do you mean? I can live on my own?"

"No. It means when the time comes, you get to decide whether you want to be adopted or not."

"Why would I want to be adopted when I can be free in two years? You think I'm stupid, don't you?" he said defensively.

"What do you mean?"

"You know exactly what I mean," he barked. "You people don't give a shit. You'll throw me into a trailer park with some other pervert drunk who wants the foster money. I know the system."

"Why would you say that? You're not in a place like that now. The O'Malleys are very nice people."

"Yeah, but they can't keep me."

"I wouldn't place you in harm's way."

"Pffft. Like you have control. You're nothing but a peon caseworker."

Karen felt her face burn with something; anger or pride, she wasn't sure which. She had to prove this boy wrong, had to give him hope for the future, had to show him that there are good people on this earth. And most importantly, she felt the need to prove to herself that she was far more than just a peon caseworker. More for her own bruised ego than anything, Karen blurted out, "As a matter of fact, I do have control. I know exactly where you'd go."

"Oh, yeah? Enlighten me," he snarled.

"You'd be with me."

They both stared at each other with surprise and then Frankie's eyes bounced nervously around the room.

"That is, if you wanted," Karen said sheepishly.

"Whatever," he shrugged, leaning back and crossing his arms. "I'm sure you'll have a boatload more terms and conditions than the O'Malleys."

"Just about the same," she nodded.

"Like what?"

"School, refrain from dropping the f-bomb, and stay clean."

Frankie said nothing, but he did unfold his arms. Karen took this to mean that he thought this wasn't a bad idea.

"Of course, I'll have to get some things in order before you can leave here," said Karen, her mind reeling with what she would have to accomplish to be a foster parent.

Frankie's eyes filled with doubt. "Sure you do."

"Hang tough. The O'Malleys are good people."

"And you're just a bleeding heart full of empty promises," Frankie muttered, flipping to a new page of his drawing pad.

*   *   *

At least the O'Malley's bed had sheets. Frankie stuck his face into the big fluffy pillow and inhaled the fresh scent of fabric softener. What a difference to lie down on something that smelled of flowers as opposed to piss. Frankie wasn't used to a good night's sleep. He was used to screaming and yelling for help that wouldn't come when a drunken pervert wandered into his bedroom.

He felt a sharp prickle in his forearm and tried to massage away the pain of the half dozen circle-shaped scars, compliments of Ray and his cigarettes. Rubbing as hard as he could was the only remedy that would alleviate the discomfort, which felt similar to a spider crawling on his arm. He grabbed a sock from his drawer and wrapped it around his forearm just tight enough so that it blocked out the weird spidery feeling, but not too tight that it cut off his circulation. Then, with the powdery scent of the soft pillow pressed against his nose, Frankie fell into a deep slumber.

* * *

Karen left the O'Malleys dumbfounded.

Did I just tell a fifteen-year-old boy I would foster him?

Yes, she thought, *I did.*

"You want to what?" asked a perplexed and somewhat alarmed Sarah.

"I want to apply to be a foster parent."

"For who?"

"Frankie Ortiz."

"The kid with the history of violence?"

"Yep."

"The one who just got his ass whopped by his mother's psycho boyfriend that no one can locate?"

"The one and only."

"Are you joking?"

"Nope."

"Okayyyy. Can I ask if you've fallen on your head or something?"

"Yep, I fell flat on my face outside the coffee shop, and now I'm crazy," Karen laughed.

"That explains it. I'll get the papers for you," Sarah said reluctantly.

It was true Frankie's history of violence would deter most foster parents from accepting him into their home, but the way Karen saw it, she had nothing to lose. Sarah begged her to rethink her decision.

"This is a big decision and a potentially dangerous choice you're making."

"Someone needs to give him a break."

"Why you?"

"Why *not* me?"

"Again I ask, why?"

"Because," Karen said, jerking the papers out of Sarah's hand, "It feels like the right thing to do."

"What happened to your bitterness toward a system that wronged you?"

"I've switched viewpoints. If you're not part of the solution, then you're part of the problem."

"What you are is soup to nuts, Karen. I sure hope you know what you're doing."

"What's that supposed to mean?"

"You know exactly what it means."

"I think it means you should mind your own business."

Sarah's face crinkled and her eyes watered. "Well, excuse me for being concerned."

Karen moaned. She hadn't meant to hurt her feelings.

"Sarah, you don't have to be concerned."

"No, it's fine," Sarah spat. "I see that I can't have an opinion or fear for your welfare."

"Of course you can and believe me, I appreciate it," Karen said, but I do know what I'm doing."

"You haven't known what you've been doing since Meg died," Sarah said, her voice leaking with pain.

"Now, you hold on a minute," Karen said defensively, her finger pointing at Sarah's face.

"No, you hold on!" Sarah shot back, her finger at Karen's face.

As if he'd been listening with his ear to the door, Marty poked his head out of his office.

"Is this a cat fight?" he smiled wickedly, rubbing his hands together. "Can you ladies hold off long enough for me to grab the popcorn? I want a front row seat."

"Screw you, Marty," Sarah sniffed.

"If you need someone to run interference, I'm your guy."

"We're fine!" they shouted in unison, scaring Marty back into his quarters.

Karen took Sarah's hand.

"I'm sorry. Are we good?"

"Yeah, we're good," Sarah grinned. "Damn hormones."

"Absolutely," Karen smiled, knowing hormones had nothing to do with it.

In her heart, Karen knew Sarah was right. She had to be half daft; a single woman fostering a fifteen-year-old with a history of violence and drug abuse. Then again, the worst thing that could happen was a vicious outburst resulting in her death, and death didn't seem like a horrible option these days.

Meg was dead.

She'd be with Meg.

How horrible was that?

When she arrived home, Karen went directly to Meg's room. She walked over to the bureau and slipped her daughter's mood ring on her pointer finger. Blue. Mood rings were such a fraud. They either turned blue or green or a muddy combination of the two. If it had any validity, the ring should have turned red for the blood that was spilled. Karen sat on the edge of the bed and hummed quietly, surveying her surroundings. She smoothed the sheets around her and then plopped herself backward in a spread eagle position, onto the soft mattress. She stared at the ceiling until it became blurry and her eyes watered, then slung her forearm over her eyes to block out the light.

Oh, Meg. My baby.

Her sobbing started quietly, building up to a full-fledged hyperventilating attack filled with moments of deep breaths and temper fits. An hour later she sat up, sniffed, wiped her nose with the back of her hand and stated aloud, "Okay, let's begin."

She left Meg's room momentarily, arriving back with a dozen large cardboard boxes she had purchased earlier that day at an office supply store. One by one, she took Meg's belongings and placed them in the boxes; jewelry, sheets, pillows, brush and comb, hairspray, Love's Baby Soft Perfume, Meg's jelly shoes, a friendship bracelet from Charlene, and some pet rock she must have bought for herself with the name *Rocky* written on it; her Big Ben wind-up alarm clock, her Converse sneakers, her oversized purple comforter set. All clothing and games were placed in black bags to be donated to a teen shelter. Karen carefully wrapped each item in sturdy plastic, treating everything in Meg's room, down to a bobby pin, like buried treasure. The rest of the things would be stored in Carl's basement, a time capsule for Karen to revisit whenever she needed the false sense of holding Meg, smelling Meg, seeing Meg. It would go without saying that Karen would keep Teddy in her room. By three in the morning, it was done. Anyone walking into her home would be unaware that a girl named Megan Jane Humble had ever lived there.

The following day, Karen told Carl about Frankie.

"You sure you want to take this kid in?" asked Carl.

"As sure as I can be. I feel like I've been called to help him."

"You've been called? What are you, a nun?"

"I can't go on thinking about Meg twenty-four hours a day. I need a distraction, and he needs help."

"And this would be the right distraction?"

"Yes."

"Really?"

"No. I mean, I'm not sure. The truth is, I'm not sure of anything anymore. I'm trying to patch this hole in my heart and there's a boy who needs a home. I don't know how else to conduct myself other than doing what my gut tells me is right. I could blame you," Karen said lightly, "You did raise me to have a benevolent nature."

"I never raised you to be no benevolent anything, or whatever it is you call yourself. What's wrong with helping out at a shelter?"

"This is better than that. It's a chance to be a mentor, to have a new experience, to offer hope where there isn't any."

"You're just like your mother," moaned Carl. "Kind-natured to a fault."

"That's benevolent," said Karen.

"Well, I'm going on record to say you didn't get that from me," said Carl.

"Then you're not going to like my next request."

"There's more to this mess?"

"I've decided to put away Meg's things, including her photos. He doesn't know about her, and I'd prefer to keep it that way. And if you plan on having any part in this boy's life, which I hope that you would, I ask that you do the same."

"Now, just you hold on a minute Missy. You're going to begin a new relationship with a lie and worse yet, you're telling me to pretend my granddaughter never existed? Have you gone off your rocker?" shouted Carl. "How do you think you'll get away with hiding the fact you had Meg? You do have neighbors and friends."

"What neighbors? No one within two blocks is under eighty. They wouldn't know if I had a girl or a boy."

"What about Charlene and Jen?"

"I don't plan on seeing them much," Karen said bitterly.

"Are you going to at least tell them?"

"Maybe, maybe not. Let's be realistic; anyone connected to me through Meg will not be a part of my future."

"That's a bit selfish, Miss Benevolent."

"Yes it is, and I couldn't care less. Jen and I had one connection, and that was our daughters. And since I don't have one of those anymore, I can't see the use in us socializing. We've nothing else in common and I don't need a Meg reminder every time I look at Charlene."

Carl cleared his throat and when he spoke, his tone was softer.

"Where's he going to school?"

"He'll finish out his sophomore year where he is, and then transfer to Cambridge High School."

"You mean away from Somerville High where Meg went."

"Right."

"And they're allowing you to cross school districts? You don't live in Cambridge?"

"I guess we're close enough to the city line that we could go either way."

"Well, lucky you," Carl said sarcastically.

"Meg's memory is impervious, Dad. No one can ever take her away. This is for Frankie's sake."

"Frankie? That's his name?"

"That's his name."

"Where is he now?"

"At a temporary foster home."

"When is he coming?"

"Four and a half months minimum. I have to go through what's called a MAPP, which takes approximately eight weeks. After that, I'm required to have a home study done by another social worker, who will ask me questions about my life and why I want to foster him. They'll wrap the whole thing up with a background check, and then I'm officially a foster parent."

"What else you gonna hit me with?"

"Just that I've decided to switch churches to avoid Meg questions in front of Frankie."

"So, if I wanted to go to church with my daughter?"

"You'll be going to Saint Catherine's."

"Perfect," Carl sighed.

"So what do you think? Do I have your blessing?"

"I'm not a goddamned priest, Karen, and I'm not going to tell you what to do. I'll never turn my back on you, but don't you think for one minute that I'll ever remove my granddaughter from my mantle or refrigerator or from anywhere else. I don't care if the kid ever comes to my house. Meg stays."

"I respect that," Karen said quickly, and then made an excuse to hang up the phone. She slouched back in her chair and stared at the ceiling.

How dare she ask her father to sacrifice Meg's photos for some boy he didn't know? How dare she presume to tell him what he could and could not keep in his own home?

If she confessed what really propelled her to foster Frankie, people would think she was certifiable. It was that damn crescent shaped scar on his face. Crazy or not, Karen believed it was a sign from Meg. For some reason, Meg had wanted them to find each other. And what that reason was, only time would tell.

JANUARY, 1981

A month after Frankie's placement, Karen received an angry call from Hal O'Malley.

"I said one offense."

"Good to hear from you, Hal," Karen said, trying to lighten up the pending conversation.

"I'm serious, Karen. I want him out."

"What happened?"

"He chose to booze and drug instead of going to school is what happened."

"Hal, please don't make any rash decisions. I promise I'll be there as soon as I can."

On the drive over, she tried to figure out the best way to convince the O'Malleys to keep Frankie until she was finished with the paperwork that would allow him to live with her. Her hand was balled into a fist and prepped to knock on the door when it flew open.

"Sun porch," barked Hal.

Averting his glare, Karen scooched sideways and squeezed past Hal through the opening. Without saying a word, she headed in the direction of the sun porch.

Frankie was seated in his usual spot, his fingers working magic with a charcoal pencil and drawing pad.

"What happened, Frankie?" Karen asked, taking a seat across from him.

"I dunno. I was tired," he said, looking out the window.

"Tired how?"

"Tired of having to try."

"Lame excuse."

"You told me to be honest."

"Yeah, well guess what? The world is tired, Frankie."

"Did I say I gave a shit about the world?"

"Fair enough," Karen replied, trying to keep her tone even, "Exactly what were you so tired of that you had to go and screw this up?"

"I was tired of being sober. I wanted to drink and get high," he said defensively.

"You wanted to get high?"

"Stoned blind," he grinned.

Karen smacked her lips and exhaled. "Let me guess. You were dropped off at school. After buying some weed from whomever, you left the building and enlisted some drunk on a street corner to buy you booze. You spent the day getting high and drinking without regard for anyone else."

"That just about covers it," he grinned, still a bit high.

"You realize you could be removed from here? The O'Malleys are afraid of keeping you, Frankie."

"So remove me."

"To where?"

"The next foster home."

"Not so easy to come by."

"To your house, then."

"I can't take you yet, and quite frankly, this wasn't part of our deal."

Karen finger combed the top of her head and leaned forward.

"Look," she said firmly, "I have moved some very big bridges to get you here. Do you remember the things I asked you to refrain from doing?"

"It's hard to remember a thousand rules."

"How about the easy ones; don't swear, be honest, stay clean?"

"Oh, those rules," he replied defiantly, meeting her gaze.

Karen looked at him calmly. "Yeah, oh those rules."

"Let me guess. I'm out on the streets."

"Not yet, but if you don't want to be, you'd better start showing some effort on your part, because no one is going to carry you, Frankie. You've got to trust that people care."

"Number one, I don't recall being asked to be carried. Number two, care for me?" he uttered with a hint of hostility, "Lady, you don't even know who the fuck I am. You can point the finger all you want, but don't pretend to know me. You crack me up," he snorted, shooing her away with his hand. "Just send me back."

"No."

"*No?*"

"No."

"What's that supposed to mean?"

"It means no. I'm not sending you back. And I do know you."

"Do tell," he dared her.

"Your entire life has consisted of one let down after another. Adults have mistreated you and have told you that you're no good and useless. They've beaten you. They've neglected you. Just when you begin to feel hopeful, something bad happens and you end up back at square one. You blow it because you don't know what else to do, because you believe you're worthless, because that is what's been pounded into your head for as long as you can remember. The only consistent thing that happens to you is inconsistency. You think that eventually I'll drop you, but I won't. I'm here to stay," she said, leaning in to lightly touch his fisted hand.

At her gentle touch, Frankie felt his fist relax and his stomach lurch. A warm, unfamiliar surge traveled through his body, like someone had come in with a broom and swept all the anger away. He swallowed hard, trying to barricade his emotions. Why was this woman screwing with his brain?

"How was that for not knowing you?"

Fearful that he might actually cry, Frankie could only nod in defeat.

"All right," said Karen, clapping her hands. "So, here's what we're going to do next. You're going to apologize profusely to the O'Malleys for this episode and assure them that it will never happen again. Starting tomorrow, I'm picking you up and driving you to school. As far as lunch goes, you have two options: eat lunch with me off school grounds, or find some kids to socialize with in the cafeteria."

Frankie grimaced. Neither option was attractive.

"I'll stay in the cafeteria."

"Good enough. Know that I'm going to speak with the principal about this. If the teacher on lunch duty doesn't note your presence, I will find out. Is that clear?"

"Yeah, it's frigging clear," he huffed.

"I'll see you after school for our usual hour visits on Tuesdays, Wednesdays, and Fridays, and trust that on the other two days, you'll be holding up your end of the bargain by producing good grades and keeping clean."

Frankie folded his long arms showing off biceps that, despite being lean, were quite defined.

A moment passed where they stared at each other like petulant children.

"Do we have a deal, Frankie?"

"Do I have a choice, Karen?"

"Not really."

Frankie did a fine job of apologizing to the O'Malleys.

"I mean it," warned Hal, his face the same color as his wooly red hair. "As it stands, this is an exception to my rule. One more time and you're out on your ass."

Karen interrupted Hal's speech with a hug.

"You're a kind man, and a lifesaver."

Hal's face softened, almost smiled, before he caught himself and cleared his throat.

"Never you mind that nonsense, Karen" he said, wriggling free from her embrace. "Now go on, you've got work to do, and Frankie promised to help me set up some shelves in the basement after his homework was done. Haven't you, boy?"

Karen eyeballed Frankie. The pot was wearing off, and he looked famished and exhausted.

"You might want to feed him first," Karen said, nodding in Frankie's general direction. "He's probably got the munchies."

As Hal shut the front door, Karen heard, "Come on, boy, it's time to bring you back to the real world. Aileen made corned beef and cabbage. It will grow hair on that chest of yours."

LIFE WITH
THE O'MALLEYS

Mrs. O'Malley served warm, open-faced corned beef sandwiches with carrots and potatoes. After dinner, she sat next to Frankie while he did his homework, humming softly and crocheting what looked like a blue blanket. Once his schoolwork was finished, Frankie helped Mr. O'Malley put up shelves in the basement. An hour and a half later, the shelves were installed, and Frankie lumbered up the stairs, ready for a rest.

Mr. O'Malley took up residence in a well used recliner.

"Frankie, will you pull up a seat for a moment?"

Frankie wasn't used to being asked to do things. Being asked meant you were given a choice, an opportunity to decline. He was used to being told what to do, like being told to go away, or forced into meeting perverts for a drug drop, or being sent to go and rifle through the neighbor's trash for scraps of food. This thing, where adults treated him like a human being, was going to take some getting used to. He knew from his previous experience with Ray that although Mr. O'Malley was a loud, hot-tempered old man, he was harmless. Just before she left, Karen whispered a suggestion, "He loves to be called Sir."

"Yes, Sir," he said, taking a seat on the blue and white plaid couch across from Hal.

"Karen Sherburne is a nice woman. She has told me of her plans to foster you. Me and the Missus have fostered over thirty kids, and I've never known a better social worker than Karen. You know what that means?"

"No," said Frankie, because honestly, he didn't.

"It means she thinks you're special. Don't disappoint her. Show her you can rise above whatever past you've had to trudge through. Control your own future, boy."

"You men want some fresh baked oatmeal cookies?" interrupted Aileen, her Irish accent thicker than Hal's.

Maybe it was pot letdown, or the accumulation of drugs he had taken over the years, but Frankie suddenly felt surreal, disconnected from himself and his surroundings.

Special? Him? How could he possibly be special when, since birth, he'd been told otherwise? The only special he'd been called was Special Olympics. To spare himself from the pain that life outside of his world was different, Frankie accepted what Ray pounded into his head. He convinced himself that no one had fresh baked cookies after dinner or clean clothes and fresh sheets that smelled of lilacs. But Frankie had been mistaken. The O'Malleys love for each other was obvious. *Could it be true that not everyone was an asshole? Assholes were easy to ignore, compassion wasn't.* It was the realization that people could be kind that damn near shattered Frankie's psyche. His heart was pounding so hard he swore it was visible through his shirt. He dropped his forehead into his hands and waited for the impending doom he was sure was about to hit.

"Frankie?" asked Aileen, placing her hand on his shoulder. "Are you okay?"

"Are you sick, boy?" questioned Hal.

"I need to go to bed," he said, his voice barely audible.

"Come, Frankie. We'll help you to your room," said Aileen.

The O'Malleys stood on either side of Frankie with their hands on his elbows, guiding him down the narrow hallway toward his bedroom.

"Here you are," said Aileen, sitting him on the edge of his bed. When she turned on the bedside light, the shadow of a crucifix, located just outside his bedroom door, was projected onto Frankie's wall.

"I think I'm going to die," he told them.

"What is it?" asked Aileen with concern, her hand automatically going to Frankie's forehead.

"I don't know. I think it's a bad trip."

Hal took a seat next to Frankie.

"Look at me, boy."

Frankie met Hal's inquisitive gaze, certain that he would confirm his suspicion.

"Aww, he's not sick, Mother," said Hal to Aileen. "Leave us be. He'll be fine."

Aileen bent over and kissed Hal's forehead, then she kissed Frankie's forehead, and Frankie felt his world spin. This love thing was worse than being beaten with a stick. At least with a beating you knew what you were getting, but with love, your emotions ran amuck.

"Let me tell you about myself," he began.

Frankie hoped this was going to be short. The back of his throat had developed a giant lump that was interfering with his swallowing.

"When I was a lad, I was a ruffian who had two kinds of behaviors; bad or worse. Then I found Aileen. Someday, you'll find an Aileen as well," he said lightly.

"If Karen wants you, it means you've got promise. Even I can tell you have potential with all them pictures you draw. Now listen up boy," he said, his hand now on Frankie's knee, "You were destined to be somebody no matter where you came from. We all are."

Frankie felt nauseous at Hal's touch. He turned and shifted almost violently.

"Shhh, easy, boy, easy," said Hal, patting his knee.

Helplessness followed frustration followed anger followed an overwhelming vulnerability he had never experienced. Frankie hung his head and began to sob, trying to hide his face with his forearm.

"No shame in it," said Hal. "No shame at all."

With his face still hidden, Frankie barked, "Get out."

Hal stood up, not out of fear, but because he recognized a fragile ego when he saw one. With his hands in his pants pockets, he said, "I met Aileen in Ireland when she was working as a waitress in a pub. I got into a brawl with a man over a bowl of peanuts. Can you imagine that? *A bowl of peanuts.* Anyway, he got the best of me, and then I like to think I got the better of him," he grinned nostalgically. "When it was over, we both lay on the floor of the pub barely conscious. Aileen got a piece of raw meat from the kitchen and put it on my eye. While I sat there with a fat piece of steak to my face, she helped the other man to his feet and sent him on his way. She kept me there and bandaged my cuts. She made sure I drank coffee and brought me ham and potatoes. She scolded me for being a fool. Once I sobered up, I thanked her and asked why she was being so nice. You know what she said? She said it was because she could see my potential. She told me what I'm about to tell you, which is don't let your past control your future. One foot in front of the other boy, step by step.

"From that day forward, I loved her. Unfortunately, it took two more miserable years and Aileen with a suitcase in her hands to stop my antics. I found myself on my knees begging for anyone to help me. As it so happened that, and remember now, boy, we're in Ireland, a priest came and found me face down just outside of a pub. I clung to his robes like a damn fool and begged for absolution. The priest looked down at me and said, *Get off your knees boy, and stop pitying yourself. Do you think you're all alone in the sinning category? Even saints have pasts boy, and your future, well, it's yours to change. Why don't you try giving up on the sinner side of things for a while?*"

"Well, let me tell you, the thought of giving up on things for a while seemed far easier a feat than giving up on them forever. And so I let go of the drinking, the cheating on Aileen, and going to pubs. And before I knew it, a while turned into twenty-five years."

Frankie wiped his eyes and looked up at Hal. A short, corpulent man, he could easily picture a younger version; cocksure and filled with booze, spewing verbal obscenities in barrooms across Ireland.

Hal walked to the doorway and stood awkwardly, jiggling the change in his pockets. As he turned to leave, he looked back at Frankie. With a wink and a grin, he said, "Remember Frankie, God loves everyone, even us assholes."

*　　*　　*

In addition to three hourly visits per week, Karen spent eight of the sixteen weeks Frankie was at the O'Malleys picking him up and driving him to school. She also went through the foster care evaluations, worked close to sixty hours a week, and prepared her home for the arrival of someone who wasn't Meg, a boy she was looking forward to helping for more selfish reasons than she could count. Maybe his presence would take away the feeling that she had ten-pound sandbags strapped to each ankle. Maybe he would bring her some happiness. If not, she'd fake it for his sake; she had become a master at acting as if her life was returning to a semblance of normal. Marty and Sarah mentioned Frankie more than they did Meg these days. Karen understood there were only so many ways to ask how she was feeling. Truth is, she would have depressed the entire office with her replies: "The same as yesterday, hopeless." "Shitty, but thanks for asking." "My daughter's dead, how do you think I'm feeling?" As the new addition into her life, Frankie was a far easier, less painful topic. So far, Karen had passed the MAPP review, her home study, and her background check. Lorraine, an old colleague of Karen's, was assigned to the case.

"It says here that parental rights were stripped?" asked Lorraine.

"Correct. And both have signed off on termination papers."

Edna, as it turned out, did not disappear. In fact, she was quite easy to locate. She was exactly where Frankie had suggested, slumming at a local bar. She signed off on her son without question. Whitey, on the other hand, spent an hour and a half trying to sell Frankie to the highest bidder.

"What are you going to give me for him? Two grand should cover it. Two grand, and he's all yours."

It was only after an illegal threat by Barry, a broad shouldered social worker with muscles on top of muscles, did Whitey begrudgingly sign off on his son.

"You understand that even with the termination of both parent's rights, you would still have to go through court to proceed with an adoption, but as long as no one contests, it should be smooth sailing," Lorraine assured her.

"Good to know," smiled Karen.

With the evaluations for foster placement underway, Karen's next step was to confront Marty.

"Listen, with all that's happened I know my attendance has been poor."

"Don't be silly," said Marty, waving his hand to dismiss her comment.

"And I know I've only been back for a short time."

"It's all to be expected."

"Well, I don't think you're expecting what I'm about to say next."

"Which is?" he asked, with a raised eyebrow.

"Because of Frankie, you know, the foster thing, well, um . . ."

Karen paused and looked around the room, trying to figure out how to word her request.

"Just get to the point. I'm going gray here, kiddo."

"I need six weeks off, but," she paused, raising her finger before he could respond, "I'll do my work from home, including all follow up calls. I'll also continue with my weekly visits, which I can reschedule for when Frankie is at school. However," and this was the part Karen was dreading, "I don't want to take on any new cases."

"No new cases? For how long?"

"For as long as it takes him to adjust."

"Karen," he started, "adjustments can take years."

"I know, I know, but I'm hoping since he's older—"

"What? That he'll adjust faster? I don't know that I can agree to this."

"Please, Marty," she pleaded, "I have to do this."

Marty sighed. "No new cases for two weeks."

"Eight weeks," Karen negotiated.

"Three weeks."

"Six weeks."

Marty shook his head, "No deal."

"How about five weeks, unless he's doing exceptionally well, and then I'll start sooner."

Marty paused and smacked his lips.

"No new cases for four weeks, and after that, you can work from home if needed. Final offer."

"Deal!"

Marty motioned for Karen to lean toward him.

"You're sure this isn't a—" Marty looked away, his words suspended in the air.

118

"Isn't a what?"

Marty opened his desk to reveal a drawer full of lollipops.

"What color?"

"Purple," said Karen, trained to pick her daughter's favorite.

Marty pulled off the wrapper and handed it to her. After taking a lick of an orange pop, he said, "Are you sure this isn't just a replacement kid, Karen? I mean he's got mondo problems. His paperwork is peppered with violence, drugs, and alcohol. I have to ask, why this particular kid?"

Pushing the pop to the side of her mouth, she replied, "Honestly? I look at this kid and I know he's redeemable. He had a shitty start, that's all."

"But he's Meg's age, Karen. You see that, don't you?"

"I see it," she said, crunching into the pop and tossing the stick into the trash.

"You also know he's not Meg, won't be Meg?"

Karen hesitated before forcing out a nervous laugh.

"Oh, Marty, don't psych 101 me! I'm fine."

"You mean you think you're fine," he corrected.

She chuckled and waved her hand at him as she walked out of the office. In the bathroom, she splashed cold water on her face and took a long, hard look in the mirror. Karen dried her hands with a paper towel and then, just to be sure she was still real, bit down hard on her lower lip until she tasted metal. Marty was right. What business did she have fostering any child, never mind a kid who came from one of the worst homes Karen had ever witnessed? On the other hand, maybe Frankie was just what she needed. Maybe having to take care of him would make her stop thinking about Meg's murderer. Daily fantasizing about killing the killer had turned into an obsession. It was what kept her going, what made her smirk with evil pleasure, what made her sleep like a baby. It was quite similar to the anticipation she felt when waiting for the new *Dynasty* to come on TV, only this was the *Karen Gets Revenge Show*, and she was the director. She wasn't sure how, or even if, she wanted to conquer these poisonous thoughts, but her hopes were pinned, maybe too much, on Frankie Ortiz easing her discomfort. She returned to her desk and was smiling like the *Grinch who Stole Christmas* when her phone startled her back to reality.

"This is Karen," she said, sounding rather dazed.

"Hi, honey," came her father's familiar voice. "Are you free for lunch?"

"Sure," she answered, closing out of the unfinished report that was due in three hours, "Let's meet at the deli around the corner from my work."

At the restaurant, Meg's long fingers visited Karen through the waitress, who set down her lunch plate. When Carl excused himself to go to the bathroom, she saw Meg inside the salt shaker she mindlessly shook on her fries. Her hands were pressed against the glass and she was smiling this silly, sly smile, and Karen couldn't help but smile back.

The waitress noticed Karen inspecting the shaker as if it were a long lost friend. She addressed Karen in a tone one would use for someone with special needs.

"The salt okay, honey?"

"It's all good," Karen said, her face flushing pink. She placed the salt shaker on the table and clasped her fingers together.

She waited until the waitress walked away before reaching for the shaker and opening the lid. She carefully poured out the contents, as if Meg would fall out with the fine white grains. She shuffled her fingers around the mound of salt until it was one thin layer on the table. She hunted through the white particles, for the small mole on the side of Meg's hand, the chicken pox mark on her right shoulder, the crescent moon scar that resembled Frankie's.

But she couldn't find any sign of her daughter.

She licked her finger and dipped it into the salt. It tasted like Meg when she was a child, mud mixed with grass mixed with baby powder. It felt like Meg, soft and grainy and pure.

"What in the hell are you doing? Have you gone off your rocker?" asked a bewildered Carl, looking anxiously from the table to Karen.

Remorse. Bitterness. Rage. Dead dreams.

None of these words could possibly relay how she felt about her daughter's death, because there were no words that could articulate how it feels to lose someone, yet sense their presence every second of every day.

"The top was loose," she said with a note of defiance, her salt-licked finger frozen on the edge of her lip.

Carl sighed heavily. He held up a hand and nodded at the waitress.

"Hi," he grinned apologetically. "There's been a mishap. Could we possibly have another shaker?"

"Not a problem," she replied, giving Karen a sweet smile that said *I knew you were bonkers.*

* * *

The week before Frankie moved in, Karen visited the O'Malley home to explain the schedule she had negotiated with Marty.

"But I'm in school all day. I'm not even here."

"But isn't it nice to come home to someone?" Karen asked, feeling a pang of guilt that she hadn't done this for her own daughter.

"It's not like me and the O'Malleys sat around all happy hour."

"But they were there in case you needed them."

"I guess."

"So, I thought me working from home was a good idea."

"It's not necessary," Frankie cut in.

"You sound disappointed. Is my being here going to pose a problem for you?" Karen asked suspiciously.

"Shit, yeah. They're going to fire you."

"Fire me?"

"For not showing up. It happened to my mother all the time."

"Is that what this is about?"

"Sort of."

"What's the other sort of?"

"Mr. O'Malley worked me like a dog. I put racks in his basement, mowed that massive lawn, and painted one whole side of the house."

Karen grinned. "And you're thinking I'm going to do that to you as well?"

"Der."

"Don't worry. I'm not as inspired by physical labor as the O'Malleys. I just want to be here for you."

When Frankie didn't respond, Karen asked, "Are you looking forward to staying with me?"

His expression said *please don't ask me that* and immediately she wished she could take it back.

"Never mind," she said, waving her arm and reaching for a bowl of chips that Hal had left for them on the table. "Silly question."

"I'm looking forward," he began slowly, "to never seeing Edna again."

To avoid saying anything stupid, Karen forced too many chips in her mouth and simply nodded.

"I know I can't stay here cause they don't want me," Frankie said, but it sounded like more of a question.

"No, you can't. But it's not that they don't want you," Karen corrected.

"I know, I know. They're old and don't want permanent kids."

"Right."

"So, if I have to go somewhere, I guess I'm kinda okay with going to your place."

Karen nodded, afraid to let out the smile that was tapping on her lips.

"Why don't we walk to the drugstore and choose a thank you card for the O'Malleys?"

"That's queer."

"It's not queer. It's respectful."

"I mean," he said without an ounce of insecurity, "It's queer to be seen with you in public."

Karen smiled. "Oh, I get it. What will people think?"

"Exactly," he nodded seriously.

"We can drive there."

"Whatever," he sighed.

In the drugstore parking lot, Karen turned her head toward a honking car. It was Jen and Charlene. Charlene was hanging out the window waving at Karen.

"Hi, Karen!"

Karen smiled uncomfortably and waved back.

"Who was that?"

"A friend of my . . . she used to work with me," she corrected.

"Oh," he said, unfazed.

The familiar thump of tears tapped her eyeballs. Karen distracted herself by fishing through her purse for a piece of gum.

"Trident cinnamon?" she offered.

Frankie took the gum from Karen and popped it in his mouth. "So if you take the summer off, they won't fire you for sure?"

"They won't fire me for sure," Karen repeated, but her mind was on Jen and Charlene, and whether or not it was possible to avoid them for the rest of her life.

LETTERS TO MEG,
SPRING OF 1981

Dear Meg,

I've heard writing was supposed to be therapeutic. Talking to Teddy, although somewhat cathartic, just doesn't cut it for me. I've never won the greatest pen pal award, but I'm going to do the best I can to keep you updated. I bought a composition book at the drugstore and titled it *Letters to Meg* so that on the days when I feel lost without you, I can connect with you through these pages.

You were my perfect presentation from God. Some days, your absence accentuates the groans in the house, and every creak and clatter, from the baseboards to the hardwood to the ice maker, hollers in my ears. Other days, I'm surrounded by a frightening dead silence; on those days, I get a Q-tip and swoop it inside my ears in case the culprit is wax build up. Last Monday, I went so far as to knock over my glass of juice just to hear it shatter.

And it felt good.

I see you constantly, Meg. You're the blur out of the corner of my eye that causes me to do a double take. I hear you, the squeaks in the floorboard and the moans of the house. I smell you, the sudden whiff of baby powder that emanates from out of the blue, filling the stale, colorless room with softness. I even feel you, a cool puff of air that tingles my spine and gives me goose bumps, telling me you're with me. Next to me. Always.

Since you've been gone, I've had this breathing problem. It feels like someone is standing behind me with a hand on each side of my ribs and slowly squeezing out my air so that by the end of the day, I'm lightheaded and woozy. I refer to it as my steel cable of remorse. It coils around my muscles, preventing me from taking a good, long breath. The way I see it, at least I feel something.

Newsflash: I'm fostering a teenage boy who will be moving into your room in just a few days. In order to protect him from thinking he's a replacement kid, I've decided to clear out everything that's yours. There's not one thing remaining in this house that says *Meg lived here.* I removed it all, down to the last bobby pin. Your grandfather, as you can imagine, is pissed. He doesn't get that tangible evidence isn't what keeps you alive; memories keep you alive.

I'm going to take a moment and imagine that you're agreeing with me so that I can rid myself of the shadow of any doubt that I'm making a huge mistake.

Karen inhaled and exhaled three times before writing, "Okay, I'm good."

Moving on: I'm not sure if you remember this kid, but he was assigned to me just before you left. He had no one and I had no one, and so I figured maybe two no ones could almost make a whole someone. Does that make sense?

I know what you're thinking. You're thinking, *here she goes again, burying herself in her work.* It's true, Meg. I never did stop to smell the roses, never allowed myself a whiff of reprieve. Well, don't worry. I've learned my lesson. I missed too many roses while you were here, and I'll be damned if I'm going to screw up again. I'm going to devote the rest of my life to making sure I don't ignore what's in front of me, that I don't put aside moments I can't get back in order to rescue the unreachable.

Did I fail you, Meg? The uncertainty torments me.

Teddy update: he's on my bed. I did a poor patch job on his foot, but he's patched nonetheless. For the most part, I keep him inside a plastic bag to retain your smell. I sleep with him, unzip the bag and smell him, have conversations with him. I look like an old lady with dementia the way I talk to that pathetic stuffed bear.

Can you hear me, Meg? Am I making sense? Am I doing the right thing?

Soon, I'll have a boy. That oughta be interesting.

Stay tuned, Meg.

Love,
Mom xoxo ☺

PART 3

New Beginnings

A FRESH START

Karen's house wasn't as neat or as big as the O'Malleys, but compared to the filthy home Frankie came from, the place was a palace. For their first official dinner, Karen ordered pizza and fries. Initially, it was supposed to be spaghetti and meatballs, but she burned the sauce and undercooked the meat, which even she wouldn't have thought possible.

"Confession time, Frankie. I can't cook. I was just trying to be a showoff. You want pizza or would you prefer a hot sub?"

"Whatever," said Frankie, who had boxed himself into a corner of the kitchen and was standing awkwardly with his hands in his pockets.

"Okay, let's go with pizza," said Karen, purposely ignoring his indifference.

She took a gallon of milk from the refrigerator and retrieved two tall glasses from the cabinet.

"Chocolate or strawberry powder?" she asked, stretching herself to reach two containers from the top shelf.

"Just white."

"Really? I have two spoons of strawberry and one spoon of chocolate. You should try it some time," she smiled.

When he responded with a blank stare, she cleared her throat and began spooning the powder into her glass.

"Tell me, Frankie, are you Catholic?"

"I dunno," he said, looking at her suspiciously.

"It doesn't matter," she quickly replied. "I just want to make sure that whatever your religious preference, I become part of it."

"I have no preference."

"Well, I'm a practicing Catholic and you're welcome to come to church with me sometime."

"Is it a *have to* or an option?"

"It's an option. I think it only fair to warn you that I sing. And it's not pretty."

"Too much information," he groaned.

Patches of awkward silence followed until the pizza arrived. In an attempt to alleviate the immediate discomfort, Karen asked, "Shall we watch TV while we eat?"

"Yeah," said Frankie, relief showing on his face.

While Frankie held both plates, Karen set up the TV dinner trays on opposite ends of the long sofa.

"What do you like to watch?"

"Doesn't matter."

"The news or a *Fantasy Island* rerun, you choose."

The only trouble with watching TV was that Frankie unwittingly linked certain shows to unwanted memories. Hearing, *The plane! The plane!* reminded him of a time when Edna had brought in not one, but three men and a woman. They disappeared into her bedroom, sparing Frankie the visual. Nonetheless, in Frankie's mind, *Fantasy Island* equaled orgy.

"The news," he answered.

After dinner, Karen scooped up the plates and headed into the kitchen. She didn't ask Frankie to help with clean up because she wanted his first night to be as stress free as possible. While she washed the dishes, Frankie channel surfed until he stumbled upon a *Three's Company* rerun, and since no distasteful Edna memories were attached with this particular sitcom, he watched it absentmindedly. Karen returned to the living room, the front of her pants soaked from leaning against the sink. He couldn't help glancing at the large wet spot that covered her midsection. She looked down and brushed at her pants, as if this would make the wet disappear.

"I know, I know," she grinned. "By now you've probably figured out that not only do I not cook, but I don't clean so much either. I usually order out and eat on plastic. I'm a poor housekeeper, Frankie."

Frankie shrugged indifferently and turned his attention back to the TV.

"I'm just going to change into sweats and prepare your room. Be back in a moment."

Karen took her time changing and preparing Frankie's room, which really didn't need any preparing. By the time she returned to the living room it was ten o'clock.

"Why don't I show you to your room? You're welcome to stay up, but keep in mind that morning comes early around here. There's only one bathroom so we have to share. I figure you need to be up around six to get dressed and ready for school."

Frankie stood, towering over Karen. He looked over her head toward the hallway and said, "Whatever."

Karen directed him down the hallway and stood in the entrance to his bedroom. She touched his forearm lightly and said, "Goodnight, Frankie. If you need anything just shout, but I hope you sleep well."

"Night," he mumbled, and with his hands glued inside his pockets, he slouched into the room.

A half hour later, he poked his head out of his bedroom. While Karen slept, Frankie wandered quietly around the small house. In the kitchen, he ran his hands along the countertops and sticky cabinets and recalled the evening's events. Watching Karen attempt to cook was like watching a comedy of errors. She absentmindedly splattered the failed spaghetti sauce onto her shirt while pouring it into the sink. She had sauce on the back of her hand that she wiped on her forehead, smearing red from just above one eyebrow to the other. Frankie felt awkward pointing it out, and let her carry on with a smudged forehead. Karen washed the saucepan and placed it upside down on a towel, leaving water dripping over the sides of the counter and onto the floor. She also seemed to be one of those obsessive hand washers who didn't believe in the use of hand towels. Several times he observed her scrubbing her hands and then rubbing them on her pants. As a result, every spice jar, every cabinet knob, even the saltshaker, felt sticky to the touch. It would have been quite clear, even without her saying so, that Karen was a slob. Betting that ninety percent of the meals would be takeout, Frankie was certainly going to miss the O'Malley's home cooked meals.

The living room held pictures of different landscapes. Not one relative or friend was displayed smiling happily from behind a glass encased photograph. Not that this surprised Frankie. Karen wasn't exactly a looker. He attempted to give her a mental makeover and came to the conclusion that on her, it would just look wrong. It was as if somehow Karen was meant to look plain. She wore big blouses covered by vests, resulting in a shapeless figure. Her slight build struggled to hold onto baggy chinos. She was pale as a ghost and her face was outlined with gray and auburn tendrils trying to escape the loose bun on the back of her head. The contrast of her graying breakaway hair highlighted thick, manly eyebrows that were in dire need of a plucking. Her cherry colored lips were thin and her cheeks were always flushed a soft shade of pink. Karen's hands were rough and cold, and the tip of her nose was often red with tiny spider veins spreading onto her cheeks. Her one redeeming feature was her eyes. They were dark walnut, so dark that they almost hid the black of her pupils. On a mean person, Karen's eyes would look demonic. But on Karen, they illuminated a tangible kindness that shocked you with their intensity. Her lashes were long and plentiful, as graceful as the wings of a butterfly. They covered every inch of her top and bottom lids so that when she blinked, they actually fluttered. Those rich eyes stood out on her bland, fair face like a beacon of hope, intent on rescuing even that which could not be rescued.

Boys like Frankie.

Once or twice, Frankie thought he saw sorrow in her eyes, as if someone stole her favorite thing in the whole wide world and she'd never get it back. Then again, what did he know? He looked for sorrow in everyone to escape the solitude of his own desolation.

Frankie poured another glass of milk, and after taking a sip told himself that pretty or not, Karen was a million times better than Edna; Edna, who smelled of body odor and tobacco, and who lived to satisfy hungry, insatiable urges. Even when he was a child, she gave blowjobs in the kitchen for twenty bucks while Frankie watched *Shazam!* and tried to ignore the sucking sound his mother made, and the moaning sound that followed when the sucking was over. The times when it got really vulgar, when his mother would take off her clothes for another five bucks, Frankie hoped he'd go blind. Karen, on the other hand, would often touch Frankie lightly when they laughed. He flinched until he got used to the fact that a hand coming his way didn't equal a slap across his face.

He scanned the house from the doorway of the living room. Large boxed rooms with high ceilings gave the impression that there was lots of space. Was this really going to be his foster home, or would he screw up like he always did?

But wait; wasn't this way too easy? What was the catch?

Was Karen a whacko?

Was she part of a secret government scheme in charge of shipping Frankie off to a foreign country to be sold as a slave?

Maybe the CIA would come at night and put a chip in his brain for some top-secret experiment.

Even worse, what if they did an anal probe?

What if the Catholic thing was just a guise and she was part of a religious cult who dressed in black robes and planned on using him as a sacrificial gift, like Rosemary's baby?

Karen couldn't really be this nice.

Nobody cared about kids like Frankie, not even people like Karen.

The thought of it all falling apart before it began caused the scars on Frankie's forearms to ache. He rubbed hard to make it stop.

Fucking asshole and his cigarettes, he thought, massaging the circular scars. He walked back to his room and sat on the edge of the bed, staring at the cream walls. He wondered what the room was used for before he came. Probably one of those junk rooms where boxes and boxes of stuff were stacked high to the ceiling.

Accustomed to sleeping fully clothed in case he had to make a narrow escape from the law or a pervert, Frankie decided to take a chance and strip down to his underwear. Just before he closed his eyes, he felt a chill followed by prickles at the nape of his neck. He sat up to grab a second blanket from the end of his bed and as he did so, he thought he saw a figure standing at the foot of his bed. He squeezed his eyes closed and shook his head. When he opened them, the room was empty. Reaching into the side pocket of his backpack, Frankie pulled out the in-case-of-emergency nip, because FYI, something like this counted as an emergency. If he only used his nips for those high anxiety moments then it really was medicinal, just like cough syrup. He opened his throat and allowed the warm vodka to wash into his system. It granted him immediate restoration. He scanned the room and, only when he was convinced he had been hallucinating guilt, did he close his eyes and allow himself to sleep heavily.

For tonight, Frankie was safe.

LETTERS TO MEG

Dear Meg,

He's already figured out I can't cook. I was kind of hoping if I played my cards right, he wouldn't notice I was homemaker-challenged for a couple of weeks. I totally burned the sauce, so I ordered pizza.

It was harder than I imagined taking him to your room and pretending I didn't see you lying stomach down on top of the comforter, your knees bent and feet twirling around in the air. You were so adorable in your farmer jeans with your giant donut-shaped black and gray headphones covering your ears, like Princess Lea hair buns! You always had a grape Tootsie Pop hanging out of the side of your mouth. You did that owl impersonation so well. How did it go? *How many licks does it take to get to the center of a Tootsie Pop?* or something like that.

Oh, that was always good for a laugh, Meg!

Frankie is definitely defensive, but that's to be expected. He acts like he couldn't care less about me or anything else, and that may be true, but I've got to keep the faith, right? He stayed with the O'Malleys before coming here, and now he's afraid I might work him as hard as Hal did. You know Hal; every time a new kid comes along a neglected room gets a new paint job or there's a new shelf built or a closet organized. I think it's great. It forces them to interact with Hal and it keeps them busy. Every kid the O'Malleys fostered has turned into a productive citizen. Of course, Frankie is older and had less of a stay time with them, but now he has me, and I'm going to follow in Hal's footsteps and push this kid to his limit.

It's resolution time.

You know how you and I went with the flow, going to bed late because we just had to watch Dallas, even if it was a rerun? We'd eat a granola bar and call it dinner. We made it to school and work by the skin of our teeth. Well, it's a brand new day. I now have a "system."☺

Shocking, I know, but without structure, I'm heading nowhere but down. Or at least that's what I read in a magazine the other day.

I know, I know. I don't like it either, but if it's going to help Frankie, I'm going to do it. And since there's no better moment than now, I'm off to sleep. No more David Letterman for me!

Stay tuned, my girl.

Love,
Mom xoxo ☺

BLESS ME, FATHER

Karen hated to switch parishes from Saint Anthony's to Saint Catherine's, but she couldn't chance anyone mentioning Meg in front of Frankie. Father Sinclair agreed.

"You'll visit for coffee sometime?" he asked hopefully.

Father Sinclair had baptized both Karen and Meg, and had been a supportive advisor to Karen throughout the years.

"Of course I will," she promised.

"I've told Father John to expect you. God bless, Karen," he said, offering his hand.

"I'll call you, Father," she said, ignoring his hand and giving him a tight squeeze.

"What am I supposed to do?" asked a tense Frankie, who had agreed to attend church with her two Sundays after his arrival.

"Just listen to the sermon. Today is penance, but you don't have to do it."

"What's that?"

"It's when you confess your sins."

"To who?"

"A priest."

"Why?"

"To be absolved."

"What gives him the right to absolve you?"

Karen thought about this a moment. "He's a priest. He's closer to God than the average person."

"That doesn't make sense. Why is he closer to God than you or me?"

"Because he took a vow of celibacy to be God's servant and . . . I'll get you a book so you can catch up on the Catholic faith."

"So just because he doesn't screw women, God listens to him more?"

Karen struggled to keep a straight face.

"It's a bit more involved."

"Whatever, but it seems pretty stupid telling another person your sins. They can use it against you."

"It's against the law for them to disclose what you say to anyone."

Frankie snorted at Karen's naivety.

"Yeah, right. Like priests don't have their own pow-wow sessions."

Karen went to confession (reluctantly, because now Frankie had cast a shadow of a doubt), leaving a restless Frankie behind in the pew.

"Bless me Father, for I have sinned, it's been two months since my last confession."

Karen confessed to giving the finger to some lady who cut her off, said she was impatient with her boss, admitted that she broke the copy machine at work and didn't fess up, even when Marty asked her personally if she knew anything about it. But these sins were chump change. What she yearned to do was have this conversation: *What do you think about impulse control, Father, because I'm not so sure it's something I own. If they called me today and said they found Meg's killer, you can be sure I'd take matters into my own hands. Would my revenge be a sin, or would it fall under the eye for an eye category? Does my daughter's murderer deserve a punishment only God has the right to bestow? Yes, Father, I was taught that forgiveness is the key to heaven. It goes something like forgive, accept, and move on. But the forgiveness factor was replaced with revenge on September 12th, 1980. I marked the event by taking on a new life's goal: kill the killer. So here's the thing, Father; I don't want to forgive and move on, pretending I've reconciled myself with my daughter's death. Someday, I'll find the killer, and until that day comes, I'm simply biding my time. Who knows, maybe what little good I do before then will cancel out the damage I plan on doing when it's time to avenge Meg's death.*

Karen knelt at the altar and recited two Hail Marys and one Our Father, then returned to the pew where an elderly man had joined Frankie. Frankie was staring at the man, who was rhythmically gliding his fingers across his rosary beads.

"What's he doing?"

"It's called a rosary," she whispered. "Think of them as prayer beads." Karen reached into her own pocket and took out the pearl rosary beads that her father had given her when she was ten years old. "See?"

Frankie examined the beads, curiously poked one with his finger and sat back, disinterested.

Already, he didn't seem like the boy she had found slumped in a corner just months ago. He was gaining weight and the black circles were getting lighter under his eyes. How hard it must have been for him to endure such a loveless environment day after day. With people like Ray in this world, Frankie could potentially have ended up dead, just like Meg.

KAREN AND FRANKIE

Summer, 1981

Karen had become a pro at budgeting her time. She was early to bed, early to rise, and bought (or occasionally attempted to cook) healthy meals for herself and Frankie. She returned to working at the office on their agreed upon date, but her hours never did go back to the way they used to be. Her resolve to be available prompted her to finish her daily workload at the office by three o'clock. There were some evenings where, after Frankie went to sleep, she would end up working until midnight, but this was a small price to pay. She berated herself for not doing this with Meg. Had she really believed the office would stop functioning without her? Some days she was certain Marty was going to fire her for her sporadic hours, but Sarah was confident that her fears were unfounded.

"Are you kidding? He can't afford to fire you. You're doing twice the work in half the time. What is there to complain about? He's just grouchy because he misses seeing you slaving away at your desk," Sarah reassured her.

Once Frankie completed his sophomore year, Karen enrolled him at Cambridge High School. She didn't want Frankie stressing over the responsibility of a full-time summer job, but she did want him to be accountable for doing something. Lorraine suggested Frankie volunteer at the Boys and Girls Club.

"I can set him up to work mornings five days a week," she told Karen.

"That's great, Lorraine. Thanks for your help."

That would leave three or more hours before Karen would be home, too much downtime for boys like Frankie. Hoping to capitalize on his talents, she came up with an idea.

"How about entering some art shows? You can paint while I'm at work, after the Boys and Girls Club."

"No," was his short response.

"I think it would be fun," she pressed, talking so quickly he couldn't interrupt. "I've called a bunch of libraries and found that Springfield is holding an exhibit at the end of June. Opening day is in two weeks. That gives you ample time to work on some projects. We can go and spend the night, see the sites. What do you say?"

"I don't want to do it."

"Why not?"

"Only fags show their work. I'm not as good as you think I am. I don't want to," he said, crossing his arms and shrugging.

"Did you at least read the flyer I left out for you?"

"No."

Karen held up Frankie's drawing of a carousel horse, "You could win a prize for this."

"Like what," he scoffed. "A paintbrush. Whoopee."

"No, like money," she grinned.

That got Frankie's attention. "How much money?"

"First place gets five hundred dollars."

Frankie paused before saying, "I'll do it, but if I don't win, I'm not doing it again."

Karen held up her pointer finger. "Let's clarify that; if you don't win first prize, or don't win at all?"

"Top three places or bust," he said flatly.

"Deal," smiled Karen, slapping him on the back and handing him his sketch book. "By the way, they're offering art classes at the YMCA. You interested?"

"Fuck, no."

"What no?"

"I meant hell no."

Karen visited the local crafts store and purchased a videocassette that taught the basics of painting, along with a large box of number two pencils and a ream of unlined paper. Each afternoon, she arrived home to a different sketch; a landscape, a sunset, even a sketch of the outside of her house.

"Wowie, you've got great range. These are quite impressive!" she marveled.

"Thanks. I tried coloring them in, but crayons make them look like shit," he said, examining his work alongside her.

The next afternoon, Karen entered the kitchen carrying a large brown shopping bag. She walked over to where Frankie sat at the table and stood over him.

Frankie met her gaze and, seeing a ridiculous grin plastered on her face, grew anxious. Edna used to look like this when she was on drugs. She would approach Frankie with a stupid smirk and say, "You need to get out. I got people coming over."

"What is it?" Frankie said, in a *get it over with* tone.

Karen held up the bag and tipped it upside down. Acrylic paints, graphite pencils, ink brushes, wax color pencils, charcoals, pastels, markers, about fifty brushes in various sizes, a color palate, and multiple sized canvases tumbled onto the table.

"Is this for me?" he asked, unable to hide his surprise.

"It sure is. Now get cracking, time's a wasting," she smiled.

Karen knew Frankie enough to know he wasn't going to jump for joy, but she wasn't prepared for his troubled expression.

"What is it?" she asked.

"I'll pay you back for this stuff if I win."

"No, you won't. This is what caretakers do. It's part of being a parent."

"Not any parent I've ever known. What's the catch?" he wondered, eyeing her suspiciously. Ray had him trained to understand that a cheeseburger from McDonald's meant a drug drop. Or a new toy, a rare commodity, meant multiple drug drops.

"There is no catch," she replied.

A foreign emotion caused Frankie's breathing to become erratic. He looked at Karen and felt the familiar detached feeling he got at the O'Malleys on the night he thought he was going to die.

"I don't feel good," he said, wiping his forehead.

"What's wrong?" Karen asked with concern.

"I dunno."

"Why don't you take a break? I'll wake you when dinner's cooked."

"You mean ordered?"

Karen laughed. "You got that right!"

Frankie paced the confines of his room. It wasn't until he dropped to the floor and did a hundred pushups that he felt back to his old self. Twenty minutes later, he returned to his drawing.

"You feeling better already?"

"Yeah."

"Huh," she said. "Maybe you just needed a break."

"Maybe," he said, giving her his trademark shrug.

Frankie wouldn't have known how to explain what was making him sick, because he didn't quite understand it himself. If he had to guess, it had something to do with accepting unsolicited help. The thought that someone cared was almost too much to absorb.

For the next couple of weeks, Frankie experimented with watercolor and various mixed mediums before coming to the conclusion that he was an acrylic on canvas painter who felt most comfortable holding his brush like a pencil. Once he began to sketch, he found it difficult to stop. If he wasn't drawing at the Boys and Girls Club, he would be thinking about what he was going to draw when he got home: scenes from across America, more carousels (he had always wanted to ride on a merry go round), fishing boats (he had begged Ray to take him in exchange for a drug drop. Ray promised and then never followed through), gingerbread houses that Adam once told him exist in a place called Martha's Vineyard. He would become so engrossed in drawing that he couldn't sleep. With the final stroke of his brush, Frankie felt a high that far exceeded any drug he'd ever taken. Sometimes he was convinced Ray must have brutally kicked his ass leaving him in a coma dreaming this life up. Other days he was sure this was the calm before the storm and that Ray, or Whitey, or maybe even Edna would come for him, sucking Frankie back into the hellish world he'd once thought existed for all humanity.

KENDRA

"Happy birthday, Patatona! I can't believe you're sixteen today!" said August, wiping the side of his eye.

"You're not going to get all emotional on me, are you, Gramps?"

"What I'm emotional about is that hairdo of yours. You look like Albert Einstein on a bad hair day."

"Oh gee, don't hold back now. Tell me how you really feel."

"If not me, then who? I look out for my own," he said, pushing a large wrapped box toward her. "This is for you."

Kendra ripped open the package, expecting to see a shirt she would hate, but would fake that she loved.

"A yellow Jordache purse!"

"Look inside," smiled August, the crown of his bald head flushing pink.

Inside were a Swatch Watch, Revlon blue glitter eye shadow, Cover Girl mascara in sapphire blue, a rainbow slap bracelet, and finally, a puffy sterling silver heart necklace.

"Oh, Gramps, this is just too much! Like, seriously too much! We can't afford all this," said Kendra, wrinkling her brow.

"Oh, what are you going on about? For my Patatona, the world," August said, grabbing her by the chin and jiggling it.

Kendra relaxed into a giant grin.

"It's all perfect! How did you know what to pick out?"

"If you can believe it, that hag Rizollo was at the store. I must've looked like a lost soul, because she offered to help," laughed August.

"Well, I'm sure glad she did!"

"Here," he said, picking up the necklace with care.

"Let me put this on you. Soon enough, some other man will own your heart."

"No worries on that. They're not exactly lining up at the door."

"That's because you're not ready for them. When you're ready, they'll come."

"No, it's because I'm a fat dweeb."

"Stop that, you're not fat. You're robust, that's all."

"Then why do you call me Patatona? I mean really, the name speaks for itself."

"What do you mean?"

"Potato puff, Gramps. You're calling me a potato puff!"

"What's cuter than a puffy little potato?" August grinned, pinching her cheeks.

Kendra didn't want to argue the point that while most girls her age wore the Madonna style laced crop tops, she had to buy long shirts to wear over leggings to hide her many bulges.

"What were you like at sixteen, Gramps? Were you skinny or fat?"

"I was robust like you. I weighed two hundred and forty pounds. Turn around," he said, fumbling with the delicate clasp.

"So, fat, like me."

"No, Patatona, robust like you!"

"What did you do with your friends for fun?"

"Nothing I would want you to do."

"Tell me," she pleaded, turning her back and gathering her hair in front so that August could clasp on the necklace.

"We used to steal nickel bottles off the soda truck."

"You were a thief?"

"Among other things."

"What did you do with the money?"

"We'd go to the movies."

"For only a nickel?"

"No, for fifteen cents."

"That's pretty cheap."

"We used to wait until we each had a quarter."

"Why a quarter?"

"In them days if you had a quarter, you lived like a king. We'd go to the movies and buy some food and then when the movie was done, we would hide under the seats and watch the burlesque girls. After that, we'd go and eat a nickel hot dog. That's why I was so robust," he laughed. "Ahhh, them were the days."

August locked the necklace into place. "There. That's nice, Patatona."

Kendra rubbed the heart with her fingers and smiled.

"Boy, you must think I'm boring," she said, rather sullenly.

"Not boring, Kendra, smart. Your Gramps is not too smart in the head, but you, you're gonna be something. Now, go look in your mirror and see how pretty you are. Try to see what I see."

Kendra went to the bathroom mirror and smiled at the necklace. Her grandfather had been both a mother and father to her over the years, and as far as Old Italian men with a questionable seedy past went, he had raised her with dignity and pride.

"It's pretty," she yelled from the bathroom.

Kendra refused to look at herself in her own bedroom mirror since the day that girl, or whatever she was, was stuck in it. Since that time, a sheer scarf hung over the mirror, obstructing any glare that might cause anyone or anything to pop in and say hello.

"Kendra, this is good frosting," her grandfather yelled through a mouthful of cake.

"Just what my fat ass needs," she mumbled.

Then, just as she had done every night since the ghost girl freaked her out, Kendra double checked the color of her eyes.

They were her usual green speckled with brown.

The bathroom mirror remained demon free.

CAROUSELS AND
GINGERBREAD HOUSES

Standing in the midst of Frankie's art exhibition, Karen could not have felt prouder. The library had done such a fine job of advertising that the room was filled to capacity with both entrants and visitors. The display area was generous, occupying an entire back portion of the library. Each artist was told they could bring four pictures, approximately half a wall's worth. The librarian in charge walked around introducing herself to the twenty-five contestants.

"You have a fine eye, young man. Vivid detail," she said, eyeballing Frankie's drawing.

"Doesn't he?" Karen beamed, placing her hand on Frankie's shoulder. Unaccustomed to being the center of attention, Frankie's stomach churned and he recoiled slightly at her touch. Anywhere else, his body language would have been misinterpreted as rude, but here at the exhibition, he'd be lucky to be thought of as a temperamental artist.

"I have to go to the bathroom," he whispered, and walked quickly away.

Karen smiled at the librarian. "He gets a bit anxious," she said protectively, crinkling her nose and nodding her head.

"Of course," agreed the disinterested librarian, who was already moving on to the next entrant.

Karen walked over to one of Frankie's drawings and lightly glided her hand along the outside edge of the canvas. After fifteen minutes, she became concerned that Frankie might have gotten ill. She was headed toward the front desk to inquire where the bathrooms were when a deep voice called out her name.

"Karen Sherburne?"

She looked over her shoulder and saw a brawny, square-faced man with a crooked nose. Though it had been years, Karen instantly recognized him as Lenny Jacobs, one of her most tragic cases back in 1972. When Lenny's mother abandoned her family of four, his father decided that Lenny's twelve-year-old twin sister was old enough to assume all responsibilities, including sexual relations. When he discovered what was going on, Lenny tried to protect her from his father and was beaten so badly he almost died. Karen was assigned to him while he was still recovering in the hospital. She was told to sit on his left side, as the beating left his right eye temporarily blind. Initially, Lenny cowered as far to the right of the bed as he could. His voice was edgy and strained, and his speech difficult to understand. Though his hearing was perfect, he sounded like he was deaf when he spoke, something neither Karen nor medical doctors understood until they later discovered that Lenny's twin, who committed suicide shortly after his hospitalization, was deaf. Although she was adept at reading lips, her father didn't provide her with hearing aids or take her to speech therapy. Lenny found himself talking at a much higher decibel than was necessary and mimicking her speech.

"It's called transference," said one psychologist.

Karen did what she could to earn Lenny's trust. When all else failed, she relied on a no-fail tactic; her weekly visits came with a can of Pepsi and a Snicker's bar. Within three weeks' time, Lenny's humorous personality punched a hole through his fear. Karen was amazed at the boy's incredible ability to transform painful experiences into lighthearted humor. Lenny, for sure, was destined to become a comedian. Karen worked with him for four years, determined to find the perfect placement for Lenny, who had seen enough sorrow for one lifetime. She found perfection in Mr. and Mrs. Meyers, an older couple who never had children of their own. Mrs. Meyers, a stout and good natured woman, was captured by Lenny's sense of humor. Mr. Meyers, a jokster in his own right, treated the boy like a long lost son.

When their time together had ended, Karen gently hugged Lenny.

"It'll be good now," she told him. "Call me if you ever need anything. Day or night, I'll come running."

Lenny narrowed his deep blue almond shaped eyes, and in a serious voice that sounded much older than his thirteen years said, "Someday, I'm gonna do you a favor, Karen."

Karen put her arm around Lenny and gave him a gentle squeeze. His narrow shoulders felt fragile under his slight frame. She wondered, with years of malnutrition, if the boy was ever going to grow.

Now, staring at the hulking man in front of her, Karen couldn't help but smile widely. She reached up and wrapped her slender arms around his thick neck.

"My word, if it isn't Lenny Jacobs!"

Lenny's guttural voice still sounded like he was deaf. "You haven't changed a bit," he grinned. "I see you still have the Annie Hall attire goin' for ya."

Karen glanced at her outfit. Yep, this was exactly the same type of clothing she wore back in the '70's.

"I guess I do," she grinned.

"You're a timeless blast from the past," he said, sighing nostalgically.

After a moment of mutual admiration, Karen asked, "What brings you to Springfield? Do you live around here?"

"Just passin' through. What about you?"

"Frankie," she began and then paused, "I mean, a boy I'm fostering, he's one of the artists."

"You should be proud," said Lenny, nodding appreciatively around the room.

"So tell me, where can I catch your comedy show?"

Lenny laughed so uproariously that some patrons looked around to see where the joke was.

"Aww, I ain't no comedian. I feel like we're back in the old days, you and me talkin' 'bout life."

Karen giggled. "If you're not making people laugh, then what are you doing for a living?"

"I'm in the business of takin' care of . . ." Lenny paused and smiled clumsily, "business. Just call me an expert in the field of organization. I help people clean up their messes."

Karen grinned, but the social worker in her felt a sense of foreboding, and because her inner voice recommended she not seek clarification, she didn't. Instead she asked, "What brings you here, to this art show?"

"I'm just passin' through. I saw the sign while I was drivin' by an' I like art. Believe it or not, I had this social worker who once gave me a book with all these drawin's in it, and I've never been the same since. Mind you, I can't make a squiggly line to save my life, but I sure do appreciate people who can."

Karen had forgotten about that book. Wasn't it funny that she ended up years later fostering a child as artistic as Frankie?

"Well, it was good to see you, Lenny. I do hope we run into each other again soon."

"It was more than good to see you, Karen Sherburne. You and my foster parents, you done good for me. I'da been a model citizen if it wasn't for this thing inside me."

"What thing inside you?"

"An itch I can't scratch."

"Can't you find a creative way to scratch yourself, like comedy skits, or working out at the gym? Look at those muscles of yours!" she exclaimed, pointing to his arm.

Lenny laughed and flexed his arms, expanding his biceps to such a degree that Karen couldn't help but touch them and murmur, "Holy bicep!"

"Comedy and weight lifting, Lenny. Think about it," she said, shaking her pointer finger at him.

"Oh, before I forget. I'm sorry about Meg," he whispered, his head bowed in respect.

Karen's face flushed with surprise. She scanned the room for signs of Frankie.

"How did you know about Meg?"

"I make it my business to look after those who looked after me. Somethin' like a periodic check-in, just like you did for me. I'm only sorry I wasn't lookin' when it happened. My foster parents, they won the lottery last year and used the money to go on a trip to Greece. Things like that happen to them all the time."

Lenny looked at Karen with a doleful expression, then reached his hand inside his jacket pocket and pulled out a Snicker's bar.

"You gave me this addiction," he grinned. "I can't leave home without one."

He slid the candy bar back into his pocket and retrieved a pack of gum. After offering a piece to Karen, he stuck one in his mouth and motioned her closer.

"Here," he said, handing her a business card. "If the time ever comes, use it."

Karen looked at the card.

Lenny Jacobs, Organizational Expert, 555-643-4321

"When what time comes?" she wondered.

"Oh, I don't know," he said, sniffing and plucking at his nose with his pointer finger. "Maybe a time will come when you'll need someone like me to help you out. That there's my beeper number. I don't plan on changin' it, ever. It don't matter if it's next week or thirty years from now. Call it and give me ten minutes tops. If I don't get back to you, then I ain't here anymore. My number won't change, and neither will my work. After all," he winked, "I love being my own boss."

Lenny offered her his hand. "I will never forget what you did for me, Karen Sherburne. You are pure goodness." He pulled Karen in a bit closer so that his peppermint breath made her eyes water. "There are many ways to organize and clean, you hear what I'm saying? I'm known for putting on quite a show."

Am I hearing what I think I'm hearing? Karen's heart was pumping fantastically and her body felt as if it would convulse. In a barely audible voice, she replied, "I hear you."

"Good," he smiled, bending down and kissing her hand.

With a mischievous glint in his eye, Lenny clucked, faux shooting her with his index finger and thumb, and then turned and walked away, leaving Karen unnerved and chilled to the bone.

"Who was that?"

"Oh, Frankie, you startled me!" Karen exclaimed, turning to see Frankie behind her. "How long have you been standing there?"

"Like, two seconds."

Her body still surging, she tried to keep her voice from shaking. "Where'd you go off to?"

"I needed some air," he said squinting at Lenny's figure in the distance. What Frankie really meant was that he needed a nip.

Satisfied he hadn't overheard their conversation, Karen steadied her voice. "I was talking to an old client of mine."

"What's he doing here?"

"Passing through," she said nonchalantly. "But enough about that, this is your day. Let's go check out the competition."

Lenny telling Karen that she was pure goodness was such a joke. Pure goodness forgives, and after years of preaching to her clients how to let go, forgive, and move on, Karen realized that she, herself, was lacking this fortitude. She should have thrown away his business card immediately, but she considered this meeting a sign from Meg. She placed the card in her wallet behind her driver's license so that when the time came to kill the killer, Lenny's services would be a mere phone call away.

* * *

Frankie was living in an unfamiliar world that held limitless possibilities. The Springfield exhibition had become a catalyst for increasing his confidence and skills as an artist. Not only had he won the grand prize of five hundred dollars, but someone had inquired about one of his paintings. Karen judiciously stepped in and negotiated a fair price of seventy-five dollars.

"Oh, Frankie, I'm so proud of you," she said handing him the cash. "How does it feel to know your artwork will be displayed in someone's home?"

Frankie reached into his pants pocket and massaged the bunched up money. "It doesn't suck," he replied dryly, but his eyes were dancing with pride.

"I bet it doesn't," she chuckled.

Throughout the summer months, Karen woke Frankie at eight-thirty sharp with a cheery *Rise and Shine, Frankie!* After showering, he ate breakfast, and then took a bus to the Boys and Girls Club, where he stayed until noontime. At twelve forty-five, he arrived home, calling Karen to tell her he was safe. That's what Karen had said:

"Call me so I know you got home safely."

Frankie knew it was more like, 'call me so I know you're not out taking drugs'. But the reason for the check-in didn't matter. What mattered was that for the first time in his life, Frankie was expected to be accountable. Karen had provided him with a quiet, structured environment and made it perfectly clear that A would follow B would follow C. He supposed she did this so that he wouldn't feel anxious about what was going to happen next . . . and next . . . and next . . . and she was right. A rigid schedule enabled him to make a very smooth transition. Having an agenda, Frankie thought, was a wonderful thing. He didn't have to guess what to eat, where to go, or what to do. There was no hustling for food or shelter, no fear of walking in the front door to a fist in his face, no worries that he'd hear his mother whoring herself out at night. The biggest mystery, if you would call it that, was what kind of sandwich Karen had prepared for him the night before: peanut butter, fluff, and jelly, or ham, cheese, and Miracle Whip. Lunch was followed by a small snack, usually a handful of way too firm chocolate chip cookies that had to be dunked heavily in milk to soften them up. The rest of Frankie's afternoon was spent drawing. He even stopped using the F-word because really, there was nothing to swear about. His days were predetermined and run of the mill, and he basked in the glory of being ordinary.

During the month of August, Karen scheduled art shows in Easton, Massachusetts, Ogunquit, Maine, and Mount Gretna, Pennsylvania. She estimated each trip would take approximately three to four days. She could tell that although he was trying to be supportive, Marty was less than thrilled.

It didn't matter. What mattered was that Karen was present for Frankie. She took care to ensure that the road trips were light and fun. She never inquired about Frankie's past or divulged hers. Conversation was light, airy and focused on the arts. For all three exhibitions, Frankie had managed to place in one of the top three spots.

After arriving home from a long weekend and winning his third prize of two hundred dollars, Frankie confided to Karen.

"I feel like this is a dream and I'm going to wake up and be living with Edna."

"That's certainly not a useful thought, is it?" Karen asked him.

"I don't know how to stop it," he worried.

"You can't stop it, but you can ignore it. Tell yourself you're good enough Frankie, because you are good enough. Thinking that you aren't not only fails to contribute to a solution, but it gets in the way of your ability to trust."

"Trust in who?"

"Trust in God, trust in yourself, trust in me," she said softly.

Frankie went to bed that night wondering if he committed to trusting in himself, Karen and God, would this be enough to remove the image of the girl that was stuck in his head? Would God do that for him? He didn't know much about this God character, but maybe, just maybe, asking was worth a shot.

*   *   *

Sunday afternoons were spent lounging around in sweats. Karen and Frankie watched movies, pigged out on popcorn and brownies, and took long afternoon naps.

Karen had spent this particular morning catching up on paperwork. By midafternoon, she was emotionally drained.

"I'm going to take a nap, Frankie. I'm pooped. Chinese tonight?"

Still not able to let his guard down, Frankie shrugged and replied, "Sure."

Karen took this as a positive. At least he wasn't saying 'whatever' to everything.

While Karen napped, Frankie slowly set out his art supplies. Remembering what Karen said, he decided to practice the art of "being good enough." To do this, he knew that he'd need to forgive and forget, so Frankie forgave himself for torturing insects and field mice, and that one stray cat when he was angry with Edna. He forgave himself for tormenting small animals out of anger and despair. He told himself he'd forget all about Edna and Ray and Whitey. In fact, he'd forget who he was entirely before he came to live with Karen just four short months ago.

The hardest memory, one that he wasn't sure he could ever forget, was that of the girl. How would he ever know for certain what had happened to her? She was a slow, germinating seed of guilt planted inside his head. Her poisonous roots would eventually invade his bloodstream and stifle Frankie, robbing him of a life he knew he didn't deserve. Her whereabouts loomed above him like a black cloud, and until he knew what happened to her, he would never be at peace. Eventually, she'd destroy him.

This wasn't a question of if, but a matter of when. He was sure of it.

It was just his luck to have two girls found inside of a week, one dead and one alive. Frankie could easily forgive himself if his was the girl who lived. But if his shit bad luck continued as it always did . . .

No.

He wouldn't buy into it. The stab had been superficial and was so very tiny it couldn't possibly have killed her. The dead girl was killed by someone else, some monster . . . that wasn't Frankie . . .

. . . because Frankie wasn't a monster . . .

. . . he was rehabilitated.

This was the truth that enabled him to sleep at night.

Trust in God, trust in yourself, trust in me, Karen had told him.

That evening, Frankie began to sketch what would become one of his finer works of art. Working from Adam's description and from photos at the local library, Frankie sketched a gingerbread cottage. For material, he shifted his choice of medium to watercolor on a 9x12 sheet. Not his favorite, but Karen had spared no expense, purchasing 300-pound watercolor paper that didn't need to be stretched prior to using. It would be perfect for this particular drawing. The project consumed him for three straight days.

"Frankie!" exclaimed Karen, staring at the picture. "This is truly amazing!"

The gingerbread cottage was set back beyond a white picket fence. The baby blue exterior boasted white scalloped trim from the Queen Anne era. There was a farmer's porch with window boxes overflowing with blue, red and pink flowers, and an entryway with such intricate trim that Karen wished she had a magnifying glass to look at the smallest details. Hedges peeked out from either side of the house while tree limbs lined the top of the drawing, as if they fell from the sky. In front of the fence was a whiskey barrel full of cascading flowers. Next to the barrel was a lamppost, and next to that, a brick walkway leading to the cottage. Karen stepped as close as she could and squinted, her face full of admiration and pride. She envisioned herself sitting on the porch of this quaint retreat.

"I cannot get over how you've shadowed the porch and the windows. This should win you first place somewhere. Hey, you know what this feels like to me?" she said, turning to face him. "It feels like coming home. You've captured something special with this one!"

Frankie, who was still holding a brush, nodded at Karen's praise. She patted him on the back and told him dinner would be ready in an hour. She left the room humming in a very zippity doo da way.

Disappointment washed over him.

Karen missed the girl. You'd think, with her nose practically touching the painting, that she would have been more observant. Frankie was certain she'd have noticed her hidden among the shadows of the second floor window, her steel grey eyes reflecting off the windowpane. The exact details of her features were a blur, so he created what he thought was a typical girl. Her hair, however, was unforgettable. Red and blonde mixed together, soft and colorful like fall leaves. How could she have missed it? As an artist, he felt insulted that she hadn't picked up on the subtlety of the girl, but more importantly, he promised himself that if she did notice, he would tell Karen everything. He'd spill his guts about the day of the stabbing, of not being sure if the girl were dead or alive, of the whole damn mess. He was desperate to confide in someone and

Karen, being the least judgmental person he knew, would be perfect. She would not, Frankie was almost certain, reject him.

"Karen," he called out to her.

"Yeah?"

"Can you come here when you get a second?"

"Sure. Let me finish these follow up calls and I'll be right in."

By the time Karen was done a half hour had passed, and Frankie had dozed off in a chair by the painting.

"I'm sorry," she apologized. "There was a, uh, problem with a client. Did you want to show me something?"

Frankie's courage had dissolved with the catnap.

"I just wanted to say thank you," he stammered.

"For what?"

"For the paints. I, uh, like them."

Karen tousled his blond hair and said, "No problem. Give me ten more minutes, and I promise we'll have supper."

Karen gave herself a mental kick in the head. Unless the feeling in her gut was mistaken, Frankie hadn't called her in to say thank you. Another missed moment because of a work call.

I'm such an idiot she cursed herself.

Frankie, on the other hand, was relieved. He wasn't prepared to suffer the consequences of his confession. What if she did reject him? What if she handed him over to the cops? He couldn't take that chance.

Not now.

Not ever.

He stared at the girl in the shadows and then reached into the side pocket of his backpack and pulled out a nip of peppermint schnapps. The cool minty flavor glided down his throat, instantly warming him. He looked behind him to make sure Karen wasn't coming and dropped to his knees. He bowed his head, like people did in church and whispered, "I vow to work laboriously against my grain if you could just get this girl out of my head. I will follow your governed laws precisely, I will believe in your existence, regardless of my past, if only you'll remove her from my mind. A-fucking-men."

The next day, Frankie woke without the girl on his conscience. Did God really hear him? Just in case it sparked bad memories, he brought the portrait to the basement and leaned it against a wall where it would remain covered with a dusty blanket for the next fifteen years. From that day forward, his thoughts rarely revisited the day of the stabbing. He tried to keep the girl out of sight, out of mind. And though his obsessive worry was somewhat lifted, his guilt took the form of a nervous stomach and migraine headaches that worsened every fall, just around the time of the stabbing.

*   *   *

Frankie came home from the Boys and Girls Club to find a wrapped box on the kitchen table. Attached to the box was a note that read, *Frankie, I think you'll enjoy this. Karen.*

The last time Frankie had received a gift was on his fourth birthday. It was a plastic dump truck that became his constant companion. The bright yellow and orange truck was perfect for loading rocks and dirt and kept him entertained for hours at a time, especially when Ray was home. Unfortunately on one of his tirades, Ray destroyed the truck by stomping on a back tire and breaking the axel. Frankie was so upset that he decided to run away. He walked a short distance before stealing a banana bike from someone's front lawn. He made it a full three blocks before the kid's parents pulled alongside him in a brown station wagon, the father screaming obscenities. Frankie jumped off the bike and tossed it toward the wagon and away from him. He made his way back home by weaving in and out of backyards. He found the truck in the trash and tried gluing the tire back on, but it wouldn't stick. Heartbroken, he asked his mother for a new one, which she promised she'd buy him when the money came. Frankie knew the money would never come.

He turned over the package a few times before eagerly tearing it open to reveal a handheld version of an electronic game called Simon.

"Cool," he said, inserting the batteries that Karen had taped to the outside of the box.

Karen arrived home a couple of hours later, deeming the day Lazy Thursday. They ate Captain Crunch cereal and a full sleeve of Nutter Butter cookies. Karen went the step further, dipping her cookies in peanut butter.

"Want to try it?" she said, offering the jar to Frankie.

"Overkill," he grimaced, waving off the jar.

After consuming half a dozen cookies dipped in peanut butter, Karen prepared a cup of tea for herself and poured Frankie a glass of soda.

"Are you looking forward to your new school?"

"Not really."

"Are you going to make an effort to meet new friends?"

"Probably not."

"Because?"

"I don't like kids my own age," was his immediate answer. The truth was kids his own age never liked smelly, delinquent Frankie.

"Care to elaborate?"

"I don't know. I just don't."

"Well, give it some thought. Remember, new school, new life."

Frankie retired to his room and sat bone straight on the edge of his bed with his hands on his knees. Tapping his knees, he considered Karen's words. It was quite possible that he could have a brand new life. Thanks to his extensive reading and quick recall, Frankie's grades were quite good. On the last quarter of his last report card he had managed to get straight B's, with just one C in math.

Because he would go to any means to ensure that he would never have to see Edna again, he decided to change both his appearance and his attitude The new kids wouldn't know him as Loser Frankie. The teachers wouldn't think of him as a pot smoking failure. He would ditch the dingy look for a preppy style, trade his layered rock 'n' roll hair for a short and shaggy cut. He would resign to making a friend or two, maybe join a sports team. This way, if anyone ever did search for him, he'd be hiding in plain sight, right under their putrid noses. Frankie took a deep breath and went to the living room to speak with Karen.

"Hey, I thought you were in bed?" she yawned, rubbing her eyes.

"I was thinking about what you were saying, about school and all. I was wondering, could we go shopping?"

"For paper supplies? Sure."

"No, for new clothes. I need shirts and shoes and pants."

Karen nodded. "Of course. We'll go shopping before school starts."

"I'll pay with the money I won from the art shows."

"You'll do no such thing. That's for your future."

"Well, then," he sulked, "it's gonna take a while to pay you back."

"Frankie, I've told you before, I'm your caretaker. It's my job to buy you clothes."

"It feels sleazy."

"Well it's not, and I'm happy to do it."

At a loss for words, Frankie nodded and returned to his room. He lay on his back staring at the ceiling, inhaling the faint smell of the fabric softener from the pillow. Soon, he'd have everything he could ever have hoped for; new home, new school, new clothes, and a new shot at life. Maybe, just maybe, Ray had been wrong and Karen had been right. Maybe Frankie was worth more than the shit off his shoes.

MEG'S OASIS

On the field, it was as if Meg were in control of the time/space continuum. Her landscape was filled with poppies one day, daisies the next, and purple and white irises the day after that. She had a waterfall, a farmhouse, a castle with a moat, and a barnyard full of the same animals as her childhood Fisher Price Toy Farm, including a cow that mooed every time she bent her neck. She wasn't sure if she slept, yet she felt refreshed and relaxed, as if she'd been dozing happily in the sun. Eating wasn't a necessity. She always had this satiated feeling like she had just finished a cheeseburger, fries, and a strawberry sundae with marshmallow and walnuts. There was no TV or Atari, but she was never bored. All Meg had to do was wish for something and it appeared. Not long ago, she was thinking she'd love to hear some music, and didn't Blondie's *Heart of Glass* permeate the skies? When she felt nostalgic about Roberto, The Ramones resounded from the leaves on the great oak tree.

In stereo.

It was truly awesome.

One day she said, "Rocky, I would kill for a chocolate frappe with whipped cream and three cherries on top!"

Didn't a table appear out of thin air with the largest chocolate frappe Meg had ever laid her eyes on?

Perhaps the weirdest part of being at the field was that Meg knew things.

If she said, "I wish I knew how Mom was," just like that, she'd know. Meg sensed her anguish and her enormous love for her. She knew her grandfather was sad and lonely and that Charlene was eating too much. In fact, every person she had ever touched was a bit gloomier without her. Megan Humble had a cosmic affect on the universe and she had to admit, it felt good to know her presence was missed.

"I wonder if Roberto knows yet?" she asked Rocky, and quicker than it takes to snap your fingers, she knew he didn't.

"Rocky, do you think my baby is okay?" and—*snap*—something told her that her baby was in his own safe haven, maybe even a field like hers.

"I wonder if those boys feel guilty, especially the bastard that off'd me."

Meg loved to think of herself as being off'd. It was very dark and seedy Hollywood mysterious to be off'd, especially the part about being dumped on a highway. The answer came: *His sorrow is eternal.*

"Well," she said, shrugging at her custom field that currently smelled like Grandpa Carl's aftershave "Looks like we both got thrown into a never-ending third dimension. I got a field, and it sounds like he got a dungeon."

Later that afternoon, Meg coasted through her fields on a banana bike and soared daringly down steep hills on roller skates and skateboards.

"You know what would be really fun?" she exclaimed, jumping off the skateboard at the bottom of the hill. "A go-cart!"

It wasn't a surprise that the go-cart appeared minutes later. What was a surprise is that it came with a helmet.

"Are you serious? I don't get it. I'm dead. What sense does this make?"

Meg obeyed the laws of her field and put on the helmet. She cruised down a perfect roller coaster hill on her go-cart screaming, "Whoopieee, this is the liffeeee!"

Meg rode the hill a few more times and then pulled over to a small pond.

Leaning in, she looked at her reflection. "Gee, I wasn't too shabby. I would dare say I was pretty," she remarked, leaning closer to pick at her braces.

And that's when the retarded angel appeared.

Right in the pond over Meg's own reflection, as if Meg was looking through a window. She was sitting on a bed playing with a really pretty heart locket around her neck. It didn't surprise Meg that she was mumbling to herself.

"I can't leave him all alone. He'll die without me," said the angel, rocking back and forth with the locket in her hand.

Wait just a minute . . . the locket . . . the bed . . . the room . . . no wings! This was no angel. This was a real girl. An alive girl!

"Hey," Meg called gently, so not to startle. Then, "Hey, you!" she said a bit louder, leaning into the pond.

The girl stopped mumbling and an abrupt silence fell upon the room. Her shoulders shivered, and she touched the nape of her neck. Refusing to look around, she sat rigid at the edge of her bed, the fingernails of her left hand digging into the palm of her right. Meg could tell she was holding her breath.

"It's okay, it's only me. Don't be afraid," said Meg, hoping to soothe this girl, who was obviously a bit off center.

The girl slowly looked in Meg's general direction. She seemed clouded by something, almost fuzzy. She got off the bed and inched toward her, peeling off some type of veil and peeking through it. She squinted, her face half turned away, like Meg used to do right before the killer attacked the victim in a scary movie. She took a deep breath and looked directly at Meg, then let go of the veil and jumped back.

"Aeeeiiiii! Holy Shit! Holy Crap! Noooo!" cried the girl, shaking her head and cupping her hands over her ears. "You are not real!"

"It's only me, Meg. Please don't spazz out," Meg pleaded. This simpleton was Meg's only connection to the world, or anything for that matter. Meg was determined to get through to her, even if she was a half-wit. She tried again, enunciating each syllable.

"Do-not-be-a-fraid. I-will-not-hurt-you."

"Go away!" the girl moaned, swatting at the mirror.

"But—"

"La, la, la, la. I can't hearrrr you!"

For the first time since she'd been at the field, Meg felt frustration. She was quite alone in her oasis save for this girl who was not here, but there. The only question was, *where was there?*

"No offense or anything, but are you retarded?"

This seemed to snap the girl back to reality.

"What?" she replied, removing her hands from her ears. "What did you call me?"

"Are you, like, slow in the head?"

"What the . . . now, why would you ask that?" she demanded, her hands forming into balls and resting on her hips. Meg was pleased to note that her anger had diminished her fear somewhat. This could work after all.

"Because you're weird."

"Well, excussseee me! It's not like every mirror in the world comes equipped with an apparition. Why did you have to come here anyway?"

"You think I chose you?" Meg asked.

"Of course. Why else are you here?"

"Beats me."

"So leave," she said, sticking out her left hip and bending her right knee.

"Geez, take a tizzy fit why don't you? I mean, what's the big deal?"

"Oh, I don't know," said the girl, tapping her chin thoughtfully, "Maybe the fact that you're clearly a dead person or ghost or God knows what!"

Meg's eyes looked up and to the left, as if she were giving this comment careful thought.

"I prefer dead person."

"So let's recap, shall we? You were once alive and now you're dead and stuck in my mirror. Super great, let the pigeons loose!" the girl scoffed, making a circular motion in the air with her pointer finger.

"Look," said Meg, "You see me. I see you. And since we're both *not* retarded, why don't you suck it up and help me?"

"Help you what?"

Good question, Meg thought to herself.

"Helloooo?" said the girl.

"Hi," smiled Meg.

The girl clucked impatiently.

"Help you what?"

"I dunno. Why else would I be here?"

"Oh, gee, I'll take that one," said the girl, mimicking shooting her brains out. "To torment me?"

"Hey," said Meg, raising a finger, "I am not tormenting you."

"Yeah, okay," she snorted.

"Well, maybe I'm here to help you," Meg pointed out.

"With what? I'm fine. I don't need your help," the girl snorted defensively. "What would I need help with?"

"Oh, I don't know. How about how not to be retarded?"

The girl's pupils grew large and her face scarlet.

"That does it!" She stomped over to her bureau and began shuffling around in her drawers. She held up a small bottle of water and gave Meg a wry smile.

"No one calls Kendra Bruno retarded! Not even some poltergeist demon ghost or whatever you are," she announced, marching toward the mirror, brandishing the bottle like a weapon.

"Is that holy water? Are you kidding me? Dude, for Pete's sake. I'm telling you I'm not ev—"

"Ha!" shouted the girl, flinging the water Meg's way. "Take that!"

Even though she knew this was more or less holographic water, Meg ducked and blocked her eyes with the back of her hand because really, the girl looked unhinged.

"Begone evil spirit! Away with you!"

"I'm evil? You're tripping, sister!"

But it was too late. The pond became the pond again.

"Damn," Meg said, standing up and brushing herself off. If she were alive, she'd have to fight herself hard not to find that girl and knock her block off.

"Why do I keep seeing her?" Meg said aloud.

"She begins the process," was the quizzical answer Meg received from the lily pads in the pond.

But before she could ask what it meant, a single butterfly glided by, distracting her with its beauty.

"Wow," said Meg. Awestruck by the exquisite butterfly, Meg walked toward her go-cart.

"Wait till Rocky hears about the butterfly!"

MIRROR, MIRROR

Kendra submerged herself in an almost too hot bubble bath. Her heart was beating in her throat and the only words coming out of her mouth were, "Shit, damn, damn, shit."

Was she going mad?

If ghost girl persisted in popping up in her mirror, drastic measures would have to be taken. Drastic, meaning voodoo or witchdoctor or something along those lines. For now, a garlic smeared mirror draped with a strand of rosary beads would have to do. She doubled up on scarves to protect her from the full brunt of the mirror's reflection.

What had she done to deserve this? She had been minding her own business in the privacy of her own room, *thank you very much*, when out of the blue this Meg appears.

Meg. Meg what's-her-last-name ghost girl.

I wonder how she died?

Was she sick?

She didn't look sick.

In fact, she looked rather healthy for a ghost.

Kinda pretty.

Skinny. Hmmphhh. Figures.

Meg had asked Kendra not to forget her. Yeah, like that would happen. Spooky girl pops into her mirror and she's supposed to forget it? Not likely. Kendra should have said: *Oh, don't you worry, spooky ghost girl, I'm damaged for life. And on that note, I'm pretty sure shitting my pants is a good indicator I'll never forget you.*

After soaking in the tub for an hour, she threw on jeans and a tee shirt and rode to the bookstore to read up on poltergeists and ghosts. Sitting on the floor of the supernatural books aisle, she scanned book after book. She read that ghosts visit for a reason. Usually, they're in limbo, and in order for them to move forward, they need to finish a task. Either they need something or you need something, and you either need to lead them to that something, or they need to show you what that something is. She read about people called mediums, who have the ability to hear and see ghosts.

Am I a medium? Kendra wondered.

She couldn't remember ever seeing a ghost before, or hearing August talk about ghosts. The only spirit mentioned in her home was the Holy Spirit. She took a moment to fantasize that maybe her parents were famous mediums helping to solve crime cases all over the country.

Okay, no and no. Reading further, Kendra determined that she was no medium. It wasn't like she was seeing many ghosts, just this one. And her parents were many things, but they were no ghost hunters.

Kendra knew something was awry the day she asked August why he only had one photograph of her parents on display.

"I don't know where the rest of them went to," he claimed.

If that wasn't a dead giveaway, Kendra didn't know what was. August knew where everything was. Determined to find out as much as she could about her parents, she crept around the house, snooping in drawers and closets. She found what she was looking for hidden in one of August's old suitcases in the basement.

Photos.

Loads and loads of photos that showed her parents dressed in black. Black nail polish, black lipstick, black hair. Nose piercings and funky haircuts. They snarled at the camera and stuck out their tongues, as if in defiance of every law that was put on this earth.

"My parents are witches, aren't they?"

"Witches?" August laughed. "Why would you say that?"

"I dunno," she shrugged, not willing to fess up to her sneakiness.

"Nayh, they ain't witches."

"Well, what are they then?"

The topic of her parents always agitated her grandfather.

"They're lost, Patatona. Sono persi delle anime."

"Lost souls? What the heck is that supposed to mean?"

"It means what it means. Why you asking about this all of a sudden?"

"Can't a girl ask about her own parents for Pete's sake?"

"Oh, Patatona, don't go getting a bee in your bonnet. What can I tell you, except I wish they were different people than they are."

Kendra knew by her grandfather's pained expression that this conversation needed to end, so she retreated to her bedroom to give them both a time out.

When Kendra left, August opened the side table containing his rosary beads and began reciting Hail Marys. How could he break his granddaughter's heart with the awful truth? Revealing that her parents were heroin addicts who left in pursuit of the next big high was a door he did not want to walk through. He kicked himself for not going along with the witch thing. Witches ain't all that bad. It would have been something they both could have lived with.

* * *

Kendra grabbed her drawing pad and began sketching a bird. She wished August had gone along with her grandiose stories of the supernatural to spare them both the gross reality of what she had heard through the whispering of neighbors over the years; that her parents were drug addicts. A witch, after all, is a far better choice of parent than a junkie. She hoped if she pushed hard enough, August would break down and tell her everything. But he wasn't going to cave. At first, she considered this a deception on her grandfather's part, but after seeing his face contort at the mere mention of his son, she realized that August himself couldn't handle the truth. All that being said, Kendra still wanted her parents back; preferably clean, but if she were to be honest with herself, she'd take them any way she could.

LETTERS TO MEG

Dear Meg,

This is Frankie's first day in a new school, and I have butterflies enough for the both of us! I couldn't send him to Somerville, where you went, where everybody knows me. Cambridge will be best, I think, for the both of us. And speaking of school, you'd be off to classes yourself, unless you decided to drop out.

That's right. *Drop out,* Meg. What do you think we would have done about the baby? And by the way, *when* were you going to tell me? God, I was so embarrassed when the coroner told me you were pregnant. Even in my grief, my pride kicked in and I pretended I knew all about your baby to protect you, to protect me, to protect the unborn baby. And it's taken me this long to realize that I'm pretty frigging pissed!

Did you never hear of a condom? Did you think you were so special that you could get away with having unprotected sex? Right under my nose you're screwing around with some kid and not protecting yourself. I mean, c'mon, it's my job to help people like you, unwed fifteen-year-old mothers from broken homes.

Were we that broken, and I didn't see it?

Charlene said you really liked Roberto. Was he big time Italian, or what? Why didn't you tell me about him? And don't say I was too busy, because that's bullshit. You were being secretive, and then you didn't tell me because you were freaked out of your tree when you didn't get your period. I wonder if you felt nauseous and bloated.

Did you?

I'll never know.☹

Do you think you would have kept it? Aborted it? Funny, I don't even know your views on abortion or, had you kept it, your favorite names. That's the thing about you being gone too soon. It's not like I can sit here and say time will tell what Meg will do, because time will never tell. I'll never know what would have been.

And that is what makes me foul.

As gruesome as it would have been, I'm angry to not know every tiny detail of your death. You remember Sergeant Flattery? He was the lead officer on your case. Right before Frankie moved in, he called and told me that they hit a wall and there were no leads on your death. I thought I was going to lose my mind. Your case is going to be forgotten, stockpiled underneath the next murder victim.

My reaction to this was an increase in my drug of choice: resentment. I'm turning rotten Meg, decaying like a half-eaten apple. Anna, the card reader, was right when she said resentment would kill me. It slowly poisons you with hate until, one day, you self-destruct. I'm sorry, baby girl. I wish I could have avenged your death.

Stay tuned,

Love,
Mom xoxo ☺

*   *   *

Frankie walked through the doors of Cambridge High School a new man. His long, white hair had been cut into a neat feather style, his

Ozzy shirt traded in for a polo, and his high-top Converse sneakers replaced with loafers.

When he appeared in the kitchen ready for his first day of school, Karen's face lit up with surprise.

"Wow, you look great! With that haircut and your new duds, I almost didn't recognize you!"

That was the plan thought Frankie, who replied, "I thought I'd try something different."

"Change can be good," Karen smiled.

"I guess so," Frankie shrugged lightly.

"Are you ready to begin a new chapter?"

"I'm ready to throw away the old one."

"Then I say it's onward and upward," Karen said eagerly, fist pumping the air above her.

Through the fucking fog Frankie finished the phrase in his head.

SUMMER, 1982

Junior year was successfully boring. Frankie was friendly to the other kids, but not overly so. Every action toward his classmates was a deliberate measure to ensure that he would remain, for the most part, unremarkable. When the school year ended, he surprised Karen by asking if he could teach art classes.

"The kids at the Boys and Girls Club are always begging me for drawing lessons. Plus, it would earn me pocket money."

The social worker in Karen warned her that letting Frankie work one-on-one in an unsupervised setting could be a recipe for disaster. One misinterpreted word, one misconstrued gesture, and everything Frankie had been working toward could be ruined, and she was not about to let that happen. She would commit to being home to assist with the students. She suggested they put an ad in the local paper for an afternoon art class to be held once a week, for six weeks, ages 9 to 13, with a cap of 12 students. The first day the ad came out, the class was filled. In fact, they had to offer an additional class to accommodate interested applicants. Frankie built makeshift drawing tables from large pieces of plywood and hung a clothesline across the length of the yard for the artwork to dry on. Karen drove to the Salvation Army Store and purchased two dozen men's dress shirts that, when put on backward, made fine cover-ups.

"I never would have imagined I'd be standing in my backyard hanging up artwork on a clothesline," smiled Karen.

"Me neither," said Frankie, looking around at the kids. Some were laughing and chatting, while others were painting with serious expressions, their brows furrowed in concentration. He could tell that the kids were cared for. He grinned at them and their parents, and tried to let go of his past, which took the form of a biting itch on the scars of his forearm.

174

FALL INTO SPRING, 1982-'83

Kendra knew she was half Italian, but had no idea about the other half. She stared at her reflection in the ghost-free bathroom mirror. Irish, Scottish, something else? In the one photo that August kept on display, her mother was a fair, redheaded, freckle-faced beauty. Kendra puckered her lips, pulled her hair away from her chubby face, and sucked in her cheeks. She had inherited most of her father's features: dark skin and hair, strong chin, and large teeth, but it was her mother's hazel eyes staring back at her. A splattering of freckles across the bridge of her nose spilled onto her cheeks. She wasn't boring or bland in the slightest. In fact, she could be model material, if only she could relinquish the damn junk food.

She couldn't.

Food was her best friend.

Big sigh.

Speaking of pudge factor, you'd think a girl of her stature would know how to cook. Kendra walked the Italian Hall of Shame when it came to the workings of the kitchen. She was an ineffective baker and chef. One determined afternoon, in an effort to prove that Italian blood did indeed course through her veins, she destroyed her grandfather's multigenerational pizzelle maker and his large saucepan. When she confessed to the murder of the pizzelle maker, August clutched his heart and whimpered like a baby. Not wanting to put him into cardiac arrest, she furtively threw out the saucepan and bought a new one. When August questioned the whereabouts of the pan, she replied, "I don't know. I couldn't find it, so I bought us a new one."

Her grandfather gave her the stink eye and sighed loudly. "If that's what you say," he said, and then she heard him mumble, "La ragazza è pazza comè una torta di frutta."

Kendra huffed and stomped down the narrow hallway to her bedroom. *She was not a fruit cake.* It wasn't her fault that she was kitchen-challenged. Her sights were set on travel and adventure, not on being Suzie Homemaker.

There was only one not so small hole in her future plans.

August.

She could never abandon him. The poor man would be lost without her. Every night during her senior year in high school, she went to bed praying for direction. One night, she received an answer from a surprising source, August himself.

"Ain't it about time you start looking into colleges?" he questioned, a gross amount of mashed potato in his mouth.

"I already told you, I'm going to the Massachusetts School of Art."

"You're killing me. That's no college."

"Is too."

"I wanna see the papers. What do the dorms look like?"

"I'm going to commute."

"Like hell you are."

"But Gramps, what about you? Who will take care of you?"

"Tell me you're kidding?" he laughed.

Trying not to sound insulted, she replied, "Of course I'm not kidding. Who will take care of you?"

"Patatona, I'm more worried about whose gonna take care of you."

"What's that supposed to mean?"

August held up his large weathered hand, and as he spoke, began counting on his fingers.

"Number one, you don't cook. Number two, you don't clean. Numbers three and four, I still do your laundry and make your bed."

Kendra's face reddened with embarrassment. It was true. She was not self-sufficient in the least. The cold hard truth was that August still washed, folded, and put away her underwear.

"Well, I'll manage," she said, sticking out her chin.

"And so will I," winked August. "Now, are you sure you won't go to Boston College or Tufts?"

"I'm a C student," Kendra snorted.

"C, B, A, it don't matter. You just keep showing up for school. I screwed myself that way. You remember what happened to me?"

Kendra had heard his story, meant as a warning cry, many times.

"Two months before graduation, I had a fight with the headmaster. He was giving me shit, and I don't take shit, so I walked out of the building. I had enough points to graduate, but never went back to ask for my certificate. I figured I was old enough to work, and so I did just that. At seventeen, I worked for a coal company that turned into an oil company. I stayed there for fifty years. I don't regret it, but I still wonder sometimes," he coughed loudly, disrupting the room.

"If you insist, I'll look into living there," agreed Kendra.

"Good," nodded August, who was having a hard time controlling his cough.

"What's wrong, are you sick?"

"Ehhh, I'm old."

"You should have that looked at."

"For what? So they can tell me I'm old? Go on now, scram."

Kendra puttered around the house, too distracted to be productive. Something wasn't quite right inside of her grandfather's chest. His voice sounded thick with stubborn mucous and his cough was sharp and deep. He wouldn't live forever, and once he was gone, she'd be all alone. How selfish it was of her to be thinking of traveling the world. She was going to stay right here and care for her grandfather, as he had done for her when her own parents left.

After dinner, Kendra retreated to her bedroom intent on sketching a white and blue parakeet that had been on her mind since early morning. Her love for drawing began in the eighth grade, after her art teacher brought in pictures from the El Greco era. Kendra's artistic talent fell more to the side of design work. She could easily have created elaborate outfits for the skinny models that pranced down catwalks, but she preferred birds and flowers. With absolute detail, she would sketch her work, using tracing paper to add in flowers and leaves until she was satisfied. Her final product would be transferred onto watercolor paper and painted. She had tried working with acrylics several times, but found them stiff and unforgiving. Watercolor had an unpredictable nature that made it an addictive medium. It flowed smoothly, and although she found the colors easy enough to manipulate, there were times when the brush took on a life of its own. It was an expression of freedom that captured Kendra, and one that she was unable to replicate anywhere else in her life.

After every sketch, Kendra felt a sense of satisfaction equivalent to waking up after a good night's sleep. She examined the parakeet for any defects and deemed it perfect. She lay back on her bed with the pad on her chest and stared at the ceiling. She sincerely hoped that the Massachusetts School of Art accepted C students. She also hoped that she would finally find some friends. Kendra had fabricated enough stories about phony friends to last a lifetime. Every now and again, August would question her social life, or lack thereof.

"How come no one ever comes over?"

"I like it quiet," she explained.

"Me too," said August, accepting her answer.

As a child, Kendra was retiring and timid. Nine times out of ten, you'd find her burrowed into August's side, especially around large crowds. Once you got to know her, she was loud and boisterous, but to a total stranger, she might as well have been a mute.

"Want to see my picture, Gramps?"

"What kind of question is that? Of course I want to see it."

When Kendra proudly displayed two brilliantly colored parakeets, August cringed.

"Jesus, Patatona, why birds? Birds are bad luck, you know, sfortuna."

"That's ridiculous."

"If you hang that in this house you're going to curse us."

Kendra kissed his forehead and gave him a squeeze.

"I'm putting it in the kitchen. It could use some color."

August shook his head in defeat. "Damn dirty birds," he mumbled. "Draw me some daisies for the kitchen instead. I don't want my meatballs maledetto."

Kendra laughed as she walked toward the kitchen. Her poor grandfather didn't realize that the house was already cursed by some dead girl who took up residence in her bedroom mirror.

SPRING, 1983

Frankie's senior year was as uneventful as his junior one. He had many acquaintances, but no real friends. Of course, he didn't expect true friends since his life was, in effect, a facade. The past two years had been devoted to four immutable principles by which Frankie tried his best to live:

1. Forgetting he was related to Whitey and Edna.
2. Pretending Karen was his birth mother (it was easy to forget about Edna and Whitey this way).
3. Ignoring the fact he might have killed someone.
4. Believing that the new and improved Frankie was the only Frankie that ever existed.

Living by these values took more effort than anyone, including Frankie, could have imagined. Not only did he have to fool others, but he had to fool himself. His social life consisted of school, work, and participating in football, a sport the old Frankie never would have had the guts to try. Any spare time was spent drawing and entering his work in local art shows.

And though he was perceived as a good-natured and friendly young man, Frankie was pushing the limits of a very palpable stress that felt close to snapping. He felt like someone had stolen his true identity and struggled with the fear that someday he'd be found out. And when the day of unveiling came, he was going to have to pay the piper, whoever that was. Half way through the year, Karen brought up the subject of college.

"Frankie, you've done so well in school. I'm really proud of you."

Internally proud and externally indifferent, he merely shrugged.

"Do you want to sit down and look at some colleges?"

"Not really. I was leaning toward a full-time job at the Boys and Girls Club."

"But you could get a degree and keep working there."

"I don't really see the big deal on going to college."

"More knowledge, more opportunities, more money. The college experience."

"The college experience doesn't seem all that appealing."

"What if you were destined to become a doctor or a lawyer, but didn't know it until you went to college?"

"If I was destined to be one, wouldn't I have had an inkling by now?"

"An accountant, a dentist, a vet . . ."

"I want to be an artist."

"But you *are* an artist! You can go to college and draw at the same time."

Frankie felt a throbbing at the nape of his neck, and craved a vodka nip.

"Isn't there an art school somewhere?"

"You mean like a college of arts?"

"Yeah."

"Sure, but . . ."

"I'll go there."

"But you could go to a place like Tufts on a scholarship, Frankie."

"You take the frigging scholarship if you want to go to Tufts so bad," he barked, slumping in his chair, and burying his head in the folds of his arms.

Karen silently cursed herself. Frankie had gone through such a systemic change that she sometimes forgot where he had come from. In fact, she sometimes forgot that he *hadn't* come from her.

"You're right. I'm sorry, Frankie. My father tried to dissuade me from social work and I'm doing the same thing to you. I just got caught up in the excitement of the great strides you've made in the past two years. It's what mothers do. We get stupid when it comes to our kids."

Frankie, who still had his face burrowed in his arms, decided this was a two nip occasion. Edna didn't get stupid over Frankie, she got stupid *in front* of Frankie. After an uncomfortable silence that felt like a year, Karen cleared her throat and said, "So, art school, huh? Let's do the research and see what we come up with."

She got up and lightly touched his shoulder before heading to the den. Frankie never acknowledged her. He kept his face buried in his arms so that Karen wouldn't see the puddle of tears that had formed on the table.

Later that evening, after dining on macaroni and cheese from a box, Karen took Frankie's plate and replaced it with a stack of paper.

"What's this?"

"I found a school that may be up your alley."

"My alley or yours?"

"Both," Karen smiled. "It's called the Massachusetts College of Art, and it offers lots of cool stuff."

"What if I don't like it?"

"If you try it and don't like it, I'd be fine with that."

"What if once I'm out, I still end up a nothing?"

"First, you were never a nothing. Second, you don't have to be a big somebody to have a successful, full life. All you have to do is make your mark," said Karen. "Just make your mark and let the world know you were here."

Oh, my mark has been made, thought Frankie.

"How much does it cost?"

"Don't worry about it."

Frankie looked down and fiddled with his fingers, preparing to ask what he considered the unmentionable. "You'd be a good mom. Why didn't you ever have kids?"

He immediately wished he hadn't said it, because Karen's eyes widened and filled with tears.

"I've been waiting to have this conversation, but it never felt right. You see . . ."

"No, forget it," he said, holding up the palm of his hand. "Sorry I asked. Not my business."

"No, it's okay. I'll tell you anything you want to know about me, Frankie."

Many times Frankie had examined Karen when she wasn't looking. She was plain looking and frumpy. His assumption was that no man bothered to see past her looks to realize what a good wife and mother she'd be. He felt a sense of protection toward her, and a veritable anger toward the men who rejected her. He decided that no, he didn't really want to hear her sob story.

"I'm good," he said, with an anxious sniff.

Karen wiped the corner of her eyes with her sleeve and said, "Okay."

"So, the Massachusetts College of Art?" he questioned, closing the subject. "I guess I could look at it."

*   *   *

Karen promised Frankie a special graduation present if he received a GPA of 3.4 or higher.

"What if it's a 3.3?"

"Then I guess it will just be nice as opposed to special," she teased.

On the morning of his last day of school, Frankie walked into the kitchen and was welcomed to the smell of pancakes and eggs. The large plate of food Karen placed in front of him looked good enough to be in a magazine, but that meant nothing. Karen's cooking was deceptively cunning. Sometimes it smelled delicious and tasted awful, and sometimes it smelled horrible and tasted surprisingly good. This morning, the very last day of school, was no day to brave a taste test.

"I'm not hungry," he said, pouring a cup of coffee.

Karen frowned. "Okay, I confess. I snuck out early and ordered this from the pancake house. I didn't cook it, but it's still sincere. So you don't have to worry about doughy pancakes or undercooked meat. It's the real McCoy, so eat with confidence."

Frankie doused his pancakes with a thick, strong smelling maple syrup. Since the day he had drawn the gingerbread house, he experienced mental blank spots where the girl was concerned; however, his stomach had grown weaker and weaker. It burned constantly, and the sight of food often made it crunch into tight knots. For Karen's sake, he took large bites and swallowed whole, ignoring the gag reflex that was trying to push the food back up his esophagus.

After two pancakes and as many spoonfuls of scrambled eggs as he could manage, Frankie washed away the sweet taste in his mouth with a bitter cup of black coffee.

"Big day today, huh?"

"I guess."

"I remember my last day of high school."

When she turned her back to pour her tea, Frankie rolled his eyes. Another *Karen in high school story* was not what he had hoped for at seven in the morning.

"A bunch of us went down to a lake and jumped in fully clothed! Can you believe it?"

Frankie gave her a dry smile. "Go Karen. What a rebel."

"Wise guy," she grinned. "That was rebel where I came from!"

"Yeah, you bad for sure," he said, toasting her with his coffee cup.

Karen laughed at his lack of interest. *Typical teenager, unimpressed by his mother,* she thought. "Call me from the Club and let me know how your last day went," she said, shrugging on a light windbreaker that didn't match her Annie Hall attire. As she headed toward the door, she stopped and rested her hand on Frankie's shoulder.

"I'm very proud of your accomplishments. I couldn't be happier for you," she said, squeezing his shoulder and tousling his hair. "Enjoy being you today," she said sweetly.

Karen's words were like a warm bath. They floated into his ears and traveled down to his stomach, mixing with the breakfast he felt obligated to enjoy. Frankie nodded, angry that his wet eyes betrayed emotion. His stomach responded by manhandling the food into a gelatinous heap of goo. He knew that the only way he could rectify the situation was to purge. Gross but effective, and Frankie thought, quite necessary.

He exited Cambridge High the same way he had for the past two years; out the side door, going directly to a bus that would bring him to the Boys and Girls Club. He didn't even smile at the sight of his report card. He merely opened it, looked at his stellar grades, and placed it in the inside pocket of his jacket, where he housed his emergency nip.

When he arrived at the club, he called Karen.

"Hi Sarah."

"Hey, it's the graduating senior! How goes it, Frankie?" she asked.

"It went okay," he replied. "Could you tell Karen 3.5? She'll get it."

"Will do," said Sarah, writing down *Frankie says 3.5* on a memo pad and sticking it to Karen's computer station.

Karen surprised Frankie by showing up at the club midafternoon.

"I was going to take the bus home," he told her, sounding a bit disappointed. The past two hours had turned today into a good day for a nip. He had just finished drawing a caricature for a boy who couldn't have been more than eight, and when Frankie handed him the drawing, he saw two familiar pink circles, tender and raw, on the boy's arm. Frankie tried to hide his anger and fear as he watched the boy smile at the picture.

"You like it, buddy?" he asked.

"Do I ever! I'm going to hang it up in my room!"

"Nicccceeee!" Frankie smiled widely, high-fiving him. But as the boy walked away, he felt the pain in his own arm return, and had to rub his scars to make it stop.

The desire for the nip didn't come then but a while later, while doing mundane work that caused his mind to wander with swooping, unwanted memories. The awareness that he was here and not watching his mother give blowjobs filtered in when he was filing. While restocking the cabinets, he shook off a sudden chill at the realization that he was no longer being abused by Ray, or starving for days on end. His emotional response wasn't one of gratefulness, but of uneasiness. Frankie knew he was fortunate, and worked diligently every day to make sure he stayed that way. His constant stomach upset carried that one remnant of his past; never being sure of the girl. A swig of alcohol was the only thing that seemed to release the cramping.

What possible harm could one or two measly nips cause?

Karen and Frankie stepped outside, Frankie focused on getting home so he could knock back the nip he had stashed in his jacket. He was about to tell Karen he had to run back into the club for something, when she said, "Over here," and began walking toward the parking lot.

"You drove here?" he asked.

"Sort of," Karen grinned, stopping in front of a black Trans Am.

"Did you lose where you parked?"

"I parked here," she replied, leaning against the car.

"Where?" he asked, and then, "Karen, I wouldn't lean on that car, it's . . ."

"Yours."

"What?"

"It's yours. Happy graduation!" she squealed, waving her hand in front of the car as if she were a hostess on a game show.

The Trans Am boasted an eagle on the hood and honeycomb gold wheels. It was showy and loud, and Frankie loved it.

"Seriously?"

"Yep. 3.5, right? You far exceeded our expectations," she said, giving him a warm hug.

"And Carl says happy graduation, too. He paid for one year of insurance."

The joy Frankie felt was weighted with guilt and frustration. Too much to absorb, his organs screamed *you're not worthy*, while Karen's pride surrounded him, her motherly love shooting beams of hope at his soul. He felt his stomach wrench, his legs turn to mush, and hoped he wouldn't throw up. Karen took his silence to be a good thing.

"So, I take it you like?"

"I love," he smiled.

"Then let's roll," she said, tossing the keys his way. "If you're not too busy with graduation plans tonight, I was hoping we could do dinner?"

"Yeah, I just have to run back and hit the bathroom."

"No problem," she said. "I'll just lean here and look cool."

Frankie headed back into the building and locked himself inside a bathroom stall. He reached inside his jacket and grabbed the nip of vodka. And just like that, Frankie's stomach settled and his cloudy judgment became clear. *A Trans Am.* He was the proud owner of a Trans Am! He popped a mint in his mouth and headed outside.

"Can we call Carl to see if he can come to dinner?" he asked, sliding into the driver's seat.

"Sure," she said. "He'd like that."

Allowing the liquid courage to do its job, Frankie looked directly ahead of him to avoid meeting Karen's eyes.

"I really appreciate the car, *Mom*."

Karen felt the air go out of her lungs.

"Shit. It was too weird," he said, gripping the steering wheel hard in an effort to transmit his shame onto it.

"No, not too weird," she replied, her lip quivering. "I'm just, well, honored is all."

"Is it okay, do you think, if I switch between calling you Karen and Mom?"

Karen pulled a tissue out of her purse.

"It's perfectly okay."

"It's just that if I have to introduce you around, sometimes it's just easier if I called you Mom. But if it's just you and me, I think I'll call you Karen."

"That works," she said, dabbing her eyes.

Frankie was sure he'd feel the impact of his statement later; and when later came, he would hunt down the filthy old drunk that lingered near the package store. For a mere five bucks, he'd supply Frankie with anything he needed.

KENDRA

"Ah, Patatona, I'm so proud of you!" beamed August, holding up her report card.

"Yeah, I actually made it through twelfth grade without one C!"

"C or no C, it don't matter. Look what remarks the teachers say about you; kind, respectful, participates in class."

"Geeky, fat."

"Oh, dite tali bugie!"

Kendra wished it were a lie. She also wished she hadn't just been called *fatty-bumbalatti* by an asshole jock who received the superlative of Most Popular.

"There must be graduation parties all over the city. I'm gonna allow you to stay out as late as you want," said August proudly.

Kendra sighed, feeling more pity for her grandfather than for herself.

"I'm staying home. I don't want to go anywhere."

"Whadda ya mean you're staying home?"

"That's whadda I mean," she said mocking her grandfather's speech. "Graduation night is nothing but one big alcohol and drug fest."

"There must be some kids who don't do that stuff who you could go out with?"

"I don't care, Gramps. Home is fine," she said, slightly embarrassed she didn't have any options.

"Awww, horseshit," he spat. "If you don't want to go out with your friends and get caught up in riffraff, I understand. But you and me, we're going out to celebrate."

Kendra squeezed into a pair of Chic jeans and, in an attempt to stretch them out, danced around her room to Van Halen.

"You ready?" August yelled through the closed door.

"Give me five minutes," she said, struggling to find a shirt that didn't cause significant muffin top.

August would only eat at Luigi's. Any other restaurant, era sporco.

"Augustino! How wonderful to see you!" said Angelo, extending his hand to August. "Come, let me get you a prime seat."

Angelo, the owner's son, personally catered to August every time he visited.

"You know me by now. I'll have the clams and the lobster," August told Angelo before they were seated.

"It will be a pleasure to cook for you tonight," smiled Angelo. "I'll be back shortly with some nice red wine."

When dinner was served, Kendra asked, "Why does he treat you so special?"

"Me and his father Luigi go way back."

"To thug days?"

"That's right. We were part of the same club."

"Should I even ask?" she questioned, stuffing a roll with two pads of butter into her mouth.

"When I was your age," he said through a slurp of red wine, "I used to go to this club with Luigi. The place was always mobbed. There were more alleyway fights, more murders in Scully Square than you wanna know about. I was lucky I never got locked up," he grunted, swallowing a clam without bothering to chew it.

Kendra looked at her chicken cacciatore and as she cut a piece, she tried not to make eye contact with August. Sometimes his slovenliness ruined her appetite, and Luigi's was no place to lose your appetite.

"You know," he said, pointing his fork toward her plate, "We used to kill our own chickens."

August had on a too small lobster bib and food particles were running amuck. An unidentifiable morsel, either a piece of roll, pasta, or lobster, was perched on his shoulder.

"Oh, that's gross," she said, referring to both the chicken killing *and* August's absent etiquette.

"Hey, if you wanted to eat it, you had to kill it yourself," he said, popping a clam into his mouth like it was a piece of popcorn.

"We used to buy live chickens and let me tell you, we used every inch of them. The feet were good for soup, the insides we fried."

"Gramps, yuck!"

"Yuck, what? You some kind of hypocrite? You can eat it, but you can't talk about it?"

"Yes, in fact I'm a colossal hypocrite, so do me a favor and skip the nasty, will ya?"

"Too bad, cause I was gonna tell you how the guy would cut the head off and give us the rest."

August made a slicing noise with his mouth, spraying food around his face. "*Swsssshhh.* Just like that, he'd cut its head off, put it in hot water and hang it up. After he removed the feathers, we took it home and gutted it. Nothing like fresh," he nodded, barbarically tearing open the lobster.

"Stop, really. *Stop.*"

August shrugged and continued massacring his food.

"So tell me more about you and Luigi and this so-called club."

"Nothing much to tell. He was part of it like I was, and then one day, he wasn't part of it no more. He opened this restaurant and made a big success of himself."

Kendra examined the room. The place was old and musty and in dire need of a facelift.

"So, where is he?"

"He's home. Remember, he's old, like me. His brother Louis—"

"Stop right there. Please tell me they did not name their boys Louis and Luigi?"

"Sure they did," he said, not seeing the humor in it. "Louis joined a large city gang."

"He did?" These were Kendra's favorite stories.

"What gang?"

"They started to materialize sometime in the 40's when all the guys were coming home from the war. I can't remember the name. They dabbled in funds." August grinned. "In those days we called them gangsters. Today they're businessmen, but they're still gangsters."

"And?" she urged, her fork in mid air.

"This particular gang wasn't that big at the beginning, but they grew and I'll tell you, they were fearless."

"Do you know stories?" she asked, hoping to God he did.

"That's all they'd be, is stories. I was in my mid-twenties back then and thought I had the world by the balls, but even I knew better than to join this gang. You either were in, or you weren't, and I decided that I wasn't."

"Did you have any friends who were in?"

"Had is the key word. My friend Mario's brother took a five hundred dollar bet on a long shot that everyone said wasn't going to win. He held it back from his boss and wouldn't you know it, the horse won. They killed him for it. They paid the guy who made the bet and buried Mario's brother in a field. They didn't find the body until they began to build in the field, and it wasn't just the one body they found. Mario's brother was crazy to get involved."

"Have you ever seen a real hit, Gramps?" Kendra asked, mechanically tearing apart a roll and bringing it slowly to her mouth.

August knew by Kendra's expression that she really wasn't absorbing the full scope of his words, that to his granddaughter, these were popcorn and movie stories. She didn't get that August had lived in a violent, corrupt world and that he was more than content with just being alive.

"I've been in places after a hit."

"Oh my God! Where?"

"My wife's cousin's house. Her cousin worked at the post office, but he was also a bookie. That's how they came to afford their house in cash. Another gang, guys from Charlestown, tried to take over. Her cousin and his people wiped them out in a shootout."

"Shootout," she repeated, enchanted by the vision.

"Look, Patatona, I ain't talking about no movie doubles getting up and walking away. These were people you stayed away from because if you got involved and they asked questions, you may say something you shouldn't. My buddy, Charlie, he knew a lot and said nothing to the cops. He went to jail so as not to squeal, and it saved his life."

"But if you were a thug, why were you so afraid?"

August laughed. "Patatona, I was a gambler and a petty thief. It's like kindergarten to college." Then he leaned forward and whispered, "Luigi had another son, Dominic. He went missing. Some say they got rid of him," August made a slicing motion across his neck. "They say that's why Luigi went straight."

Kendra's mouth popped open. Over the years she had perfected her look of surprise. "And no one called the cops?"

"The cops?" he laughed. "The cops were involved. Let me tell you something, Patatona. You know these stories you hear about crooked cops? Well, some of them are true."

"Oh, Gramps, it all sounds so Hollywood."

August's concerned face prompted her to ask, "What's wrong?"

"I think maybe I tell you too much. Since you were a little girl, I've told you my stories so that you would see that your grandfather, he ain't perfect. And my stories, they ain't no bedtime tales. Always remember that bad people hide in plain sight. They live right under your nose. I might'a been in a two-bit club where petty thieves gathered to gamble, but I never got involved with the big spenders. Some of these guys, they had ferocious reputations. It was best to keep to yourself, especially if you had a family that you wanted to see live."

Angelo came over and placed fried ice cream in front of Kendra.

"Sulla casa," he bowed, "Congrats on making it through high school. Most of us should've paid more attention. Ain't that so, August?"

"You speak the truth," August nodded. "Tell me, how is your papa?"

"Lui va morbido in testa."

"Ah, we all go soft at some point. Tell him I was asking after him."

The two men paused to look at Kendra who was contentedly filling her face with dessert. "That's a girl, lei mangia," giggled August. "Angelo, she's gonna make a good wife, ain't she?"

"La tua ragazza, è buona ma è un po piena."

"I can understand Italian, Angelo. Thanks for calling me fat."

Angelo shrugged in surprise. "What? I no call you fat. Good peasant stock is what we look for in our women."

"Then I'm going to Italy stat."

"It was a good meal, Angelo," August told him.

Kendra covered her mouth and released a loud burp, causing Angelo to beam.

"Good girl!" he said, folding his hands together in prayer and then pointing them toward Kendra. "See, you love'a my food!"

"Yes, Angelo, I love'a your food."

On their way home, Kendra asked, "What will you do when I leave for school?"

"What do you mean? Am I a cripple or something?"

"I worry about you."

"Enough of your nonsense," said August, forcing out one of his guttural coughs that unnerved Kendra. "Your old grandfather ain't your problem to take care of."

FRANKIE

To celebrate Frankie's graduation, Carl suggested dinner at an Italian restaurant named Luigi's.

"It's supposed to have old fashioned Italian food," he told them.

Frankie had no idea what that meant, but hoped his stomach could handle it.

The restaurant had old world appeal with a cozy, intimate setting. It smelled of seafood, beef, and gravy.

"This reminds me of an Italian grandmother's kitchen," said Carl.

"We don't have an Italian grandmother," stated Karen.

"Yes, but if we did, this is what her kitchen would smell like," he said, inhaling deeply.

"Really? Because I feel like I'm in a mob movie and am about to be approached by Al Pacino."

"Uh, I'm going to side with Carl on this one. Here comes the Italian grandmother," whispered Frankie.

They turned their attention to a short gray-haired woman shuffling toward them. She wore an outdated powder blue dress and flat, furry tan shoes that resembled house slippers. When she was a few feet away from them, Frankie noted that they were, indeed, house slippers. Her gait was sluggish but steady, and her back hunched. Her overall size and shape reminded Frankie of an orange sitting on top of portable tree stumps. She glanced at the trio and with a slight smile, directed them to a small circular table with giant goblets, bulky white plates, and blood red napkins.

"Good evening, my name is Marie. I'll be'a your server tonight. Is this your first time eating at Luigi's?"

Fully mesmerized by their surroundings, they shook their heads yes.

"Well in that case, Angelo, he the owner, will come and say'a hello. He like to greet all new patrons."

"Thank you," nodded Carl, whose chair was up against a wood paneled wall, circa 1970.

"Not to mention it," nodded Marie. "I will go get you sum'a rolls."

Marie turned slowly, as if her brain were instructing her body to *go now* and it was taking a while to respond. With her feet never leaving the ground, she shuffled and waddled her way to a table across the room where a man, who was obviously Angelo, was talking and laughing with an older man and a teenage girl.

"That's got to be Angelo," said Karen.

"This is a very interesting world," said Carl, almost to himself.

Frankie didn't participate in the conversation because he was too preoccupied with the girl, whom he found striking. Her green eyes had him so captivated that he hadn't noticed Angelo making his way to their table until he stood in front of Frankie and obstructed his view.

"Greetings!" he smiled, his arms out as if he were going to hug the table. "I'm Angelo, the proprietor. Welcome to Luigi's!"

Angelo's voice was deep and jovial, true game show host material. Frankie was immediately suspicious. It was the kind of voice that could promise you something, and no matter what it was, you'd believe he could deliver.

You need a car, I'll get you a car. You need money, I'll get you money. You need a hit, I'll take care of it.

Frankie had known people like Angelo. They could be dangerous. *Red napkins*, thought Frankie, *to hide the blood stains.*

"Thank you, Angelo," smiled Karen.

"You're very welcome, beautiful lady," he bowed.

The inflection in his voice caused Frankie to look at Karen, who was blushing from the flattery.

"We're waiting for bread," he said, interrupting the moment.

"He just graduated tonight," added Karen apologetically, like this were an excuse for curt behavior.

"Ah, that's two graduates tonight!" he exclaimed. "I bring you the house specials, and for the young man, he gets a free dessert!"

Throughout the evening, Angelo appeared at their table, which Frankie found quite irritating. Karen, on the other hand, was enjoying every minute of it.

"I think that Angelo is taken by you, Karen," winked Carl.

"Oh, he's probably like that to everyone," blushed Karen.

Oh you can bet your ass he is, thought Frankie.

"You still drawing at the Boys and Girls Club?" asked Carl.

"Yeah, every day."

"Tell him how many caricatures you've drawn," beamed Karen.

"I forget," he lied.

"I'll tell him, then. Since he's been there, he's drawn an estimated eight hundred caricatures."

"That's something all right," nodded Carl.

"It sure is," Karen replied. "Someone put a donations jar on the counter marked *Caricature Funds* and it raised six hundred dollars for the club. They donated it to a family who lost everything in a house fire."

Carl nodded at Frankie and said, "Good job."

Frankie liked Carl very much. He showed up for dinner every Tuesday with a crock pot full of stew that the three of them quickly devoured. He made sure to attend some of Frankie's games alongside Karen, and showed up at sports banquets and the award ceremony that honored top students.

Carl didn't try to give Frankie advice, nor did he push him toward or away from him. For some inexplicable reason, this didn't seem to be enough for Karen. It was clear to Frankie that she desperately wanted her father to participate in Frankie's life more than he did, whereas Frankie thought he couldn't have gotten a better deal with Carl. The way he saw it, Karen's expectations were either more than Carl was willing to give, or more than he was capable of giving. The one odd thing was that Frankie had never been to Carl's house. He always came to them. Every so often, Karen would call and tell Frankie she had stopped by Carl's and would be an hour late, but she never included Frankie in these visits. He didn't question why, nor did he want to know. Carl, Frankie knew, had been broken. By what or whom it was unclear, but whatever it was, it caused Carl to keep Frankie at arm's length. His wound was permanent and he, along with Frankie, would forever be damaged goods. Contrary to what Karen thought, this made Frankie more fond of Carl, feel more akin to Carl than she could ever understand.

Halfway through the evening, Angelo approached the girl's table. When she stood up, he hugged her, pinched her cheeks, and then handed her an envelope. She was shaking her head in refusal, but Angelo persisted. She looked at the old man, who nodded, and only then did she accept it. The old man was trying to hand Angelo money, but Angelo shook his head saying, "Sulla casa, sulla casa." As they walked past his table, Frankie felt his heart skip a beat. He took a few more bites of shrimp before his stomach protested, and then pushed his dish aside. Angelo, who was like a hawk, must have mistaken this gesture as a sign of him wanting more, and promptly emerged with a plate of pastries.

"For the graduate, we got tiramisu, custard, gelato, rum cake, and cannoli," he announced genially.

"Oh, my!" exclaimed Karen, hands on her cheeks. "This is great, Angelo!"

"I am glad the beautiful lady is pleased," he bowed.

Frankie wondered if the rum cake had enough alcohol in it to take the edge off, and decided there was no harm in trying a slice.

"We have to come here more often," smiled Karen.

"The food is good, no doubt about it," agreed Carl. "And I'm sure it wouldn't do Angelo harm to see you again," he winked.

While Karen and Carl enjoyed a laugh, Frankie took a giant bite of the rum cake, sucking on the gelatinous center, hoping to absorb the rum. The last thing he needed was a man complicating Karen's life. "And," she paused, "I have some other news I was going to save for later, but now is as good a time as any. Your adoption forms were processed," she announced, her magnificent walnut eyes lighting up Luigi's dim atmosphere, as well as Frankie's heart.

LETTERS TO MEG

Dear Meg,

Your grandfather and I took Frankie out for a graduation dinner. We went to an Italian place called Luigi's, and let me tell you, we're talking heavy Italian food. My stomach feels like a heap of dough, and I'll be burping garlic for a month! You would have liked its retro/mafia atmosphere.

Frankie was checking out this girl across the room. Of course, he wasn't aware that I noticed him noticing her, because he was far too concerned with the owner, Angelo. It's obvious he feels threatened by male figures, but who can blame him? I can say this to you, Meg, because I would have said it had you been there, but I only *wish* the owner was coming on to me! I'm sure he's acquired hefty tips and returning customers with his flattery. Heck, I fell for it. I can't wait to go back and be fed compliments, even if they come with a penalty of garlic breath and heavy indigestion.

Frankie loved his car. Your grandfather paid for his insurance for the year, which was more than I could have asked for, but I do wish he'd reach out more. I don't think he has any desire to get close to another child. I stop by his house every week, not to see him, but to see your face. And what a beautiful face it was, Meg! Your eighth grade school picture is my personal favorite. I lose myself in those large almond eyes of yours and stroke your red and blonde hair on top of the glass, pretending I can feel its softness. I kiss your cheek, and if I close my eyes, I can feel your smooth white skin against my lips. On some days I find it utterly painful, while on others I find it incredibly comforting. Problem is I never know what kind of reaction I'm going to have until I'm holding your photo against my heart.

Confession: I thought with Frankie I'd feel less empty, but I don't. Every so often, I get this craving to fill something. I eat, I sleep, I put more time in at work. Nothing helps. There's an empty spot in my heart that leaks into the very essence of my being. There's no remedy for that.

It's a deplorable feeling.

The good news is that in a very short time, Frankie has changed so much I doubt anyone from his past would recognize him. I mean, I barely recognize him. He went from being this overaggressive kid to a reserved and polite young man. And boys are totally different than we are, Meg. I mean *totally*. When they change and grow, they really change! Frankie was tall as it was, but since he's been here, he's put on twenty needed pounds and has grown another two inches. And then there was the shaving experience; Carl stopped by and went over the basics with him, and while he was at it, he offered to teach him how to tie a tie, just in case he needed it for college. He looked so very handsome dressed up for dinner. How can I describe his looks? His father is from Scandinavian descent and his mom is Dominican. Frankie has olive skin, a square face, an upturned nose and unique amber colored eyes that seem to look right through you. He has a triangular mouth with full lips and dimples. And he has a scar, just like yours that only adds to his appeal. It's my favorite feature. He really should be on a magazine cover for best looking humans in the world, but he doesn't seem to notice how handsome he is. Years of damage does that to a kid.

In my new world, people don't see me as a woman who has unwillingly survived the death of her daughter. They see a woman who has raised a well-rounded son. I will always feel like the former, and as unkind as this may sound, because I don't mean it to be, the latter will have to suffice. Stay tuned,

Love,
Mom xoxo ☺

FAMILY AT LAST

Even though both his parents had relinquished their rights, Frankie didn't trust the system. Primitive survival instincts told him that as long as he remained a free-floating foster kid, his future was uncertain. There was only one way to ensure that neither of his parents could ever legally touch him again, and that was to change his name to Frankie Sherburne.

"Isn't it great it went through so fast?"

"What do I have to do?" he said anxiously, wanting to purge his past as quickly as he could.

"Show up at the courthouse at three o'clock."

"Courthouse? You never said anything about having to go to court. Is Edna going to be there?"

"Oh, it's nothing formal. We're just going to meet a judge in his chambers to finalize the adoption by signing a few papers. It shouldn't be more than half an hour, and then we'll be family," Karen said hopefully.

"And then what happens?"

"What do you mean?"

"What happens to me?"

"Nothing happens. You stay here doing the same thing you've been doing."

"When do I have to go back again?"

"Go back where?"

"To court to renew it."

"Never. This is it."

"Really?"

"Really."

"So Edna can't touch me after this?"

"That's right."

Frankie racked his brain for anything that could keep him tied to his mother.

"She has my birth certificate. She can come get me."

"No, she can't. A new one will be issued in about a month. After the meeting with the judge, we'll go to City Hall and request one."

"What about *before* the month? Can she or Whitey or Ray . . ." Frankie began, his scarred arm pulsing with worry.

"Both your parents relinquished their rights and Ray has no authority over you. It's done, Frankie. This will seal the deal."

"Cool," he said, but Karen could see the worry in his eyes.

"Do you have any more questions?"

"What if I get sick? Can I see a doctor?"

Karen maintained a neutral expression. Frankie once told her of a winter when he suffered with chronic bronchitis and asthmatic bouts that left his sore lungs gasping for air and feeling as if he were breathing through a straw.

"You'll fall under my healthcare plan."

"What if I need clothes or art supplies?"

"That's part of my role as your guardian. I'm responsible for providing for your shelter and clothing. It won't change."

"But that doesn't mean you have to buy me art supplies."

"No, it doesn't. But I want to."

"And what if I don't want you to? What if you buying everything makes me feel like a scab?"

"Frankie," said Karen, lightly touching his arm, "I don't ever want you to feel as if you're a burden. All I expect from you is that you keep your end of the bargain by striving to be the best person you can. Everything else we'll work out together. Okay?"

Karen walked to the refrigerator and produced a small cake that said, *Congratulations to Us!!* She asked the bakery to add a second exclamation point in the hopes that Frankie would understand how important the day was to her. They each had two pieces with a full glass of milk, and then Karen retired to her den to catch up on some work. It seemed like yesterday that Meg had disappeared, and in a whirlwind of a few years, Karen had buried her daughter then fostered and planned an adoption for a troubled boy. She vowed to do the best she could to provide for his welfare, because God only knew, she had dropped the ball with Meg.

*　　*　　*

Frankie's head felt like it was spinning off its axis. People like him didn't luck out. Just to be sure that he wasn't hallucinating, he knocked over a vase on an end table, sending it shattering into a million pieces. The noise drew Karen back into the room.

"Is everything . . . oh, the vase. Bummer."

"It was an accident," he said, feeling no inward remorse, because the broken vase had validated his security. Karen had not freaked out and attacked him. She didn't kick him out for breaking it. She was still going to keep him.

"Of course it was. Why don't you get the broom and a trash bag and I'll start collecting the pieces. And put on some shoes, I don't want your feet getting cut."

Exactly a month to the day of the adoption, Frankie and Karen walked into City Hall, where Frankie was issued a brand new birth certificate.

"I'll put this in the den in the file cabinet under your name."

He glanced at the certificate in her hand.

> *Full name of Child: Francis Sherburne.*
> *Date of Birth: 1/17/65.*
> *Name of Mother: Karen Louise Sherburne*

Wow.

It was true.

He was no longer Frankie Ortiz.

And if he were no longer Frankie Ortiz, he thought diplomatically, then he never had a mother named Edna. He was never beaten by a bastard named Ray. And most importantly, Frankie never stabbed a girl. He smiled briefly, allowing himself to go forward with this train of thinking until his stomach revolted. His gut felt like a tightly wound knot of sloshing liquid, publicizing his lies and fears to the rest of his body by way of rapid, uncontrolled spasms. It was his stomach's response that told Frankie that no matter how far he ran from his past, he would never truly be free.

PART 4

Convergence

FRANKIE AND KENDRA

Having to skip meals due to time constraints proved most annoying. Between full-time college classes, a part-time job, and little wiggle room for anything else, crabbiness had become a way of life for Kendra. She yearned for August's fried pork chops and green peppers, meatballs, baked haddock, and pasta fagioli. Once her schedule was under control, she promised herself that she would visit her grandfather once during the week. She was home every weekend, but the poor man was probably lonely as hell Monday through Thursday.

"I hope you're at least getting out," she asked him, during one of her daily calls.

"What are you talking about?"

"It's just, I don't want you to be alone all the time."

"What, you think I rolled over and died?"

"Okay," Kendra challenged, deciding to embarrass her grandfather for his own good, "What did you do today?"

"Had coffee and banana bread with Sheri Rizollo."

Kendra laughed at the thought of it.

"A fine yarn, Gramps, but really, what did you do?"

"I had coffee and banana bread with Sheri Rizollo."

"Oh, *real-ly* now?" she replied, her voice tinted with jealousy.

"She comes and visits a couple days a week."

"And how long has this been going on?"

"For the past two months."

"Gramps, I only left two months ago!"

"What can I say? She moves fast," he said in an amused voice.

"But I thought you hated her?"

"Ah, Patatona, she's a lonely old hag visiting a lonely old thug. I admit, she ain't much to look at and she's no Italian, but she sure can bake banana bread."

"Well, I guess I don't have to worry about you then," she sulked.

"You never did have to worry about me, Patatona. All you gotta worry about is getting good grades. You got that?"

Kendra's digital watch beeped, alerting her that she was running out of time.

"I gotta go eat something before the next class. Love you, Gramps."

"Love you more, Patatona."

Kendra started to replace the phone on the receiver, but quickly brought it back to her ear. "And by the way," she said, a snit in her voice, "I'll be coming home this Wednesday, so you can tell Sheri Rizollo that you're all set for company." And with August's laughter ringing in her ears, Kendra dashed down Huntington Avenue in search of the nearest sandwich shop.

The one positive side effect to being food deprived was losing weight. In two short months, Kendra had dropped nearly fifteen pounds. As she walked briskly past a group of four boys in her now saggy acid-washed Levi's and loose fitting tee shirt, one of them wolf whistled and began singing, *"Dum Da Dum, Foxy Lady."*

This was not a good day to be heckled. Starving, anxious over her afternoon test, and thanks to Sheri Rizollo, feeling dispensable, Kendra turned and faced them, quieting them with a threatening stare. It was hard enough to walk past boys if you were thin, but if you were fat, well, it was horrific. She recognized one of them from her art history class.

"Who said that?" she demanded.

The boys looked around awkwardly.

"I said, who said that?"

"I did," said a very tall boy.

"I know you," said Kendra. "You think it's fun to pick on girls walking down the street, huh? You think it's really cutesy-cute to mock people, don't cha?" she said, lifting her chin in a challenging way.

The boy smiled warmly, as if misunderstood. "Not at all."

"No," she challenged, hands on her hips.

"No," he said, careful to keep his voice non-confrontational. "I thought you were, uh, foxy."

The group chuckled at his comment, causing Kendra's temper to flare.

"Yeah, well, try it again, and you'll get a book in your face," she warned, brandishing the biggest book she had and shaking it in his direction.

"Chill," he said, holding up both hands.

Kendra stared every one of them down before swiveling on her heel to leave. She moved two steps and heard, "You're still *da, da, dum, foxy.*"

Feeling like an out of control Chuck Norris, she whipped the book violently, just missing the culprit's shoulder.

"Whoa!" he shouted and ducked.

"I warned you," she snarled, fists balled at her side.

He laughed, picked up the book and handed it to her.

"You sure did. I'm sorry, but I can't help it. You're very pretty."

Kendra's eyes filled with tears. "You're a liar. I am not pretty. I'm fat."

As if wanting to shield her from embarrassing herself, the boy turned to his three friends and said, "Catch you guys later."

The boys took their cue, mumbled, "See ya, man," and walked away.

"Listen," he began, "You might want to switch out whatever funhouse mirror you own for a real one, Foxy."

Kendra found herself speechless.

"So you weren't joking?"

"Not even a little."

I'm sorry," she stammered, and then in one quick breath said, "It's just, well, I've always been what my grandfather would call robust, but I recently lost weight, without even trying I might add, which is odd, because when I have tried in the past of course it doesn't work, in fact I gain weight trying to lose weight hands down every time, but now because I don't have time to eat it's just melting off and I haven't even really noticed because I still feel, as my grandfather would say, robust.

Phew," she said, before going on, "And to be honest, I was on my way to eat and I never get to eat and it pisses me off, as you can see. And right now, I'm really hungry. Plus," she paused, for another intake of breath, "I'm not used to being noticed by boys, especially good looking ones. If you only saw me a few months ago," she blushed.

"I have," he replied.

"Come again?"

"I've seen you before."

"Well, duh, you're in my class."

"Before that. I was at Luigi's for dinner, and I saw you."

"Yeah?" she cocked her head to the side and studied his face for a moment like she was trying to remember.

"Yeah, funny thing, though," he smiled. "I never noticed your weight."

"Oh puh-leassse," she snorted.

"It's true."

Kendra wanted to fire back a clever retort, like how he must be blind, but stifled her big mouth by gnawing on her fingernail. While she awkwardly examined her raw cuticle, he asked, "Can we try this again?"

She looked up at the tall boy who could easily grace the cover of Teen Beat Magazine and nodded.

"Hi," he said, sticking out his hand.

Kendra wiped her soggy nail bitten hand off on her pants and offered it to him. "Hi."

"What's your name, Foxy?"

"Kendra," she replied, and now that she knew he was sincere, Foxy wasn't such a bad thing to be called.

"I'm Frankie."

"Nice to meet you, Frankie. Care to grab a quick bite?"

"Only if I treat."

"You've got yourself a deal," she smiled, "But I have to warn you, I know how to eat and I'm not afraid to go large."

After scarfing down her dream lunch, Kendra ordered a chocolate frappe with whipped cream and a cherry.

"I should be embarrassed, but I'm not. Sorry."

"For what, being real? Help yourself."

"I'm finding it tough adjusting to school and my vice is to eat, but since I can't eat that much because there is no flipping time, I find myself forced to stockpile," she said, swiping a lump of whipped cream off of the straw and sticking it in her mouth. "I feel like a damn rodent who squirrels away food for the winter."

"So," he interrupted, "Did you do the assignment on Van Gogh yet?"

Kendra looked alarmed.

"Isn't it due next week? Did I screw up and miss the deadline?"

"Next week," he confirmed. "I was going to get a jump on it. We could study together, tonight if you want?"

"Can't."

"Other plans?" he asked. Kendra was both pleased and surprised to hear a hint of disappointment in his voice.

"If you want to call my part-time job plans, then yeah, I have other plans."

"Maybe some other time?" Frankie asked hopefully.

"I'd like that," smiled Kendra, who wiped her mouth with the back of her hand. "Listen, I don't mean to pull a chew and screw, but I've seriously got to fly. See you in class?"

"Yeah, sounds good," he said.

Kendra brushed the crumbs off her lap, grabbed her books, and went to the counter to purchase a Coke. She came back to the table, popped open the can and poured in a sugar packet.

"You're kidding?"

"Sadly, no," she said, grabbing two more packets and stuffing them in her pocket.

"Wherever I go, I clip a few of these," she said patting her pocket. "Just in case I need the rush."

She waved quickly, and as she spun around her ankle buckled and her Coke splashed out of the can. Pink with embarrassment and struggling to maintain her balance, she cried out, "Whoops!"

"You okay?" Frankie asked, starting to get up.

"No, sit there. I'm fine. This is par for my course. I'm kind of clumsy."

"You sure?"

Kendra motioned for Frankie to sit back down and in as gracious a voice as she could muster said, "Thanks for lunch. Catch ya later!"

* * *

Frankie watched as Kendra missed the full swing of the door and smacked her hip on the corner as it swung shut. Once outside, she bumped into a large, baldheaded man, which caused her to stumble back a few steps and trip over the curbstone, nearly losing everything in her hands. Instead of viewing Kendra's trilogy of errors as comic relief, Frankie felt a warm heat massaging his chest. Kendra was perfect.

Frankie impatiently counted down the days until history class. He waited for Kendra outside of the classroom, and when she walked up to him he smiled, handing her a small, white object.

"What's this?"

"My ear," he smirked.

Kendra's hearty burst of laughter echoed through the corridors.

"You're kidding, right?" she asked, examining the molded work.

"Nope. I borrowed some quick dry compound from Professor Graham."

"Oh, you did, did you? You do realize that Van Gogh offered his ear to a prostitute?" she remarked, in a husky sensual voice that made Frankie blush.

"Er," was all Frankie could manage.

"I think it's hilarious," she bellowed.

"Hilarious enough to let me buy you another lunch?" he asked hopefully.

"You seriously want to watch me eat again? I eat like a cow."

"You eat like you love it."

"I do," she snorted.

"I wish I could eat like that, but I've got a nervous stomach," he said, and following in Karen's footsteps, he reached out and lightly touched Kendra's arm. It worked. He could feel her relax upon his touch.

"Oh," she replied. "All righty, then. My non-nervous stomach would be happy to oblige. Lunch it is."

*   *   *

A month into their blissfully new relationship, Karen met Kendra at an art show. Frankie and Kendra had each paid a fifteen dollar fee to exhibit five pieces of work. Frankie could tell that Kendra was a bit surprised by Karen's mousy appearance. Petite and ordinary, her auburn hair was loosely pulled back in a messy bun. Her wardrobe was baggy and loose and she appeared stuck in the 70's.

"Ah, you're a realist. Nice work," said Karen, admiring Kendra's pieces.

Kendra smiled broadly and replied, "Thanks!"

"What type of medium do you prefer?"

"Watercolor."

"On what kind of paper?"

"Ideally 300-pound, but it can get a bit pricey, so I usually slum it."

"Well, great work. I can tell you're very talented."

Thanks to the nip he greedily downed ten minutes ago in the restroom stall, Frankie felt giddy and a bit sentimental that the two women he loved were by his side. He closed his hand around Kendra's and said, "After the show, I thought we could all go out for lunch. There's an Italian place that just opened down the street."

"I'd love to," smiled Karen. "We can talk more then, Kendra. I'm just going to walk around and check out the competition."

When Karen was out of earshot, Kendra whispered, "She's great!"

Frankie smiled and put his arm around her. Since the onset of their relationship, he had upped his drinking, consuming anywhere from one to four nips a day. Whether it was nerves or fear of losing what he had, the nips were the only thing that helped to put his perspective, which was growing more warped by the day, into a somewhat normal reality.

Leaning into him, she asked, "Are you really real, or am I dreaming, because if I'm dreaming, don't wake me up."

"It's real, baby," he said, giving her shoulder a squeeze.

"But you're too perfect to be real."

Frankie winced at the flattery. If people only knew how exhausting it was, how much strength it took to conceal his past.

"You've got it backwards. You're the perfect one," he whispered.

"And you're going to get rewarded for that," she said, raising her eyebrows and slapping his backside.

*   *   *

Pretending to admire a piece of work that resembled the splattering of a two-year old, Karen observed young love from across the room. She slowly rubbed her chest trying to rid herself of the jealousy that had presented in the form of indigestion. Sarah had told her that mothers of boys tend to feel threatened by their son's first girlfriends, but Karen never suspected she would be one of them. After all, it wasn't as if she'd given birth to him, wasn't as if she'd raised him from infancy. She shook her head firmly.

It's grin and bear it time, Karen. Put on your big girl panties, paste on a smile, and let it go. It's out of your control.

She brushed the nonexistent lint off of her shirt and approached her son and the girl she was sure was going to steal him away.

*   *   *

August picked up the phone on the second ring.

"Hi, Gramps, how's it going?"

"Never mind me, are your grades good?"

"Define good."

"Kendra—"

"One of the professors wants to show my work at his adult education classes in Cambridge."

"That's my girl! Tell me, which drawing of yours does this professor guy like?"

"It's a parakeet with flowers."

"Oh, Madonna, you're still drawing them rats with wings?"

"For the last time, birds are not rats with wings!"

"They're bad luck, I tell you. Dirty creatures. Why don't you draw math problems, make pretty numbers? You'll learn math and be an accountant and make lots of money. Then I won't worry so much about you."

"Whatever," Kendra sighed.

"Lookit, I know I've done too much bad to tell you what you have to do, but take it from an old man who learned too late; it pays to be smart. Now, are you getting enough to eat? You need food or money?"

"Neither. Can't I call without you thinking I need anything?"

"Of course you can, Patatona."

"Or are you too busy with Sheri occupying your time?"

"Oh, you're a funny girl," giggled August. "But wipe off the pout face because it will make you ugly. Tell me about this boy Frankie. Is he treating you like the princess you are?"

"As a matter of fact, he is."

"He telling you you're a ten and treating you like a twenty?"

"You're annoying me. I call to say hi and you grill me."

August laughed. "Maybe if you brought him around, I could see for myself."

"I'm not ready to show him how annoying you are."

"If I had a nickel for every time you annoyed me, I'd be rich by now!"

"Bye, you pain in the—"

"Ah, ah, none of that. Hang up nicely, Patatona. You'll feel bad otherwise."

"Will not."

"I know my girl."

Kendra muttered *shit* under her breath because she knew he was right.

"Fine. I Love you, Gramps."

"I love you too, my Patatona. Even if you are annoying."

Kendra hung up the receiver to August's roaring laughter.

Sometimes talking to her grandfather could incite such rage. Why did she subject herself to his nonsense? After all, she *was* eighteen

215

years old now, *totally* an adult. She wandered the halls of the school, procrastinating on her way back to her studies. She thought of Frankie and smiled, grateful that she no longer had to make up stories about nonexistent friends or pretend to be happy when she was miserable. But perhaps best of all, the ghost girl Meg hadn't followed her to any college mirrors.

Kendra could think of only two missing items in her life; a mother and a best girlfriend. These past few days she had walked around with a permanent grin, wishing she had another woman to confide in. She and Frankie had made love in a fit of giggles, mostly because Kendra couldn't stop talking.

"Please turn off the lights."

"Why?"

"You'll see my fat rolls."

"I don't care if you have fat rolls."

"That's because it's not your fat!"

Fit of giggles, lights off, then Frankie tripped finding his way back to bed.

"Where'd ya go?"

"I'm under the covers, hiding my body."

Fit of giggles.

"I think you're missing the point of what we're about to do!"

"Fine, but promise you won't laugh."

"At what?"

"At me. I think one boob is bigger than the other."

More giggles.

"Kendra, c'mere," said Frankie, feeling for her hand. He pulled her close and kissed her lightly.

"Do I have bad breath? I can gargle, I brought some Listerine."

"Shhh," said Frankie, tracing the outline of her lips and kissing her again.

Kendra was drawn to utter silence as he slid his hand down the center of her spine, sending chills throughout her body. She had never felt such lust before. When the big moment came, Kendra began talking anxiously.

"Don't look at it."

"At what?"

"My coochie."

"Your *what?*"

"My no-no, my coochie, my hoo-ha. Just don't look at it."

"How can I not look at it? It's beautiful."

"My hoo-ha is beautiful? Really?"

"Really."

"So is yours."

"I don't have a hoo-ha."

Giggles.

"You ready?" Frankie said, his voice laden with sleepy lust.

"As ready as I'll ever be. Stick it to me."

"You really are romantic," Frankie smiled, gently easing his way in.

"Oh!"

"What?!"

"Nothing. Just oh. I thought I should say something."

And then, much quicker than she had liked, the event ended.

Frankie gave a final moan. Kendra moaned back in return, not because she had an orgasm, but because she didn't want him to think she didn't. He leaned over and kissed Kendra, then flipped onto his back.

"You didn't get off, did you?" he asked apologetically.

Not wanting to hurt his feelings, she replied, "If I didn't, I was damn close. It was great!"

Frankie's smile faded into a worried frown.

Kendra poked his side. "It's okay, Frankie. I had fun. Honestly, I don't know if I could've handled more!"

"It's not that," he said, absently chewing on his bottom lip.

"What is it?"

"This is going to sound foolish, but I almost feel too lucky. It's like I'm waiting for the shit to hit the fan."

"Well, I won't toss anything into the wind if you promise not to," she laughed.

"What if I told you I wasn't always such a nice guy?"

"None of us are always nice, Frankie. Wait," she said over dramatically, "Did you pick on fat girls?"

"I did more than pick on fat girls," he replied guiltily.

Kendra nuzzled into Frankie's neck. "We're not even nineteen years old, Frankie. Get real. Every kid has regrets. That's part of growing up. Kids can be crummy. You shouldn't have such a guilty conscience," she said, reaching over him to grab a bag of chips off the nightstand.

* * *

After they made love, Frankie confessed he hadn't always been a nice guy, but shied away from details.

"So you'd still like me even if I did some bad things?" he asked.

"Do you still do bad things?" she questioned, through a mouth full of chips.

"No."

"Then what does it matter? You can't change what you did. Besides, my grandfather was worse than you could ever be."

"He was?"

"Sure, he was a *real* thug. He smoked and drank and gambled and hung out with street gangs. His mother shot his father."

"She did?" asked Frankie, hoping to hear even worse to alleviate his own conscience.

"Yeah," said Kendra, in a dramatic voice. "So you can just feel better about yourself. I mean c'mon, it's not like you ever killed anybody," she winked.

And then Kendra began singing Barry Manilow's *Can't Smile Without You.*

Frankie closed his eyes and listened to Kendra's raspy voice, but found it hard to ignore the sense of oxygen deprivation. Air was leaving his lungs, but none was returning. When he couldn't stand the sense of suffocation a second longer, he excused himself.

"Need some water, be right back."

As Kendra dozed contentedly, Frankie stood in the bathroom breathing in through his nose, slowly out through pursed lips. He tipped his head sideways and took a few sips from the sink nozzle. Instant nausea. He turned on the shower and, kneeling as close as he could without immersing his head, vomited his past into the toilet bowl.

AUGUST'S PAST, IN BRIEF

August's harsh cough startled him awake.

"Kendra, did you finish your homework? Kendra, don't be a pain in the arse girl, answer me."

Met with silence, August looked at the time. It was four in the morning. He'd been dreaming again. Kendra had been gone for months now, off to college and dating that Frankie boy. With his granddaughter away, August seemed to lose track of time, intermittently sleeping through the days and nights. If it weren't for Sheri's visits, Sunday Mass, and his trips to Kmart, he was sure he'd slowly go mad.

On the side table next to the clock was a picture of Kendra as an infant. Two young people were holding her, smiling widely into the camera. August's son, Sal, and his girlfriend, Heidi, had sworn eternal love after only two weeks of dating. August mistook their relationship for immature puppy love that wouldn't last, but a year later, Kendra was born. When Kendra was two months old, Heidi and Sal asked August to babysit so they could go to a friend's wedding. Eighteen years and counting, and they still hadn't returned. It took August two years to come to terms with the fact that his son had abandoned his daughter, and another year before he contacted Heidi's mother, Mary Catherine.

Mary Catherine had offered to take Kendra, but August refused to let her go. She lived clear across town, tucked away in an Irish Catholic neighborhood, which was nothing like the Italian one in which August resided, and no place that he wanted his granddaughter raised. Mary Catherine's neighborhood was stagnant and smelled of moss, while a walk through August's neighborhood was like taking your nose on a date. The Contrado's smelled of meatballs, the Pappeleo's of sausage, pepper and onion, the Scaccia's of fish fried to perfection, and Sheri

219

Rizollo's (who wasn't Italian at all, but who cooked like one) of warm baked goods.

This neighborhood, unlike Mary Catherine's, would never know a boiled dinner or gravy from a jar. Everyone was dark and loud and prattled on in different Italian dialects. The front of every home was lined with small, tight, neatly clipped bushes that were surrounded by pansies and snapdragons. Porches were filled with rocking and folding chairs, and cars were parked in front of houses so that driveways could be utilized as a spectator arena. Seated in folding chairs in the driveways were rows of older Italians who overfed cookies to the neighborhood kids and crammed their ears with stories from their youth. If you did own a backyard, you didn't use it because the action was out front. Side yards, visible to the street with bocce courts, were the new backyard. No one asked about anyone's business because the walls were thin enough, the doors and windows always open; no one had to ask because everyone knew each other's business. However, when challenged by the cops or a lawyer, no one knew anything. If the neighborhood felt the need to intervene in your life, they did so without your permission, descending upon you like a mini mob.

Kendra blended perfectly with this environment. Believing his granddaughter's dark features would have clashed in an Irish neighborhood, he informed Mary Catherine she was welcome to visit any time, but that Kendra would stay with him. Mary Catherine grudgingly agreed and visited Kendra weekly for six months before suffering a fatal heart attack, proof from God himself that August did the right thing to keep Kendra by his side.

When Kendra asked August about her parents and her mother's side of the family, he claimed to know nothing about nothing. He thought it best to cut all ties and start from scratch.

"You don't even know how my parents met?"

"I think they were in high school together."

"You remember stories about hoodlums and movies that cost a quarter, but you can't recall how my parents met? Geez, Grampy."

"Ah, give an old man a break, will ya?"

"Will you at least try to remember?"

"I'll try."

"Promise you'll try?"

"I promise I'll try."

"Swear to God, and may God strike me dead right now if you're not telling the truth that you'll try?"

"What the hell kinda crap is that? I said I'd try. Now, make like an egg and beat it. And stop gnawing on your fingers. Pretty soon you'll start eating your fingertips off."

This is what August didn't tell Kendra: Sal and Heidi began dating at the end of their senior year in high school, when they both seemed what August would call normal. After graduation, Sal announced he was not going to college, but instead was getting a full-time job. August didn't see any harm in Sal's decision. There was nothing wrong with a hardworking man, so he encouraged his son to do whatever made him happy.

Sal said he was going to take a few weeks off to relax, but at the end of the summer he remained jobless, and August suspected, on drugs. And as if his son being a druggie and a bum weren't enough to give August heartburn, the couple announced that they were leaving the Catholic Church and converting to witchcraft. That's when Mary Catherine went off her rocker and disowned Heidi. Heidi cleaned out her savings and rented a shanty of an apartment with peeling wallpaper and a queen size mattress that lay on the floor. She and Sal got jobs at a fast food restaurant and against August's better judgment, Sal moved in with Heidi, but still they stopped by August's for a home cooked meal three days a week. After two months their funds dried up. Sal begged August to take pity on them, and August reluctantly agreed to let them live in the basement.

As much as he loved his son, it disgusted August to see Sal in such a state of disease. August blamed himself for the way Sal turned out. For the first ten years of his life, Sal had been exposed to drinking, gambling, eviction threats, and a prodigal father.

"Can I have a sip of your wine?" Sal had asked when he was nine.

"Go ahead," said August, pushing his glass toward him.

Sal took a small sip and spit it all over the table. He scrunched his face in disgust and wiped his tongue off with a napkin.

"Bleck!"

August laughed. "You don't want to start that habit, son."

"When did you start the habit?" asked Sal.

"When I was six years old."

"Na-ah," said Sal.

"It's true. It was normal to have wine in my house. In fact, we used to make our own wine."

"How do you do that?"

"At first, my sisters stomped on the grapes. Then someone up the street bought a grape churner and we borrowed it. That churner saved their poor feet."

"Did you drink all the time?"

"Yes."

"How much?"

"I was drunk more than not. I think that's why when I got older I could consume so much and not be affected."

"What's so much? Like three glasses or something?" asked an innocent faced Sal.

"No, like twenty shots in a row."

"Twenty?"

"Sure, then I drove home cause I didn't even feel drunk," he said, with almost too much swank.

"You're lucky you didn't die," scolded Sal.

"We all die, son," shrugged August. "It's just a matter of when."

On any given workday, it was nothing for August to down seven shots of whiskey before work. To keep his body from getting the shakes, he hid liquor bottles along his truck route, under bushes and behind sheds.

"Mom says if you drink too much you become an alcoholic."

"Well, I drink too much and I'm not one."

"How do you know you're not one?"

"I'm a drunk, not an alcoholic."

"That makes no sense."

"Sure it does. An alcoholic doesn't go to work. I never miss a day's work. An alcoholic can't stop boozing. Every Lent, I stop drinking the hard stuff," he said proudly. "If I was an alcoholic, I couldn't have stopping drinking four to five quarts of whiskey a week now, could

I have? The booze never had me by the throat and I've never felt I couldn't live without it," August said proudly.

"I don't know about that, Papa."

"Aw, what the hell do you know, you're just a kid."

August's wife would often announce that with all he put her through, she was sure to die of a broken heart. He laughed lightly, misinterpreting her stress for drama. One evening, while he was out gambling the rent money, his wife had a heart attack in front of Sal. August came home to his wife on the floor and his son weeping on top of her stomach.

Sobering instantly, he asked, "What happened here?"

"You must've really broke her heart this time, Papa!" sobbed Sal.

From that night forward, August put down the hard liquor and only gambled for chump change. Even though he tried to make up for lost time, he was sure those early years affected Sal. He confessed to a priest that he was over his head with raising the boy, and for a brief second, he questioned whether sending him to live with his sister would be a better alternative than living with his own father. The priest talked him out of it, and August did the best he could. Throughout the rest Sal's childhood, August lived with the guilt of his past and worst of all, with the fear of not knowing he lost Sal until after he had lost him. And now, August believed that he was being punished for his sins through his son.

"Your son's a drug addict," Sheri Rizollo told him.

"Mind your own damn business."

"You just keep him on your side of the fence. If anything goes missing, he'll be the first one people blame."

"My son is no thief."

"No, August," she said harshly, "Not yet. But he is a drug addict, and drug addicts are desperate people."

"Keep your opinions to yourself," he barked.

"If you'll allow me to help—"

"I don't want that kind of help, Sheri. I don't want *you.*"he barked, ignoring her very pink face.

Sheri Rizollo spun on her heel and stormed off. Of course, she turned out to be right. Sal was caught stealing by August on many occasions. He would swipe money from his father's wallet and hock anything he could get his hands on, including August's thick gold rope chain. He received multiple final warnings, but August never followed through on his threats. When Heidi got pregnant, August threatened to kick them both out on the street if she didn't put down the drugs. To his great relief, she managed to stay clean, but it was a frenetic clean. She was jittery and trembled and had to be force fed. Her face was covered in acne and her personal hygiene was horrible. Her greasy, straggly hair hung in front of her eyes and she had pungent body odor. August had to remind the girl to shower.

"I'm kinda scared," she confessed to August not long before she was due to give birth.

"You should be. Look at you. You don't even know how to care for yourself. How you gonna be a momma?"

"Do you think Sal will get a job now?"

Beyond the surface mess that she was, August saw a fearful child with sparkly green eyes and freckly skin.

"Let's hope so," he said, pessimistically.

"Will you help, August? Help with the baby if I can't do it?"

"What the hell you talking about? You can do it, Heidi. You just need to keep doing what you're doing and you'll be fine."

"What if I'm not? What if I start taking drugs again?"

"What are you saying, girl?"

Heidi broke down into tears. "I can't watch Sal use without aching for it, August. I'm frightened."

August placed a dish of asparagus mixed with egg, cheese, and tomato in front of her.

"Stop that baloney and eat this food I cooked for you. It will make the baby strong."

"First promise me you'll help," she said, blinking back tears. "Promise you'll help with this baby."

"All right, all right," he huffed. "I'll help you. Now, eat girl. You don't look big enough to have a baby in your stomach."

That night August gave Sal an ultimatum.

"Stop using or you're out. Heidi will stay, but you're gone. You're having a kid, *stupida pazza di merda*, now snap out of it."

Sal was able to remain clean for close to four weeks. August had regained hope for the couple, until Kendra was born. Instead of making things better, the child's birth seemed to worsen matters. Within weeks, August witnessed Heidi's lack of interest in her child. Her desire for a high overrode all else. Soon enough, her eyes carried the familiar glazed over expression of a heroin addict; one that no longer was shooting up to get high, but that needed to get high to feel normal.

To this day, August waited hopefully for his son's return. It didn't matter which Sal returned; the shadow of a son who lived in a chemical euphoria, or the son in the photograph, the one who looked like he was gonna make something of himself. August loved them both. His eyes welled with tears and his raspy cough filled the empty house. Maybe it was a good thing this Frankie came along when he did, because his Kendra needed a man who would look after her. Time, August knew, was not on his side.

FALL, 1984

August wanted to meet Frankie right away, but Kendra held off in case she and Frankie didn't work out. The last thing she wanted was to open her home to a man just to be dumped by him.

"It's been a year."

"Yep."

"Why you hiding him?"

"I'm not. I told you, I'm just not ready to bring him round."

"He's black, isn't he? That's why you won't bring him here. You're dating a black boy."

"No, he's not black. And what if he was?"

"Don't give me any liberal shit now," he warned. "You don't mix races. We're different colors for a reason. He's a Chinese then?"

"I'm just nervous. What if we break up?"

"So what if you do?"

"Then I'll be embarrassed."

"About what?"

"Him knowing all about me. I'll be vulnerable and exposed."

"Exposed? What's he gonna find out here? Are we aliens or something? Bring the boy around, Patatona."

"Okay, okay! Calm down, geez."

"Don't you geez me. You just get him here. Frankie's a spic name."

"Gramps, stop it. You might be racist, but I'm not."

"I don't care what you are. You just ain't dating any spics."

"He's not Spanish. He's not black. He's not Chinese. He's white. Very white."

"Not too white, I hope? He doesn't look like a harp, does he?"

"He looks like a blond-haired Italian boy."

226

"That's perfect," he smiled. "If he's too pink you get the babies that look like ghosts and burn in the sun."

Kendra looked at him with disgust. Was it any wonder she didn't want Frankie to come here?

"I'm warning you, don't you dare open your mouth and say anything stupid in front of him."

"What, me? I never say stupid things. You know that."

She rolled her eyes to heaven. "Frankie comes from a quiet home. It's just him and his mother, and his mother is very educated."

"Meaning what?"

"Meaning you might offend him by making stupid comments like you're doing now. And you'll embarrass me by shoving giant meatballs into that pie hole of yours and then talking with your mouth full."

"You ashamed of me, Patatona?"

"Of course not, Gramps."

"Well, you're telling me how to act it seems."

"No, no. Act like you, only not as harsh."

"I get it," he shook his head. "Pretend I have manners."

"Exactly!"

*   *   *

"But it's our one year anniversary. I thought we could celebrate the entire weekend, starting with drinks and a movie," sulked Frankie.

"Yeah, me too," she said, squeezing his hand. "But I can't leave my grandfather alone all weekend. He looks forward to me being there."

"Aw, c'mon, Ken, one weekend won't kill him."

"Well, now that you said that, I have to go. You could have cursed him," she said, making the sign of the cross.

"Stop crossing yourself, it's not going to help," Frankie laughed, trying to push her hand away from her forehead.

Kendra leaned back. "Just let me do it three times to be sure," she said, her face set in concentration.

"What about the old hag bag, or whatever you call her? Can't she keep him company?"

Kendra snorted out a laugh. "Ms. Rizollo doesn't come on the weekends. She respects our privacy."

"More like she's scared of you," he joked.

"She'd better be. She's not stealing my grandfather away! Besides, you're coming over to meet him on Sunday. It's not like we won't see each other at all, and you should really go visit your mother. You haven't seen her in a while, and I don't want her to think I'm keeping you from her."

Knowing he wasn't going to get his way, Frankie pouted.

Kendra yanked him by the collar and kissed him hard on the lips.

"Sunday, Frankie, is only two days away."

*   *   *

By nine o'clock Saturday morning, August was already making Sunday's gravy. Kendra walked lazily toward the kitchen inhaling the aroma of her childhood.

"Morning Gramps."

"Morning Patatona, you ready for some breakfast?"

"I think I'll shower first. Call me when the mailman comes."

"Why, you waiting for an invitation to the White House or something?"

"For your information, I'm waiting for my anniversary card," she replied, a bit too surly before stomping off down the hall.

"Women," August mumbled, taste testing the thick red sauce.

Normally, Kendra wouldn't have given her body a second glance while undressing, but this time she scrutinized it, turning this way and that.

Thighs not too flabby, small waist, soft round stomach, large breasts, arms, eh, too jiggly. Other than that, she thought, slapping her behind, *not bad.*

She reached for the Prell and shampooed her long, black hair that Frankie loved to run his fingers through. *Silky smooth* is what he called it. Moments like that made Kendra pinch her arm to make sure she wasn't dreaming. During her high school years she stayed home most weekends, isolating herself with movies and food. In college, she transformed into the free-spirited party girl she'd always wanted to be. Now almost twenty pounds lighter and more self-assured than she had ever been, she'd give her left arm for the kids back home to see her driving around in a Trans Am with her handsome boyfriend.

Beside her grades, which were in the average to below average range, it was a fair assessment that college had been kind to Kendra. She wasn't planning on doing anything but drawing for the rest of her life, so what did a C here and there matter? Besides, Frankie was a straight A student. He'd take care of the finances and manage their bills, and all that other complicated stuff.

At eleven o'clock, Kendra ran to the door and flung it wide open startling the mailman, whose hand almost got stuck in the slot.

"Er, sorry, Earl," she said, biting her lower lip.

"Kids," Earl mumbled, handing her a magazine, some bills, and an envelope with Kendra's name on it. She rushed to the kitchen table and tore open the envelope. The card was a picture of two lovebirds with their beaks touching, the space between them shaped like a heart. She read the inside aloud.

"We do fine apart, but we're better together, you fill up my heart, we're like birds of a feather. Happy Anniversary, Ken. Love, Frankie."

The best part was that when Kendra opened the card, ten sugar packets fell onto the floor. She skipped lightly to the stove and held it up to August's face.

"Lookit this, isn't he adorable!"

August made a gagging reflex. "Damn birds."

"Just admit it, he's good!"

"Okay, okay," said August, still stirring the sauce. "He seems like a fine boy. He'd better treat you right, is all I got to say."

"He does," she replied, leaning in and smelling the sauce. "Can I have a meatball?"

"They're for tomorrow, for you and *loverrrrboy*," he taunted.

"What's for lunch?"

"What are you making?" teased August.

"You know I can't cook."

"No, I know you don't cook. I spoiled you."

"Good point," she agreed. "You need to teach me soon."

"So you can cook for your *loverrrrboy?*"

"In fact, yes," she beamed. "I want to learn how to cook fine Italian cuisine."

August went to the fridge and took out ham, eggs, and cheese. He walked back to the stove where a skillet was heating up. Cracking the eggs into the hot oil, he gestured to a chair. Kendra sighed and sat down.

"What. You want me to learn to cook now?"

"No, I'm not prepared for my kitchen's downfall just yet."

"Uh-oh, what did I do?" she said, shifting in her seat.

"Patatona, I don't want to ask, but as your only guardian, I got to. Besides, I didn't think you'd appreciate Sheri coming and asking."

Kendra's stomach did a flip flop. "Ask what?"

"You need to discuss anything?"

Kendra flushed. "Oh God, is this a lame attempt at a sex talk?"

"Shhh, don't say the word out loud."

"Are you kidding me? With all that you tell me, you can't say the word sex?"

August cringed and closed his eyes. "I can't do this. You need a woman."

"No, I'm fine. It's fine, Gramps," she said, opening a bag of chocolate chip cookies.

"You two been going out for a while. You might need something sometime. A doctor, or something else."

Kendra crossed herself, folded her hands in prayer, and began reciting, "Hail Mary, full of grace . . ."

"I've got a responsibility to ask, but I beg of you, lie to me."

". . . the Lord is with thee," she continued, covering her ears.

"I got to ask."

"Don't . . . blessed art thou among women . . ."

"Here it comes."

"Shoot me now . . . and blessed is the fruit of thy womb . . ."

"Are you two bumping uglies yet?"

Kendra's jaw dropped open and her hands fell to her lap. They stared at each other, and then broke out into a gale of laughter.

"Don't be silly," she said, wiping her teary eyes. "Nothing is going on," she said, honoring August's request that she lie.

"All kidding aside," he said, taking her hands in his, "I'm your grandfather. You come to me first if you need anything. I may faint from the shock, but I'll give it my best try."

"Will it rival the shock of the pizzelle machine?" she asked, quickly adding the sign of the cross and saying, "May it rest in peace."

August copied her by crossing himself and then said, "The pizzelle machine, may it rest in peace, was pebbles compared to my love for you."

Kendra hugged her grandfather. "I love you, Gramps."

"I love you more, Patatona."

"But can I just say, *bumping uglies*? You couldn't think of a nicer way to approach that?" she asked.

They laughed out of embarrassment, out of silliness, and because both parties knew that they were lying horribly. August didn't want her confessing anything to him, and she would never disclose she had sex before she got married. He would swallow a rosary whole if she began blabbering, and she would rather die a thousand horrible deaths than discuss her sex life with her grandfather. She wasn't about to admit that she'd been on the pill for three months and before that had used condoms. Technically, she should still be using condoms, but she was foolishly in love. She believed Frankie when he said that before she came along he wasn't big on sex and had no reason to think he had any diseases.

And if it turned out he did have a disease that would kill them both, they'd die together, just like Bonnie and Clyde. Well, except for the robberies, police chases, and a climactic bloody shootout.

But together nonetheless.

* * *

Kendra phoned Frankie on Saturday night.

"You're still coming?"

"Of course I am."

"I've warned him to be on his best behavior," she said, her voice full of worry.

"I'm sure he'll be fine," Frankie reassured her. If Kendra had only known where he came from, she wouldn't be worrying about an old man like August.

Kendra's grandfather tried his best to remain composed during Sunday dinner. Though this was their first time meeting, Frankie had heard enough about August to tell that he was struggling, and that sooner or later, he'd have to resort back to being himself. His attempt at being polite lasted approximately twenty minutes.

"What's your nationality?"

Frankie tried to remember what Karen said she was. "English."

"Just plain English?"

"Just plain English," Frankie repeated.

"You look too dark to be just plain English. You looked mixed with somethin'."

To listen to August, you could tell he wasn't all that bright. Frankie took a chance by replying, "We're from the dark side of England." He doubted August would chance embarrassing himself by asking where the dark side of England was. He also knew that Kendra, though a brilliant painter, was not a student. The lie was a small risk, one he was certain he would get away with.

August shrugged, "Eh, that's okay. We can put lots of sun protector on the babies if they come out light."

"Babies?" Frankie questioned.

"Gramps!" Kendra bellowed.

Frankie suppressed a grin at the look on Kendra's face; she was flushed red with embarrassment.

"Whhhattt? With you kids, everything's a crisis," he laughed.

"So Frankie," said August, pausing to slurp his wine, "Did you bring any dessert? Kendra said you were going to bring something."

Frankie produced a box that had been sitting on the chair next to him. "It's from an Italian pastry shop," he smiled proudly. "It's called ricotta cake."

"Ricotta pie," Kendra corrected.

"My favorite," said August, clearly impressed. "Hand it over, boy, and I'll cut it up."

Frankie watched in awe as August engulfed a whole slice in two large chomps. He leaned into Kendra and giggled, "Now I know where you get it from."

"Yeah," she replied. "Imagine what I'd look like if I didn't hold back!"

Frankie took one bite and pushed the plate aside. Thick like paste and sweet like a cookie, Ricotta pie had to be an acquired taste.

"That was the best!" Kendra said, licking her lips.

"Anything Italian is the best," August remarked.

"Almost everything," she said, glancing at Frankie.

"Pass the pie," said August, ignoring Kendra's lovesick remark.

"Here's a fast fact," said Kendra, licking her lips. "This pie is one of our many Christmas traditions, so thank you for bringing Christmas early."

"No problem," smiled Frankie, inwardly cursing himself for sounding stuffy.

"What are the traditions at your house? What do you people do for the holidays?" asked August.

"The holidays?"

"Yeah, like for Christmas, where did you go?"

"Church," was the first thing that came to Frankie's mind.

"There's a good boy," nodded August, crumbs flying out of his mouth.

Under the table, Frankie drummed his fingers nervously along his scarred arm. How could he tell Kendra where he had come from? How could he say he was adopted at fifteen years old and rescued from a world that offered nothing but bleak chaos?

"And we make apple cobbler," he added, replacing his traumatic childhood with false memories.

AUGUST

August was having an exceptional week. Last Sunday's dinner with Kendra and Frankie went better than expected. The boy seemed like a standup character. The knowledge that Kendra was cared for must be the reason he had been feeling like a million dollars. His sensory perceptions were heightened. His vision was sharp, food tasted and smelled delicious, and his body ached less than it had in ten years. He was in such good spirits that if a hurricane swept up his house, he would find a way to smile about it. Sheri's banana bread tasted like the best bread in the world, warm and moist and loaded with walnuts and chunks of banana that melted in your mouth. Kendra called to say she got an A-minus on her math test, her first ever A-minus in math! Jerry Springer had an all new episode about *Who's my real Dad?* with paternity testing where you had to wait on the edge of your chair for the results. And just for today, even his cough had subsided. August wondered if this were a sign that his son was finally coming home. He glanced at the familiar picture of two young parents with a beautiful baby cupped between them and smiled.

"Ah, mio figlio," he said, daydreaming of the good old days when he used to push Sal on a tire swing at the playground. The ringing of the phone tore him from his thoughts.

"Hal-llo."

"Hi, Gramps."

"Patatona, what gives?"

"For starters, Happy Birthday!"

"Awww, shit on my birthday. I'm too old for those anymore. What's second?"

"I'm feeling like an A student in math for once in my life!"

"See, I told you them brains were in there somewhere. Good girl, Patatona. I'm proud of you."

"Thanks. I'm proud of me, too! I can't wait to eat a good meal, which reminds me, what are you making for dinner? You remembered Frankie and his mother are coming, right?"

"What am I, a restaurant?"

"Gramps, she's all alone. And we both know how that feels."

"Eh, I'm pulling your leg, Patatona. Of course his old lady can come. I got fried eggplant and pasta all ready."

"Gramps?"

"What is it?"

"Ti amo."

"In Italian, Patatona? What did I do to deserve that?"

"Nothing. It just came over me."

"I love you, too, Kendra. Now, get the hell off the phone. I got things to do."

August hung up the phone with a smile. If his Isabella were alive, she would have adored Kendra. And Sal would be proud of her sarcastic personality and strong will. Although Kendra hadn't mentioned that she'd bring anything, August was sure she'd show up with balloons, a cake, and her annual photo mug. He decided to surprise her as well with a homemade ricotta pie. He whistled tunes from his past while he dressed for the market. He shrugged on his jacket and placed his hat on his head. His hand was on the doorknob when he felt a small tickle at the back of his throat and began to cough. He paused, trying to decide whether to get a glass of water or to bring some cough drops with him on his walk.

"I'll bring some cough drops," he mumbled.

He crossed the kitchen and opened the cabinet, his cough escalating with each step. He poured himself a glass of cold water and tried to take a sip, but the cough prevented him from swallowing. Short of breath, he leaned onto the sink for support. Two massive coughs later, August spit up a chunk of blood the size of a small teacup. Still unable to catch his wind, he backed himself into his kitchen chair and tried to calm himself. A suffocating panic overwhelmed him, and just when he thought he wasn't going to catch his breath, he inhaled sharply.

"Ah, that's better," he said.

Then, to his surprise, August heard a voice that he hadn't heard for years, a voice he had yearned for, a voice that could melt his heart.

"August?"

Just to his left stood a small, blurry figure.

"Chi è? Isabella?"

The tiny woman smiled and held out her hand. Relieved, August raised his arm and his hand met hers. He rose, leaving behind the limp body slumped in his favorite kitchen chair.

"Time to go?" he asked his wife.

"Time to go," she repeated, escorting her husband to a room that suddenly appeared next to his kitchen, like it had always been there if only he had been paying attention. It was occupied with loved ones from his past. Just before he crossed the threshold, he hesitated.

"What's wrong, August?"

"What about Kendra?"

"She'll be taken care of."

"How can I be sure?"

Isabella smiled warmly. "You did fine by yourself, didn't you?"

"I was lonely by myself. I don't want that for her."

"But you were never truly alone. I was just over here," she said, pointing toward the room. "I was waiting for you right here."

August looked past his wife to the extravagant room that held a long dining table filled with August's favorite foods. The room was adorned with Tuscan-style furniture that was occupied by his mother, his sisters, his favorite aunt, and even Sully and Crazy Louie.

"Something smells good," he smiled.

"Come, August," said Isabella warmly.

"Are you sure my Patatona will be okay?"

"She's a strong woman who takes after her grandfather."

"Then I guess it will be okay to wait right here for her, like you did for me. Will you wait with me?"

"For as long as it takes," smiled Isabella, leading August into the arms of his loved ones.

* * *

Kendra had it all figured out. She and Frankie would pick up Karen and then drive to August's for his birthday. Originally, it was just going to be Frankie and Kendra, but when Frankie mentioned to Karen that it was August's birthday, Karen offered her services as official shopper and cake purchaser.

Before she could ask, Kendra explained to Karen that her parents had abandoned her when she was an infant.

"I'm sorry that happened to you," said Karen.

"Yeah, it sucks. Since I was a kid, I've been trying to figure out what I've done wrong."

"You've done nothing wrong," Karen said, and then, "You know that, right?"

"Most of the time I do, but sometimes I'm not so sure."

While Frankie and Kendra studied for midterms, Karen followed the list that Kendra had given her; fluffy foam slippers with extra arch support, a dozen balloons, rum cake. Kendra had bought August a mug with her picture on it like she did every year for his birthday. As a result, August's cabinet was lined with mugs that had the ever changing face of Kendra Bruno imprinted on them.

Arriving at the house, the trio quietly shut the car doors. They opened the back door and tiptoed through a small hallway to a door that opened into the kitchen. When they reached the threshold, Kendra turned to them and brought her finger to her lips.

"I want to sneak up on him. He'll be so happy!" she smiled.

"Will we frighten him?" wondered Karen.

"No, but I have an idea," giggled Kendra. "You go first, Frankie. Peek in and see what he's doing."

Frankie eased open the door, took one last look at Kendra and then, with a wink and a smile, crept into the room. Kendra felt, more than saw, Frankie's entire body stiffen. He automatically dropped his arm down, pushing back against Kendra's thigh and blocking the entrance.

"What is it, Frankie? Look out, will ya?" said Kendra.

When she tried to muscle past him, his other hand, which had been strategically balancing the rum cake, gave way, spilling its contents onto the floor.

Kendra shook her head and said, "What's wrong with you? Move right now, you silly—"

"Gramps? Gramps? Grampy!" Kendra screamed, running toward August who lay slumped in the chair. Beneath her shoes, almonds and frosting from the rum cake crunched and smeared the brown linoleum. In her haste to reach him, Kendra slipped on the mess and fell to her knees. Not bothering to get up, she crawled hastily to her grandfather.

"Gramps?" she whimpered, stroking his shoe like a kitten.

"Kendra, honey. Let me help," said Karen, gently urging Kendra to her feet. Kendra rose slowly, vertebra by vertebra, and as she did she noted August's blood stained shirt.

"Oh, Gramps!" she bawled, hiding her face in her hands.

Karen motioned for Frankie to come and take her place beside Kendra.

"I'll be back in a minute, honey," she whispered. "I'm going to get some things to clean him up." She removed her hand and quickly placed Frankie's in its spot, but Kendra shook it off.

"I need a minute alone," she said.

"No problem," said Frankie, relieved of his duty.

As soon as Frankie and Karen tiptoed down the hallway, Kendra, who still had her face burrowed in her hands, collapsed at her grandfather's feet. She made a V with her right pointer and middle finger and peeked through it. Sure enough, he was dead. She closed the V and continued to sob until she felt a chill at the nape of her neck and heard a very faint voice that sounded as if it were coming from outside.

"*Hey,*" it said.

She recognized that voice. She dropped her hand and slowly raised her eyes. Behind August, less translucent than she had ever appeared, stood the ghost girl. Aggravation overshadowed both grief and surprise.

"You," she whispered harshly.

"Yes, it's me, Meg!" said the ghost, quite pleased to be noticed and remembered.

"What are you doing here?"

"I don't know. One minute I was enjoying the sunset and the next thing you know—ZAP," she said, snapping her fingers in genuine amazement.

Looking at Meg standing over August reminded Kendra of a show she once saw that described how ghosts come and take dead people away, almost like an escort.

"No, please don't take him! Please don't take him away!" she begged, crisscrossing her hands over her heart.

"What?"

"My grandfather. Don't take him," sobbed Kendra, holding August's hand.

Her sudden movement caused Meg to look down.

"Ohhhhh. Oh, my. This looks bad. Is he? Who is he?"

"My grandfather. And stop pretending like you don't know what's happening. You're here to take him away."

"I am?" she asked. "Cuz nobody told me that."

"Oh, don't give me that," Kendra spat accusingly "Now put back his soul, you soul-sucking wench, you evil demon spawn, you put back his soul right now!"

"But I don't have his soul. I'm just as confused to be here as you are to see me."

"Hey, wait a minute. How come I can see you like this, outside of a mirror and all?"

"Beats me," shrugged Meg.

Kendra looked from August to Meg, then behind Meg into the empty pantry.

"C-can you see him? Is he with you?"

"I dunno. I don't think so."

"Well, look behind you or something. Is there something there I can't see?"

Meg did as Kendra instructed.

"I don't see anyone else. I'm alone, as usual."

Then Meg squinted at Kendra.

"Do *you* see anyone else?"

Kendra huffed, "Now why would I be asking you the same question if I could see for myself, you numbskull?"

"Chill out, geez. I'm not the one seeing ghosts, you are," Meg sulked.

"Oh, like I'm an expert."

Both parties fell silent long enough for Meg to examine the man Kendra called her grandfather. He was old and gruff looking with thick, sharp whiskers.

"If you're not here to steal his soul, then why the hell are you here?" barked Kendra, her voice like a metal blade trying to slice through Meg.

"God, don't snap a cord," said Meg.

Meg wasn't sure why she was here, but this Kendra girl was nasty. Why God would make her the only human Meg could see was just plain cruel. Away from the peace of her field where all her wishes were granted, Meg felt a bubbling anger toward Kendra. In fact, she kind of felt like her hormonal teenage self again. She stuck out her chest and said, "If I were alive, you'd be cruisin' for a brusin'."

Kendra leaned forward and snarled, "Oh, really? You think you can take me, ghost girl?"

"You're all talk," spat Meg.

"Yeah? You're an asshole."

"Shit stain."

"Dweeb."

"Hemorrhoid."

A slight grin passed across Kendra's tear stained face. "Good one. You're a turd face, ghost girl, you know that?"

Meg grinned back.

"So I've been told."

After a momentary silence, Kendra whispered, "Meg?"

"Yes?" Meg whispered back.

"Where's my grandfather? Is he in heaven already?"

Meg's eyes filled with pity. "I don't know, but I'm sure that wherever he is, he's okay."

"How do you know that?"

"Because when I'm not here, I'm in the best place in the world. I'm sure you're grandfather is in his own best place."

"If you ever run into him, will you let me know?"

"Kendra?" Karen and Frankie stood in the doorway, Karen wearing an expression of uncertainty. She had clearly witnessed Kendra speaking to something that wasn't there. Frankie looked empty, like he had taken leave from his body.

"Mom?" cried Meg.

Kendra's head snapped back toward Meg. "Mom?"

"Who's that boy . . . wait a minute. I know him."

"You know who?"

"Him."

"What are you talking about?" Kendra hissed under her breath.

"I'm talking about my mom and that boy," said Meg, pointing toward Karen.

"Whose mom? No, she's not my—", but Meg was fading in and out like a holographic image.

"Kendra? Are you okay?" asked Karen, in a *I'm a social worker and do you need medication* way.

Kendra looked at Karen and when she looked back to Meg, she was gone.

"I'm fine. I thought I saw," she began, pointing to where Meg stood.

Frankie's face became pinched with worry.

"Ken?"

"You see," she sniffed, "A few years ago, I went to the library and got this book to bring back my—"

Kendra stopped when she saw Frankie and Karen exchange a cautionary glance.

"I'm just a bit disoriented is all," she whimpered.

What was she thinking? If she told them what she saw, they'd think she was bonkers. This was definitely a case where the truth wouldn't set her free. In fact, now all alone in the world, the truth would certainly end her in a nuthouse.

"Honey?" Karen said, lightly touching Kendra's shoulder. "Let's clean him up a bit."

Kendra didn't answer.

"Frankie, could you come and help Kendra?"

Karen might as well have been talking to infants.

"Frankie?" It wasn't until Karen said a stern, "Frank-kie." that Frankie seemed to return to planet earth.

"Come help Kendra," she repeated in an encouraging tone you would give to a small, insecure child who got lost on task.

Frankie obediently walked over and knelt beside Kendra, and Kendra felt the familiar touch of the man she loved lifting her away from the grandfather she would never get to love again.

"No, no, no, don't you touch me!" she wriggled.

"Shhh," said Frankie, folding Kendra into his arms. "Shhh. We'll just sit over here while Mom cleans up."

"Don't hurt him," Kendra whimpered.

"I won't," Karen said, recalling the night she saw Meg at the morgue. "I'll be as gentle as I can," she promised.

*   *   *

"You feeling okay?" Karen asked her father anxiously.

"Perfectly. Why?"

"No coughs or anything?"

Carl laughed. "What are you going on about?"

"I've had a day from hell. We just got back from Kendra's house. We found her grandfather in the kitchen. He passed."

"Passed out?" he questioned.

"Passed on," she corrected.

"As in dead?"

Karen licked her lips and recounted the day's events. "And so the minute Frankie realized what he was looking at, he tried to block her view. The cake fell to the floor and Kendra was hysterical. The place was a mess. Dad, there was blood. I can't even think about."

"What did you do?"

"Initially, we all panicked. Kendra screamed bloody murder. Frankie stood stiff as a board. I rushed to the phone and dialed the police, who were not at all happy I tampered with the body."

"You what?"

"I cleaned him up a bit before they got there."

"Why on earth would you do that?"

"Because I wanted to help calm her down."

Karen didn't want to explain that it would have helped if someone had straightened Meg out before she saw her. Identifying her dead daughter was hard enough, but identifying a murdered and left for dead daughter was utter torture.

"Is everyone okay?"

"Sort of. I don't know. Probably not. According to Kendra, August has had a brutal cough for months. And then there was something else, something weird going on with Kendra. She asked for a minute alone, and when we came back she seemed to be in the midst of a conversation."

"With her grandfather?"

"Nope. With something near him."

"She was probably talking to him, saying goodbye or praying."

"See, that's what I thought at first, but it wasn't like that. It was like she was arguing with someone. I thought I heard her say Mom, but I can't be sure. It was almost," Karen paused, "like she was talking to a ghost."

"Did you ask her about it?"

"What was I going to ask, Dad? I'm forgetting it happened, chalking it off to near hysteria. Everything moved so quickly from there. The police came, the funeral director came, and then a woman named Sheri came. She must be an old family friend because the minute she saw her,

Kendra ran into her embrace and sobbed even louder. She offered to help Kendra with the funeral arrangements, which she gladly accepted. She's staying with her tonight."

"And where are her parents?" asked Carl.

"MIA."

"Dead as well, or gone missing?"

"From what I surmised, those words are interchangeable," sighed Karen.

SHERI'S SECRET LOVE

Kendra had no way of contacting her parents, and even if she did, she wasn't sure she'd bother. She was alone, the executor in charge of her grandfather's possessions. If they did come, it would probably be to swindle what they could out of August's funds, and Kendra couldn't bear that reality. It was time to let her parents go and move on with her life. Because most of the neighbors had already passed on themselves, she didn't expect much of a turnout at the wake.

"Mind if we stand with you?" Frankie asked.

"Mind? I would love it," she wept, burrowing so close into Frankie's side that their breathing synchronized.

Sheri Rizollo was the first to arrive. Dressed in black with a preposterously outdated brimmed hat, she nodded at Frankie and Karen before turning to Kendra.

"Your grandfather was a good man," she said, dabbing her eyes with a tissue.

Kendra appreciated all of Sheri's help, but tonight she was too raw to listen to this woman's babble. Big deal that she and August shared banana bread for a few months. What could that possibly have done to redeem the nasty gossip she had been spreading around for close to a decade?

"Thanks," she replied, forcing a small grin.

"Did he ever tell you we were childhood friends? That after his father's death, his mother and my father became good friends?"

Kendra was baffled. She had heard every thug story in the book, but this, this was going to be interesting.

"Sorry, no, he didn't."

Sheri nodded in August's direction, the past swirling into the present. "We even dated for a short time," she blushed.

245

Kendra's eyes widened at the promise of a juicy story. "I never knew."

"I'm not sure this is the right time or place, my dear. It's a bit drawn out and complicated, but I'd be happy to tell you some other time."

Kendra visually swept the empty room. She would welcome a long, complicated story about now.

"Now is good, Ms. Rizollo. That is, if you don't mind."

"Course not," she replied, motioning to two chairs in the front row.

"My father's name was Enrique Rizollo. He was born and raised in Curitiba, Brazil. Have you heard of it?"

"I'm not too smart in the history department."

"Curitiba isn't a poor place. It's not like here, but it's not poor. There are disparities in Curitiba, and my father was a statistic of those disparities. He grew up in a poor area, living at the edge of a river in a small home, or to be more exact, a small, wooden shack with no proper sanitation. When he was sixteen he married, and when he was twenty he had a son."

"A son? You have a brother?"

"Well, not exactly, no. The hospital was four miles away and he had no means of transportation, save his own two feet. When his wife gave birth she bled and the baby, he was sick. It took him hours to get to the hospital, and then another six to be seen. By the time he arrived home twelve hours later, both his wife and son were dead." Sheri sighed. "He moved here when he was twenty-five years old. He learned to speak English while working as a janitor and took advantage of night courses. At thirty-eight, he became an obstetrician. He had planned to move back to Brazil where he could help women, so that giving birth wouldn't be a death sentence, but then he met my mother and fell in love. But," she said, holding up one finger, "even though he stayed here, he regularly sent money to relief groups and encouraged others to do the same."

"My grandfather never mentioned any of this," said Kendra.

"Yes, well I suppose he had his reasons," said Sheri, looking at August admiringly. "It was your great-grandmother who found a place to live for my father when he first came to this country. Enrique Rizollo was the reason your great-grandfather attacked your great-grandmother. He thought they were having an affair, but they weren't. She was a kind woman, herself an immigrant, who only wanted to help."

"You mean that's why the shooting happened?"

"That's why it happened," nodded Sheri.

"But I don't get it. You've both said such rotten things over the years," said Kendra, who bit her lip to stop herself from saying too much.

"I was jealous."

"Of what?"

"I loved your grandfather."

"Did he know?"

"Sure he did," Sheri smiled sadly. "He just didn't love me. I used to badger him to marry me so much that he began to call me a hag," she giggled at the memory. "Then when he fell in love and got married, it was like a heavy congestion settled in my breastbone. And still to this day," she sniffled, "It's never quite left."

"Is that why you never got married?"

"Oh, I've had my offers but yes, mainly I suppose that's why. No one could ever compare to Augustino. When your grandmother died, God rest her soul, I offered to step in and help take care of Sal. He declined. When you came along, I offered again. He told me it wasn't such a good idea and that he'd be just fine. And you know," she said, touching the tip of Kendra's nose, "As usual, he was right."

"I'm sorry, Sheri," was all Kendra could manage.

"So you see, Kendra, what you've heard all these years are the words of a lonely and bitter woman who didn't want anything more than a thug named Augustino Bruno."

"Thug?" Kendra grinned. "You know that word?"

"My dear, all us old folks know it. I've wasted my life pining after a man who never wanted me, and after all these years we were finally enjoying each other. Silly to think I almost imagined that now that we were old . . ." her voice trailed off. "Oh, I'm just an old fool," she said, dabbing her eyes with a white handkerchief she pulled out of her sleeve.

"I don't know," said Kendra, seeing Sheri in a new light. "He really enjoyed your banana bread."

"Yes, he certainly did."

"And that has to mean something," she said, wrapping her arm around Sheri's shoulder.

Kendra's compassion must have moved Sheri because she sat up taller and said, "I could make it for you sometime. You could take it to college with you."

Feeling like half a person without her grandfather, Kendra wanted nothing more than to latch onto anyone who held a key to his past. Sheri was as good as she was going to get.

"I think banana bread is yummy," smiled Kendra.

"Then for now," decided Sheri, "We'll have to stick together, you and me."

LETTERS TO MEG

Dear Meg,

I'm too drained to chronicle this week's events, but I will say one thing, it was a riptide of emotions. Italian people are very expressive. They touch and hug and kiss, even if they have no idea who you are. And when a loved one is mentioned in a story, their name is followed by a sign of the cross and they say or mumble, God rest his soul.

I wanted to tell Kendra that I understood her grief, and that when people say they're sorry for your loss it doesn't quite cut it, because the human language inadequately describes the despair you feel when a loved one dies. I also wanted to warn her that when people become displaced, like in death, it removes your center of gravity and you feel this vertigo, a spinning out of control.

But I didn't tell her anything.

Instead, I stood beside her, rubbing my heart necklace until the metal felt warm against my skin. The necklace with your ashes that I never take off, except in the shower because I'm afraid if it opens up, I'll lose you forever.

Funny thing, Meg, I felt a twinge of envy for Kendra. It was no mystery how August died. But with you, your killer remains this anonymous face.

A dreg of society.

And I can't see my soul resting here or in the afterlife until he's caught and punished.

Stay tuned,

Love
Mom xoxo ☺

KENDRA

Kendra needed advice on some very large decisions. Would she sell or keep the house? Until now, her life had been on autopilot: school, work, August, Frankie, school, work, August, Frankie. And however she had felt before about not having a family was nothing compared to what she felt now.

"I don't know what to do with the house," Kendra told Sheri.

"Do you have to decide now?"

"I don't know if I have to or not, that's the problem."

"I don't want to pry, but did your grandfather ever mention a will?"

"Yes, it's in his safety deposit box. Everything is mine, but I'm not sure what everything includes. I don't know what he owes."

"I have a friend who's a lawyer. Let's give her a call."

A week after August died, Kendra found out that the house had been paid off years ago, and on top of that, August had left her fifty thousand dollars.

"You can pay off your school loans and still have a nest egg," said Sheri.

"Then for now, I guess I'll keep the house. I need my own place and besides, why pay for an apartment when I can live there?"

"I agree," said Sheri.

A month after the funeral, Kendra went home to clear out her grandfather's belongings. It still smelled of August; Barbisol shaving cream mixed with a strong minty mouthwash. Sheri must have been spying out the window because not two minutes after her arrival, she was ringing her doorbell.

"Helllllooo?" she sang out.

"Hi, Ms. Rizollo. How are you?"

"I'm fine, honey, and how are you?"

"Good as I can be."

"Of course," said Sheri sympathetically. "Is there anything I can help you with?"

"I was going to start sorting through his things for Goodwill."

"Would you like a hand?"

"If you can spare the time. It's not going to be easy giving his things away."

While they sorted and bagged August's clothing, Sheri admitted that she had tried to contact Kendra's parents over the past few weeks.

"How did you know where to look?"

"Just before he died, your grandfather, (sign of the cross), God rest his soul, told me that their last known address was in Salem. I thought it funny he mentioned it, until . . ." she trailed off. "Well, now I see why. There's a reason for everything, I guess."

"But how did he know where to look? He told me he hadn't a clue where they were."

"It was the last place Sal called from, but that was years ago. Anyway, they weren't there and I've no idea where to go from here. I could keep trying if you'd like?"

Kendra surprised herself with a defensive tone. "For what? So they can move back and shoot up and rip me off? I don't want two druggies up my ass sniffing around the place and touching my grandfather's things."

Sheri looked astonished. "Is that what you were told?"

"Not exactly. I sort of figured it out in bits and pieces."

"I see."

"You're not correcting me," Kendra noted, stuffing a dress shirt into an almost filled garbage bag.

"I wish I could," said Sheri apologetically, fiddling with the sleeve of her sweater.

That night, Kendra cried herself to sleep. She was virtually an orphan. An orphan with a ghost. If Meg hadn't come for August that day, why had she come? If you asked Kendra, this was one ill-informed ghost. And how weird was her reaction to Karen? Meg the ghost looked like she'd seen a ghost when Karen walked in. For a fraction of a second, a thought crossed Kendra's mind, but no . . . Frankie never mentioned having a sister, not even a dead one. There would be evidence, like the mention of her name or pictures on the mantel. Clearly ghost girl was a simple-minded halfwit, as Kendra had suspected from the beginning.

* * *

"Drat, drat, drat!"

While Meg paced back and forth in front of the great oak tree, Rocky appeared to be leaning against its massive trunk enjoying the shade.

"Was that really my mother or was it someone who only looked like her? I wished I knew, Rocky. Oh, how I wished I knew!

"But if it was Mom, what the heck was she doing? And that boy, he looked familiar. I can't quite place his face. Was he some distant cousin, maybe?"

Meg plopped herself next to Rocky and scratched her chin.

"Hmmm. How are that girl and my Mom connected? And why don't I automatically know, like I know everything else around here?"

Meg thought hard about her mother just like she'd done in the past when she wanted to know how she was. And just like in the past, it worked. She heard her mother's voice, as if she were on the telephone asking how her day went. She could sense her mother's heart laced with distress, yet it was lighter than it was the last time she checked. But that was all she got.

"Rocky," she said, glancing down at the rock by her side, "I got nothin'."

Then Meg decided to concentrate on the mystery boy, the one who looked familiar. Picturing his face, she heard these words: *His sorrow is eternal.*

"Huh, that's funny," she said, trying to remember where she'd heard that line before. To Meg, being eternally sorrowful took on new meaning. Where she lived time was infinite. For all she knew seconds were minutes and minutes were hours and hours were years. The thought of aging never crossed her mind until she saw her mother with her graying hair and wrinkled eyes. And now that she thought about it, the girl looked older. And thinner.

"Just how long have I been dead, Rocky? Why do I keep being zapped in and out of that girl's life?"

Meg leaned against the tree and closed her eyes, focusing on the boy. He looked older too. She imagined what he might look like younger; preppy haircut, tucked in flannel shirt, loafers, Levi's.

Wait a minute. You know who he sort of reminds me of? That boy who . . . nayh, that's not possible. That would be weirdness to infinity if he were the boy who . . . Meg furrowed her brow, her mind churning in a concerted effort to make sense of anything that had happened, and just when she felt a twinge of recollection—ZAP—she became distracted by a beautiful sunset, one that came and went as often as she wished, one that offered ADD or amnesia, or sometimes both.

"Oh, look at that, Rocky! Isn't that the most beautiful sunset you've ever seen? It's gotta be the best one yet!"

And just like that, Meg's worries were carried away. They were lifted off her shoulders by beautiful bluebirds, more purple than blue, to a far-off horizon where they could no longer burden her.

* * *

For the next three years, Kendra plunged into her schoolwork, determined to honor the memory of her grandfather with good grades. When she wasn't in school she was working; when she wasn't working or studying, she was with Frankie. Every other Sunday, she had gotten into the habit of visiting Ms. Rizollo, who had turned out to be an angel in disguise. She was not only emotionally supportive, but she taught Kendra how to cook basic entrees, like pot roast and homemade macaroni and cheese.

During Kendra's senior year, Sheri asked if she had plans after graduation.

"In fact, I do," replied Kendra, slicing into a log of extra sharp cheddar. "Frankie and I plan on hitting the open road. We want to travel and see the country while we're still young."

Sheri Rizollo was a woman who never left the safety of her own neighborhood, never mind her hometown.

"Are you sure you want to do that? It sounds so . . . unpredictable," said Sheri in a concerned voice.

"And that's just what I'm looking for," smiled Kendra. "We'll kick around for a few years and then find a place to settle down."

"What about your house?"

Kendra handed a plate of sliced cheese to Sheri. "Well, about all that. I was kind of hoping you could help me sell it. I could use some of the cash for the road, and the rest I'll put away in an account for when I get back."

"Oh," said Sheri, putting down the plate and walking toward the stove. "I suppose I could help. My cousin's best friend is a real estate agent. No harm in asking her how the market is doing these days," she mumbled, bending over and adjusting the flame on a pan of boiling water, which in truth needed no adjusting.

"That's great! I can't wait to go," said Kendra excitedly. "We've already mapped out art exhibitions for the next twelve months."

Sheri nodded, but continued to face the stove. She retrieved a magic handkerchief from under her sleeve and lightly wiped her cheeks.

"Boy," said Kendra, walking over to Sheri, "Am I ever gonna miss you. I was thinking if it's all right, I could stay with you when I was in town? We could swap August stories and reminisce about the good old days."

Sheri turned and hugged Kendra. She allowed only a moment to pass before pushing herself away and wiping her nose with the handkerchief before tucking it back up her sleeve.

"Okay, down to business," she said, clearing her throat. "We need to be sure the pasta is cooked al dente or the entire dish will come out all wrong."

SPRING, 1987

"You're graduating in two weeks, and you're just now informing me that you've decided to go on a world tour?" Karen snapped, unable to comprehend Frankie's short notice.

"I wasn't sure for sure, and now I am."

"You wasn't *sure for sure*?" she mocked, hands on her hips. "When were you sure for sure, then?"

Frankie sighed, but Karen didn't care. This was going to be one of those conversations he wasn't going to win. She watched as he flopped down in the kitchen chair.

"If you want the truth, I didn't say anything because I didn't want you to try and talk me out of it," he admitted.

"I see," said Karen, who was staring out the window, her expression a map of fear and anger.

"I'm sorry for the lack of notice."

"How about no notice at all, because that's what it feels like. How could you think procrastinating on this would be a better idea?" she barked, turning to face him. "Do you plan on coming back anytime soon?"

"We have no real plans, but I'm sure we'll be back soon-ish."

"Mmm, hmm," she said, sucking in her lips.

"I'm sorry if I—"

Karen put her hand up. "I can't talk about this now, Frankie. I feel shitty about the entire thing. I did want you to go out and explore the world, and I was worried Kendra might hold you back, but she didn't. And what a great adventure the two of you will share, but . . ." Karen's voice crackled. "But it seems like I just got you. I just got you six short years ago, and now you're leaving, and you couldn't even give me a head's up. I've no time to process this turn of events."

"I'm sorry," he said. Karen knew by the look on his face that his apology was authentic. She could also tell by the way he was rubbing his stomach that he was in pain.

"I don't know what to say," he replied guiltily.

Karen wiped her eyes with the back of her hand. "No, I'm sorry. I'm really not mad. The whole thing just took me by surprise. If you'll just give me twenty minutes to absorb the news, you'll see how genuinely happy I am for you."

"I'll give you fifteen," he grinned.

Relieved that Frankie was trying to make light of the situation, Karen sniffed, "Deal," then left the room to blow her nose and collect herself.

On graduation day, Frankie and Kendra packed their belongings into a beat up Winnebago that Frankie acquired from trading in his Trans Am.

"I think this will do just fine," he smiled, running his hand along the dusty side of the van.

For their graduation present, Karen had bought them a tent, art racks, and stocked the Winnebago with two months worth of food.

"You spent too much on us," scolded Frankie.

"Not that we don't appreciate it," Kendra cut in, "But you did go overboard."

Karen placed herself between them and slung one arm around each of their shoulders.

"All I want is for you guys to go out and experience life."

"That there," said Frankie, "sounds like the perfect exit speech."

Karen nodded, and hugged each one separately before letting them go. They climbed into the van looking ridiculously happy.

As the van pulled away, Karen shouted, "Don't forget to call once a week!"

"Will do," waved Kendra, half her body hanging out the window.

Karen watched them turn the corner and sighed heavily. This was a lesser version of how she felt the day Meg went missing.

Abandoned. Frightened. Uncertainty itching at her body like mosquito bites.

"Well," she said to no one at all, "Guess it's time for me to get a life."

LETTERS TO MEG

Dear Meg,

Frankie and Kendra left me.

I'm being dramatic.

They left to seek fame, fortune, and adventure.

I'm jealous.

And pouty. I wished I were driving away with them. Instead, I'm sitting here with my two favorite security blankets: a pan of almost cooked brownies and Teddy. This is the first time in a long time I haven't been focused on someone else, and to be honest, it's a bit scary. Living vicariously through others is the only thing that's gotten me through the years. To prevent myself from going mad, I've decided to sign up for a few continuing education courses. First up is *Power-Packed Communication Skills for Women*. Why this course? Because I'm interested in growing and improving my skills. I'm open to change and new ideas. I want to prepare for upcoming challenges successfully.

Or at least that's what the brochure told me I wanted.

I'll be learning about non-verbal behaviors, speech patterns, grammar rules, negative word use, how to handle my anger and emotions no matter what my situation, and the five dimensions of self awareness.

Whatever.

At least it will get me out.

Should I get a dog?

No. Too much work.

Maybe a bird?

No. The early morning chirping would annoy me.

A fish?

I know, why bother.

The second course starts immediately after the first one and is called *Conflict Resolution: Useful Skills for Handling Difficult People and Dangerous Situations.*

I'll be learning about proxemics, kinesics, and supportive stances. Sarah said they do self defense demonstrations like the front choke release, bite release, and kick block. This is a course I should have taken when you were alive so I could have taught you these skills.

Maybe you'd be here right now.

Maybe you'd be living with me and going to college while I helped take care of the baby.

Or married to Roberto.

The very last course, and the one I'm most looking forward to, is *Criminal Personality Profiling.* I'm going to learn about psychopaths and crime scenes and organized and disorganized murders. I'm going to pay particular attention in this class. I want to know everything about the bastard that killed you.

Stay tuned,

Love,

Mom xoxo ☺

ON THE ROAD

Frankie and Kendra began their adventure just twenty minutes from home, selling their artwork at small street fairs along the Charles River in Medford. Kendra exhibited her modern/realistic approach and Frankie his traditional, impressionistic style.

They traveled throughout New England, and then journeyed to Maryland, Pennsylvania, Virginia, Georgia, and Florida. They explored much of the southwestern United States, then to California and back across the country toward Massachusetts. They sold just enough to survive, their profits barely paying for their depleting art supplies. Kendra thought she had allotted them a sufficient amount of money for a two-year trip, but her budget skills failed her and she came up short by a full year. She also didn't take into consideration her lack of impulse control. She convinced Frankie to spend one week at Hershey Park and two weeks at Disney World. Frankie took it in stride, not becoming overly concerned with Kendra's spending habits.

"I told you I sucked at budgeting, Frankie. I knew the A-minus was a fluke."

"It's fine, Ken. I should have spoken up sooner."

"Why didn't you talk me out of Disney?"

"Because you seemed intent on getting your way."

Kendra blushed. "I did, didn't I? But now you have to suffer."

"I'm not suffering at all," he said, caressing her cheek.

"Well, I am. I haven't had a frigging Three Musketeers in a week," she sulked. "I'd kill for some nougat."

"That *is* slumming it," Frankie agreed with a smirk.

"I can call Sheri and ask her to wire us more money," she suggested.

"I thought we decided to put that toward a home?"

"Eh, what's another couple thousand?"

"It's a couple of thousand we won't have towards a better home."

"Frankie, c'mon, let's just call her."

"Ken, we're not going to die and believe me, this isn't close to roughing it."

Frankie knew what it felt like not to eat for a week. He knew what it was like to be cold or hot or smelly because the water and electricity had been shut off. Having to live hand to mouth didn't bother him one bit.

As long as he had his nips.

And although they didn't make much money, they did have a taste of fame. Frankie won first place in the Willimantic Art Festival in Connecticut, two prizes at the Ocean Beach show in Florida, and first place in Neptune, West Virginia. Kendra won first in Mandarin, Florida, second in Longmeadow, Massachusetts, and took home a ribbon for best in category at the Osbornedale Art Festival in Derby, Connecticut.

It took one solid week of living off of peanut butter and crackers before Kendra broke down.

"I can't do it anymore!" she whined. "I'm sick of smelling like a beast and sleeping in a beat up Winnebago."

"But we've spent half the journey in hotels, not in the Winnebago."

"Yeah, thanks to me and my spendthrift ways."

"Kendra—"

"I know it's my fault," she interrupted. "Who'd have thunk I'd be this irresponsible with money?"

Frankie sighed. "Let's dissect that nonsensical sentence."

"Oh, stop with the grammar," she pouted. "I know I dug us into this hole."

"And I don't care. We can stick it out a bit longer."

"Why? What's the point?"

"I just would feel like a . . ." and he shook his head and looked away.

"A what?"

Examining the dusty window, Frankie shrugged.

"A failure, Frankie? Would you feel like a failure?"

He looked at her. "Maybe."

"Hey," she said, taking his chin in her hand, "This doesn't mean we won't be traveling. We're not quitting. We're regrouping. We're going to reinvent ourselves."

Frankie looked doubtful.

"Don't ya trust me, honey?"

"Definitely not with finances," he grinned.

"I hear you, and I concur."

"You drive me nuts!" he said, folding her into his arms and giving her a passionate kiss.

"That's because I'm full to the rim with peanut butter."

"What am I going to do with you?" Frankie sighed.

Kendra made a small space between her pointer finger and thumb as if she were squeezing something. "I do have one teeny tiny suggestion."

"You've already beat me down, so you might as well spit it out."

"Why don't we stay with Karen until we can get our heads on straight? That way if I really am an incorrigible spendthrift, we won't get the boot."

"Absolutely not."

"Why not?"

"Too imposing."

"She'd love it."

"No."

"Yes."

"I said no, Ken. It's no, for sure."

One week and many beat downs later . . .

"Why, of course you two are more than welcome to live here until you find a place of your own!" Karen blurted to Frankie.

"It's just for a short time," Frankie assured her.

"No rush at all," she said excitedly.

While Frankie was unloading, Kendra wrapped her arms around Karen's small neck and said, "I am never going to eat peanut butter again."

*   *   *

Frankie and Kendra filled Karen's den with suitcases, art supplies, trophies, and ribbons. Once settled, they each got part-time jobs to supplement their incomes. Frankie was hired to do restoration work on furniture for the local museum, as well as painting signs for professional storefronts. Kendra, not knowing what she would do or what she was capable of doing, circled everything that was available in the newspaper.

"I'm off to find work," she announced to Karen and Frankie, who were sitting at the table drinking coffee.

"Good luck," they said in unison.

As soon as the door closed behind her, Frankie looked at Karen.

"I give her three hours tops before she's back here complaining that her feet are sore from pounding the pavement."

Kendra did come back within three hours, but with a job.

"I was just hired as director of field services for the local Girl Scouts!"

"What? I mean, wow, really?"

"I guess they liked me," she smiled.

"Well, who wouldn't?" Karen said, giving Kendra a squeeze. "Congratulations honey."

For the next six months, Kendra and Frankie worked more than they painted. Kendra immersed herself in the world of scouting and began organizing monthly staff meetings on the importance of being involved in the arts. Every night, unless one of them was working, the threesome ate dinner together.

"So, you know how I've been having these meetings at work?"

"The art meetings?"

"Yeah. We were discussing a crafts fair to support the local Girl Scouts and I donated some of my artwork, just a few small pictures," she said, preparing to put a meatball in her mouth. "Anyway," she said, her mouth full of meatball, "my work circulated around the area and landed in Springfield."

"That's where Frankie sold his very first painting," said Karen, with a hint of nostalgia.

"So someone must have really loved my paintings, because I got a call from the Museum of Fine Arts in Springfield and they want to exhibit my work," she beamed, slathering a thick glob of butter on a roll, and then ripping open a few sugar packets to pour into her Coke

"Good for you, Ken."

Even though he had a smile on his face, Kendra thought she heard a hint of envy in his tone. She shook it off, telling herself she was being ridiculous.

"Yeah, I'm quite excited."

"Oh," said Frankie, glancing at the clock and pushing his chair out. "I just remembered I've got to paint a sign before tomorrow."

"Okay, but will you come with me to Springfield?"

"For what?"

"They're going to have this thing for me," Kendra said, waving her hand like it was nothing.

"What are they going to have?" asked Karen.

"It's silly, really," Kendra clucked. "They're calling it a *One Woman Show*. It's sort of a big deal, I guess."

"Of course we'll come!" exclaimed Karen. "We wouldn't miss it for the world! In fact, I have an idea. With my work schedule, I'm never home and that den is gathering dust bunnies. Why don't you two take it over as an art room?"

"We couldn't," said Frankie.

"Of course you can," Karen insisted. "With the new policies we're trying to implement for DSS services, I doubt I'll be around very often. Just give me a week to clear out my stuff."

*   *   *

The couple set up their art studio and painted side by side, Kendra's long, silky hair pinched up in an orange banana clip and Frankie's whitish blond hair falling in short, messy wisps around his face. It wasn't long before Frankie began telling himself lies about his artwork. He'd walk into the room and note that his work seemed vapid compared to Kendra's blindingly colorful paintings. He tried to put up an air of normality, but his chest ached and he felt like a drowning man. Frankie's coffee break was a nip. His mid-morning snack was a nip. A nip preceded lunch and dinner. To hide his addiction, he began to stagger their painting time so that one of them either had to go to work or take a break. Then he got sloppy and Kendra noticed.

"Have you been drinking?"

"Why?"

"You smell like alcohol."

"Only for inspiration," he said lightly.

"Well, geez, wait for me!" she smiled. "I'd like to be inspired by a good buzz now and then!"

Before she bounced out of the room, she gave Frankie one of her haunting kisses that penetrated his soul. He envisioned them laughing in bed tangled up in the sheets, and silently berated himself for lying to the most wonderful woman in the world.

There were times when Frankie had to increase his daily dosage of nips, and after calculating how much he was spending, he decided to upgrade to bottles, on the condition that he would drink the equivalent of a shot glass or two, maybe four at the most, at any given time.

He went to the liquor store and purchased twelve bottles of gin, figuring it would last him roughly three weeks.

When Kendra left for work, Frankie took his coffee/gin break. He downed two shots, paused, and then threw back a third for good measure. His mind thrashed, a destructive neurosis taunting him with lies. He thought he wanted a symbiotic relationship with Kendra, but that was before this so-called One Woman Show. What he wanted was a relationship that was skewed in his favor, with Kendra working miserable side jobs and Frankie receiving kudos for his artwork. Although it was obvious her designs were progressing artistically, Kendra was wildly disorganized. She was Pigpen on steroids. When she walked, things flew out of her pockets of their own accord. But she was unbelievably talented and had an attribute Frankie lacked: she could see twenty-five strokes ahead of herself before she even finished a rough sketch.

Kendra's One Woman Show was a hit. Her work was exhibited at the Museum of Fine Arts, the Springfield Public Library, the Westfield State Teachers College, and a musical instrument company who liked her colorful drawing of two macaw parrots perched on flutes. She had joined a couple of artist guilds and the Academic Artist's Association and, with Karen's urging, had flyers made. Even though Frankie felt his dreams being buried as Kendra's flourished, he tried to rise above his own insecurities. For Valentine's Day, he painted her a sign that read *Kendra Bruno Watercolors*.

"I love, love, love it!" she squealed.

While in Springfield, the couple decided to enter a small exhibit sponsored by the Fine Arts Center at the University of Massachusetts Amherst.

Kendra's detailed painting of three peonies won her the grand prize of a thousand dollars.

"This is unbelievable! I'm in shock," she told Frankie.

"Congrats," he said, halfheartedly, but Kendra didn't seem to notice.

"Honestly, I expected you to win, because you're so damn good," she said, letting out a snort, "and they called me instead! Hot dog, I'm so excited!" she laughed, hugging Frankie tightly.

"You deserve it," he said, and he meant it.

Frankie received honorable mention. He thought he deserved more.

For their six-year anniversary, Kendra surprised Frankie with two plane tickets to California.

"Three weeks of travel and fun, and I've signed us up for a few exhibits!"

"What about work, Ken?"

"I got the time off. I was hoping furniture restoration could wait until you got back?"

"How are we going to get our art there?"

"Have it shipped."

"The cost of that would be ridiculous."

"We're only young once, Frankie. Let's go!"

"Spendthrift."

"Scrooge."

"I can't."

"You *can*. Puh-leassse?"

"No."

"Yes."

"It's no, Ken, no for sure."

FALL, 1989

"Have fun kids!" Karen waved from the airport gate.

The California trip helped lift Frankie's spirits. His mood and ego improved when his paintings started to become a hot commodity.

"I'm glad you talked me into this," he said, pulling Kendra close and kissing the side of her head.

"Frankie, you're doing so well. You've sold just about everything," she said.

Frankie thought he noted a hint of surprise in her voice, but shook it off.

By the end of two weeks, the couple had become quite adept at haggling. They even discovered a system that wealthy people used; they would come dressed in rags, haggle, leave, and then return fifteen minutes before you closed to see how much of your work was sold. This way, they could gauge how much they needed to barter.

Right before closing, Kendra shook a stalky gray-haired man's hand and walked over to Frankie.

"The bastard cut me down by four hundred, but I managed to sell three pictures," she said, wiping her brow with the back of her forearm.

"Selling art isn't just about the money, Ken."

"Oh, really, Mr. Philosopher? Because this trip cost a pretty penny."

"Is that why you draw?"

"Well, no, and yes. What about you?"

"I draw for myself, and if I had to be honest, for the recognition."

"Not the money?"

Frankie put his arm around her and spoke in a whisper, "Selling your art means that somebody likes your work enough to buy it. Sure you get paid, but for the rest of your life you know that someone felt highly enough about your masterpiece to display it within the boundaries of their home. Now, how does that feel?"

"If you put it that way, it feels damn good! Oh, and by the way," she said slapping his behind, "He wants us to deliver them."

They loaded the large paintings into the rented van and drove for an hour.

"This looks like the place," Frankie said, nodding at a prominent looking mansion on a hill.

"You're shitting me," said Kendra. "What an ass I am for letting this guy talk me down four hundred bucks."

"Remember," reminded Frankie, "Money is transient, artwork is forever."

"Blah, blah, blah," she pouted at Frankie, causing him to laugh.

Kendra's paintings were normally sixty inches long, making delivery a two-man job. Crossing the threshold, she found it difficult to keep her tongue from hanging out of her mouth. A housekeeper directed them across a long entrance and up three steps to a room that could have been a home in itself. Cathedral ceilings housed a grand piano in one corner and an inground swimming pool, encased in glass, in the other. In the middle were two sectionals and a television the size of a movie theater screen. The windows of the room were at least forty feet high.

The gray-haired man was waiting for them at the top of the stairs. Without any salutation, he explained, "I needed something strong and striking right there on that center wall, and I believe your paintings are just the thing."

"This is so marvelous," she mumbled, holding onto her colorful parrot and flower painting with both hands.

"Yes, well then," began the man, "You can lean them against that wall and pick up the check at the front door."

And with that, the couple was dismissed.

It took Kendra five days to stop bragging, and another three to stop daydreaming about houses of the rich and famous. It wasn't until she was back on planet earth that she realized Frankie seemed distant and scattered.

"You okay?"

Nice of you to finally notice is what Frankie wanted to say. What he did say was, "Perfectly. Why?"

*　　*　　*

When they arrived home, Karen noticed Frankie's darkening mood. He looked frayed and unkempt and didn't bother to change out of his running clothes. He stuck to his regimented schedule, but barely ate. Scruffy whiskers framed his too thin face and his weight plummeted by fifteen pounds. When she walked by the den to watch Frankie through the French door, she knew he was aware of her presence, yet he never acknowledged her.

"I'd refer to his attitude as good old-fashioned jealousy," snipped Kendra, who was preparing turkey club sandwiches.

Karen shook her head and clucked. "Working together can be a tenuous balance."

"Indeed," sighed Kendra. "But it's not like he hasn't seen his day in the sun. Wasn't it Frankie who won two one thousand dollar prizes in California and Pennsylvania?"

"Ah, but you're the one who got your work displayed in an extravagant home and had an art show named after you," reminded Karen.

"Yeah, that was way cool," she agreed.

"Still," Karen said, her voice laced with worry, "It seems as if it's something more than that, like something went missing inside him, almost like he were on something."

Kendra spun around and faced Karen.

"You think so? Oh, my God. We've got to put an end to this shit!"

Karen held out her arm, palm facing down, and pumped it lightly. "Calm down, Kendra."

"I can't calm down," she said, stuffing a slice of tomato in her mouth.

"Let's talk to Frankie and see what he has to say before jumping to conclusions."

"Okay, but whatever's up his ass, he's got nine months to pluck it out."

"Why . . . oh, Kendra, really?"

"Really," she smiled. "I'm eating for two, and I like to eat as it is, so Frankie's going to need to get a grip on reality damn fast!"

"Does he know yet?"

"Nope, I just took a test this morning. I was going to tell him later, but seeing as it just leaked out of me, there's no time like the present."

Kendra hugged Karen and walked toward the den. Karen counted to five and then jumped out of the chair. She tiptoed down the hall to where she could position herself within eye and earshot. Kendra approached Frankie in her usual bubbly manner. She began talking animatedly, her hand flailing around her head. Frankie nodded, and then put his hand to his forehead as if he were thinking. After a moment, Kendra put her hands on her hips and Karen thought she heard her say, "Well, say something." With that, Frankie grabbed her around the waist and swung her in a circle. Kendra allowed her head to tip backward, filling the room with her raspy laugh. When the spinning stopped, she grabbed Frankie by the cheeks and kissed him passionately.

"Life is good," Karen said to no one in particular, and feeling like the voyeur she was, turned and walked away.

*   *   *

David Letterman had become a nightly ritual for Frankie and Kendra. They half watched the show, half discussed their future.

"I think I want to go back to school," said Frankie.

"What's wrong with the career you have now?" asked a pallid looking Kendra, who since the announcement of her pregnancy, had suffered from chronic nausea and a high libido.

"It's not much of a career. A good father should be more responsible."

"First off, you'll be a great father, no matter what. And as far as careers go, what did you have in mind?"

"I want to teach."

Kendra nodded at him. "Yeah, you'd be a fine teacher, babe. And now the million dollar question: how are we going to afford it?"

"We'll manage."

"Well, I was sort of hoping now that I'm pregnant we could start looking for a place of our own."

Frankie sighed and took her by the hand. "I know I was the one who wanted to be here short term, but it's important that my kid have a stable home. Can we bite the bullet until we figure out if college is even feasible?"

"Fine by me," Kendra said in a sultry tone, "Why don't you begin your career by sliding over and teaching me some lessons in love."

*   *   *

Kendra told Frankie she feared she'd never be able to paint again. The mere sight of paint tubes made her gag, and thanks to her supersonic nostrils, smelling it was worse. In fact, most odors, including food smells, caused Kendra's stomach to curdle.

"Thank God for Sheri's banana bread! It's the only thing that doesn't make me puke!" she'd exclaim, when a new batch was given to her.

Frankie was thankful for both Sheri and the bread. She would send Kendra home with four loaves at a time; all of which Kendra consumed August-style.

In four months the nausea subsided and Kendra was painting with a vengeance. Her skin was radiant, her mind sharp as a tack, and her sex drive was off the charts. If she could, she'd spend every moment in bed with Frankie. Frankie, on the other hand, was busier than ever, so busy that he almost didn't have time to feel a disquieting pinch of dissatisfaction. He spent his days in school and his nights refurbishing furniture, forgetting that only a few years ago he had dreamt of becoming an artist.

"I'm so proud of us!" said Kendra, lightly stroking Frankie's hair as they lay in bed with the sheets puddled around their feet.

Fundamentally life was good, but Frankie wasn't. He hadn't a clue where the aching loneliness was coming from and worse, had no idea how to prevent it from spreading into every aspect of his life. Kendra mentioned his drinking a couple of times, but it was done lightheartedly. The other day, she had walked in on him discarding a bottle of gin into the trash.

"Hey, no fair. The pregnant lady feels left out!"

"I was just——"

Kendra waved him off. "You were just letting loose, right? It's fine, Frankie. I don't know why you get so embarrassed or feel the need to hide it when you have an occasional drink. For Pete's sake, we drank our asses off in college."

"That was college," he said stiffly.

"And we're like, twenty-four," she smiled. "I do appreciate you trying to be considerate, but don't worry. I don't feel left out. I'm aware I'm in a no-alcohol zone with bambino here." Kendra patted her stomach.

"I didn't want you to feel slighted," he lied, the guilt mounting inside of him. Frankie wasn't trying to be considerate of Kendra. He was trying to hide from her. He knew full well he was in the throes of an insidious addiction, one he'd had for years. One that up until now, he thought he had under control.

LETTERS TO MEG, 1990

Dear Meg,

Frankie and Kendra are expecting. Do you know what that means? It means I'm going to be a grandma! I think I'll ask to be called Nana K. It has a ring to it, don't you think? I don't want to say anything to them, but really, it's about time they got married.

Poor Kendra was sick for the longest time, but now she's this rocket of energy blasting here and there. I think you'd like her, Meg. She's feisty like you were, smart like you were, and she's stubborn, like you were. Some days I find myself wondering what you would have morphed into as a young adult.

Would you have turned out to be a famous painter? No. You were too fidgety for the patience it takes to create anything with fine details.

Maybe you would have been a nurse? No. You didn't like to touch anything gross. You never would have made it.

How about an accountant? You were good with numbers.

A policewoman? You did like to take control and intimidate people. But you were kind of klutzy and that, combined with being able to brandish a gun, could be a recipe for disaster!

Maybe you would have chosen to have your baby and then worked slowly toward a college degree?

Anything's possible, I guess. Whatever you would have been, I would have been proud of you.

Stay tuned for more baby news,

Love,
Mom xoxo ☺

THE NAMESAKE

Meg was having her usual 'every day's a holiday' at the field. One minute she was chatting with Rocky about the beautiful rainbow in the distance, and the next thing she knew she was standing in a hospital room. For some reason the transition didn't go smoothly and Meg found everything around her blurry.

"What in the name of?" she began to say, and then was zapped back to the field.

"Whooo that was funky weird," she told Rocky. And then, "Oh, look at that rainbow!"

*   *   *

Kendra had been in labor for seventy-two hours, not including what she would later refer to as the pansy-ass labor that hit previous to the real McCoy. The pansy-ass labor was similar to really bad period cramps, which she foolishly mistook for full-blown labor. But the real McCoy, it was indescribable. Kendra knew a contraction was coming because of the hot flash that preceded it. She felt like a blowfish, expanding as the heat rose from the bottom of her feet to the tip of her puffed out hair follicles. Just when her head felt like a pressure cooker, her stomach contracted and a fist of fury gripped, releasing momentarily before picking up in intensity. She found it too much effort to utter anything other than, *ow, ow,* with an occasional, *frig,* thrown in. Forty-eight hours, countless cool facecloths and continuous glasses of ice chips later, she begged for the epidural she swore she'd never ask for. Unfortunately, it didn't fully take and she was left with a numb left side and intense contractions.

"Ow, ow, ow, ow, ow, frig, ow, frig, ow, ow."

"It's time to push," said the nurse.

"No, I'm done," said Kendra despondently.

"But this is the final stretch," Karen coached. "Let's get this done so we can see the baby!"

"I don't see the use. Really, I don't. I bet you I could push my ass off and this thing wouldn't budge. It hasn't budged for three frigging days, so why would it budge now?"

Kendra turned her head away and closed her eyes.

"If you don't push, you'll be facing a cesarean," warned the doctor.

"Is it less painful because if it is, I'll take it."

"Honey," said Karen, "You don't want a cesarean. Trust me, it's no fun."

"Why? Did you have one with Frankie?"

"My friend from college had one. It was tough going."

"Owwwww."

"That's the one," coached the nurse. "Push!"

Kendra bravely pushed for the next forty-five minutes before announcing once again that she was throwing in the towel.

"I've made a decision. I'm just not going to do it. *Fuck it,*" she said, sweat dripping off of her face. "If this little shit wants to come out, he's just going to have to do it on his own."

"Let's focus on the positive," said the doctor.

"You're so close," said the nurse.

"You need to focus, Ken," added Frankie.

"I'll tell you what *I need,* Frankie," she spat. "I *need* to sleep. I *need* to not be in pain anymore. I *need* this out of me now!"

Frankie patiently leaned in and with his classic magical touch that relaxed Kendra every time said, "Then push, Ken."

*   *   *

Meg stood up to stretch her legs and—ZAP—back to the hospital room. She found herself standing next to a nurse and staring between the legs of the somewhat wicked human, Kendra. Unfortunately for

Meg, no blurry vision was accompanied with this trip. She could see everything perfectly.

*   *   *

Kendra nodded at Frankie, indicating that she was back in the game, but another familiar voice stopped her dead in her tracks.

"This is pretty gross territory down here. I'd push that sucker out fast if I were you. Trust me, you *do not* want it staying there."

Kendra felt a chill as she maneuvered her head around her giant lump of a stomach. Meg was standing next to the nurse peering between Kendra's legs in gross, but utter fascination.

"You! Get out of there!" she screamed accusingly, and since the nurse couldn't see Meg, she assumed that Kendra was speaking to her.

"But this is where the baby comes out," she said, a bit sarcastically.

"Oh, sorry, not you," she apologized.

The doctor leaned toward the nurse and asked, "What meds is she on?"

"Point of interest," Meg told her, "I was pregnant when I died."

"You're too young to have kids."

"You're sweet to say that," said the nurse, who thought Kendra was speaking to her. "I actually have four children. Kids keep you young," she said. "Now, please honey, push."

"Don't be a dill weed. Just push it out," repeated Meg. "You can do it. I know you can."

"Why are you here?"

"Well, I always wanted to be a nurse."

Kendra felt like an idiot. She nodded at the poor nurse, frustrated that everyone in the room thought she was going certifiably insane.

"I don't know, really. One minute I was in the field and the next minute I'm here," Meg said, opening her arms to encompass the room. She walked away from the nurse and walked up behind Karen, who was holding Kendra's hand.

"You need to leave," she said sternly.

"Oh, you want me to . . . sure, I'll just be outside," said Karen, her voice full of hurt.

"Why did you do that?" Frankie whispered, his voice tinged with agitation.

"Ow, ow, ow, ow."

"Push!" cried the doctor. "Push, Kendra!"

"Is that my mom?" asked Meg.

"Karennnn! Come baaackk!" moaned Kendra.

Karen, who looked like she was taking forever sauntering toward the door, rushed back to Kendra's side and reached out for her hand. "I'm here," she assured her.

"That *is* my mom. What is she doing here? Mom, can you hear me?" Meg yelled, screaming in Karen's ear.

"Shut up!" shouted Kendra. "Go away!"

"Me?" asked Karen, withdrawing a step.

"No, Karen, not you," said Kendra, who really wanted to cry out, *Not you, the ghost behind you!*

"Ken, who are you talking to, babe?"

"The frigging pain," lied Kendra.

"That's very therapeutic," said the nurse. "Good girl, you tell that pain to go away!"

Kendra smiled at everyone and then began to laugh at the ridiculousness of her situation. The laughing lasted for thirty seconds before her face turned bright red.

"Ooo, here comes a whopper," warned Meg. "I can tell by your face. You look like a human blow torch!"

"Go away!"

"Keep pushing," said the doctor.

"Push on the next one, and you'll be home free," Meg coached.

"Please, you're upsetting me. Please, go."

"Pain begone," chanted the nurse, in a soothing mantra-like tone.

"I'm not trying to upset you, I swear. I can't help where I land. And that *is* my mom," insisted Meg, pointing at Karen. "Why is she here?"

Before Kendra could answer, the whopper that Meg predicted hit full force.

"Push it out, push it out!" cheered Meg.

"Ow, ow, frig, owwwwwww," and with one last push, a small, beautiful bundle fell into the doctor's hands.

"I did it! Oh, thank God it's over," she said, collapsing back onto the bed.

"Whoopee! I knew you could!" exclaimed Meg.

"Congratulations, it's a girl!" smiled the doctor.

"She's beautiful," laughed Frankie, admiring his handiwork. "What should we name her?"

Kendra looked at Meg, who was outlined in a brilliant sunbeam, her steel gray eyes glowing with pride. It was surreal to think that in this room, among nurses, a doctor, and loved ones, stood a ghost watching over her. She was definitely one egg short of a dozen, but she was Kendra's ghost, nonetheless.

"Megan, but I'd like to call her Meg."

Right before she vanished, Meg stuck out her tongue, flung her arms in the air, made a peace sign with both hands and bopped her head up and down like she was at a rock concert.

"Yessss!" were the last words Kendra heard her say.

"Meg it is," Frankie said, kissing the newborn on the forehead. "You like that name, Mom?"

"Mom? Karen?"

When Karen didn't answer, Kendra propped herself up on her elbows and scanned the room. She saw Frankie rushing to Karen, who was out cold on the floor.

"Someone help her!" shouted Kendra.

The nursing staff hoisted Karen to her feet and settled her into a chair with a cold glass of water.

"You sure you're okay?" Frankie asked.

"I forgot to eat is all," she said weakly.

Frankie nodded, patted Karen's shoulder, and turned back to Kendra.

"I know we're kind of late in the game, but will you marry me?"

"Anytime, anyplace," said Kendra, placing her hand on Frankie's cheek.

For the next couple of hours, maternity staff came in and out of the room to poke and prod mother and child, who were both very sleepy. Many *ooohed* and *ahhhed* over the peaceful olive-skinned beauty who jackhammered her way into the world.

"Doesn't she rock?" Kendra asked Karen.

"She's absolutely precious," Karen answered.

Before they knew it, both women had tears streaming down their cheeks.

Later in the evening while nursing Meg, Kendra revisited ghost Meg's visit.

What was it Meg was saying about Karen? She's my mother, your mother? Whose mother was she? She was speaking nonsense. Poor, lost ghost girl.

*   *   *

Karen's tears weren't for the new Meg. Her tears were for the old Meg, and the sense that somewhere someone had made it so that Karen's daughter had a namesake.

"Dad, it's me."

"What's the good word?"

"It's a girl."

"Hey, now that is good news!" Karen could hear the smile in Carl's voice.

"They named her Meg."

"You're joking, right? Where on earth did they get that from?"

"Oh, earth had nothing to do it with it," Karen smiled. "Come and visit when you can."

*   *   *

In her strawberry and pound cake scented field, Meg was pacing back and forth.

"I tell you, Rocky. It was wild. She named the baby after me! And my Mom was there and . . . hey," Meg pondered, "Why was Mom there?"

But before she could give this serious thought, *poof*, it vanished, and Meg continued talking rapidly.

"And there was a man there who must be Kendra's husband, and . . . wait just a minute," Meg paused again. "I'm feeling a serious sense of déjà vu."

The man reminded her of something. A memory, perhaps? Almost like a memory that she forgot to remember.

"I've seen him somewhere when I was alive, but where?" Meg asked Rocky, just before going pale with the recollection of a scorching memory that seemed to have happened centuries ago. It was a memory that didn't belong to a girl who lived in a field that had fruit-flavored grass and giant oak trees.

"He sort of looks like a grown up version of that cute boy who did this to me. But if it is him, I don't get it. Why was he with my mother and Kendra? Is he going to hurt them too?" Meg wondered to Rocky. Her voice became weak and she trembled as the forgotten past attacked her like a virus. "Oh no! I've got to stop him, Rocky! I've got to get back there somehow!"

Meg raced across the field in a fit of panic and tears.

"Moommmm, Mommmmyyyy!"

At the crest of her hill she was stopped dead in her tracks by the incoming sunset.

Poof.

The glory of the perfect sky deleted her memory, filling her with a profound peace that caused her to drop to her knees.

"Oooo, will you look at that? Have you ever seen anything so beautiful?"

Meg allowed herself to sink down into the perfectly mowed grass that felt soft as a kitten and smelled of fabric softener. She closed her eyes, dreaming of sunsets and baby giggles.

TRANSITIONS

The next few years were monumental, not only for Frankie and Kendra, but for Karen as well. Although she loved having her family around, Karen's life had become quite full and work so busy that when she came home in the evenings she yearned for quiet, something beautiful baby Meg seemed incapable of. Meg, Karen knew, would be an exotic beauty. Her features were identical to Frankie, she had Edna's dark coloring, and Kendra's green kaleidoscope eyes. Bald as a cue ball when she was born, Meg began sprouting hair at three months old, which Karen first noticed on an afternoon when she had offered to babysit. She was holding Meg by a sunny window when she first took notice of the wiffle of color on her head. Blonde with a scattering of tiny red streaks, baby Meg's hair was undeniably the same exact color as her own Meg's hair.

"But, how can this be?" she said in amazement, lightly touching Meg's downy hair.

By one year of age, Meg had her own paint brush, which she wielded freely around the house, splattering washable paint colors as she toddled about. If someone told her there was a cuter baby on earth, Karen would beg to differ.

Frankie quit his restoration job and began the process of changing the course of his life. He became a full-time student at UMASS Boston and began working at Bradlees Department Store in Somerville. Starting off at register, he quickly was promoted to night manager, sometimes working up to fifty hours a week. Between work and school, Frankie was lucky to get three to four hours of sleep a night. Just before Meg's fourth birthday, he graduated with a bachelor's degree in industrial arts. He continued working for Bradlees while earning his masters degree in vocational education, which he received when Meg turned five.

Additionally, he took a course in technology training, which qualified him to teach computer repair and build networks. He landed his first teaching job at a vocational school, only five miles from home. Karen couldn't have been prouder of Frankie's accomplishments, but she was also concerned. The stress of the past five years had taken its toll on her son. A new baby combined with a professional and educational facelift would challenge anyone's resilience. What was worrisome was Frankie's lack of enthusiasm. Her son no longer smiled or laughed, except to put up a false air when Meg was around. She hoped now that he was done with his degree the old Frankie would return.

*   *   *

Karen was both right and wrong. The old Frankie was returning, but not the *new* old Frankie, the one who had been adopted and turned his life around. Remnants of Frankie Ortiz were starting to materialize. He had worked his way up to a dozen or so shot glasses of hard liquor a day. Anything would do, but if given a choice, he'd rather have whiskey. He hid the smell by sloshing Listerine in his mouth and carrying peppermint or cinnamon drops in his pocket. What he had accomplished in the past five years hadn't registered with him. Instead, he beat himself up for not being a good enough provider.

"We need to move, Ken. We're beyond encroaching in my mother's space."

Now that she had Meg, Kendra's decision to move had changed course. She enjoyed having as many helping hands around as possible.

"Karen doesn't seem to mind," was the usual answer she gave.

The conversation usually ended in a battle of wills, one that left Frankie guzzling nips in the bathroom and Kendra's voice scratchy and raw from screaming. Frankie wasn't sure why she was so reluctant to move, but he did have a guess. Kendra's spending habits were excessive. Despite Frankie's many requests, she planned expensive trips without consulting him. Disney put them in the hole four grand because she insisted on staying on the grounds, purchasing every princess outfit that existed for Meg, and wanted to spend two weeks theme park hopping instead of one. Kendra didn't want them to feel rushed. That Christmas, without running it by Frankie, she bought Karen a new stove.

"You're living in the dark ages with that old thing. You'll love this one!" beamed Kendra.

Karen accepted the gift gracefully, but Frankie knew Kendra really bought the stove for herself. Why on earth would a woman who burned toast want a stove? He said nothing, swallowing his anger along with a nip.

* * *

Without having a discussion, Karen and Frankie were on the same wavelength about their cramped living arrangements, and Karen had made a mental note to make it her personal business to keep an eye out for potential real estate deals. One afternoon while visiting a client, Karen accidentally drove down a side street and knew immediately that her wrong turn was no accident. Directly in front of her was a yellow Colonial that looked to be perfect for Frankie and Kendra.

When she arrived home, Kendra was at the new stove cooking something in a pot.

"Mmm, smells good."

"Escarole soup," said Kendra. "I'm on my hundredth diet of the month."

Karen laughed. "Is Frankie going to be home for dinner?"

"He's here now."

"Oh, good. I wanted to talk to you guys."

Kendra stopped stirring and looked at Karen.

"Oh my God, you have cancer."

"No, I don't."

"You have heart disease."

"Wrong again, Ken."

"What is it, Karen? Tell me, because I heard you coughing the other day."

Ever since August's death, Kendra had somatic bouts, especially around hoarse coughs. In her mind, if you had a hoarse cough, you were going the way of August.

"Kendra, I am not sick in any way."

"Really and truly?"

"Promise."

"Then what's the emergency?"

"I don't remember saying there was one."

Kendra inspected the soup and turned down the flame.

"Oh. Okay, then," she said, hugging Karen tightly. "If you're not sick, what's up? Oh," she began in a sing-song voice, "Kar-en's got a boyyy-friend!"

"No such luck," laughed Karen.

Kendra shrugged and turned toward the den.

"Frankie," she yelled, "Get yer butt out here. Karen's got an announcement."

Frankie came into the kitchen with Meg trailing behind him. She was holding a paintbrush dripping with orange goop.

Kendra put her hands up in defeat and said, "It's totally washable, Karen. Totally."

"It's fine, Kendra," she sighed. "Now, let's say we sit and talk for a second, but let me assure you, there is nothing wrong."

"Were you going on about the coughing again?" Frankie snipped. "I told you, I had a tickle in my throat."

"No, I wasn't saying it was you. She came in here all, *I've gotta speak to you two.*"

"Shush!" Karen scolded them like children and wondered if they were actually going to be mature enough to pull this off. Once everyone was seated, she looked from Frankie to Kendra and said, "I love having you here . . ."

"And we love being here!" Kendra interrupted.

"Yes, honey. But I was thinking it might be time for a change."

"Change?" asked Kendra.

"Yes."

"Of what?"

"Of residence."

"You're moving?"

"Ken, she wants *us* to move," said Frankie, who turned to Karen. "I totally get it. I'm relieved, actually. We'll start looking this week."

"You don't have to do that."

"Don't you want us?" Kendra sulked. "I cook, you know. If it wasn't for me, you'd all be skin and bones."

"And I'm so grateful for that Kendra, but I think it's time you moved out on your own. Be more independent."

"I agree," said Frankie, nodding his head at Kendra in an encouraging way.

"Well, it's going to take a while to find the perfect home," Kendra sulked, a slight warning that she wasn't going to be gotten rid of easily.

"Not necessarily," Karen smiled.

Kendra went to the stove to check on her soup. "What do you mean?"

"I found a home you might like."

"How far away is it?" Kendra asked.

"Twenty minutes tops. Here's the agent's number. I don't think you'll be disappointed."

The couple went out that evening to look at the house. As Karen predicted, they immediately fell in love and signed an offer to purchase. Kendra used the remaining money her grandfather had left her for the down payment. They closed in just two months' time and settled quickly into their new home. At first, Meg couldn't understand where Nana K was, and for a full week scampered from room to room calling out "Nana K!, Nana K!, where are you, Nana K?" It wasn't until they visited Karen that Meg realized her grandmother was staying put.

"But Nana K," said Karen's blonde girl with a hint of fire in her hair. "I want you to live with us."

"Oh Meg, I'd love to live with you, but Nana K has to stay here," said Karen, who for many reasons considered this child to be the beginning and the end of all that was pure and good.

"Why?"

"Well, for starters, I want to. Won't it be fun to come and visit? We'll go shopping and play games and go out to dinner."

"Mommy says you won't eat now. She says you can't cook."

Karen looked at Kendra, who blushed and lightly patted Meg's head. "Thanks for throwing Mommy under the bus, kiddo. But Karen, let's face it, you burn toast, even with the knob on a light setting."

"Fair enough," Karen smiled. "But I'll be coming to visit you once a week for dinner. So you see, Meg, between Grandpa Carl, your mom, and leftovers, Nana K will be eating like a queen!"

PART 5

Kill the Killer

THE SLIPPERY SLOPE

On the days Karen ate dinner or stopped by for a cup of tea, Frankie was nowhere to be found. "He's busy trying to paint his next masterpiece in the basement or he's out for a run or I'm not sure where he went," were one of three replies a bitter Kendra would offer.

And then there was his full-time teaching job that he had worked years to acquire.

"Frankie's teaching experience hasn't been all that smooth," admitted Kendra.

"How do you mean?"

"Well, it's a large school system and he's the new kid on the block. He got the bottom of the barrel for classrooms, students, and books. He has four prep classes in three different classrooms and teaches out of a cart."

"That is tough," Karen agreed.

"And last week, he was accused of stealing tools from someone who should have been in a psych ward instead of teaching."

"He never told me," Karen spoke into her tea, which was cupped in her hand.

"He doesn't like to worry anyone. And he's so structured that it's maddening," said Kendra, running her fingers through her hair. "Everything has to be scheduled exactly. His morning run has to be at the same time every day, he has to eat at the same time, things have to be in a certain place. If not, it's like his entire world is turned upside down. And Karen, I think he's drinking. I mean *a lot*."

"Did you try talking to him about it?"

"Do I ever shut my mouth?" Kendra asked.

"True," Karen grinned. "What did he say?"

"He's in denial. Lately, it's been getting worse, but as a compulsive eater and shopaholic, I've been reluctant to judge."

Karen glanced at Meg, who was happily playing with her giant dollhouse that she received on her sixth birthday.

"Is it affecting our little one?"

"I don't think so, not yet. But I'm considering drastic measures soon."

"Like what?"

"Like going to Sheri's for a while."

"I had no idea things were this bad, Kendra."

Kendra shrugged and began fiddling with her fingernails.

"We haven't had sex in months. It's like I don't exist anymore. I feel more like his rival than his lover."

"How so?"

"C'mon, Karen. He's so jealous of whatever success I have, and I don't even care about it anymore. I'd rather quit painting and forfeit the spotlight to him than to spend my life worrying about bruising his fragile ego."

Karen reached out and placed her hand on top of Kendra's.

"I'm so sorry, Kendra. Should I speak with him?"

"If you think it will help," she said, biting her lower lip in an attempt to force back inevitable tears. "But be gentle. He's very sensitive to criticism."

Kendra momentarily let go of Karen's hand to wipe her nose on her sleeve. She let out a loud, unladylike snort and said, "There's something else I have to tell you. Brace yourself," she warned, flipping her hand over to give Karen's hand a squeeze. "I might be crazy."

Suppressing a smile, Karen replied, "Sweetie, we're all crazy. It just depends on what level. What you've been going through, and alone I might add, can easily make a person feel insane."

"Oh, this isn't about Frankie . . . well it is . . . but it's not. It's about me, about a situation I've been going through for years."

"A situation?"

"That's the best word I can think of to describe it. You see, for a while now, I've been seeing this . . ." Kendra paused and her face blushed.

"Seeing who?" asked Karen. "You're not having an affair, are you?"

"God, no. When would I have time for an affair?"

"Are you seeing a therapist then?"

"Karen, you keep interrupting me."

"Sorry," said Karen. "Go on. You were saying you're seeing someone."

"More like *something*."

"Something?"

"A ghost."

"A ghost?" Karen blinked.

"Yes," said Kendra, who was looking between the cuticle she was about to rip off and Karen.

"You mean like an apparition?"

"Uh-huh."

"Like, Boo?" Karen asked, splaying her hands in front of her.

"Yes, that's what I mean," Kendra said, in a heat of embarrassed tears that slid down her cheeks.

"And what is this ghost saying to you?"

"Not much. One minute I'm minding my own business and the next minute she's standing in my kitchen. At first she was a super pest, but over time I've grown fond of her."

A thought raced through Karen's mind. It was quicker than the blink of an eye and something Karen logically wanted to dismiss, but emotionally couldn't separate from. Maybe Kendra was like Anna, that psychic Karen had seen many years ago.

"Has this been a normal part of your life, seeing ghosts?"

"I don't see ghosts, as in plural. I see one ghost, and one ghost only."

"Okay," Karen spoke slowly, trying to process the information. "And have you always seen this one ghost?"

"Not always. When I was fourteen . . . don't laugh . . . I did a spell thing and that's when she came."

"A spell thing?" Karen confirmed, to be sure she was hearing her correctly.

"Yes, I cast a spell."

"Hmmm," was all Karen could respond.

The two sat quietly for a moment while Karen considered Kendra's past. This ghost could easily be a contrived fantasy, something Kendra didn't really see, but felt, like an imaginary friend. Karen was sure what she was hearing was a girl's coping abilities to make up for her parents' abandonment. During times of stress, Kendra's subconscious directed her to manufacture a ghost as a distraction to keep her from the reality and pain of what was occurring. Once Karen analyzed the situation, it made perfect sense. It was a healthy coping skill.

"And is this ghost here now?" Karen asked, not because she thought it were true, but to pacify Kendra, who was clearly distressed.

"Meg? No. She bops in now and again whenever I feel sad, it seems. Whenever," she paused thoughtfully, "I need a friend. And she loves my Meg, brags about her like she's her own."

Karen kept her face neutral, nodding supportively.

Poor Kendra . . . wait. Did she say Meg?

"Kendra, you just said Meg."

"That's her name."

"The ghost's name is Meg?"

"Uh-huh," Kendra said, matter-of-factly. "Where do you think I got my Meg's name from? The damn ghost was in the delivery room driving me nuts. Do you remember when you thought I was telling you to go away? I was saying go away to her."

Karen tried to keep a doubtful expression from covering her face.

"Okay," said Karen, waving her hands in front of Kendra. "Can we go back to this spell you claimed to have cast. Do you actually think it worked, Kendra? Is that why you think you see this ghost?"

"Karen, I don't *think* I see a ghost. I *see* a ghost. And yes, it has to have been the spell. It's the only thing that makes sense to me. If you promise you won't call one of your social worker friends to commit me, I'll tell you my ghost story."

Karen inhaled deeply. Kendra and her long-winded tales equaled a long afternoon. As patiently as she could, she replied, "Sure, let's hear your ghost story."

In one long breath, Kendra came out with it.

"Well, you know how my parents abandoned me, right? Back then, I would have done just about anything to get them to come home. I went to the library and rented a book that had a promising spell in it, one that would bring my parents home. It was my first time, mind you, I'm not a witch or anything. I don't craft, if that's what you're thinking. Because if I were a true witch, the spell wouldn't have misfired, which is obviously what happened. The spell called for a concoction and, come to think of it, I wonder if I didn't cheap out on the herbs and cup if any of this would have happened?"

Karen looked at Kendra blankly. The girl could tangent like no other. Kendra noted the impatience in her eyes and continued.

"Anyhoo, the next thing I know, poof, there she was."

"Poof?" questioned Karen.

"Well, not exactly. I recited the spell for a while, days, weeks, I can't remember, and then it was poof," Kendra said, opening her hands.

"And you named her Meg?"

"No, she told me her name was Meg."

"Do you remember the year and month you began seeing her?"

"I would say the fall of 1980, maybe September, but I can't be sure."

The date caught Karen's attention, who had begun to feel invisible fingers lightly running up and down the nape of her neck. If Kendra was fourteen that would have made Meg fifteen. But that would be ludicrous. No, it would be impossible. Sweat formed under her armpits anticipating Kendra's next response.

"Kendra, have you ever physically seen this ghost?"

"I've always seen her," Kendra said crisply. "I told you Karen, I'm not crazy."

"I never said you were," Karen tried to reassure her. "What's she look like?"

"A cute teenager, someone I would have been jealous of in high school," Kendra smiled. "We were around the same age when I first saw her. Course, she's still that age but I'm not, so now she looks like a kid. She's the same old feisty ghost she always was. Funny thing was, at first I thought she was retarded. I know that sounds harsh, but wait until you hear this—"

"Sorry," Karen interrupted, "but can you describe her physically?"

"Well, let me see. She has pretty gray eyes, she's about yay high and average sized."

Kendra turned her eyes up and to the right as if searching her brain for more information. "Oh, and her hair is funky cool."

"What does funky cool mean?"

"It's blonde and red at the same time, like highlights. Come to think of it," said Kendra thoughtfully, "It's the same color as my Meg's. Isn't that a hoot? I mean, it's not every day you see hair color that unique and . . . Karen, are you okay?"

Karen was clutching her heart locket and breathing hard, like she'd just run a marathon.

"Karen? Hey, Karen!" Kendra said, snapping her fingers in front of Karen's face.

"Oh, I knew I shouldn't have told you anything. This is exactly what happened when I told Frankie."

Karen felt as if she were struck by a bad virus. Her hand shook as she raised it to wipe the sweat that had begun to form on her brow.

"Karen," Kendra said, her voice full of concern, "Speaking of ghosts, you're as white as one. What can I get you?" she asked, leaning in toward Karen's face. Before she could react, Karen vomited all over Kendra and the kitchen table.

Kendra hopped to her feet, ran a dish towel under cool water and stuck it on Karen's forehead.

"Ewwww, you poor thing! Should I call the doctor or something?" she asked, pulling the chair away from the table with Karen still in it.

When Karen didn't answer, Kendra said, "Are you catatonic? Look, I didn't mean to scare you. It's all good. I lied. I've never seen a ghost."

Still no answer. At that point, Meg wandered into the room.

"Nana K, you got sick. Bleck! You need to go potty?"

"Nana K's fine," said Kendra. "Catatonic thanks to me, but fine. Do Mommy a favor and go turn on Sesame Street. I'll be right in to check on you."

Little Meg looked Karen up and down and, determining her grandmother would be okay, shrugged and walked toward the television. Kendra turned her attention back to Karen.

"Karen, I'm about to dial 911, stay calm."

As she turned to walk toward the phone, Karen grabbed her by the back of her tee shirt.

"No. I'm fine."

"If you're fine, mind telling me why you blew chunks everywhere?"

Karen couldn't bring herself to answer.

"I'm so sorry. Total overshare," Kendra sighed. "I spooked Frankie, and now I've spooked you."

"You didn't spook me, Kendra. It's just that, oh, how I can say this? My daughter," Karen's lower lip quivered, "looked exactly like this ghost you're describing."

Kendra felt Karen's forehead with the back of her hand. She kneeled in front of her and placed a hand on either side of Karen's arms. She talked slowly and deliberately.

"Ka-ren, re-main calllmmmm. You're hallucinating and might be having an aneurism or something. I am going to call for help."

Karen gently pulled Kendra's hands away and held them in hers. Looking directly into her sparkly, concerned eyes, she said, "I'm quite sane. For whatever reason, my daughter has come to you."

Now it was Kendra's turn to go pale.

"But I don't understand what you're saying to me. Karen, you don't have a daughter."

"But I *did*," Karen said.

"What happened to her?"

"She was murdered."

"Holy shit, that's horrible!" exclaimed Kendra, both hands covering her mouth. "How old was she?"

"Fifteen."

"I have a feeling I already know the answer to this next question; what was her name?"

"Meg. My daughter's name was Meg."

"Holy chills up and down my spine," Kendra shuddered. "But what makes you think my ghost is your Meg?"

When Karen spoke, her voice was strained with indifference. "I don't think. I'm not thinking. Meg died in 1980, during the dates you were doing that spell. You suddenly see a girl that looks and acts like her, a girl with the same name. If you really are seeing a ghost, I can't help wondering if it isn't Meg. I mean, how many coincidences can there be in this world? There has to be a connection."

"Wait a minute, I'm having a delivery room flashback. Meg pointed at you. She said you were her mother. I was confused and chalked it off as a crazy ghost moment."

"She told you that?"

"Yes, but then Meg came and ghost Meg left and I forgot all about it. Well then, no wonder Frankie freaked out. He had a twin. The pain must be too much for him to bear."

Karen shook her head. "Frankie doesn't know."

Kendra raised an eyebrow. "Frankie doesn't know his sister died?"

Karen swallowed hard. "Frankie didn't have a sister."

Kendra threw her arms in the air and slapped them against her thighs.

"Okay, time for a visit to our local hospital. I know a little pill called valium that will help. Let's go," she said, reaching for Karen's arm.

"Kendra," Karen pulled back, "Frankie was adopted."

"Adopted?"

"Correct."

"So, he's not your kid?"

"Biologically speaking, no."

"When did you adopt him?"

"Not long after Meg died."

"Shit," Kendra said, slouching back on her thighs. "It's obvious you two look nothing alike, but I figured he resembled his dad."

"He's a good mix of his biological parents," Karen said softly.

"But why keep such a secret, Karen? I mean, it's not like you lost a pet. This was your daughter, for Chrissake. No offense, but you call yourself a social worker?"

"I thought it was the right thing to do. Frankie came from a bad place," she explained, grabbing a tissue and blowing her nose. "I didn't want him to feel like a replacement child."

Kendra shook her head in disbelief. "First off, bad place? What in the hell does that mean? What kind of bad place did my husband come from? Secondly, if he's not Frankie Sherburne, who is he?"

"His real name is Frankie Ortiz," Karen said quietly.

"Ortiz? What is that? Spanish? Puerto Rican?"

"His mother was Dominican."

"This is just *super* great!" Kendra huffed. "I can't believe you thought keeping the fact you had a kid a secret was a good idea. And that you and Frankie kept his adoption from me outright sucks. What if my daughter ever needed a transplant? I mean, what in the hell were you two thinking?"

Karen ignored, may not have even heard, Kendra's ranting.

"Was she happy?"

"Was who happy?"

"Meg."

"Karen, I don't think talking about this is a good idea. I'm too wigged out right now."

Karen grabbed Kendra's wrist. "Please. You don't know what it's been like for me to live without her. She was my life. She was all I had in this world and she was taken from me by some monster. I need to know, Kendra, I need to know about my baby girl," she pleaded, her face etched with pain and remorse.

Kendra nodded. "I'm sorry, I'm being selfish. It was the shock of it all."

"I don't blame you one bit for being angry with me."

"I am angry, but I understand your reasoning, and Meg's death is far more important. The first time I saw her," Kendra began, "I was too busy shrieking like a screech owl to pay attention to the finer details. She asked me for help and . . . Karen? How was she murdered?"

"They think she was stabbed. She was found on the side of the highway, thrown away like trash."

"Oh my God," cried Kendra, slapping the back of her hand against her forehead. "Do you think she was still alive when she asked me for help?"

Karen hid her face in her hands and wept like a baby.

"Oh, God, Oh, God, Oh, God!"

"Oh, shit!" Kendra screamed, waving her hands nervously, as if she were shaking them dry. "Karen, I swear, there was nothing I could do."

Karen interrupted her by holding her hand up. "Where was she when you first saw her?" she sniffed.

"I don't know. She looked disheveled, like she'd fallen or something."

"So, no landmarks? Nothing you can recall that could help find the killer?"

Kendra's eyes opened wide. "They didn't find the killer?"

Karen slowly shook her head, her somber expression answering the question.

"Oh, Karen! I am so, so sorry!"

Karen had so many questions that she couldn't think of where to begin. She asked the first thing that came to mind.

"What did Frankie say?"

"Frankie said it was impossible, that there was no such thing as ghosts. He told me he never wanted to hear about it again."

They sat for a moment in silence before Karen asked hopefully, "Can you contact her for me?"

Kendra's eyes filled with pity and she bit her lower lip.

"I can't. It doesn't happen that way."

"Next time you see her will you tell her you know me? Ask her if she has a message for me?"

"I promise I will," said Kendra, hugging Karen tightly.

Karen nodded her head in understanding. "Will you call me the second it happens? Maybe she'll speak to me if she knows I'm there."

"I will. And, Karen?"

"Yeah," she said, wiping her eyes with a wad of tissue.

"I know this is an intense conversation and both of us are pretty shaken up. But since you're not having a heart attack or anything, do you think you can help me clean your vomit off my table?"

Karen looked with disgust at the kitchen table. When her wet eyes met Kendra's, the two let out a light chuckle before returning to solemn faces.

"Listen," said Karen, "I'd like to be the one to tell Frankie about Meg."

"You think that I was going to tread on that water? He's all yours," Kendra said, handing her a hot dishtowel and a bottle of disinfectant. "When do you think you'll tell him?"

"He stops by on Wednesdays, so I'll plan on doing it then."

"That's a week from yesterday."

"Then a week from yesterday it is," Karen said, exhaling loudly.

"Karen," wondered Kendra, "If this is your Meg, do you think it's almost like she knew our paths would eventually cross and came to protect us or something?"

"I'd like to think that," agreed Karen.

Just then, baby Meg appeared in the doorway.

"Nana K, are you better?"

"I'm all better Meg," said Karen, bending over to give her a squeeze.

"Good. Want to watch Sesame Street with me?"

"I'd love to, honey. Let me clean up this mess with mommy and I'll be right in."

That night, Karen tossed and turned, unable to sleep. It wasn't going to be easy for Frankie to hear that after all these years, Karen had been lying about her past. Would he reject her for the secrets she had kept from him, or would he understand that everything Karen did was for his own security and well being? She put herself in Frankie's shoes and tried to imagine how she would feel if he had kept an equally large secret from her. The answer was easy: she'd feel hurt and furious. She knew all there was to know about Frankie and yet she had never felt she could let her guard down enough to tell him about Meg. The topic felt off limits in a way Karen couldn't explain, like she had to protect Meg from Frankie, and Frankie from Meg. She drifted into a guilty sleep, hoping that her son would find it in his heart to forgive her deceit.

*   *   *

The following Wednesday, just like clockwork, Frankie appeared at the back door.

"Hey," he said, approaching Karen with a kiss on the cheek. "What's the good word?"

"Nothing much. You having your usual?"

"Sure am," he replied.

Karen walked over to the coffee pot and poured Frankie a small black coffee. Handing it to him, she suggested, "Let's sit in the living room where we can both relax."

Upon entering the room, which was dimly lit with scented candles, Frankie said, "Uh-oh. Candles and living room talk. This must be serious!"

They sat facing each other, bookends on the couch.

"Just wanted to have a heart to heart."

"Did Kendra talk to you about my drinking? I admit it's a little out of control, but I promised to cut back. She exaggerates everything, you know that."

"It's not about your drinking, though I would like to get to that later. It's about me," Karen said, lightheaded with anxiety. "I've kept some things from you that I feel guilty about."

"What kind of things?"

"Things that happened before you came along."

Frankie shifted uncomfortably. "You don't have to do this. If I never asked about it, it means I was okay with not knowing."

"Well, I'm not okay with it," she said guiltily.

"Karen, there's plenty you don't know. Let's not make this a big deal."

Karen held up her pointer finger. "You forget I was your social worker. I know everything there is to know about your past."

"Not quite."

"Then this will be the perfect time for us to clear the air so that we both feel worlds better."

"I doubt that," he said, sipping the hot coffee.

"Kendra told me that you two have been having a tough time and I think what I have to say will help clarify some things."

"About what?" he asked defensively.

"She told me about the ghost and I just thought—"

Frankie lifted up his hand. "Stop right there."

"There's nothing to be afraid of, Frankie. Let's talk about it."

"If I tell you everything, you'll hate me," he moaned.

"But she already told me everything; how you were spooked and didn't believe her, and asked her not to speak of it again."

"I only said that so she would stop."

"Why on earth would you do that to her?"

Frankie looked down at his hands. "The gingerbread house."

"I'm sorry?" said Karen.

"The drawing of the gingerbread house."

"What about it? It was one of your best drawings."

"Did you ever wonder why I refused to exhibit it?"

"You said you didn't like it."

"I was hiding something in it."

"Hiding something? What were you hiding, and what's this got to do with our conversation now?"

"I hid her in the gingerbread house. I tried to show you, to come clean that night, but you didn't see her. Then I lost my nerve."

"Hid who? What are you talking about? I don't understand you, and I'm confused enough as it is," Karen sighed.

Frankie got up and left the room. "Where are you going?" asked Karen.

"Give me a second," he called walking toward the kitchen. Karen heard the cellar door open and thought *this entire family is certifiable.*

Frankie reappeared with a backward facing painting. He turned the painting over to reveal the gingerbread house and leaned it against the coffee table in front of Karen.

"Look."

Karen looked at it.

"Okay."

"Look again."

Karen looked again and shrugged. "Still one of my favorites but Frankie, can we stay on topic? What on earth does this have to do with anything?"

"You can't see it?" he said, running his fingers through his hair in frustration.

"Yes, I can see the damn picture, Frankie," Karen said, her voice rising.

"But you don't see *her*?" he asked meekly.

"See her? See who? Who am I supposed to see?"

She stood up, and with her finger pointed at the picture, she looked at Frankie.

"You gotta throw me a bone here, Frankie, because to be honest, I'm about to lose my cool!"

"Just look at it," he insisted calmly. "Take a moment to really look at it."

Karen huffed and lowered her hand. She squatted in front of the painting and sarcastically recited what she saw.

"I spy with my little eye . . . a cottage, white picket fence, scalloped trim work, farmer's porch, window boxes, lamppost, brick walkway. I spy . . . a first floor, I spy . . . a second floor, I spy . . . who's that?" Karen whispered.

"I put her there to get her out of my head."

She dropped to her knees in front of the canvas and traced the outline of the girl.

"It happened right before you left the first time," he said quietly. "No one ever found out. What I remember most was her hair. It was like the colors of fall, like my Meg's."

Karen stared, captivated by the sharp gray eyes reflecting off the windowpane.

"How did I miss her?" she mumbled, lightly stroking the painting.

"The night that I drew it, I tried to tell you. I promised myself that if you noticed, I'd tell you everything. But then you left to make a phone call and by the time you came back, I lost my nerve."

Lost in a whirling dervish of disbelief, Karen mumbled, "Yes, I remember that night. I thought there was something more you had to say, but I didn't want to press you. I thought whatever it was, you'd work it out."

"It was an accident, a horrible accident," Frankie began.

Karen stopped stroking the picture and slowly turned to face Frankie.

"What was an accident?"

"The girl in my picture, she's the same girl Kendra described. She's Kendra's ghost," he blurted, his voice laced with panic.

"I think she wants revenge. I'm afraid she'll take Meg!" he cried.

"But why would she do that?"

Frankie swallowed hard and told Karen everything he remembered about that day.

"I was walking with my friend Adam, and there she was. She looked so damn happy and full of herself. I only meant to scare her, but I was way too stoned. I told her to give me her purse and she yelled something at me, something like, eat my shorts. She was feisty; she reminded me of everything I wasn't and of everything I wanted, and of all the kids who called me trailer trash. Until Kendra mentioned her, I thought she may have been alive. All these years, I've been telling myself she was alive and that I couldn't have killed her."

"Go on," Karen said, her voice barely audible.

"Me and Adam, we put her in his car. We put her—" Frankie's voice crackled with pain. "I thought she'd be found alive."

"You put her where, Frankie?"

"We drove to a spot on the highway. We walked down a ways and placed her on the ground. I thought eventually she'd climb up and go home. I only wanted to scare her," he said, dropping his head into his hands. "And this ghost, at first I thought it was just Kendra being Kendra, but then she started to describe her. It was her hair that caught my attention; I've only seen two people in my entire life with that hair color," Frankie laughed bitterly. "What were the odds of my daughter having that same hair color?"

Karen returned to the painting, running her fingers across the girl in the portrait, "How sure are you that the ghost that Kendra claims to see is the same girl you hurt, the same girl you drew here?"

"I would bet my life on it."

"Then, your life it is," Karen muttered.

"What?" Frankie sniffed. "Did you say something?"

Karen removed her hand from the painting and said, "I need you to leave. Please, go."

"I knew you'd hate me."

"I don't hate you, Frankie. It's just, this is a lot of information to absorb."

"Do you think I should tell Kendra?"

"I think she has the right to know," Karen said coldly. "Don't you?"

Frankie nodded stiffly. "Yeah."

Karen rose to her feet and pointed Frankie toward the back door. Just before he left, he turned his cheek toward his shirt and wiped his red, swollen eyes on his collar. He paused, waiting for something; a hug, a word of assurance, anything that would ease his discomfort, but Karen just stared blankly at him, like she never saw him before in her life. He nodded once and quietly shut the door.

* * *

Karen stood stiffly by the door until she heard the car drive down the road, then she dropped to her knees and clutched her stomach, folding her body into itself. After a few deep breaths, she allowed herself to sink onto the floor where she lay on her side. She opened her mouth and let out a silent scream. Her mind raced with incoherent thoughts. If someone were to walk in, they would have thought her insane. Laying there motionless with a blank expression and hollow eyes, she experienced a flood of caseload flashbacks. Some had grown into productive human beings, others had gone the way they were predicted to go. An estimated guess would be a recovery rate of 60/40.

Was that good enough? Was that worth her life? Actually, that was a misstatement.

Was it worth her daughter's life?

Were Harry and David and Patty, Angelo, Carlos, and Melissa, Roseann, Rebecca, and Travis, and the list went on, all worth Meg's having lived as a latchkey kid?

And what about Sonia? She was a Hole fanatic who, when she wished to terminate a meeting would begin singing Doll Parts.

Karen listened to Sonia sing that song every week for almost a year. At the fourth meeting, she asked Sonia why she liked it so much. "It's about love and rejection. I especially like when it talks about being able to fake it so much that you don't even know you're faking it anymore."

Karen could see the girl's reasoning; Sonia's history was a father who sexually abused her and a mother who had blamed and rejected her daughter for her husband's actions.

"Not everyone you love will reject you, Sonia."

Because this was a topic she wasn't ready to broach, Sonia stared past Karen and in a haunting voice began singing the song, about how someday Karen would ache, just like Sonia did.

Where was she today? Did Sonia survive the demons in her life, or was she married to a man like her father, a heroin addict with a penchant for sexually abusing young children?

In too short a time, Karen had lost her husband, her mother and her daughter. It had taken her so long to feel right. Never better, but just 'right'. Now, she'd never be right again. In that moment, she understood how deeply Sonia ached and could hear the girl singing that haunting song, the one she had used to separate herself from the rest of the world. Karen's ache burned straight to her core, and she could feel the softness around her heart hardening, shellacked by a thick, black paste. Her voice began with a soft hum before progressing into a scream that, had the neighbors not been eighty years old and deaf, would have come running to her rescue. Karen sang until her throat was raw and then allowed herself a moment to regain her composure. She struggled to her feet, scampering unsteadily to her purse. In a blind rage, she fumbled for her wallet. Behind her license was a crumpled card with a pager number on it. Without considering the consequences of her actions, Karen picked up the phone and dialed. She waited for the beep, punched in her number, and hung up. She walked into the bathroom, vomited, and when the phone rang five minutes later, she was ready.

"Lenny, it's Karen Sherburne."

"Hey-ho, Karen. Isn't this a nice surprise! To what do I owe the pleasure of your voice?"

"How are you, Lenny?" Karen asked, avoiding his question.

"I'm fine, Karen," Lenny said slowly. "How is yourself?"

"Not so fine," Karen wept softly.

"I kinda figured you didn't call to shoot the shit."

"You figured right."

"In that case, I'm all ears. Whatever you need, I won't let you down."

"I need, how did you put it, an organizational expert."

"What kind of mess are we looking at?" Lenny asked cautiously.

"A pretty big one."

"Well, I got a couple packages. An organizational fix, where I hafta to go in and help folks get on the right track, then I got what I'd refer to as a reality slap, where clean up goes a bit deeper and things have to be broken down in order to be rebuilt. Lastly, I got a total reorg, where things are such a mess that the only cure is to demolish everything. The reorg," Lenny clarified, "equals final."

Karen interpreted Lenny's packages: *a threat, a beating, or kill the killer.*

"I want the reorg," she answered vehemently.

"You're certain? Because I want ya to know that once the reorg begins, there's no stoppin'it. What's taken apart is taken apart."

Stunted by anger and grief, she blurted, "I know what I want, and I want the reorg. I found him, Lenny."

Karen sensed Lenny's lips forming a twisted grin.

"Well then," he said, "I guess it's showtime. Let's meet for coffee soon so we can formulate a plan. Call me in a couple days and I'll tell you where we can meet."

Karen hung up expecting to feel remorse, but remorse didn't come. Abhorrence came. And for this, she was grateful.

* * *

While Karen was speaking with Lenny, Meg was enjoying an area of the field scented with daffodils and sucking on grass that tasted like dill pickles. For the first time since being in her grassy field, she experienced a sensation from another lifetime, one that caused her to bring her hand to her side, fingering the area. She withdrew her hand expecting to see, for reasons she couldn't recall, blood.

"That's odd," she said, sniffing the tips of her fingers, which emanated an acrid combination of rotten vegetables and dog poo. If she could have put a name to it, Meg would have said the smell on her fingers leaked of revenge.

"Huh," she said turning her hand over in front of her face. "That's just freaky."

From the vast, colorful field Meg heard a soft, familiar voice say *Almost time, Megan.*

"Grandma Vicki, is that you?"

Meg stood and scanned the area. She was about to shout her grandmother's name when the bluest blue jay she'd ever seen landed on her shoulder and began chirping.

"You have blueberry breath!" laughed Meg.

And everything else melted away.

*   *   *

Frankie came home in such a bad mood that Kendra didn't dare ask what he and Karen had discussed. An entire week passed before she decided to brave the topic.

"So, did Karen speak with you about anything in particular last week?"

"Like what?" he snipped.

"Like my ghost?"

"Of course," Frankie snorted. "I should have known."

"Should have known what?"

"That everything always has to revolve around you."

"That's not true," Kendra snapped. "She mentioned she was going to speak to you about it, is all. Excusssee me for asking."

Frankie looked at his wife's hurt expression and relaxed his shoulders. "She didn't have a chance to speak to me about anything because I dropped my own bomb."

"You had a bomb? What bomb?" asked Kendra.

Frankie painstakingly divulged his past; who his parents were, where he grew up, and finally, stabbing Meg. Kendra listened patiently to everything, until he revealed what had happened with Meg.

"No, this can't be true. You murdered someone? You," she paused, shaking her finger at him, "took a girl's life?"

Frankie looked vacantly past Kendra. His eyes were red and puffy, his face blotchy.

"I may vomit right here," said Kendra pacing back and forth. "Yep, I'm gonna hurl," she gagged, racing to the kitchen sink. She wretched violently until her stomach was empty, then continued to dry heave for a number of minutes before splashing water on her face and dabbing herself dry with a hand towel. She turned and faced Frankie, and with a hoarse voice asked, "What did Karen have to say?"

"She told me to leave."

"That's it?"

"Pretty much," he said, sniffing. "She was in shock, and who could blame her. After all she did for me, it's like a slap in the face. I should have told her years ago, when it happened."

Frankie was missing pieces of the puzzle, but Kendra wasn't. As they stared at each other in silence, Kendra's puzzle fell into place: *If Meg was Karen's kid, and Frankie killed Meg, my husband killed his adoptive mother's daughter. On top of this, my Meg's namesake is none other than Karen's murdered daughter, who once again, was killed by my husband. This is some sick, twisted, stomach churning shit. August must be turning over in his grave.*

"This is un-fucking forgivable, Frankie. You do know that?" yelled Kendra, who was praying that Meg remained asleep through the commotion.

"I haven't asked for your forgiveness, Kendra. I don't expect it. But please believe me, it wasn't intentional. I never meant to hurt her."

"You've got to right this. You've got to get your ass to the police and tell them everything."

"What? Are you crazy? They won't care that this was an accident. They'll fry me. Is that what you want? Do you want me to go to jail for an accident that happened years ago? Trust me, the boy who killed that girl died along with her."

"Well, I'm sure her parents don't feel like it was years ago, and you look alive to me. You owe her . . . er, them . . . you owe her parents, Frankie, whoever they are. I'm sure the authorities would be lenient considering you were underage, it was an accident, and you didn't know you actually . . . killed her," Kendra's voice trailed off. "I'll go with you to the station."

"I can't do it," he sobbed.

"There could be some statue of time or whatever they call it, who knows."

"It's statute," Frankie corrected.

"Are you really going there and correcting me?" Kendra howled, then lowering her voice asked, "Don't you want to clear your soul?"

"Clear my soul?" he asked. "Ken, I'm not sure I ever owned a clear soul. I was born damaged goods."

"Well, I don't believe that and quite frankly, it sounds like a copout. Please don't let the past strangle our future, Frankie. If you turn yourself in, talk to someone . . ."

"I said no," Frankie growled, banging his fist on the countertop. "I won't sacrifice what I have now for a fucking accident! Don't you see, they'll find out who I was and they'll think I did it on purpose. I'll end up in jail like the white trailer trash everyone always thought I was. I will not give my life away for a fucking dead girl!"

Kendra looked at Frankie in shock and disgust.

"I promised to stand by you for better or for worse, but I refuse to stand by this. I will not allow our daughter to live here, with the blood of a dead girl on your hands," Kendra said softly. Within an hour, she packed herself and Meg each a suitcase and phoned Sheri to let her know they were coming to stay indefinitely.

She carried a groggy Meg to the car and then came back for the suitcases. Picking up one in each hand, she turned to face Frankie. The man she fell in love with had vanished and in his place was someone she didn't know, someone she wished had never floated to the surface.

"Kendra," Frankie pleaded. "We can work this out."

Kendra let out a puff of air that said *are you kidding me?* "No, Frankie. We can't. Please don't come over or call. I'll let you speak with Meg, only because I can't bring myself to tell her that her father is a murderer. But come near us and I swear I'll get a restraining order against you, and believe you me, I won't hesitate to tell them why."

"You're killing us, Ken."

Kendra stared at Frankie as if he were an alien. Remembering her grandfather's warning—*You have an obsession with thugs, don't go marrying a thug*—she replied, "You killed us, Frankie. You . . . you . . . *thug.*"

She turned on her heel and headed to the car. She didn't look back to see that Frankie had dropped to his knees and was covering his face in his hands, nor did she notice ghostly Meg standing behind him, looking confounded by the turn of events.

RELIVING THE LAST

Meg plopped down under the oak tree beside Rocky. She grabbed a blade of grass and sucked hard.

"Cream soda," she nodded. "Good choice."

She threw the blade behind her and animatedly explained what she had witnessed to Rocky. "Kendra left Frankie, called him a murderer. What do you suppose that means? Do you think it means he's *really* a murderer? I can't believe it, I just can't . . . ow," Meg moaned, "my aching side." Momentarily distracted by the pain, Meg didn't hear the voices right away. She only stopped examining her side when she heard herself say, *She thinks I'm defiant.*

"What the?" she wondered, her attention drawn to a giant movie screen that had materialized five feet away from her. Meg stared at herself on the big screen, her image paused with a phone to her ear. It wasn't until she sat in the theater seat that appeared for her use that the movie commenced.

Are you? the woman on the other end of the phone asked.

"That's Sarah," Meg grinned. "She was always nice to me."

Of course I am. I'm a teenager. Meg watched herself smirk on screen in that cocky way teenagers do when they think they're cool.

I'll tape a note to her computer that her defiant, but adorable daughter called.

Love it. See ya, Sarah.

The movie screen flashed white then showed Meg in front of the grocery store flipping her headphones around her neck. She walked into the store and the screen flashed again, showing her exiting with a gallon of milk and humming a Blondie song.

"Oooo, I love that song!" she smiled.

Meg watched herself rummage through her purse. She was so engrossed, she almost collided with a girl.

Whoops! On screen Meg said.

"Man, I was a rude one," Meg remarked, her cheeks blushing pink. "I almost took out that . . . hey, that's Kendra." Meg stood and pointed firmly at the screen. She turned to Rocky, who was still under the tree and shouted, "Rocky, look, it's Kendra!"

When she turned back the screen flashed white again. Meg was in an alleyway and two boys were trying to steal her purse.

Eat my shorts!

"That's right, sister. You tell them," Meg said proudly. No one messes with . . . hold everything. Rocky, come here," she motioned. "Come look at this." Though Rocky remained under the oak tree, Meg acted as if he were sitting next to her. "Isn't that Frankie? Kendra's Frankie? What's he doing?" Meg watched as Frankie produced a small object and pierced her side. She mirrored the movie screen Meg by touching her own side. She withdrew her hand and held it up to her face. There was blood on her fingers, but as soon as she blinked, the blood disappeared. Scary movie music brought her attention back to the screen. It flashed white and the boys were carrying Meg down a steep hill. The screen flashed again and Meg saw herself lying on the ground and heard the sound of the car abandoning her. The screen flashed one last time, and with tears rolling down her cheeks, Meg watched herself die.

LETTERS TO MEG

Dear Meg,

My permanent brain setting is locked on the channel of broken dreams, and now with this incomprehensible discovery, I find myself thinking that my life after your death has been nothing but a sick joke. I mean, did God really think it would be a good idea that I raise your murderer as my own son? Did he really think I was strong enough to forgive such a trespass? I've searched my soul, and guess what? I can't find an ounce of Mother Teresa inside of me.

I've been deprived of your humor and sarcasm, your quick wit and contagious giggle, and even your belligerence. I find it extremely unfair we didn't get to experience monumentally explosive fights that ended with us clinging apologetically to each other and then ordering a pepper and onion pizza. Those days were yet to come; those bonding days of mother and daughter, where age releases childhood disclosures that had been hidden in the closet for years. I'll never find out your deepest secrets or see your dreams realized as you grow into the woman you were meant to be. I have ached every single day of my life without you, vowing vengeance on the person that stole you from me.

What a twist of fate that person happens to be my adoptive son. But I can't let the little details get in my way, can I Meg? I've done something wonderfully horrible. And in doing so, I'm pretty damn sure I've crossed that fine line that separates the sane from the totally fucked up. But I don't care.

Frankie and I will always have three things in common: you and the fact that no matter what we do for the rest of our lives, we'll always hate ourselves. Him for killing you, and me for opening my heart to my daughter's killer. And both of us, no matter what good we do in this life, will be murderers. It's time to end the pain, Meg.

Kendra and Meg moved out. They're safe at Sheri's. Lenny said that it's time to go big or go home. After all these years, revenge will finally be mine.

Stay tuned,

Love,
Mom xoxox ☺

LASSO OF TRUTH

"What did I just see?" Meg asked, and then more emphatically, "What did I just see!" She closed her eyes and, as they did with Kendra, the puzzle pieces fell into place.

I was killed by Frankie who married Kendra who are both connected to Mom. Little Meg, who is named after me, is the daughter of the man who murdered me.

"Rocky, I've got to somehow tell Mom about this. Maybe if I concentrate hard enough, I can zap myself to Kendra and tell her everything and then she can tell Mom and then . . ." the movie screen distracted her with the theme song from *Wonder Woman.*

And there she was, the Amazon warrior princess, with her superhuman strength and invisible plane. In a skimpy outfit that resembled the American flag, she conquered villains with the help of her indestructible bracelets and lasso of truth.

A large table appeared next to Meg. On it were a bucket of popcorn, a giant Snickers bar and a large Pepsi.

"Yummmm," she said cheerfully, and then, "Ooo, I know all of the episodes by heart. Rocky, come watch Wonder Woman!"

As Meg watched Wonder Woman swing her lasso of truth, her own truths were obliterated, and she forgot all about her last days on earth.

"Ha, ha," she laughed pointing at the screen. "I love this episode. Rocky, you're gonna love this!" Meg smiled, forcing a handful of buttery popcorn into her mouth.

TRUE NORTH

Karen and Lenny had two more conversations, a virtual one and a face to face meeting. First was a brief phone discussion where Lenny spoke cryptically, inviting her to a coffee shop across town.

"Is your aunt still ill?"

"My aunt?"

"Yeah, you're aunt. The one you said didn't look like she was gonna make it."

"Oh, my *aunt*. Yes, she's still ill."

"You still hoping she'll get rid of her sickness?"

"Very much so."

"Why don't we meet for a cup of coffee so's we can continue our discussion in person? We can meet at the new coffee shop downtown."

"But won't it be crowded?" she asked, worried that they'd be overheard, then becoming paranoid about phone taps added, "I mean, I don't want to go to a busy shop where it's hard to hear and we'd have to shout and all."

"Naw, it tends to be empty mid afternoon."

"Okay then, where is this new place?"

"Right in the center next to Tony's Cleaners. It's called True North. The lattes are to die for." Karen could hear the slight chuckle in Lenny's voice and knew he was pleased with his play on words.

"When?"

"Tomorrow, let's say three o'clock."

When Karen entered the shop, she found Lenny tucked in a corner by the door, at a table that was separate from the rest of the patrons. In front of him were a half-eaten chocolate chip muffin and a blueberry scone. He was sipping a frothy coffee.

"I'm sorry," Lenny apologized. "I was starving and started without you."

"I have to admit," grinned Karen, "I'd never have guessed you for a frothy coffee kind of guy."

Lenny dabbed the corner of his mouth with his napkin and with smiling eyes answered, "I'm fulla surprises."

Karen ordered a black coffee and joined Lenny at the table. They conversed quietly, Karen so worried about being overheard that her lips hardly moved when she spoke. Lenny asked about logistics; where Frankie lived, was there a garage, what kind of car did he drive, what time he usually left and arrived home during the week, did they own any pets, were the neighbors nosey, did Karen trust that Kendra wouldn't stop in without warning.

"Because if they do stop by unexpectedly, it will become a most unfortunate situation for all involved. If you can control anything, control his wife from bringing your grandkid over in two days."

"Two days? It's going to happen in two days?"

"If what you're tellin' me is accurate, two days is a fine time to visit," Lenny's eyes shone wickedly.

Karen looked at Lenny, acknowledged with a head nod, but was unable to verbally reply.

Was she really having this conversation?

"Karen?" Lenny snapped his fingers in front him. "Unless you've changed your mind?"

"What?" Karen replied, responding to his action. "No, I haven't changed my mind."

Unconvinced, Lenny reached his thick arm across the table and patted Karen's hand. "Karen, maybe you're feelin' numb right now. Afta'all, you just found out who murdered your kid, which is quite a shock to one's system. Maybe we should wait it out a bit because if you change your mind once it's too late, you'll have a hard time gettin' over the ball you got rollin'."

"Lenny," Karen said firmly. "I've been waiting to have a change of heart ever since I contacted you. But," she said, briefly closing her eyes, "I haven't. I'm standing by my vow to Meg."

"Vows are broken all the time, Karen."

"Not by me," she said with the same anger she had used on Anna the psychic many years ago.

Lenny examined Karen, his eyes searching hers for traces of indecision.

"What?" she asked, in an adolescent *stop looking at me* way.

"I don't know," he shrugged.

"Don't know what?"

"I'm trying to forward think, Karen."

He kept his eyes on Karen for a minute longer before nodding to himself.

"What?" she asked again, fidgeting in her chair.

Lenny looked down and, with the tip of his broad pointer finger, collected the scattered crumbs into a single small pile in the center of his plate.

"I've been comin' here since this place opened," he said. "The lady who owns it, her name is Paula."

"That's nice Lenny, but this matters because?"

"Do you know why she named this place True North?" he asked, but before she could reply, he answered his own question. "I do, cause I liked the name an' asked her about it. She told me that everyone has a true north an' that finding your own true north means knowing your purpose in life, knowing what your values are. It's about trusting your instincts. She told me opening this shop was her destiny, her true north. Now, if there is the tiniest bit of doubt about what's going on between you an' me, you got exactly two days to call it quits."

Karen's agitation drove her to push back her chair and stand up. "Whatever the hell my true north was died with my daughter. I need you to finish it, Lenny." Karen rubbed her face with the palm of her hand. "I've got things to do. Contact me when it's done."

"As you wish, Karen. Just remember," he said, popping a mint in his mouth and motioning for her to lean in. When they were nose-to-nose, Lenny whispered, "This ain't something you can shout do-over on once it's done."

"I understand that," she whispered back.

"Good. Now remember, in two days, you make sure you know where your grandkid and her mother are at. And here," he said handing her a mint, "You got coffee breath."

Karen accepted the mint, turning it over in her hand. *So this is my life. I'm with a killer who is worried about coffee breath.* She popped the mint in her mouth, patted Lenny's shoulder, and walked briskly out of the coffee shop.

SCENTS OF MEG

Two days later, Karen called Kendra to ensure she wasn't going to be visiting Frankie.

"Any plans tonight?" she asked, trying to sound nonchalant.

"None. I'm pretty wiped out."

"Have you seen Frankie at all?"

"You know I haven't seen him since we left. I'm not ready to see him. I don't know if I'll ever be ready." Kendra sounded miserable.

"Would you and Meg like to go out for ice cream?"

"What part of me being wiped didn't you understand?" Kendra teased.

"How about I come over, just for a short visit?"

"I appreciate the offer, but honestly, I think I'm going to hit the sack soon. Can we do breakfast tomorrow morning?"

"We sure can," Karen said, wondering if she should police Sheri's house to make sure Kendra and Meg stayed put.

"Karen, regardless of what happens with me and Frankie, I think you need to tell him about your Meg, our Meg; I mean, my ghost Meg. I don't know how much longer we can all go on like this."

"It won't be much longer," Karen assured her. "I'm working on it now, I promise. I'll pick you up tomorrow morning around nine."

"Mind if I leave Meg with Sheri so that we can speak adult freely?"

"You read my mind," answered Karen.

Karen hung up the phone and decided that good and drunk was the only way she was going to get through the evening. She poured a shot of scotch, swigged it, and promptly helped herself to another, allowing the alcohol to steal her lucidity and swarm her head with the unbelievable circumstances since Meg's death.

More scotch.

Lifting the glass to her lips, she told herself that she didn't really love Frankie. Never had. The selfish truth was that none of it had anything to do with saving Frankie. It was, as Marty and her father had suspected, about replacing Meg. It had always been about replacing irreplaceable Meg.

Another shot down the hatch.

Karen had assumed that Frankie's anger and bouts of violence stemmed from being beaten, molested, and neglected. Once those factors were removed, she was certain he'd reform. And he did, but not in time to prevent Meg's death. Did she miss something that would have indicated what he was capable of when they first met? *No,* she thought, *I worked with Lenny for years, and look at him. He's a contract killer who I hired to kill my adopted son who killed my daughter.*

She laughed insanely, laughed so hard she graduated into a coughing fit. Trying to catch her breath, she closed her eyes and inhaled a mixture of familiar smells. It was the sweet powdery scent of Love's Baby Soft and grape lollipops. Leaning forward to sniff the air, she whispered, "Meg? Is that you?"

* * *

Frankie turned on the shower then leaned on the counter, watching his image evaporate in the mirror. He switched on the radio and began undressing. Sliding the shower curtain aside, he inserted his hand to make sure that the temperature was hot enough to feel the burn, but not hot enough to scald him.

* * *

Kendra, Meg, and Sheri were enjoying a cup of tea and banana bread when Kendra asked, "Do you smell that?"

"Smell what? Don't tell me I left the oven on," said Sheri, who had turned her attention to the stove.

"No, not hot food," replied Kendra curiously. "I smell grapes and baby powder."

"You're weird, Mommy," giggled Meg, picking the walnuts out of her banana bread.

"Weird is my middle name," Kendra grinned, rustling Meg's unique colored hair. "Now, what say we wrap it up and get you ready for bed? I've been working on a sketch and feel compelled to finish it."

* * *

Lenny was walking toward his car whistling, "Whistle while you work" when a strong whiff of berry and powdery perfume stopped him dead in his tracks. His eyes darted around, while he sniffed like a dog, searching for the source of the smell. Not so much as a leaf was rustling in the wind.

"Must be my imagination," he shrugged, proceeding with his tune.

* * *

"Meg?" pleaded Karen, who was mourning the loss of the already faded smell that was her daughter. She slumped back against the couch. Hoping to escape through sleep, she closed her eyes and drifted into an uncomfortable state, the glass of scotch still in her hand. Expecting to be haunted with visions of Meg, she was instead assaulted with memories of Frankie. The night she found him beaten to a pulp. The honors he had received in school. The first time he referred to her as his mother. The granddaughter he had given her.

Karen's eyes popped open. How foolish had it been to think that she was in charge of the delicate balance of the universe? Avenging Meg's death would destroy too many lives, including Kendra's and Meg's. And though her emotions now swung like a pendulum on speed . . . she despised and loved Frankie . . . it was simply not her place to destroy him.

"What have I done!" she cried, releasing the glass of scotch so that it fell to the floor and shattered into pieces.

"Ow, ow, ow, shit," she cursed, plucking out shards of glass from her heel, hopping on one foot and searching for her car keys.

"Keys, keys, where are my fucking keys!" she panicked, before reciting the Saint Anthony prayer and remembering they were in her jacket pocket. Head buzzing from the effects of the alcohol, Karen formulated a plan. She'd race to Frankie's to head off Lenny, putting an end to the horrible wheels she had set in motion. She shrugged on her jacket and ran for the car, but lost her balance and slipped on the wet pavement, resulting in a nasty scrape on her left knee.

"Frankie," she moaned, scrambling to her feet. Karen ran, almost sideways, toward her sedan. Flooring the gas pedal, she raced down the street, praying no cars or pedestrians would cross her path.

THE COSMIC COLLISION

After four days of zero hygienic care, Frankie decided to shave. He filled his hand with a mound of shaving cream and mashed it on, like a pie in the face. It smelled of grapes and baby powder, a very odd thing as the can clearly said unscented shaving cream. He looked at the razor and wondered if he were capable of ending what seemed to be a life doomed to misery. As early as he could remember, he had witnessed sex, drugs, and prostitution. Throughout his early years, he had felt hungry and tired and constantly ill, living with a nagging stomachache that stole his natural desire to eat. And the girl, who could forget about the girl? He didn't stab her for her purse. He had seen her before.

And not just once, many times.

She didn't go to his school, but must have lived close by because she pranced by the supermarket and in front of the five and dime, laughing with her friends and puffing on cigarettes. She was cute, confident, and definitely cared for.

And she disturbed Frankie.

Who was she to strut around like 'Her Highness of the Royal Court' with her Parliaments and fancy purse and seemingly perfect life? The girl wouldn't know a shitty day if it walked up and bit her on the ass. All Frankie had was shitty days.

No, Frankie didn't hurt her because of a few lousy bucks in her wallet. And he didn't hurt her by accident. Her existence had made a mockery out of his own life. She represented everything he would never have, a security that he would never know. He had stolen her life because he was envious, and now there was no way to amend it. With a shaking, untrustworthy hand, he brought the razor to his neck and ever so slowly, began to shave.

* * *

"Time for bed, Meg," said Kendra, leading her daughter into Sheri's spare bedroom.

"When are we going home, Mommy? I miss my own bed. I miss Daddy."

"When Daddy's cold gets better," sighed Kendra, tucking the covers under her daughter's chin.

* * *

Driving with her left hand like a demon on speed, Karen leaned toward the passenger seat and into her pocketbook, fumbling blindly for Lenny's pager number.

Where was the damn card? It was always tucked just inside her wallet. On any other day, she could have placed her hands on it a million times over and now that she wanted it, it wasn't there.

"God dammit!" she cursed, spanking the steering wheel.

* * *

Lenny pulled onto Frankie's street ten minutes early. If there was one thing he abided by over the course of his career, it was keeping to his schedule. He drove by Frankie's house and turned around, parking five houses down and to the left, where he could keep an eye out in case Frankie decided to leave the premises unexpectedly. He swung his large body sideways and stepped onto the curb without a sound. He took care closing the car door so that only the slightest click could be heard. His size fourteen shoes turned to the right, collecting grains of sand that made a light scratching noise against the cement. As was customary for Lenny, he reached into his brown leather aviator jacket

Jodi Blase

and pulled out two Marlboros, sticking one behind his ear and one between his lips. He bit it, and then moved it from side to side before finding a satisfactory spot in the left hand corner of his mouth.

Lenny struck a match and took a hit off his cigarette. He walked slowly up the stone walkway, counting his steps; *one, two, three, four.* Though he appeared simple-minded, Lenny was a calculating man who was always processing; *five, six, seven, eight.* He had the uncanny ability to see at least twelve moves ahead right from when his shoe touched the grainy pavement; *nine, ten, eleven, twelve.* He inhaled deeply and exhaled slowly, tipping his chin upward and blowing billows of smoke toward heaven. The air was breezy and the stars peeked out through the darkness. *What a beautiful night,* he thought to himself, *a fine night to die.* As cumbersome as he appeared, Lenny moved as deftly as a cat hunting its prey. He smiled to himself, knowing that he was going to enjoy tonight. Usually his feelings were impersonal, but this hit was going to be a pleasure. This guy had the nerve to kill Karen's daughter and then assume the role of her son, sucking off of her like a bloody leech. It was downright perverse.

Lenny did his due diligence in deciding how he was going to kill Frankie . . . gunshot, strangulation, poisoning, hypodermic needle . . . in the end, he chose blowing his brains out. To him, shooting a person was as gratifying as shattering a dish against the floor. The impact, the sound of something breaking, the little pieces flying everywhere. It was a real stress reliever. He couldn't wait to smell the stench of this guy's death.

* * *

Karen dovetailed around corners, ignoring stop signs and pedestrian walkways, cursing at the yellow light that prevented her from moving forward. She was looking from left to right, debating whether to run the light, when a crinkled card on the floor of the passenger's seat caught her eye.

"Yes!" she exclaimed, grabbing the card, before screaming, "You've *got* to be kidding!"

328

She banged her hands against the steering wheel when she realized that in her harried rush, she'd left her cell phone on the table in the hallway.

*   *   *

Kendra pulled out her drawing pad and examined her nearly finished sketch.

"Who's that?" asked Sheri, who had quietly approached her from behind.

"Oh, this? No one. Just a face I couldn't get out of my head."

"I've never seen you draw a person before. This is quite good," beamed Sheri.

Kendra looked at Sheri quizzically.

"What is it, dear?"

"You sure you don't have perfume on?"

"Nothing I haven't worn before."

"I smell it again. That perfume all the girls used to wear in high school. What was the name of it again? Oh yeah," Kendra remembered, "Love's Baby Soft."

"Kendra," sighed Sheri. "I don't smell a thing. Your mind is playing tricks on you. I don't know everything that happened and I won't pry, but don't you think it's high time you phoned Frankie to clear the air?"

"I'm afraid I won't be able to forgive him for what he did."

"Maybe not, but having a conversation couldn't hurt, could it?"

"I don't know. As it stands now, I don't think I'll ever trust him again."

Sheri nodded sympathetically and patted Kendra's shoulder.

"You know, the more I look at this drawing, the more lifelike it becomes. It's almost as if her eyes are speaking to you."

"What are they saying?" asked Kendra.

"They look," Sheri said thoughtfully, "like they're saying thank you."

When Sheri retired to her room, Kendra struggled with her thoughts. *I should call him . . . screw him . . . God, I love him . . . call him to say I need more time . . . time for what? He's a murderer.* Kendra thought of August, of all their thug talks, of his warnings to steer clear of anyone that seemed like trouble. He had only wanted her to find a nice man, someone that wasn't damaged like he was, like her father and mother were, like she had become. And then she thought of her daughter and of her namesake. She headed toward the phone, her heart sinking with one final thought, *I've got to end it.*

* * *

Frankie stepped out of the shower and dried off. Wrapping the white bath towel around his waist, he made his way toward the bedroom. He threw on a pair of checkered boxers and headed down to the kitchen. He glanced at the front door, but missed the shadow that was standing just to the left at the bottom of the steps.

After dropping wheat bread into the toaster, he poured himself a glass of Riesling. Not his first choice of drink, it was all that was left in the house, and at this point, any buzz was better than no buzz at all. He promised himself that first thing in the morning, he'd contact Alcoholics Anonymous. It was time to get his family back.

* * *

Lenny watched the figure walk toward the back of the house. He took one last, lengthy hit off his cigarette and then bent down to snuff it out under his boot. He reached into his pocket, pulled out a sandwich baggie, and slipped the cigarette inside. He finger combed his hair, squared his shoulders, and rang the bell.

* * *

Frankie had the wine glass to his lips when he heard the doorbell. He put the glass down and headed for the front door when the ringing of the phone stopped him. He paused in the hallway, halfway between the phone and the door. His first thought was that Kendra and Meg were home, and Karen was on the phone. But Kendra wouldn't be ringing the bell. His second thought was of Karen at the door and Kendra on the phone, but Karen usually rang and then entered, calling out his name.

He heard the toaster pop and the sound of both bells ringing in his ears. He decided to ignore the doorbell and answer the phone. If it wasn't Kendra or Karen, he didn't give a shit who it was.

*   *   *

Meg was leaning against her favorite oak tree sucking on a piece of grass that tasted like a grape lollipop when she noticed a small figure in the distance.

"Grandma Vicki? Is it really you?"

*   *   *

Karen sat in her car beseeching the red light to change. She counted to ten and quickly looked around. Revving the gas, she said, "Screw this."

Swerving around a corner toward another intersection, she was just about at Frankie's house. Ignoring all rules of the road, she went straight through the intersection. Halfway across, she heard a honking sound. She turned her head to the left, saw a tractor-trailer heading directly at her, and realized that neither stepping on the brake nor speeding up would help. While the repeated honking of the truck pleaded for her to disappear from its path, the faces of Frankie, Kendra, and little Meg flashed before her eyes and she recalled Anna the psychic's prediction from so many years ago. *In the end, it won't just be his blood; it will be your blood as well.*

The impact of truck hitting car caused a magnificent sound of metal scraping against the pavement.

*   *   *

Frankie picked up the receiver just as Kendra had given up.

"Hello?" he said, into the empty line, and then, "Oh well, guess it's the door."

Upon opening the door, a large, cumbersome man whose frame encompassed the doorway said, "Hello, Frankie."

"Do I know you?"

"I'm a friend of Karen's."

"Well," Frankie began, "any friend of Karen's is a friend of mine."

* * *

Kendra hung up the phone, somewhat relieved that Frankie hadn't answered. Breaking up their marriage over the phone wasn't exactly fair. She closed her eyes and said a prayer to her grandfather, asking him for strength. Inside of a minute, she had an answer. Tomorrow over breakfast, she'd tell Karen that she was going to turn her husband in. Wherever their lives went from there couldn't possibly be as bad as where they were now. Meg's murder wasn't a secret that Kendra was willing to keep.

* * *

Frankie offered his hand to the man standing in his doorway.

Ignoring the gesture, Lenny nodded slightly and muscled his way forward so that Frankie automatically took a step back. Safely inside, Lenny leaned against the door until it quietly closed. Frankie's smile faded as Lenny produced a silenced Beretta that he aimed at Frankie's head.

"Hey, whoa there!" shouted Frankie, his hands automatically drawing up to block his face.

"This is for Meg."

Frankie peeked through his fingers.

"Meg? Meg is my daughter."

"No. Meg was Karen's daughter, and you off'd her then left her for dead, you asshole."

Frankie lowered his hands in disbelief while a vivid recollection of the day he and Adam stabbed the girl flooded his senses.

"But this has to be a mistake," he said, trying to buy time. "Karen didn't have any kids. If she had a daughter, she would have told me."

Lenny faux yawned, as if he were bored. "Yeah, well, I'm not sure what her reasoning was behind that bright idea, but Karen did have a kid, and her name was Meg."

Frankie stalled, calculating his chances of escape.

"Look, you have the wrong guy. You're making a huge mistake here."

"You tellin' me you never murdered a girl?"

"Never," lied Frankie.

"Tsk, tsk," scolded Lenny. "You're a bigger coward than I expected."

A flashback of his life with Ray hit Frankie hard. This asshole in front of him was treating him just like Ray used to, and Frankie was utterly helpless. Blind with anger, he snapped, "Coward? Put the gun down and we'll see who the coward is, fuck face."

"There you are," grinned Lenny. "Now, do you want to confess before I pull the trigger or what?"

"I told you, you've got the wrong guy."

"Have it your way," Lenny shrugged indifferently.

"Do you think this is what Karen wants? In case you weren't aware of it, I'm her adopted son. C'mon, man," he said, trying to sound calm, "do you really think this would make her happy?"

Lenny smiled, a cynically evil smile. "Who do you think sent me here, dumbass?"

The blood drained from Frankie's face and vomit pooled in his throat.

"That bitch," Frankie mumbled.

"Yeah, I could see why you'd think that," Lenny agreed.

"What a joke," Frankie chuckled. "Un-fucking real. I mean, what are the chances?" he asked Lenny, his palms toward the ceiling. "What are the fucking chances that the only person I truly trusted would be the mother of a girl I stabbed?"

"I'm going to have to go with you on this one," Lenny nodded. "Ain't karma a bitch?"

"All right, you've got me. I'll turn myself in."

"I ain't no cop," Lenny laughed.

Frankie closed his eyes and brought his hands to the sides of his head like he were warding off a headache. His abusive childhood flooded his psyche, and his only thought was protecting himself from people like Ray, and at the present moment, Lenny was the new Ray.

"Have you collected yourself yet? I want to be sure you get the full scope of this before we say goodnight."

Frankie dropped his hands and opened his eyes. "I'm going to rip your heart out," he growled. "And then I'm going to find Karen and take care of her, just like I took care of her snotty daughter."

Lenny smiled, baring his yellow teeth like a rabid animal. "Say goodnight, Frankie."

Frankie took one step toward Lenny before hearing the fatal thud of the gun.

*   *   *

Lenny stuck the gun inside his jacket, and quietly stepped outside. Before closing the door, he double checked that the splattered mess on the floor wasn't so much as twitching a finger. Satisfied at the lack of movement, Lenny walked quickly back to his car and entered it as silently as he had exited. He turned the corner onto the main road and swore under his breath. A crowd had gathered at the scene of an accident and officers were detouring traffic. A tractor-trailer was pulled off to the side, and just beyond it was a car with one side resembling crumpled tin. Lenny could just make out the bottom half of a woman lying on the ground. She appeared lifeless. He slouched down and casually put on a baseball hat he kept in the car for these kinds of situations. Pulling the cap down as close to his eyes as he could, Lenny looked straight ahead waiting for the police officer in charge to motion a direction. He glanced over at the accident, but didn't crane his neck to see the particulars. Lenny's line of work afforded him all the gory details he needed. A mere accident, fatal or not, was almost unimpressive. Medics worked diligently, trying to resuscitate her with fancy machines.

"Give it up, boys," he mumbled to himself. "If you gotta go, tonight's a fine night to die."

∗   ∗   ∗

Vicki cupped Meg's face in her hands and brushed back her hair.

"Let me look at you, Megan. My, you're so pretty," beamed Vicki.

"Oh, Grandma, what took you so long?"

Vicki smiled and held out her hand.

"You know me, it takes me forever to primp," she winked. "Now, you ready to go, Megan?"

"Go where?"

"With me, of course."

"Are you kidding? I've been ready!"

Meg walked hand in hand with her grandmother. They ventured through the field and up a medium-sized hill. When they reached the crest, Meg caught her breath. In the distance, at the base of the hill, there had been a horrible accident.

"Holy collision! They're going to have one heck of a headache," said Meg, shaking her head at the scene below.

"Looks bad, doesn't it?" replied Vicki, her voice edged with concern.

"It sure does. I haven't seen anything this bad since," Meg paused and looked at her grandmother. "Since I was alive."

Vicki squeezed Meg's hand and nodded.

"Grandma, why are we here?"

Vicki pointed to the wreckage, "Because your mother needs us."

Meg squinted, and recognized her mother's small figure lying on the ground. She hesitated, taking a step backward.

"Let's go, honey," Vicki said, gently pulling Meg forward.

"Is this because she's . . . will she be coming with us?"

"Honestly, I don't know," answered Vicki.

"I don't understand. Why are we here if not to get her?"

"Moral support, just to be by her side."

"Can we talk to her?"

"We can try."

"Do you think she'll hear us?"

"I'm betting some part of her will."

"Okay then, let's go," said Meg, leading the way. "It was awful lonely when I was in Mom's shoes. If Kendra hadn't come along, I would have gone totally bonkers," Meg grinned, remembering her first impression of Meg as a retarded angel.

"Grandma?"

"Yes, Megan?"

"What should we say to her?"

"Oh, this and that, fill her head with happy thoughts."

"Could we ask her what she wants to do?"

"I don't see why not," smiled Vicki, tapping the tip of Meg's nose. They took one step before Meg paused again.

"What do you suppose she'll say when we ask her what she wants to do?"

Vicki thought for a moment before replying, "I'm not quite sure. Your mother always has been a willful and strong woman. And let's not forget that she's got enough fight in her for twenty people."

"So if she says she's not coming with us, what happens next?"

Vicki and Meg scanned the distant figure for signs of life.

"Next?" Vicki smiled, wrapping her arms around Meg. "We do what we've been doing all along. We wait."

To Dylan d
Kevin

ACKNOWLEDGEMENTS

Damaged Goods has been a slow evolution. A massive thanks to my family and friends who listened as I plotted the storyline, who read and reread draft after draft, who helped me with logistics and Italian, and who patiently heard me say, "It's finished this time, for sure." You, all of you, were the light and motivation that kept me sane. Thanks to Mel Robbins, Talk Radio Personality and host of A&E's show Monster In-Laws for taking time out of her busy schedule to write a book review, and to Mark Saia, NREMT-P, RRT for his extensive medical know-how. Deep gratitude to my parents, Pat and Tony Bruno, for their never-ending encouragement, editor Lawrence H. Brown for his expertise and much needed humor during our many hours of editing, and to photographer E. J. Landry, who captured the book cover perfectly, as well as producing a very decent author photo. I cannot express the gratefulness I feel for my family, for meine wahre liebe, Dennis, my daughter Jocelyn, the beautiful model for the book cover, and my two awesome sons, Nico and Danny. You provided me with the support, patience and love that I needed to keep calm and write on.

EJ Landry you're welcome

Made in United States
North Haven, CT
22 May 2022

19428050R00211